THE TALE

OF THE

BODY THIEF

THE TALE
OF THE
BODY THIEF

THE VAMPIRE CHRONICLES

ANNE RICE

ALFRED A. KNOPF

New York

1992

For my parents,
Howard and Katherine O'Brien.
Your dreams and your courage will be with me
all of my days.

Sailing to Byzantium

by W. B. Yeats

I

That is no country for old men. The young
In one another's arms, birds in the trees
—Those dying generations—at their song,
The salmon-falls, the mackerel-crowded seas,
Fish, flesh, or fowl, commend all summer long
Whatever is begotten, born, and dies.
Caught in that sensual music all neglect
Monuments of unageing intellect.

II

An aged man is but a paltry thing,
A tattered coat upon a stick, unless
Soul clap its hands and sing, and louder sing
For every tatter in its mortal dress,
Nor is there singing school but studying
Monuments of its own magnificence;
And therefore I have sailed the seas and come
To the holy city of Byzantium.

III

O sages standing in God's holy fire
As in the gold mosaic of a wall,
Come from the holy fire, perne in a gyre,
And be the singing-masters of my soul.
Consume my heart away; sick with desire
And fastened to a dying animal
It knows not what it is; and gather me
Into the artifice of eternity.

IV

Once out of nature I shall never take
My bodily form from any natural thing,
But such a form as Grecian goldsmiths make
Of hammered gold and gold enamelling
To keep a drowsy Emperor awake;
Or set upon a golden bough to sing
To lords and ladies of Byzantium
Of what is past, or passing, or to come.

THE TALE
OF THE
BODY THIEF

T HE Vampire Lestat here. I have a story to tell you. It's about
something that happened to me.

It begins in Miami, in the year 1990, and I really want to
start right there. But it's important that I tell you about the dreams I'd
been having before that time, for they are very much part of the tale
too. I'm talking now about dreams of a child vampire with a woman's
mind and an angel's face, and a dream of my mortal friend David
Talbot.

But there were dreams also of my mortal boyhood in France—of
winter snows, my father's bleak and ruined castle in the Auvergne, and
the time I went out to hunt a pack of wolves that were preying upon
our poor village.

Dreams can be as real as events. Or so it seemed to me afterwards.

And I was in a dark frame of mind when these dreams began, a
vagabond vampire roaming the earth, sometimes so covered with dust
that no one took the slightest notice of me. What good was it to have
full and beautiful blond hair, sharp blue eyes, razzle-dazzle clothes, an
irresistible smile, and a well-proportioned body six feet in height that
can, in spite of its two hundred years, pass for that of a twenty-year-old
mortal. I was still a man of reason however, a child of the eighteenth
century, in which I'd actually lived before I was Born to Darkness.

But as the 1980s were drawing to a close I was much changed from
the dashing fledgling vampire I had once been, so attached to his classic
black cape and Bruxelles lace, the gentleman with walking stick and
white gloves, dancing beneath the gas lamp.

I had been transformed into a dark god of sorts, thanks to suffering
and triumph, and too much of the blood of our vampire elders. I had
powers which left me baffled and sometimes even frightened. I had
powers which made me sorrowful though I did not always understand
the reason for it.

I could, for example, move high into the air at will, traveling the night winds over great distances as easily as a spirit. I could effect or destroy matter with the power of my mind. I could kindle a fire by the mere wish to do so. I could also call to other immortals over countries and continents with my preternatural voice, and I could effortlessly read the minds of vampires and humans.

Not bad, you might think. I loathed it. Without doubt, I was grieving for my old selves—the mortal boy, the newborn revenant once determined to be good at being bad if that was his predicament.

I'm not a pragmatist, understand. I have a keen and merciless conscience. I could have been a nice guy. Maybe at times I am. But always, I've been a man of action. Grief is a waste, and so is fear. And action is what you will get here, as soon as I get through this introduction.

Remember, beginnings are always hard and most are artificial. It was the best of times and the worst of times—really? When! And all happy families are not alike; even Tolstoy must have realized that. I can't get away with "In the beginning," or "They threw me off the hay truck at noon," or I would do it. I always get away with whatever I can, believe me. And as Nabokov said in the voice of Humbert Humbert, "You can always count on a murderer for a fancy prose style." Can't fancy mean experimental? I already know of course that I am sensuous, florid, lush, humid—enough critics have told me that.

Alas, I have to do things my own way. And we will get to the beginning—if that isn't a contradiction in terms—I promise you.

Right now I must explain that before this adventure commenced, I was also grieving for the other immortals I had known and loved, because they had long ago scattered from our last late-twentieth-century gathering place. Folly to think we wanted to create a coven again. They had one by one disappeared into time and the world, which was inevitable.

Vampires don't really like others of their kind, though their need for immortal companions is desperate.

Out of that need I'd made my fledglings—Louis de Pointe du Lac, who became my patient and often loving nineteenth-century comrade, and with his unwitting aid, the beautiful and doomed child vampire, Claudia. And during these lonely vagabond nights of the late twentieth century, Louis was the only immortal whom I saw quite often. The most human of us all, the most ungodlike.

I never stayed away too long from his shack in the wilderness of uptown New Orleans. But you'll see. I'll get to that. Louis is in this story.

The point is—you'll find precious little here about the others. Indeed, almost nothing.

Except for Claudia. I was dreaming more and more often of Claudia. Let me explain about Claudia. She'd been destroyed over a century before, yet I felt her presence all the time as if she were just around the corner.

It was 1794 when I made this succulent little vampire out of a dying orphan, and sixty years passed before she rose up against me. "I'll put you in your coffin forever, Father."

I did sleep in a coffin then. And it was a period piece, that lurid attempted murder, involving as it did mortal victims baited with poisons to cloud my mind, knives tearing my white flesh, and the ultimate abandonment of my seemingly lifeless form in the rank waters of the swamp beyond the dim lights of New Orleans.

Well, it didn't work. There are very few sure ways to kill the undead. The sun, fire . . . One must aim for total obliteration. And after all, we are talking about the Vampire Lestat here.

Claudia suffered for this crime, being executed later by an evil coven of blood drinkers who thrived in the very heart of Paris in the infamous Theatre of the Vampires. I'd broken the rules when I made a blood drinker of a child so small, and for that reason alone, the Parisian monsters might have put an end to her. But she too had broken their rules in trying to destroy her maker, and that you might say was their logical reason for shutting her out into the bright light of day which burnt her to ashes.

It's a hell of a way to execute someone, as far as I'm concerned, because those who lock you out must quickly retire to their coffins and are not even there to witness the mighty sun carrying out their grim sentence. But that's what they did to this exquisite and delicate creature that I had fashioned with my vampiric blood from a ragged, dirty waif in a ramshackle Spanish colony in the New World—to be my friend, my pupil, my love, my muse, my fellow hunter. And yes, my daughter.

If you read Interview with the Vampire, *then you know all about this. It's Louis's version of our time together. Louis tells of his love for this our child, and of his vengeance against those who destroyed her.*

If you read my autobiographical books, The Vampire Lestat *and*

The Queen of the Damned, *you know all about me, also. You know our history, for what it's worth—and history is never worth too much—and how we came into being thousands of years ago and that we propagate by carefully giving the Dark Blood to mortals when we wish to take them along the Devil's Road with us.*

But you don't have to read those works to understand this one. And you won't find here the cast of thousands that crowded The Queen of the Damned, *either. Western civilization will not for one second teeter on the brink. And there will be no revelations from ancient times or old ones confiding half-truths and riddles and promising answers that do not in fact exist and never have existed.*

No, I have done all that before.

This is a contemporary story. It's a volume in the Vampire Chronicles, make no mistake. But it is the first really modern volume, for it accepts the horrifying absurdity of existence from the start, and it takes us into the mind and the soul of its hero—guess who?—for its discoveries.

Read this tale, and I will give you all you need to know about us as you turn the pages. And by the way, lots of things do happen! I'm a man of action as I said—the James Bond of the vampires, if you will—called the Brat Prince, and the Damnedest Creature, and "you monster" by various and sundry other immortals.

The other immortals are still around, of course—Maharet and Mekare, the eldest of us all, Khayman of the First Brood, Eric, Santino, Pandora, and others whom we call the Children of the Millennia. Armand is still about, the lovely five-hundred-year-old boy-faced ancient who once ruled the Théâtre des Vampires, and before that a coven of devil worshiping blood drinkers who lived beneath the Paris Cemetery, Les Innocents. Armand, I hope, will always be around.

And Gabrielle, my mortal mother and immortal child will no doubt turn up one of these nights sometime before the end of another thousand years, if I'm lucky.

As for Marius, my old teacher and mentor, the one who kept the historical secrets of our tribe, he is still with us and always will be. Before this tale began, he would come to me now and then to scold and plead: Would I not stop my careless kills which invariably found their way into the pages of mortal newspapers! Would I not stop deviling my mortal friend David Talbot, and tempting him with the Dark Gift of our blood? Better we make no more, did I not know this?

Rules, rules, rules. They always wind up talking about rules. And I love to break the rules the way mortals like to smash their crystal glasses after a toast against the bricks of the fireplace.

But enough about the others. The point is—this is my book from start to finish.

Let me speak now of the dreams that had come to trouble me in my wanderings.

With Claudia, it was almost a haunting. Just before my eyes would close each dawn, I'd see her beside me, hear her voice in a low and urgent whisper. And sometimes I'd slide back over the centuries to the little colonial hospital with its rows of tiny beds where the orphan child had been dying.

Behold the sorrowful old doctor, potbellied and palsied, as he lifts the child's body. And that crying. Who is crying? Claudia was not crying. She slept as the doctor entrusted her to me, believing me to be her mortal father. And she is so pretty in these dreams. Was she that pretty then? Of course she was.

"Snatching me from mortal hands like two grim monsters in a nightmare fairy tale, you idle, blind parents!"

The dream of David Talbot came once only.

David is young in the dream and he is walking in a mangrove forest. He was not the man of seventy-four who had become my friend, the patient mortal scholar who regularly refused my offer of the Dark Blood, and laid his warm, fragile hand on my cold flesh unflinchingly to demonstrate the affection and trust between us.

No. This is young David Talbot of years and years ago, when his heart didn't beat so fast within his chest. Yet he is in danger.

Tyger, tyger burning bright.

Is that his voice, whispering those words or is it mine?

And out of the dappled light it comes, its orange and black stripes like the light and shade itself so that it is scarcely visible. I see its huge head, and how soft its muzzle, white and bristling with long, delicate whiskers. But look at its yellow eyes, mere slits, and full of horrid mindless cruelty. David, its fangs! Can't you see these fangs!

But he is curious as a child, watching its big pink tongue touch his throat, touch the thin gold chain he wears around his throat. Is it eating the chain? Good God, David! The fangs.

Why is my voice dried up inside me? Am I even there in the mangrove forest? My body vibrates as I struggle to move, dull moans coming from behind my sealed lips, and each moan taxes every fiber of my being. David, beware!

And then I see that he is down on one knee, with the long shiny rifle cocked against his shoulder. And the giant cat is still yards away, bearing down on him. On and on it rushes, until the crack of the gun stops it in its tracks, and over it goes as the gun roars once again, its yellow eyes full of rage, its paws crossed as they push in one last final breath at the soft earth.

I wake.

What does this dream mean—that my mortal friend is in danger? Or simply that his genetic clock has ticked to a stop. For a man of seventy-four years, death can come at any instant.

Do I ever think of David that I do not think of death?

David, where are you?

Fee, Fie, Fo, Fum, I smell the blood of an Englishman.

"I want you to ask me for the Dark Gift," I'd said to him when first we met. "I may not give it to you. But I want you to ask."

He never had. He never would. And now I loved him. I saw him soon after the dream. I had to. But I could not forget the dream and perhaps it did come to me more than once in the deep sleep of my daylight hours when I am stone cold and helpless under literal cover of darkness.

All right, you have the dreams now.

But picture the winter snow in France one more time, if you would, piling about the castle walls, and a young male mortal asleep on his bed of hay, in the light of the fire, with his hunting dogs beside him. This had become the image of my lost human life, more truly than any remembrance of the boulevard theatre in Paris, where before the Revolution I'd been so very happy as a young actor.

Now we are truly ready to begin. Let's turn the page, shall we?

I

THE TALE

OF THE

BODY THIEF

O N E

MIAMI—the vampires' city. This is South Beach at sunset, in the luxurious warmth of the winterless winter, clean and thriving and drenched in electric light, the gentle breeze moving in from the placid sea, across the dark margin of cream-colored sand, to cool the smooth broad pavements full of happy mortal children.

Sweet the parade of fashionable young men displaying their cultured muscles with touching vulgarity, of young women so proud of their streamlined and seemingly sexless modern limbs, amid the soft urgent roar of traffic and human voices.

Old stucco hostelries, once the middling shelters of the aged, were now reborn in smart pastel colors, sporting their new names in elegant neon script. Candles flickered on the white-draped tables of the open-porch restaurants. Big shiny American cars pushed their way slowly along the avenue, as drivers and passengers viewed the dazzling human parade, lazy pedestrians here and there blocking the thoroughfare.

On the distant horizon the great white clouds were mountains beneath a roofless and star-filled heaven. Ah, it never failed to take my breath away—this southern sky filled with azure light and drowsy relentless movement.

To the north rose the towers of new Miami Beach in all their splendour. To the south and to the west, the dazzling steel skyscrapers of the downtown city with its high roaring freeways and busy cruise-ship docks. Small pleasure boats sped along the sparkling waters of the myriad urban canals.

In the quiet immaculate gardens of Coral Gables, countless lamps illuminated the handsome sprawling villas with their red-tiled roofs, and swimming pools shimmering with turquoise light. Ghosts walked in the grand and darkened rooms of the Biltmore. The massive mangrove trees threw out their primitive limbs to cover the broad and carefully tended streets.

In Coconut Grove, the international shoppers thronged the luxurious hotels and fashionable malls. Couples embraced on the high balconies of their glass-walled condominiums, silhouettes gazing out over the serene waters of the bay. Cars sped along the busy roads past the ever-dancing palms and delicate rain trees, past the squat concrete mansions draped with red and purple bougainvillea, behind their fancy iron gates.

All of this is Miami, city of water, city of speed, city of tropical flowers, city of enormous skies. It is for Miami, more than any other place, that I periodically leave my New Orleans home. The men and women of many nations and different colors live in the great dense neighborhoods of Miami. One hears Yiddish, Hebrew, the languages of Spain, of Haiti, the dialects and accents of Latin America, of the deep south of this nation and of the far north. There is menace beneath the shining surface of Miami, there is desperation and a throbbing greed; there is the deep steady pulse of a great capital—the low grinding energy, the endless risk.

It's never really dark in Miami. It's never really quiet.

It is the perfect city for the vampire; and it never fails to yield to me a mortal killer—some twisted, sinister morsel who will give up to me a dozen of his own murders as I drain his memory banks and his blood.

But tonight it was the Big-Game Hunt, the unseasonal Easter feast after a Lent of starvation—the pursuit of one of those splendid human trophies whose gruesome modus operandi reads for pages in the computer files of mortal law enforcement agencies, a being anointed in his anonymity with a flashy name by the worshipful press: "Back Street Strangler."

I lust after such killers!

What luck for me that such a celebrity had surfaced in my favorite city. What luck that he has struck six times in these very streets—slayer of the old and the infirm, who have come in such numbers to live out their remaining days in these warm climes. Ah, I would have crossed a continent to snap him up, but he is here waiting for me. To his dark history, detailed by no less than twenty criminologists, and easily purloined by me through the computer in my New Orleans lair, I have secretly added the crucial elements—his name and mortal habitation. A simple trick for a dark god who can read minds. Through his blood-soaked dreams I found him. And tonight the pleasure will be mine of finishing his illustrious career in a dark cruel embrace, without a scintilla of moral illumination.

Ah, Miami. The perfect place for this little Passion Play.

I always come back to Miami, the way I come back to New Orleans. And I'm the only immortal now who hunts this glorious corner of the Savage Garden, for as you have seen, the others long ago deserted the coven house here—unable to endure each other's company any more than I can endure them.

But so much the better to have Miami all to myself.

I stood at the front windows of the rooms I maintained in the swanky little Park Central Hotel on Ocean Drive, every now and then letting my preternatural hearing sweep the chambers around me in which the rich tourists enjoyed that premium brand of solitude— complete privacy only steps from the flashy street—my Champs Élysées of the moment, my Via Veneto.

My strangler was almost ready to move from the realm of his spasmodic and fragmentary visions into the land of literal death. Ah, time to dress for the man of my dreams.

Picking from the usual wilderness of freshly opened cardboard boxes, suitcases, and trunks, I chose a suit of gray velvet, an old favorite, especially when the fabric is thick, with only a subtle luster. Not very likely for these warm nights, I had to admit, but then I don't feel hot and cold the way humans do. And the coat was slim with narrow lapels, very spare and rather like a hacking jacket with its fitted waist, or, more to the point, like the graceful old frock coats of earlier times. We immortals forever fancy old-fashioned garments, garments that remind us of the century in which we were Born to Darkness. Sometimes you can gauge the true age of an immortal simply by the cut of his clothes.

With me, it's also a matter of texture. The eighteenth century was so shiny! I can't bear to be without a little luster. And this handsome coat suited me perfectly with the plain tight velvet pants. As for the white silk shirt, it was a cloth so soft you could ball the garment in the palm of your hand. Why should I wear anything else so close to my indestructible and curiously sensitive skin? Then the boots. Ah, they look like all my fine shoes of late. Their soles are immaculate, for they so seldom touch the mother earth.

My hair I shook loose into the usual thick mane of glowing yellow shoulder-length waves. What would I look like to mortals? I honestly don't know. I covered up my blue eyes, as always, with black glasses, lest their radiance mesmerize and entrance at random—a real nuisance—and over my delicate white hands, with their telltale glassy fingernails, I drew the usual pair of soft gray leather gloves.

Ah, a bit of oily brown camouflage for the skin. I smoothed the lotion over my cheekbones, over the bit of neck and chest that was bare.

I inspected the finished product in the mirror. Still irresistible. No wonder I'd been such a smash in my brief career as a rock singer. And I've always been a howling success as a vampire. Thank the gods I hadn't become invisible in my airy wanderings, a vagabond floating far above the clouds, light as a cinder on the wind. I felt like weeping when I thought of it.

The Big-Game Hunt always brought me back to the actual. Track him, wait for him, catch him just at the moment that he would bring death to his next victim, and take him slowly, painfully, feasting upon his wickedness as you do it, glimpsing through the filthy lens of his soul all his earlier victims . . .

Please understand, there is no nobility in this. I don't believe that rescuing one poor mortal from such a fiend can conceivably save my soul. I have taken life too often—unless one believes that the power of one good deed is infinite. I don't know whether or not I believe that. What I do believe is this: The evil of one murder is infinite, and my guilt is like my beauty—eternal. I cannot be forgiven, for there is no one to forgive me for all I've done.

Nevertheless I like saving those innocents from their fate. And I like taking my killers to me because they are my brothers, and we belong together, and why shouldn't they die in my arms instead of some poor merciful mortal who has never done anyone any willful harm? These are the rules of my game. I play by these rules because I made them. And I promised myself, I wouldn't leave the bodies about this time; I'd strive to do what the others have always ordered me to do. But still . . . I liked to leave the carcass for the authorities. I liked to fire up the computer later, after I'd returned to New Orleans, and read the entire postmortem report.

Suddenly I was distracted by the sound of a police car passing slowly below, the men inside it speaking of my killer, that he will strike soon again, his stars are in the correct positions, the moon is at the right height. It will be in the side streets of South Beach most certainly, as it has been before. But who is he? How can he be stopped?

Seven o'clock. The tiny green numerals of the digital clock told me it was so, though I already knew, of course. I closed my eyes, letting my head drop just a little to one side, bracing myself perhaps for the full effects of this power which I so loathed. First came an amplification of the hearing again, as if I had thrown a modern technological switch. The soft purring sounds of the world became a chorus from hell—full of sharp-edged laughter and lamentation, full of lies and anguish and random pleas. I covered my ears as if that could stop it, then finally I shut it off.

Gradually I saw the blurred and overlapping images of their thoughts, rising like a million fluttering birds into the firmament. *Give me my killer, give me his vision!*

He was there, in a small dingy room, very unlike this one, yet only two blocks from it, just rising from his bed. His cheap clothes were rumpled, sweat covering his coarse face, a thick nervous hand going for the cigarettes in his shirt pocket, then letting them go—already forgotten. A heavy man he was, of shapeless facial features and a look full of vague worry, or dim regret.

It did not occur to him to dress for the evening, for the Feast for which he'd been hungering. And now his waking mind was almost collapsed beneath the burden of his ugly palpitating dreams. He shook himself all over, loose greasy hair falling onto his sloping forehead, eyes like bits of black glass.

Standing still in the silent shadows of my room, I continued to track him, to follow down a back stairs, and out into the garish light of Collins Avenue, past dusty shop windows and sagging commercial signs, propelled onward, towards the inevitable and yet unchosen object of his desire.

And who might she be, the lucky lady, wandering blindly and inexorably towards this horror, through the sparse and dismal crowds of the early evening in this same dreary region of town? Does she carry a carton of milk and a head of lettuce in a brown paper bag? Will she hurry at the sight of the cutthroats on the corner? Does she grieve for the old beachfront where she lived perhaps so contentedly before the architects and the decorators drove her to the cracked and peeling hostelries further away?

And what will he think when he finally spots her, this filthy angel of death? Will she be the very one to remind him of the mythic shrew of childhood, who beat him senseless only to be elevated to the nightmare pantheon of his subconscious, or are we asking too much?

I mean there are killers of this species who make not the smallest connection between symbol and reality, and remember nothing for longer than a few days. What is certain is only that their victims don't deserve it, and that they, the killers, deserve to meet with me.

Ah, well, I will tear out his menacing heart before he has had a chance to "do" her, and he will give me everything that he has, and is.

I walked slowly down the steps, and through the smart, glittering art deco lobby with its magazine-page glamour. How good it felt to be moving like a mortal, to open the doors, to wander out into the fresh air. I headed north along the sidewalk among the evening strollers, eyes drifting naturally over the newly refurbished hotels and their little cafés.

The crowd thickened as I reached the corner. Before a fancy open-air restaurant, giant television cameras focused their lenses on a stretch of sidewalk harshly illuminated by enormous white lights. Trucks blocked the traffic; cars slowed to a stop. A loose crowd had gathered of young and old, only mildly fascinated, for television and motion picture cameras in the vicinity of South Beach were a familiar sight.

I skirted the lights, fearing their effect upon my highly reflective face. Would I were one of the tan-skinned ones, smelling of expensive beach oils, and half naked in friable cotton rags. I made my way around the corner. Again, I scanned for the prey. He was racing, his mind so thick with hallucinations that he could scarce control his shuffling, sloppy steps.

There was no time left.

With a little spurt of speed, I took to the low roofs. The breeze was stronger, sweeter. Gentle the roar of excited voices, the dull natural songs of radios, the sound of the wind itself.

In silence I caught his image in the indifferent eyes of those who passed him; in silence I saw his fantasies once more of withered hands and withered feet, of shrunken cheeks and shrunken breasts. The thin membrane between fantasy and reality was breaking.

I hit the pavements of Collins Avenue, so swiftly perhaps I simply seemed to appear. But nobody was looking. I was the proverbial tree falling in the uninhabited forest.

And in minutes, I was ambling along, steps behind him, a menacing young man perhaps, piercing the little clusters of tough guys who blocked the path, pursuing the prey through the glass doors of a giant ice-cooled drugstore. Ah, such a circus for the eye—this low-ceilinged cave—chock-full of every imaginable kind of packageable and preserved foodstuff, toilet article, and hair accoutrement, ninety percent of which existed not at all in any form whatsoever during the century when I was born.

We're talking sanitary napkins, medicinal eyedrops, plastic bobby pins, felt-tip markers, creams and ointments for all nameable parts of the human body, dishwashing liquid in every color of the rainbow, and cosmetic rinses in some colors never before invented and yet undefined. Imagine Louis XVI opening a noisy crackling plastic sack of such wonders? What would he think of Styrofoam coffee cups, chocolate cookies wrapped in cellophane, or pens that never run out of ink?

Well, I'm still not entirely used to these items myself, though I've watched the progress of the Industrial Revolution for two centuries with my own eyes. Such drugstores can keep me enthralled for hours on end. Sometimes I become spellbound in the middle of Wal-Mart.

But this time I had a prey in my sights, didn't I? Later for *Time* and *Vogue*, pocket computer language translators, and wristwatches that continue to tell time even as you swim in the sea.

Why had *he* come to this place? The young Cuban families with babies in tow were not his style. Yet aimlessly he wandered the narrow crowded aisles, oblivious to the hundreds of dark faces and the fast riffs of Spanish around him, unnoticed by anyone but me, as his red-rimmed eyes swept the cluttered shelves.

Lord God, but he was filthy—all decency lost in his mania, craggy face and neck creased with dirt. Will I love it? Hell, he's a sack of blood. Why push my luck? I couldn't kill little children anymore, could I? Or feast on waterfront harlots, telling myself it's all perfectly fine, for they have poisoned their share of flatboatmen. My conscience is killing me, isn't it? And when you're immortal that can be a really long and ignominious death. Yeah, look at him, this dirty, stinking, lumbering killer. Men in prison get better chow than this.

And then it hit me as I scanned his mind once more as if cutting open a cantaloupe. He doesn't know what he is! He has never read his own headlines! And indeed he does not remember episodes of his life in any discerning order, and could not in truth confess to the murders he has committed for he does not truly recall them, and he does not know that he will kill tonight! He does not know what I know!

Ah, sadness and grief, I had drawn the very worst card, no doubt about it. Oh, Lord God! What had I been thinking of to hunt this one, when the starlit world is full of more vicious and cunning beasts? I wanted to weep.

But then came the provocative moment. He had seen *the* old woman, seen her bare wrinkled arms, the small hump of her back, her thin and shivering thighs beneath her pastel shorts. Through the glare of fluorescent light, she made her way idly, enjoying the buzz and throb of those around her, face half hidden beneath the green plastic of a visor, hair twisted with dark pins on the back of her small head.

She carried in her little basket a pint of orange juice in a plastic bottle, and a pair of slippers so soft they were folded up into a neat little roll. And now to this she added, with obvious glee, a paperback novel from the rack, which she had read before, but fondled lovingly, dreaming of reading it again, like visiting with old acquaintances. *A Tree Grows in Brooklyn.* Yes, I loved it too.

In a trance, he fell in behind her, so close that surely she felt his breath on her neck. Dull-eyed and stupid, he watched as she inched her way closer and closer to the register, drawing out a few dirty dollar bills from the sagging collar of her blouse.

Out the doors they went, he with the listless plodding style of a dog after a bitch in heat, she making her way slowly with her gray sack drooping from its cut-out handles, veering broadly and awkwardly around the bands of noisy and brazen youngsters on the prowl. Is she talking to herself? Seems so. I didn't scan her, this little being walking faster and faster. I scanned the beast behind her, who was wholly unable to see her as the sum of her parts.

Pallid, feeble faces flashed through his mind as he trailed behind her. He hungered to lie on top of old flesh; he hungered to put a hand over an old mouth.

When she reached her small forlorn apartment building, made of crumbling chalk, it seemed, like everything else in this seedy section of town, and guarded by bruised palmettos, he came to a sudden swaying stop, watching mutely as she walked back the narrow tiled courtyard and up the dusty green cement steps. He noted the number of her painted door as she unlocked it, or rather he clamped on to the location, and sinking back against the wall, he began to dream very specifically of killing her, in a featureless and empty bedroom that seemed no more than a smear of color and light.

Ah, look at him resting against the wall as if he had been stabbed, head lolling to one side. Impossible to be interested in him. Why don't I kill him now!

But the moments ticked, and the night lost its twilight incandescence. The stars grew ever more brilliant. The breeze came and went.

We waited.

Through her eyes, I saw her parlour as if I could really see through walls and floors—clean, though filled with careless old furniture of ugly veneer, round-shouldered, unimportant to her. But all had been polished with a scented oil she loved. Neon light passed through the Dacron curtains, milky and cheerless as the view of the yard below. But she had the comforting glow of her small carefully positioned lamps. That was what mattered to her.

In a maple rocking chair with hideous plaid upholstery, she sat composed, a tiny but dignified figure, open paperback novel in hand. What happiness to be once more with Francie Nolan. Her thin knees were barely hidden now by the flowered cotton robe she had taken from her closet, and she wore the little blue slippers like socks over her small misshapen feet. She had made of her long gray hair one thick and graceful braid.

On the small black-and-white television screen before her, dead movie stars argued without making a sound. Joan Fontaine thinks Cary Grant is trying to kill her. And judging by the expression on his face, it certainly did seem that way to me. How could anyone ever trust Cary Grant, I wondered—a man who looked as though he were made entirely of wood?

She didn't need to hear their words; she had seen this movie, by her careful count, some thirteen times. She had read this novel in her lap only twice, and so it will be with very special pleasure that she revisits these paragraphs, which she does not know yet by heart.

From the shadowy garden below, I discerned her neat and accepting concept of self, without drama and detached from the acknowledged bad taste that surrounded her. Her few treasures could be contained in any cabinet. The book and the lighted screen were more important to her than anything else she owned, and she was well aware of their spirituality. Even the color of her functional and styleless clothes was not worth her concern.

My vagabond killer was near paralysis, his mind a riot of moments so personal they defied interpretation.

I slipped around the little stucco building and found the stairs to her kitchen door. The lock gave easily when I commanded it to do so. And the door opened as if I had touched it, when I had not.

Without a sound I slipped into the small linoleum-tiled room. The stench of gas rising from the small white stove was sickening to me. So was the smell of the soap in its sticky ceramic dish. But the room touched my heart instantly. Beautiful the cherished china of Chinese blue and white, so neatly stacked, with plates displayed. Behold the dog-eared cookbooks. And how spotless her table with its shining oilcloth of pure yellow, and waxen green ivy growing in a round bowl of clear water, which projected upon the low ceiling a single quivering circle of light.

But what filled my mind as I stood there, rigid, pushing the door shut with my fingers, was that she was unafraid of death as she read her Betty Smith novel, as she occasionally glanced at the glittering screen. She had no inner antenna to pick up the presence of the spook who stood, sunk into madness, in the nearby street, or the monster who haunted her kitchen now.

The killer was immersed so completely in his hallucinations that he did not see those who passed him by. He did not see the police car prowling, or the suspicious and deliberately menacing looks of the uniformed mortals who knew all about him, and that he would strike tonight, but not who he was.

A thin line of spit moved down his unshaven chin. Nothing was real to him—not his life by day, not fear of discovery—only the electric shiver which these hallucinations sent through his hulking torso and clumsy arms and legs. His left hand twitched suddenly. There was a catch at the left side of his mouth.

I hated this guy! I didn't want to drink his blood. He was no classy killer. It was her blood I craved.

How thoughtful she was in her solitude and silence, how small, how contented, her concentration as fine as a light beam as she read the paragraphs of this story she knew so well. Traveling, traveling back to those days when she first read this book, at a crowded soda fountain on Lexington Avenue in New York City, when she was a smartly dressed young secretary in a red wool skirt and a white ruffled blouse with pearl buttons on the cuffs. She worked in a stone office tower, infinitely glamorous, with ornate brass doors on its elevators, and dark yellow marble tile in its halls.

I wanted to press my lips to her memories, to the remembered sounds of her high heels clicking on the marble, to the image of her smooth calf beneath the pure silk stocking as she put it on so carefully, not to snag it with her long enameled nails. I saw her red hair for an instant. I saw her extravagant and potentially hideous yet charming yellow brimmed hat.

That's blood worth having. And I was starving, starving as I have seldom been in all these decades. The unseasonal Lenten fast had been almost more than I could endure. Oh, Lord God, I wanted *so* to kill her!

Below in the street, a faint gurgling sound came from the lips of the stupid, clumsy killer. It cleared its way through the raging torrent of other sounds that poured into my vampiric ears.

At last, the beast lurched away from the wall, listing for a moment as if he would go sprawling, then sauntered towards us, into the little courtyard and up the steps.

Will I let him frighten her? It seemed pointless. I have him in my sights, do I not? Yet I allowed him to put his small metal tool into the round hole in her doorknob, I gave him time to force the lock. The chain tore loose from the rotten wood.

He stepped into the room, fixing upon her without expression. She was terrified, shrinking back in her chair, the book slipping from her lap.

Ah, but then he saw me in the kitchen doorway—a shadowy young man in gray velvet, glasses pushed up over his forehead. I was gazing at him in his own expressionless fashion. Did he see these iridescent eyes, this skin like polished ivory, hair like a soundless explosion of white light? Or was I merely an obstacle between him and his sinister goal, all beauty wasted?

In a second, he bolted. He was down the steps as the old woman screamed and rushed forward to slam the wooden door.

I was after him, not bothering to touch terra firma, letting him see me poised for an instant under the street lamp as he turned the corner. We went for half a block before I drifted towards him, a blur to the mortals, who didn't bother to notice. Then I froze beside him, and heard his groan as he broke into a run.

For blocks we played this game. He ran, he stopped, he saw me behind him. The sweat poured down his body. Indeed the thin synthetic fabric of the shirt was soon translucent with it, and clinging to the smooth hairless flesh of his chest.

At last he came to his seedy flophouse hotel and pounded up the stairs. I was in the small top-floor room when he reached it. Before he could cry out, I had him in my arms. The stench of his dirty hair rose in my nostrils, mingled with a thin acidic smell from the chemical fibers of the shirt. But it didn't matter now. He was powerful and warm in my arms, a juicy capon, chest heaving against me, the smell of his blood flooding my brain. I heard it pulsing through ventricles and valves and painfully constricted vessels. I licked at it in the tender red flesh beneath his eyes.

His heart was laboring and nearly bursting—careful, careful, don't crush him. I let my teeth clamp down on the wet leathery skin of his neck. Hmmm. My brother, my poor befuddled brother. But this was rich, this was good.

The fountain opened; his life was a sewer. All those old women, those old men. They were cadavers floating in the current; they tumbled against each other without meaning, as he went limp in my arms. No sport. Too easy. No cunning. No malice. Crude as a lizard he had been, swallowing fly after fly. Lord God, to know this is to know the time when the giant reptiles ruled the earth, and for a million years, only their yellow eyes beheld the falling rain, or the rising sun.

Never mind. I let him go, tumbling soundlessly out of my grip. I was swimming with his mammalian blood. Good enough. I closed my eyes, letting this hot coil penetrate my intestines, or whatever was down there now in this hard powerful white body. In a daze, I saw him stumbling on his knees across the floor. So exquisitely clumsy. So easy to pick him up from the mess of twisted and tearing newspapers, the overturned cup pouring its cold coffee into the dust-colored rug.

I jerked him back by his collar. His big empty eyes rolled up into his head. Then he kicked at me, blindly, this bully, this killer of the old and weak, shoe scuffing my shin. I lifted him to my hungry mouth again, fingers sliding through his hair, and felt him stiffen as if my fangs were dipped in poison.

Again the blood flooded my brain. I felt it electrify the tiny veins of my face. I felt it pulse even into my fingers, and a hot prickling warmth slide down my spine. Draught after draught filled me. Succulent, heavy creature. Then I let him go once more, and when he stumbled away this time, I went after him, dragging him across the floor, turning his face to me, then tossing him forward and letting him struggle again.

He was speaking to me now in something that ought to have been language, but it wasn't. He pushed at me but he could no longer see clearly. And for the first time a tragic dignity infused him, a vague look of outrage, blind as he was. It seemed I was embellished and enfolded now in old tales, in memories of plaster statues and nameless saints. His fingers clawed at the instep of my shoe. I lifted him up, and when I tore his throat this time, the wound was too big. It was done.

The death came like a fist in the gut. For a moment I felt nausea, and then simply the heat, the fullness, the sheer radiance of the living blood, with that last vibration of consciousness pulsing through all my limbs.

I sank down on his soiled bed. I don't know how long I lay there.

I stared at his low ceiling. And then when the sour musty smells of the room surrounded me, and the stench of his body, I rose and stumbled out, an ungainly figure as surely as he had been, letting myself go soft in these mortal gestures, in rage and hatred, in silence, because I didn't want to be the weightless one, the winged one, the night traveler. I wanted to be human, and feel human, and his blood was threaded all through me, and it wasn't enough. Not nearly enough!

Where are all my promises? The stiff and bruised palmettos rattle against the stucco walls.

"Oh, you're back," she said to me.

Such a low, strong voice she had, no tremor in it. She was standing in front of the ugly plaid rocker, with its worn maple arms, peering at me through her silver-rimmed glasses, the paperback novel clasped in her hand. Her mouth was small and shapeless and showing a bit of yellow teeth, a hideous contrast to the dark personality of the voice, which knew no infirmity at all.

What in God's name was she thinking as she smiled at me? Why doesn't she pray?

"I knew you'd come," she said. Then she took off the glasses, and I saw that her eyes were glazed. What was she seeing? What was I making her see? I who can control all these elements flawlessly was so baffled I could have wept. "Yes, I knew."

"Oh? And how did you know?" I whispered as I approached her, loving the embracing closeness of the common little room.

I reached out with these monstrous fingers too white to be human, strong enough to tear her head off, and I felt her little throat. Smell of Chantilly—or some other drugstore scent.

"Yes," she said airily but definitely. "I always knew."

"Kiss me, then. Love me."

How hot she was, and how tiny were her shoulders, how gorgeous in this the final withering, the flower tinged with yellow, yet full of fragrance still, pale blue veins dancing beneath her flaccid skin, eyelids perfectly molded to her eyes when she closed them, the skin flowing over the bones of her skull.

"Take me to heaven," she said. Out of the heart came the voice.

"I can't. I wish I could," I was purring into her ear.

I closed my arms around her. I nuzzled her soft nest of gray hair. I felt her fingers on my face like dried leaves, and it sent a soft chill through me. She, too, was shivering. Ah, tender and worn little thing, ah, creature reduced to thought and will with a body insubstantial like a fragile flame! Just the "little drink," Lestat, no more.

But it was too late and I knew it when the first spurt of blood hit my tongue. I was draining her. Surely the sounds of my moans must have alarmed her, but then she was past hearing . . . They never hear the real sounds once it's begun.

Forgive me.

Oh, darling!

We were sinking down together on the carpet, lovers in a patch of nubby faded flowers. I saw the book fallen there, and the drawing on the cover, but this seemed unreal. I hugged her so carefully, lest she break. But I was the hollow shell. Her death was coming swiftly, as if she herself were walking towards me in a broad corridor, in some extremely particular and very important place. Ah, yes, the yellow marble tile. New York City, and even up here you can hear the traffic, and that low boom when a door slams on a stairway, down the hall.

"Good night, my darling," she whispered.

Am I hearing things? How can she still make words?

I love you.

"Yes, darling. I love you too."

She stood in the hallway. Her hair was red and stiff and curling prettily at her shoulders; she was smiling, and her heels had been making that sharp, enticing sound on the marble, but now there was only silence around her as the folds of her woolen skirt still moved; she was looking at me with such a strange clever expression; she lifted a small black snub-nosed gun and pointed it at me.

What the hell are you doing?

She is dead. The shot was so loud that for a moment I could hear nothing. Only ringing in my ears. I lay on the floor staring blankly at the ceiling overhead, smelling cordite in a corridor in New York.

But this was Miami. Her clock was ticking on the table. From the overheated heart of the television came the pinched and tiny voice of Cary Grant telling Joan Fontaine that he loved her. And Joan Fontaine was so happy. She'd thought sure Cary Grant meant to kill her.

And so had I.

SOUTH BEACH. Give me the Neon Strip once more. Only this time I walked away from the busy pavements, out over the sand and towards the sea.

On and on I went until there was no one near—not even the beach wanderers, or the night swimmers. Only the sand, blown clean already of all the day's footprints, and the great gray nighttime ocean, throwing up its endless surf upon the patient shore. How high the visible heavens, how full of swiftly moving clouds and distant unobtrusive stars.

What had I done? I'd killed her, his victim, pinched out the light of the one I'd been bound to save. I'd gone back to her and I'd lain with her, and I'd taken her, and she'd fired the invisible shot too late.

And the thirst was there again.

I'd laid her down on her small neat bed afterwards, on the dull quilted nylon, folding her arms and closing her eyes.

Dear God, help me. Where are my nameless saints? Where are the angels with their feathered wings to carry me down into hell? When they do come, are they the last beautiful thing that you see? As you go down into the lake of fire, can you still follow their progress heavenward? Can you hope for one last glimpse of their golden trumpets, and their upturned faces reflecting the radiance of the face of God?

What do I know of heaven?

For long moments I stood there, staring at the distant nightscape of pure clouds, and then back at the twinkling lights of the new hotels, flash of headlamps.

A lone mortal stood on the far sidewalk, staring in my direction, but perhaps he did not note my presence at all—a tiny figure on the lip of the great sea. Perhaps he was only looking towards the ocean as I had been looking, as if the shore were miraculous, as if the water could wash our souls clean.

Once the world was nothing but the sea; rain fell for a hundred million years! But now the cosmos crawls with monsters.

He was still there, that lone and staring mortal. And gradually I realized that over the empty sweep of beach and its thin darkness, his eyes were fixed intently on mine. Yes, looking at me.

I scarce thought about it, looking at him only because I did not bother to turn away. Then a curious sensation passed over me—and one which I had never felt before.

I was faintly dizzy as it began, and a soft tingling vibration followed, coursing through my trunk and then my arms and legs. It felt as if my limbs were growing tighter, narrower, and steadily compressing the substance within. Indeed, so distinct was this feeling that it seemed I might be squeezed right out of myself. I marveled at it. There was something faintly delicious about it, especially to a being as hard and cold and impervious to all sensations as I am. It was overwhelming, very like the way the drinking of blood is overwhelming, though it was nothing as visceral as that. Also no sooner had I analyzed it than I realized it was gone.

I shuddered. Had I imagined the entire thing? I was still staring at that distant mortal—poor soul who gazed back at me without the slightest knowledge of who or what I was.

There was a smile on his young face, brittle and full of crazed wonder. And gradually I realized I had seen this face before. I was further startled to make out in his expression now a certain definite recognition, and the odd attitude of expectation. Suddenly he raised his right hand and waved.

Baffling.

But I knew this mortal. No, more nearly accurate to say I had glimsed him more than once, and then the only certain recollections returned to me with full force.

In Venice, hovering on the edge of the Piazza San Marco, and months after in Hong Kong, near the Night Market, and both times I had taken particular notice of him because he had taken particular notice of me. Yes, there stood the same tall, powerfully built body, and the hair was the same thick, wavy brown hair.

Not possible. Or do I mean probable, for there he stood!

Again he made the little gesture of greeting, and then hurriedly, indeed very awkwardly, he ran towards me, coming closer and closer with his strange ungainly steps as I watched in cold unyielding amazement.

I scanned his mind. Nothing. Locked up tight. Only his grinning face coming clearer and clearer as he entered the brighter luminous glare of the sea. The scent of his fear filled my nostrils along with the smell of his blood. Yes, he was terrified, and yet powerfully excited. Very inviting he looked suddenly—another victim all but thrown into my arms.

How his large brown eyes glittered. And what shining teeth he had.

Coming to a halt some three feet from me, his heart pounding, he held out a fat crumpled envelope in his damp and trembling hand.

I continued to stare at him, revealing nothing—not injured pride nor respect for this astonishing accomplishment that he could find me here, that he would dare. I was just hungry enough to scoop him up now and feed again without giving it another thought. I wasn't reasoning anymore as I looked at him. I saw only blood.

And as if he knew it, indeed sensed it in full, he stiffened, glared at me fiercely for one moment, and then tossed the thick envelope at my feet and danced back frantically over the loose sand. It seemed his legs might go out from under him. He almost fell as he turned and fled.

The thirst subsided a little. Maybe I wasn't reasoning, but I was hesitating, and that did seem to involve some thought. Who was this nervy young son of a bitch?

Again, I tried to scan him. Nothing. Most strange. But there are mortals who cloak themselves naturally, even when they have not the slightest awareness that another might pry into their minds.

On and on he sped, desperately and in ungainly fashion, disappearing in the darkness of a side street as he continued his progress away from me.

Moments passed.

Now I couldn't pick up his scent anymore at all, save from the envelope, which lay where he had thrown it down.

What on earth could all this mean? He'd known exactly what I was, no doubt of it. Venice and Hong Kong had not been coincidence. His sudden fear, if nothing else, had made it plain. But I had to smile at his overall courage. Imagine, following such a creature as me.

Was he some crazed worshiper, come to pound on the temple door in the hopes I'd give him the Dark Blood simply out of pity or reward for his temerity? It made me angry suddenly, and bitter, and then again I simply didn't care.

I picked up the envelope, and saw that it was blank and unsealed. Inside, I found, of all things, a printed short story clipped apparently from a paperback book.

It made a small thick wad of pulp pages, stapled together in the upper-left-hand corner. No personal note at all. The author of the story was a lovable creature I knew well, H. P. Lovecraft by name, a writer of the supernatural and the macabre. In fact, I knew the story, too, and could never forget its title: "The Thing on the Doorstep." It had made me laugh.

"The Thing on the Doorstep." I was smiling now. Yes, I remembered the story, that it was clever, that it had been fun.

But why would this strange mortal give such a story to me? It was ludicrous. And suddenly I was angry again, or as angry as my sadness allowed me to be.

I shoved the packet in my coat pocket absently. I pondered. Yes, the fellow was definitely gone. Couldn't even pick up an image of him from anyone else.

Oh, if only he had come to tempt me on some other night, when my soul wasn't sick and weary, when I might have cared just a little—enough at least to have found out what it was all about.

But it seemed already that eons had passed since he had come and gone. The night was empty save for the grinding roar of the big city, and the dim crash of the sea. Even the clouds had thinned and disappeared. The sky seemed endless and harrowingly still.

I looked to the hard bright stars overhead, and let the low sound of the surf wrap me in silence. I gave one last grief-stricken look to the lights of Miami, this city I so loved.

Then I went up, simple as a thought to rise, so swift no mortal could have seen it, this figure ascending higher and higher through the deafening wind, until the great sprawling city was nothing but a distant galaxy fading slowly from view.

So cold it was, this high wind that knows no seasons. The blood inside me was swallowed up as if its sweet warmth had never existed, and soon my face and hands wore a sheathing of cold as if I'd frozen solid, and that sheathing moved underneath my fragile garments, covering all my skin.

But it caused no pain. Or let us say it did not cause enough pain.

Rather it simply dried up comfort. It was only dismal, dreary, the absence of what makes existence worth it—the blazing warmth of fires and caresses, of kisses and arguments, of love and longing and blood.

Ah, the Aztec gods must have been greedy vampires to convince those poor human souls that the universe would cease to exist if the blood didn't flow. Imagine presiding over such an altar, snapping your fingers for another and another and another, squeezing those fresh blood-soaked hearts to your lips like bunches of grapes.

I twisted and turned with the wind, dropped a few feet, then rose again, arms outstretched playfully, then falling at my sides. I lay on my back like a sure swimmer, staring again into the blind and indifferent stars.

By thought alone, I propelled myself eastward. The night still stretched over the city of London, though its clocks ticked out the small hours. London.

There was time to say farewell to David Talbot—my mortal friend.

It had been months since our last meeting in Amsterdam, and I had left him rudely, ashamed for that and for bothering him at all. I'd spied upon him since, but not troubled him. And I knew that I had to go to him now, whatever my state of mind. There wasn't any doubt he would want me to come. It was the proper, decent thing to do.

For one moment I thought of my beloved Louis. No doubt he was in his crumbling little house in its deep swampy garden in New Orleans, reading by the light of the moon as he always did, or giving in to one shuddering candle should the night be cloudy and dark. But it was too late to say farewell to Louis . . . If there was any being among

us who would understand, it was Louis. Or so I told myself. The
opposite is probably closer to the truth . . .

On to London I went.

TWO

THE Motherhouse of the Talamasca, outside London, silent in
its great park of ancient oaks, its sloped rooftops and its vast
lawns blanketed with deep clean snow.

A handsome four-storey edifice full of lead-mullioned windows,
and chimneys ever sending their winding plumes of smoke into the
night.

A place of dark wood-paneled libraries and parlours, bedrooms
with coffered ceilings, thick burgundy carpets, and dining rooms as
quiet as those of a religious order, and members dedicated as priests and
nuns, who can read your mind, see your aura, tell your future from
the palm of your hand, and make an educated guess as to who you
might have been in a past life.

Witches? Well, some of them are, perhaps. But in the main they
are simply scholars—those who have dedicated their lives to the study
of the occult in all its manifestations. Some know more than others.
Some believe more than others. For example, there are those members
in this Motherhouse—and in other motherhouses, in Amsterdam or
Rome or the depths of the Louisiana swamp—who have laid eyes upon
vampires and werewolves, who have felt the potentially lethal physical
telekinetic powers of mortals who can set fires or cause death, who
have spoken to ghosts and received answers from them, who have
battled invisible entities and won—or lost.

For over one thousand years, this order has persisted. It is in fact
older, but its origins are shrouded in mystery—or, to put it more
specifically, David will not explain them to me.

Where does the Talamasca get its money? There is a staggering
abundance of gold and jewels in its vaults. Its investments in the great
banks of Europe are legendary. It owns property in all its home cities,
which alone could sustain it, if it did not possess anything else. And
then there are its various archival treasures—paintings, statues, tapes-

tries, antique furnishings and ornaments—all of which it has acquired in connection with various occult cases and upon which it places no monetary value, for the historical and scholarly value far exceeds any appraisal which could be made.

Its library alone is worth a king's ransom in any earthly currency. There are manuscripts in all languages, indeed some from the famous old library of Alexandria burnt centuries ago, and others from the libraries of the martyred Cathars, whose culture is no more. There are texts from ancient Egypt for a glimpse of which archaeologists might cheerfully commit murder. There are texts by preternatural beings of several known species, including vampires. There are letters and documents in these archives which have been written by me.

None of these treasures interest me. They never have. Oh, in my more playful moments I have toyed with the idea of breaking into the vaults and reclaiming a few old relics that once belonged to immortals I loved. I know these scholars have collected possessions which I myself have abandoned—the contents of rooms in Paris near the end of the last century, the books and furnishings of my old house in the tree-shaded streets of the Garden District, beneath which I slumbered for decades, quite oblivious to those who walked the rotted floors above. God knows what else they have saved from the gnawing mouth of time.

But I no longer cared about those things. That which they had salvaged they might keep.

What I cared about was David, the Superior General who had been my friend since the long ago night when I came rudely and impulsively through the fourth-storey window of his private rooms.

How brave and poised he had been. And how I had liked to look at him, a tall man with a deeply lined face and iron-gray hair. I wondered then if a young man could ever possess such beauty. But that he knew me, knew what I was—that had been his greatest charm for me.

What if I make you one of us. I could do it, you know . . .

He's never wavered in his conviction. "Not even on my deathbed will I accept," he'd said. But he'd been fascinated by my mere presence, he couldn't conceal it, though he had concealed his thoughts well enough from me ever since that first time.

Indeed his mind had become like a strongbox to which there was no key. And I'd been left only with his radiant and affectionate facial expressions and a soft, cultured voice that could talk the Devil into behaving well.

As I reached the Motherhouse now in the small hours, amid the snow of the English winter, it was to David's familiar windows that I went, only to find his rooms empty and dark.

I thought of our most recent meeting. Could he have gone to Amsterdam again?

That last trip had been unexpected or so I was able to find out, when I came to search for him, before his clever flock of psychics sensed my meddlesome telepathic scanning—which they do with remarkable efficiency—and quickly cut me off.

Seems some errand of great importance had compelled David's presence in Holland.

The Dutch Motherhouse was older than the one outside London, with vaults beneath it to which the Superior General alone had the key. David had to locate a portrait by Rembrandt, one of the most significant treasures in the possession of the order, have it copied, and send that copy to his close friend Aaron Lightner, who needed it in connection with an important paranormal investigation being carried on in the States.

I had followed David to Amsterdam and spied on him there, telling myself that I would not disturb him, as I had done many times before.

Let me tell the story of that episode now.

At a safe distance I had tracked him as he walked briskly in the late evening, masking my thoughts as skillfully as he always masked his own. What a striking figure he made under the elm trees along the Singel gracht, as he stopped again and again to admire the narrow old three- and four-storey Dutch houses, with their high step gables, and bright windows left undraped, it seemed, for the pleasure of the passersby.

I sensed a change in him almost at once. He carried his cane as always, though it was plain he still had no need of it, and he flipped it upon his shoulder as he'd done before. But there was a brooding to him as he walked; a pronounced dissatisfaction; and hour after hour passed during which he wandered as if time were of no importance at all.

It was very clear to me soon that David was reminiscing, and now and then I did manage to catch some pungent image of his youth in the tropics, even flashes of a verdant jungle so very different from this wintry northern city, which was surely never warm. I had not had my dream of the tiger yet. I did not know what this meant.

It was tantalizingly fragmentary. David's skills at keeping his thoughts inside were simply too good.

On and on he walked, however, sometimes as if he were being driven, and on and on I followed, feeling strangely comforted by the mere sight of him several blocks ahead.

Had it not been for the bicycles forever whizzing past him, he would have looked like a young man. But the bicycles startled him. He had an old man's inordinate fear of being struck down and hurt. He'd look resentfully after the young riders. Then he'd fall back into his thoughts.

It was almost dawn when he inevitably returned to the Mother-house. And surely he must have slept the greater part of each day.

He was already walking again when I caught up with him one evening, and once again there seemed no destination in particular. Rather he meandered through Amsterdam's many small cobblestoned streets. He seemed to like it as much as I knew he liked Venice, and with reason, for the cities, both dense and darkly colored, have, in spite of all their marked differences, a similar charm. That one is a Catholic city, rank and full of lovely decay, and the other is Protestant and therefore very clean and efficient, made me, now and then, smile.

The following night, he was again on his own, whistling to himself as he covered the miles briskly, and it soon came clear to me that he was avoiding the Motherhouse. Indeed, he seemed to be avoiding everything, and when one of his old friends—another Englishman and a member of the order—chanced to meet him unexpectedly near a bookseller's in the Leidsestraat, it was plain from the conversation that David had not been himself for some time.

The British are so very polite in discussing and diagnosing such matters. But this is what I separated out from all the marvelous diplomacy. David was neglecting his duties as Superior General. David spent all his time away from the Motherhouse. When in England, David went to his ancestral home in the Cotswolds more and more often. What was wrong?

David merely shrugged off all these various suggestions as if he could not retain interest in the exchange. He made some vague remark to the effect that the Talamasca could run itself without a Superior General for a century, it was so well disciplined and tradition bound, and filled with dedicated members. Then off he went to browse in the bookseller's, where he bought a paperback translation in English of Goethe's *Faust*. Then he dined alone in a small Indonesian restaurant, with *Faust* propped before him, eyes racing over the pages, as he consumed his spicy feast.

As he was busy with his knife and fork, I went back to the bookstore and bought a copy of the very same book. What a bizarre piece of work!

I can't claim to have understood it, or why David was reading it. Indeed it frightened me that the reason might be obvious and perhaps I rejected the idea at once.

Nevertheless I rather loved it, especially the ending, where Faust went to heaven, of course. I don't think that happened in the older legends. Faust always went to hell. I wrote it off to Goethe's Romantic optimism, and the fact that he had been so old by the time he wrote the end. The work of the very old is always extremely powerful and intriguing, and infinitely worth pondering, and all the more perhaps because creative stamina deserts so many artists before they are truly old.

In the very small hours, after David had vanished into the Mother-house, I roamed the city alone. I wanted to know it because he knew it, because Amsterdam was part of his life.

I wandered through the enormous Rijksmuseum, perusing the paintings of Rembrandt, whom I had always loved. I crept like a thief through the house of Rembrandt in the Jodenbreestraat, now made into a little shrine for the public during daylight hours, and I walked the many narrow lanes of the city, feeling the shimmer of olden times. Amsterdam is an exciting place, swarming with young people from all over the new homogenized Europe, a city that never sleeps.

I probably would never have come here had it not been for David. This city had never caught my fancy. And now I found it most agreeable, a vampire's city for its vast late-night crowds, but it was David of course that I wanted to see. I realized I could not leave without at least exchanging a few words.

Finally, a week after my arrival, I found David in the empty Rijksmuseum, just after sunset, sitting on the bench before the great Rembrandt portrait of the Members of the Drapers' Guild.

Did David know, somehow, that I'd been there? Impossible, yet there he was.

And it was obvious from his conversation with the guard—who was just taking his leave of David—that his venerable order of moss-back snoops contributed mightily to the arts of the various cities in which they were domiciled. So it was an easy thing for the members to gain access to museums to see their treasures when the public was barred.

And to think, I have to break into these places like a cheap crook!

It was completely silent in the high-ceilinged marble halls when I came upon him. He sat on the long wooden bench, his copy of *Faust*, now very dog-eared and full of bookmarks, held loosely and indifferently in his right hand.

He was staring steadily at the painting, which was that of several proper Dutchmen, gathered at a table, dealing with the affairs of commerce, no doubt, yet staring serenely at the viewer from beneath the broad brims of their big black hats. This is scarcely the total effect of this picture. The faces are exquisitely beautiful, full of wisdom and gentleness and a near angelic patience. Indeed, these men more resemble angels than ordinary men.

They seemed possessed of a great secret, and if all men were to learn that secret, there would be no more wars or vice or malice on earth. How did such persons ever become members of the Drapers' Guild of Amsterdam in the 1600s? But then I move ahead of my tale . . .

David gave a start when I appeared, moving slowly and silently out of the shadows towards him. I took a place beside him on the bench.

I was dressed like a tramp, for I had acquired no real lodgings in Amsterdam, and my hair was tangled from the wind.

I sat very still for a long moment, opening my mind with an act of will that felt rather like a human sigh, letting him know how concerned I was for his well-being, and how I'd tried for his sake to leave him in peace.

His heart was beating rapidly. His face, when I turned to him, was filled with immediate and generous warmth.

He reached over with his right hand and grasped my right arm. "I'm glad to see you as always, so very glad."

"Ah, but I've done you harm. I know I have." I didn't want to say how I'd followed him, how I'd overheard the conversation between him and his comrade, or dwell upon what I saw with my own eyes.

I vowed I would not torment him with my old question. And yet I saw death when I looked at him, even more perhaps for his brightness and cheerfulness, and the vigor in his eyes.

He gave me a long lingering thoughtful look, and then he withdrew his hand, and his eyes moved back to the painting.

"Are there any vampires in this world who have such faces?" he asked. He gestured to the men staring down at us from the canvas. "I am speaking of the knowledge and understanding which lies behind these faces. I'm speaking of something more indicative of immortality than a preternatural body anatomically dependent upon the drinking of human blood."

"Vampires with such faces?" I responded. "David, that is unfair. There are no *men* with such faces. There never were. Look at any of Rembrandt's paintings. Absurd to believe that such people ever existed, let alone that Amsterdam was full of them in Rembrandt's time, that every man or woman who ever darkened his door was an angel. No, it's Rembrandt you see in these faces, and Rembrandt is immortal, of course."

He smiled. "It's not true what you're saying. And what a desperate loneliness emanates from you. Don't you see I can't accept your gift, and if I did, what would you think of me? Would you still crave my company? Would I crave yours?"

I scarce heard these last words. I was staring at the painting, staring at these men who were indeed like angels. And a quiet anger had come over me, and I didn't want to linger there anymore. I had forsworn the assault, yet he had defended himself against me. No, I should not have come.

Spy on him, yes, but not linger. And once again, I moved swiftly to go.

He was furious with me for doing it. I heard his voice ring out in the great empty space.

"Unfair of you to go like that! Positively rude of you to do it! Have you no honor? What about manners if there is no honor left?" And then he broke off, for I was nowhere near him, it was as if I'd vanished, and he was a man alone in the huge and cold museum speaking aloud to himself.

I was ashamed but too angry and bruised to go back to him,

though why, I didn't know. What had I done to this being! How Marius would scold me for this.

I wandered about Amsterdam for hours, purloining some thick parchment writing paper of the kind I most like, and a fine-pointed pen of the automatic kind that spews black ink forever, and then I sought a noisy sinister little tavern in the old red-light district with its painted women and drugged vagabond youths, where I could work on a letter to David, unnoticed and undisturbed as long as I kept a mug of beer at my side.

I didn't know what I meant to write, from one sentence to the next, only that I had to tell him in some way that I was sorry for my behavior, and that something had snapped in my soul when I beheld the men in the Rembrandt portrait, and so I wrote, in a hasty and driven fashion, this narrative of sorts.

You are right. It was despicable the way I left you. Worse, it was cowardly. I promise you that when we meet again, I shall let you say all you have to say.

I myself have this theory about Rembrandt. I have spent many hours studying his paintings everywhere—in Amsterdam, Chicago, New York, or wherever I find them—and I do believe as I told you that so many great souls could not have existed as Rembrandt's paintings would have us believe.

This is my theory, and please bear in mind when you read it that it accommodates all the elements involved. And this accommodation used to be the measure of the elegance of theories . . . before the word "science" came to mean what it means today.

I believe that Rembrandt sold his soul to the Devil when he was a young man. It was a simple bargain. The Devil promised to make Rembrandt the most famous painter of his time. The Devil sent hordes of mortals to Rembrandt for portraits. He gave wealth to Rembrandt, he gave him a charming house in Amsterdam, a wife and later a mistress, because he was sure he would have Rembrandt's soul in the end.

But Rembrandt had been changed by his encounter with the Devil. Having seen such undeniable evidence of evil, he found himself obsessed with the question What is good? He searched the faces of his subjects for their inner divinity; and to his amazement he was able to see the spark of it in the most unworthy of men.

His skill was such—and please understand, he had got no skill from the Devil; the skill was his to begin with—that not only could he see that goodness, he could paint it; he could allow his knowledge of it, and his faith in it, to suffuse the whole.

With each portrait he understood the grace and goodness of mankind ever more deeply. He understood the capacity for compassion and for wisdom which resides in every soul. His skill increased as he continued; the flash of the infinite became ever more subtle; the person himself ever more particular; and more grand and serene and magnificent each work.

At last the faces Rembrandt painted were not flesh-and-blood faces at all. They were spiritual countenances, portraits of what lay within the body of the man or the woman; they were visions of what that person was at his or her finest hour, of what that person stood to become.

This is why the merchants of the Drapers' Guild look like the oldest and wisest of God's saints.

But nowhere is this spiritual depth and insight more clearly manifest than in Rembrandt's self-portraits. And surely you know that he left us one hundred and twenty-two of these.

Why do you think he painted so many? They were his personal plea to God to note the progress of this man who, through his close observation of others like him, had been completely religiously transformed. "This is my vision," said Rembrandt to God.

Towards the end of Rembrandt's life, the Devil grew suspicious. He did not want his minion to be creating such magnificent paintings, so full of warmth and kindness. He had believed the Dutch to be a materialistic and therefore worldly people. And here in pictures full of rich clothing and expensive possessions, gleamed the undeniable evidence that human beings are wholly unlike any other animal in the cosmos—they are a precious mingling of the flesh and immortal fire.

Well, Rembrandt suffered all the abuse heaped upon him by the Devil. He lost his fine house in the Jodenbreestraat. He lost his mistress, and finally even his son. Yet on and on he painted, without a trace of bitterness or perversity; on and on he infused his paintings with love.

Finally he lay on his deathbed. The Devil pranced about, gleefully, ready to snatch Rembrandt's soul and pinch it between evil little fingers. But the angels and saints cried to God to intervene.

"In all the world, who knows more about goodness?" they asked, pointing to the dying Rembrandt. "Who has shown more than this painter? We look to his portraits when we would know the divine in man."

And so God broke the pact between Rembrandt and the Devil. He took to himself the soul of Rembrandt, and the Devil, so recently cheated of Faust for the very same reason, went mad with rage.

Well, he would bury the life of Rembrandt in obscurity. He would see to it that all the man's personal possessions and records were swallowed by the great flow of time. And that is of course why we know almost nothing of Rembrandt's true life, or what sort of person he was.

But the Devil could not control the fate of the paintings. Try as he might, he could not make people burn them, throw them away, or set them aside for the newer, more fashionable artists. In fact, a curious thing happened, seemingly without a marked beginning. Rembrandt became the most admired of all painters who had ever lived; Rembrandt became the greatest painter of all time.

That is my theory of Rembrandt and those faces.

Now if I were mortal, I would write a novel about Rembrandt, on this theme. But I am not mortal. I cannot save my soul through art or Good Works. I am a creature like the Devil, with one difference. I love the paintings of Rembrandt!

Yet it breaks my heart to look at them. It broke my heart to see you there in the museum. And you are perfectly right that there are no vampires with faces like the saints of the Drapers' Guild.

That's why I left you so rudely in the museum. It was not the Devil's Rage. It was merely sorrow.

Again, I promise you that next time we meet, I shall let you say all that you want to say.

I scribbled the number of my Paris agent on the bottom of this letter, along with the post address, as I had done in the past when writing to David though David had never replied.

Then I went on a pilgrimage of sorts, revisiting the paintings of

Rembrandt in the great collections of the world. I saw nothing in my travels to sway me in my belief in Rembrandt's goodness. The pilgrimage proved penitential, for I clung to my fiction about Rembrandt. But I resolved anew never to bother David again.

Then I had the dream. *Tyger, tyger* . . . David in danger. I woke with a start in my chair in Louis's little shack—as if I'd been shaken by a warning hand.

Night had almost ended in England. I had to hurry. But when I finally found David, he was in a quaint little tavern in a village in the Cotswolds which can only be reached by one narrow and treacherous road.

This was his home village, not far from his ancestral manor, I quickly divined from scanning those around him—a little one-street place of sixteenth-century buildings, housing shops and an inn now dependent upon the fickleness of tourists, which David had restored from his own pocket, and visited more and more often to escape his London life.

Positively eerie little spot!

All David was doing, however, was guzzling his beloved single-malt Scotch and scribbling drawings of the Devil on napkins. Mephistopheles with his lute? The horned Satan dancing under the light of the moon? It must have been his dejection I had sensed over the miles, or more truly the concern of those watching him. It was their image of him which I had caught.

I wanted so to talk to him. I didn't dare to do it. I would have created too much of a stir in the little tavern, where the concerned old proprietor and his two hulking and silent nephews remained awake and smoking their odoriferous pipes only on account of the august presence of the local lord—who was getting as drunk as a lord.

For an hour, I had stood near, peering through the little window. Then I'd gone away.

Now—many, many months later—as the snow fell over London, as it fell in big silent flakes over the high facade of the Motherhouse of the Talamasca, I searched for him, in a dull weary state, thinking that there was no one in all the world whom I must see but him. I scanned the minds of the members, sleeping and awake. I roused them. I heard them come to attention as clearly as if they had snapped on their lights on rising from bed.

But I had what I wanted before they could shut me out.

David was gone to the manor house in the Cotswolds, somewhere, no doubt, in the vicinity of that curious little village with its quaint tavern.

Well, I could find it, couldn't I? I went to seek him there.

The snow was falling ever more heavily as I traveled close to the earth, cold and angry, with all memory of the blood I'd drunk now wiped away.

Other dreams came back to me, as they always do in bitter winter, of the harsh and miserable snows of my mortal boyhood, of the chill stone rooms of my father's castle, and of the little fire, and my great mastiffs snoring in the hay beside me, keeping me snug and warm.

Those dogs had been slain on my last wolf hunt.

I hated so to remember it, and yet it was always sweet to think I was there again—with the clean smell of the little fire and of those powerful dogs tumbled against me, and that I was alive, truly alive!— and the hunt had never taken place. I'd never gone to Paris, I'd never seduced the powerful and demented vampire Magnus. The little stone room was full of the good scent of the dogs, and I could sleep now beside them, and be safe.

At last I drew near to a small Elizabethan manor house in the mountains, a very beautiful stone structure of deep-pitched roofs and narrow gables, of deep-set thick glass windows, far smaller than the Motherhouse, yet very grand on its own scale.

Only one set of windows was lighted, and when I approached I saw that it was the library and David was there, seated by a great noisily burning fire.

He had his familiar leatherbound diary in his hand, and he was writing with an ink pen, very rapidly. He had no sense at all that he was being watched. Now and then he consulted another leatherbound book, on the table at his side. I could easily see that this was a Christian Bible, with its double columns of small print and the gilt edges of its pages, and the ribbon that marked his place.

With only a little effort I observed it was the Book of Genesis from which David was reading, and apparently making notes. There was his copy of *Faust* beside it. What on earth interested him in all this?

The room itself was lined with books. A single lamp burned over David's shoulder. It was as many a library in northern climes—cozy and inviting, with a low beamed ceiling, and big comfortable old leather chairs.

But what rendered it unusual were the relics of a life lived in another clime. There were his cherished mementos of those remembered years.

The mounted head of a spotted leopard was perched above the glowing fireplace. And the great black head of a buffalo was fixed to the far right wall. There were many small Hindu statues of bronze here and there on shelves and on tables. Small jewel-like Indian rugs lay on the brown carpet, before hearth and doorway and windows.

And the long flaming skin of his Bengal tiger lay sprawled in the very center of the room, its head carefully preserved, with glass eyes and those immense fangs which I had seen with such horrid vividness in my dream.

It was to this last trophy that David gave his full attention suddenly, and then taking his eyes off it with difficulty, went back to writing again. I tried to scan him. Nothing. Why had I bothered? Not even a glimmer of the mangrove forests where such a beast might have been slain. But once again he looked at the tiger, and then, forgetting his pen, sank deep into his thoughts.

Of course it comforted me merely to watch him, as it had always done. I glimpsed many framed photographs in the shadows—pictures of David when he'd been young, and many obviously taken of him in India before a lovely bungalow with deep porches and a high roof. Pictures of his mother and father. Pictures of him with the animals he'd killed. Did this explain my dream?

I ignored the snow falling all around me, covering my hair and my shoulders and even my loosely folded arms. Finally I stirred. There was only an hour before dawn.

I moved around the house, found a back door, commanded the latch to slide back, and entered the warm little low-ceilinged hall. Old wood in this place, soaked through and through with lacquers or oil. I laid my hands on the beams of the door and saw in a shimmer a great oak woodland full of sunlight, and then only the shadows surrounded me. I smelled the aroma of the distant fire.

I realized David was standing at the far end of the hallway, beckoning for me to come near. But something in my appearance alarmed him. Ah, well, I was covered with snow and a thin layer of ice.

We went into the library together and I took the chair opposite his. He left me for a moment during which time I was merely staring at the fire and feeling it melt the sleet that covered me. I was thinking of why I had come and how I would put it into words. My hands were as white as the snow was white.

When he appeared again, he had a large warm towel for me, and I took this and wiped my face and my hair and then my hands. How good it felt.

"Thank you," I said.

"You looked a statue," he said.

"Yes, I do look that way, now, don't I? I'm going on."

"What do you mean?" He sat down across from me. "Explain."

"I'm going to a desert place. I've figured a way to end it, I think. This is not a simple matter at all."

"Why do you want to do that?"

"Don't want to be alive anymore. That part is simple enough. I don't look forward to death the way you do. It isn't that. Tonight I—" I stopped. I saw the old woman in her neat bed, in her flowered robe, against the quilted nylon. Then I saw that strange brown-haired man watching me, the one who had come to me on the beach and given me the story which I still had, crammed inside my coat.

Meaningless. You come too late, whoever you are.

Why bother to explain?

I saw Claudia suddenly as if she were standing there in some other realm, staring at me, waiting for me to see her. How clever that our minds can invoke an image so seemingly real. She might as well have been right there by David's desk in the shadows. Claudia, who had forced her long knife through my chest. "I'll put you in your coffin forever, Father." But then I saw Claudia all the time now, didn't I? I saw Claudia in dream after dream . . .

"Don't do this," David said.

"It's time, David," I whispered, thinking in a vague and distant way how disappointed Marius would be.

Had David heard me? Perhaps my voice had been too soft. Some small crackling sound came from the fire, a bit of kindling collapsing perhaps or sap still moist and sizzling within the huge log. I saw that cold bedchamber in my boyhood home again, and suddenly, I had my arm around one of those big dogs, those lazy loving dogs. To see a wolf slay a dog is monstrous!

I should have died that day. Not even the best of hunters should be able to slay a pack of wolves. And maybe that was the cosmic error. I'd been meant to go, if indeed there is any such continuity, and in overreaching, had caught the devil's eye. "Wolf killer." The vampire Magnus had said it so lovingly, as he had carried me to his lair.

David had sunk back in the chair, putting one foot absently on the fender, and his eyes were fixed on the flames. He was deeply distressed, even a little frantic, though he held it inside very well.

"Won't it be painful?" he asked, looking at me.

Just for a moment, I didn't know what he meant. Then I remembered.

I gave a little laugh.

"I came to say good-bye to you, to ask you if you're certain about your decision. It seemed somehow the right thing to tell you I was going, and that this would be your last chance. It seemed sporting, actually. You follow me? Or do you think it's simply another excuse? Doesn't matter really."

"Like Magnus in your story," he said. "You'd make your heir, then go into the fire."

"It wasn't merely a story," I said, not meaning to be argumentative, and wondering why it sounded that way. "And yes, perhaps it's like that. I honestly don't know."

"Why do you want to destroy yourself?" He sounded desperate.

How I had hurt this man.

I looked at the sprawling tiger with its magnificent black stripes and deep orange fur.

"That was a man-eater, wasn't it?" I asked.

He hesitated as if he didn't fully understand the question, then as if waking, he nodded. "Yes." He glanced at the tiger, then he looked at me. "I don't want you to do it. Postpone it, for the love of heaven. Don't do it. Why tonight, of all times?"

He was making me laugh against my will. "Tonight's a fine night for doing it," I said. "No, I'm going." And suddenly there was a great exhilaration in me because I realized I meant it! It wasn't just some fancy. I would never have told him if it was. "I've figured a method. I'll go as high as I can before the sun comes over the horizon. There won't be any way to find shelter. The desert there is very hard."

And I will die in fire. Not cold, as I'd been on that mountain when the wolves surrounded me. In heat, as Claudia had died.

"No, don't do it," he said. How earnest he was, how persuasive. But it didn't work.

"Do you want the blood?" I asked. "It doesn't take very long. There's very little pain. I'm confident the others won't hurt you. I'll make you so strong they'd have a devil of a time if they tried."

Again, it was so like Magnus, who'd left me an orphan without so much as a warning that Armand and his ancient coven could come after me, cursing me and seeking to put an end to my newborn life. And Magnus had known that I would prevail.

"Lestat, I do not want the blood. But I want you to stay here. Look, give me a matter of a few nights only. Just that much. On account of friendship, Lestat, stay with me now. Can't you give me those few hours? And then if you must go through with it, I won't argue anymore."

"Why?"

He looked stricken. Then he said, "Let me talk to you, let me change your mind."

"You killed the tiger when you were very young, didn't you? It was in India." I gazed around at the other trophies. "I saw the tiger in a dream."

He didn't answer. He seemed anxious and perplexed.

"I've hurt you," I said. "I've driven you deep into memories of your youth. I've made you aware of time, and you weren't so aware of it before."

Something happened in his face. I had wounded him with these words. Yet he shook his head.

"David, take the blood from me before I go!" I whispered suddenly, desperately. "You don't have a year left to you. I can hear it when I'm near you! I can hear the weakness in your heart."

"You don't know that, my friend," he said patiently. "Stay here with me. I'll tell you all about the tiger, about those days in India. I hunted in Africa then, and once in the Amazon. Such adventures. I wasn't the musty scholar then as I am now . . ."

"I know." I smiled. He had never spoken this way to me before, never offered so much. "It's too late, David," I said. Again, I saw the dream. I saw that thin gold chain around David's neck. Had the tiger been going for the chain? That didn't make sense. What remained was the sense of danger.

I stared at the skin of the beast. How purely vicious was his face.

"Was it fun to kill the tiger?" I asked.

He hesitated. Then forced himself to answer. "It was a man-eater. It feasted on children. Yes, I suppose it was fun."

I laughed softly. "Ah, well, then we have that in common, me and the tiger. And Claudia is waiting for me."

"You don't really believe that, do you?"

"No. I guess if I did, I'd be afraid to die." I saw Claudia quite vividly . . . a tiny oval portrait on porcelain—golden hair, blue eyes. Something fierce and true in the expression, in spite of the saccharine colors and the oval frame. Had I ever possessed such a locket, for that is what it was, surely. A locket. A chill came over me. I remembered the texture of her hair. Once again, it was as if she were very near me. Were I to turn, I might see her beside me in the shadows, with her hand on the back of my chair. I did turn around. Nothing. I was going to lose my nerve if I didn't get out of here.

"Lestat!" David said urgently. He was scanning me, desperately trying to think of something more to say. He pointed to my coat. "What's that in your pocket? A note you've written? You mean to leave it with me? Let me read it now."

"Oh, this, this strange little story," I said, "here, you may have it. I bequeath it to you. Fitting that it should be in a library, perhaps wedged somewhere on one of these shelves."

I took out the little folded packet and glanced at it. "Yes, I've read this. It's sort of amusing." I tossed the packet into his lap. "Some fool mortal gave it to me, some poor benighted soul who knew who I was and had just enough courage to toss it at my feet."

"Explain this to me," said David. He unfolded the pages. "Why are you carrying it with you? Good Lord—Lovecraft." He gave a little shake of his head.

"I just did explain it," I said. "It's no use, David, I can't be talked down from the high ledge. I'm going. Besides, the story doesn't mean a thing. Poor fool . . ."

He had had such strange glittering eyes. Whatever had been so wrong about the way he came running towards me across the sand? About his awkward panic-stricken retreat? His manner had indicated such importance! Ah, but this was foolish. I didn't care, and I knew I didn't. I knew what I meant to do.

"Lestat, stay here!" David said. "You promised the very next time we met, you would let me say all I have to say. You wrote that to me, Lestat, you remember? You won't go back on your word."

"Well, I have to go back on it, David. And you have to forgive me because I'm going. Perhaps there is no heaven or hell, and I'll see you on the other side."

"And what if there is both? What then?"

"You've been reading too much of the Bible. Read the Lovecraft story." Again, I gave a short laugh. I gestured to the pages he was holding. "Better for your peace of mind. And stay away from *Faust*, for heaven's sake. You really think angels will come in the end and take us away? Well, not me, perhaps, but you?"

"Don't go," he said, and his voice was so soft and imploring that it took my breath away.

But I was already going.

I barely heard him call out behind me:

"Lestat, I need you. You're the only friend I have."

How tragic those words! I wanted to say I was sorry, sorry for all of it. But it was too late now for that. And besides, I think he knew.

I shot upwards in the cold darkness, driving through the descending snow. All life seemed utterly unbearable to me, both in its horror and its splendour. The tiny house looked warm down there, its light spilling on the white ground, its chimney giving forth that thin coil of blue smoke.

I thought of David again walking alone through Amsterdam, but then I thought of Rembrandt's faces. And I saw David's face again in the library fire. He looked like a man painted by Rembrandt. He had looked that way ever since I'd known him. And what did we look like—frozen forever in the form we had when the Dark Blood entered our veins? Claudia had been for decades that child painted on porcelain. And I was like one of Michelangelo's statues, turning white as marble. And just as cold.

I knew I would keep my word.

But you know there is a terrible lie in all this. I didn't really believe I *could* be killed by the sun anymore. Well, I was certainly going to give it a good try.

THREE

THE Gobi Desert.

Eons ago, in the saurian age, as men have called it, great lizards died in this strange part of the world by the thousands. No one knows why they came here; why they perished. Was it a realm of tropical trees and steaming swamps? We don't know. All we have now in this spot is the desert and millions upon millions of fossils, telling a fragmentary tale of giant reptiles who surely made the earth tremble with each step they took.

The Gobi Desert is therefore an immense graveyard and a fitting place for me to look the sun in the face. I lay a long time in the sand before the sunrise, collecting my last thoughts.

The trick was to rise to the very limit of the atmosphere, into the sunrise, so to speak. Then when I lost consciousness I would tumble down in the terrible heat, and my body would be shattered by this great fall upon the desert floor. How could it then dig in beneath the surface, as it might have done, by its own evil volition, were I whole and in a land of soft soil?

Besides, if the blast of light was sufficiently strong to burn me up, naked and so high above the earth, perhaps I would be dead and gone before my remains ever struck the hard bed of sand.

As the old expression goes, it seemed like a good idea at the time. Nothing much could have deterred me. Yet I did wonder if the other immortals knew what I meant to do and whether or not they were in the least concerned. I certainly sent them no farewell messages; I threw out no random images of what I meant to do.

At last the great warmth of dawn crept across the desert. I rose to my knees, stripped off my clothing, and began the ascent, my eyes already burning from the faintest bit of light.

Higher and higher I went, propelling myself well beyond the place where my body tended to stop and begin to float of its own accord. Finally I could not breathe, as the air was very thin, and it took a great effort to support myself at this height.

Then the light came. So immense, so hot, so blinding that it seemed a great roaring noise as much as a vision filling my sight. I saw yellow and orange fire covering everything. I stared right into it, though it felt like scalding water poured into my eyes. I think I opened my mouth as if to swallow it, this divine fire! The sun was mine suddenly. I was seeing it; I was reaching for it. And then the light was covering me like molten lead, paralyzing me and torturing me beyond endurance, and my own cries filled my ears. Still I would not look away, still I would not fall!

Thus I defy you, heaven! And there were no words suddenly and no thoughts. I was twisting, swimming in it. And as the darkness and the coldness rose up to envelop me—it was nothing but the loss of consciousness—I realized that I had begun to fall.

The sound was the sound of the air rushing past me, and it seemed that the voices of others were calling to me, and through the horrid mingled roar, I heard distinctly the voice of a child.

Then nothing . . .

Was I dreaming?

We were in a small close place, a hospital smelling of sickness and death, and I was pointing to the bed, and the child who lay on the pillow, white and small and half dead.

There was a sharp riff of laughter. I smelled an oil lamp—that moment when the wick has blown out.

"Lestat," she said. How beautiful her little voice.

I tried to explain about my father's castle, about the snow falling, and my dogs waiting there. That's where I had wanted to go. I could hear them suddenly, that deep baying bark of the mastiffs, echoing up the snow-covered slopes, and I could almost see the towers of the castle itself.

But then she said:

"Not yet."

IT WAS night again when I awoke. I was lying on the desert floor. The dunes bestirred by the wind had spread a fine mist of sand over all my limbs. I felt pain all over. Pain even in the roots of my hair. I felt such pain I couldn't will myself to move.

For hours I lay there. Now and then I gave a soft moan. It made no difference in the pain I felt. When I moved my limbs even a little, the sand was like tiny particles of sharp glass against my back and my calves and the heels of my feet.

I thought of all those to whom I might have called for help. I did not call. Only gradually did I realize that if I remained here, the sun would come again, naturally enough, and I would be caught once more and burned once more. Yet still I might not die.

I had to remain, didn't I? What sort of coward would seek shelter now?

But all I had to do was look at my hands in the light of the stars to see that I was not going to die. I was burnt, yes, my skin was brown and wrinkled and roaring with pain. But I was nowhere near death.

At last I rolled over and tried to rest my face against the sand, but this was no more comforting than staring up into the stars.

Then I felt the sun coming. I was weeping as the great orange light spilled over all the world. The pain caught my back first and then I thought my head was burning, that it would explode, and that the fire was eating my eyes. I was mad when the darkness of oblivion came, absolutely mad.

When I awoke the following evening, I felt sand in my mouth, sand covering me in my agony. In that madness, I'd apparently buried myself alive.

For hours I remained so, thinking only that this pain was more than any creature could endure.

Finally I struggled to the surface, whimpering like an animal, and I climbed to my feet, each gesture pulling at the pain and intensifying it, and then I willed myself into the air and I started the slow journey west and into the night.

No diminishing of my powers. Ah, only the surface of my body had been deeply harmed.

The wind was infinitely softer than the sand. Nevertheless it brought its own torment, like fingers stroking my burnt skin all over and tugging at the burnt roots of my hair. It stung my burnt eyelids; and scraped at my burnt knees.

I traveled gently for hours, willing myself to David's house once more and feeling the most glorious relief for a few moments as I descended through the cold wet snow.

It was just before morning in England.

I entered by the rear door again, each step an excruciating ordeal. Almost blindly, I found the library and I went down on my knees, ignoring the pain, and collapsed upon the tigerskin rug.

I laid my head beside the tiger's head, and my cheek against its open jaws. Such fine, close fur! I stretched out my arms on its legs and felt its smooth, hard claws under my wrists. The pain shot through me in waves. The fur felt almost silky and the room was cool in its darkness. And in faint shimmers of silent visions, I saw the mangrove forests of India, I saw dark faces, and heard distant voices. And once very clearly for a full instant I saw David as a young man, as I'd seen him in my dream.

It seemed such a miracle, this living young man, full of blood and tissue and such miraculous achievements as eyes and a beating heart and five fingers to each long slender hand.

I saw myself walking in Paris in the old days when I was alive. I was wearing the red velvet cloak, lined with the fur of the wolves I'd killed back in my native Auvergne, never dreaming that things lurked in the shadows, things that could see you and fall in love with you, just because you were young, things that could take your life, just because they loved you and you'd slain a whole pack of wolves . . .

David, the hunter! In belted khaki, with that magnificent gun.

Slowly, I became aware that the pain was already lessened. Good old Lestat, the god, healing with preternatural speed. The pain was like a deep glow settling over my body. I imagined myself giving a warm light to the entire room.

I picked up the scent of mortals. A servant had come into the room and quickly gone out. Poor old guy. It made me laugh to myself in my half sleep, to think what he had seen—a dark-skinned naked man, with a mop of unkempt blond hair, lying atop David's tiger in the darkened room.

Suddenly, I caught David's scent, and I heard again the low familiar thunder of blood in mortal veins. Blood. I was so thirsty for blood. My burnt skin cried for it, and my burning eyes.

A soft flannel blanket was laid over me, very light and cool-feeling to me. There followed a series of little sounds. David was pulling the heavy velvet draperies closed over the windows, which he had not bothered to do all winter. He was fussing with the cloth so that there would be no seams of light.

"Lestat," he whispered. "Let me take you down into the cellar, where you'll surely be safe."

"Doesn't matter, David. May I stay here in this room?"

"Yes, of course, you may stay." Such solicitude.

"Thank you, David." I started to sleep again, and snow was

blowing through the window of my room in the castle, but then it was wholly different. I saw the little hospital bed once more, and the child was in it, and thank God that nurse wasn't there but had gone to stop the one who was crying. Oh, such a terrible, terrible sound. I hated it. I wanted to be . . . where? Home in the deep French winter, of course.

This time the oil lamp was being lighted, instead of going out.

"I told you it wasn't time." Her dress was so perfectly white, and look, how very tiny her pearl buttons! And what a fine band of pretty roses around her head.

"But why?" I asked.

"What did you say?" David asked.

"Talking to Claudia," I explained. She was sitting in the petit-point armchair with her legs straight out before her, toes together and pointed at the ceiling. Were those satin slippers? I grabbed her ankle and kissed it, and when I looked up I saw her chin and her eyelashes as she threw back her head and laughed. Such an exquisite full-throated laugh.

"There are others out there," David said.

I opened my eyes, though it hurt to do it, hurt to see the dim shapes of the room. Sun almost coming. I felt the claws of the tiger under my fingers. Ah, precious beast. David stood at the window. He was peering through a tiny seam between the two panels of drapery.

"Out there," he went on. "They've come to see that you're all right."

Imagine that. "Who are they?" I couldn't hear them, didn't want to hear them. Was it Marius? Surely not the very ancient ones. Why would they care about such a thing?

"I don't know," he said. "But they are there."

"You know the old story," I whispered. "Ignore them and they'll go away." Almost sunrise anyway. They have to go. And they certainly won't hurt you, David.

"I know."

"Don't read my mind if you won't let me read yours," I said.

"Don't be cross. No one will come into this room or disturb you."

"Yes, I can be a danger even in repose . . ." I wanted to say more, to warn him further, but then I realized he was the one mortal who did not require such a warning. Talamasca. Scholars of the paranormal. He knew.

"Sleep now," he said.

I had to laugh at that. What else can I do when the sun rises? Even if it shines full upon my face. But he sounded so firm and reassuring.

To think, in the olden times, I always had the coffin, and sometimes I would polish it slowly until the wood had a great luster to it, and then I'd shine the tiny crucifix on top of it, smiling at myself, at the care with which I buffed the little twisted body of the massacred Christ, the Son of God. I'd loved the satin lining of the box. I'd loved the shape, and the twilight act of rising from the dead. But no more . . .

The sun was truly coming, the cold winter sun of England. I could feel it for certain, and suddenly I was afraid. I could feel the light stealing over the ground outside and striking the windows. But the darkness held on this side of the velvet curtains.

I saw the little flame in the oil lamp rise. It scared me, just because I was in such pain and it was a flame. Her small rounded fingers on the golden key, and that ring, that ring I gave her with the tiny diamond set in pearls. What about the locket? Should I ask her about the locket? *Claudia, was there ever a gold locket . . . ?*

Turning the flame higher and higher. That smell again. Her dimpled hand. All through the long flat in the Rue Royale, one could catch the scent of the oil. Ah, that old wallpaper, and the pretty handmade furniture, and Louis writing at his desk, sharp smell of the black ink, dull scratch of the quill pen . . .

Her little hand was touching my cheek, so deliciously cold, and that vague thrill that passes through me when one of the others touches me, *our skin.*

"Why would anyone want *me* to live?" I asked. At least that was what I started to ask . . . and then I was simply gone.

FOUR

TWILIGHT. The pain was still very great. I didn't want to move. The skin on my chest and on my legs was tightening and tingling and this only gave variation to the pain.

Even the blood thirst, raging fiercely, and the smell of the blood of the servants in the house couldn't make me move. I knew David was there, but I didn't speak to him. I thought if I tried to speak, I would weep on account of the pain.

I slept and I know that I dreamed, but I couldn't remember the dreams when next I opened my eyes. I would see the oil lamp again, and the light still frightened me. And so did her voice.

Once I woke talking to her in the darkness. "Why you of all people? Why you in my dreams? Where's your bloody knife?"

I was grateful when the dawn came. I had sometimes deliberately clamped my mouth shut not to cry out over the pain.

When I woke the second night, the pain was not very great. My body was sore all over, perhaps what mortals call raw. But the agony was clearly past. I was lying still on the tiger, and the room felt just a little uncomfortably cold.

There were logs stacked in the stone fireplace, set way back under the broken arch, against the blackened bricks. The kindling was all there, with a bit of rumpled newspaper. All in readiness. Hmmm. Someone had come dangerously close to me in my sleep. I hoped to heaven I had not reached out, as we sometimes do in our trance, and pinioned this poor creature.

I closed my eyes and listened. Snow falling on the roof, snow tumbling down into the chimney. I opened my eyes again and saw the gleaming bits of moisture on the logs.

Then I concentrated, and felt the energy leap out from me like a long thin tongue and touch the kindling, which burst at once into tiny dancing flames. The thick crusted surface of the logs began to warm and then blister. The fire was on its way.

I felt a sudden flush of exquisite pain in my cheeks and on my forehead as the light grew brighter. Interesting. I climbed to my knees and stood up, alone in the room. I looked at the brass lamp beside David's chair. With a tiny soundless mental twist, I turned it on.

There were clothes on the chair, a pair of new pants of thick soft dark flannel, a white cotton shirt, and a rather shapeless jacket of old wool. All these clothes were a little too big. They had been David's clothes. Even the fur-lined slippers were too big. But I wanted to be dressed. There were some undistinguished cotton undergarments also, of the kind everyone wears in the twentieth century, and a comb for my hair.

I took my time with everything, noting only a throbbing soreness as I pulled the cloth over my skin. My scalp hurt when I combed my hair. Finally I simply shook it until all the sand and dust was out of it, tumbling down into the thick carpet, and disappearing conveniently enough from view. Putting on the slippers was very nice. But what I wanted now was a mirror.

I found one in the hallway, an old dark mirror in a heavy gilded frame. Enough light came from the open library door for me to see myself fairly well.

For a moment, I could not quite believe what I beheld. My skin was smooth all over, as completely unblemished as it had ever been. But it was an amber color now, the very color of the frame of the mirror, and gleaming only slightly, no more than that of a mortal who had spent a long luxurious sojourn in tropical seas.

My eyebrows and eyelashes shone brightly, as is always the case with the blond hair of such sun-browned individuals, and the few lines of my face, left to me by the Dark Gift, were a little bit more deeply etched than before. I refer here to two small commas at the corners of my mouth, the result of smiling so much when I was alive; and to a few very fine lines at the corners of my eyes, and the trace of a line or two across my forehead. Very nice to have them back for I had not seen them in a long time.

My hands had suffered more. They were darker than my face, and very human-looking, with many little creases, which put me in mind at once of how many fine wrinkles mortal hands do have.

The nails still glistened in a manner that might alarm humans, but it would be a simple thing to rub a bit of ash over them. My eyes, of course, were another matter. Never had they seemed so bright and so iridescent. But a pair of smoke-colored glasses was all that I needed there. The bigger mask of black glasses was no longer necessary to cover up the shining white skin.

Ye gods, how perfectly wonderful, I thought, staring at my own reflection. You look almost like a man! Almost like a man! I could feel a dull ache all over in these burnt tissues, but that felt good to me, as if it were reminding me of the shape of my body, and its human limits.

I could have shouted. Instead I prayed. May this last, and if it doesn't I'd go through it all again.

Then it occurred to me, rather crushingly—I was supposed to be destroying myself, not perfecting my appearance so that I could move around better among men. I was supposed to be dying. And if the sun over the Gobi Desert hadn't done it . . . if all the long day of lying in the sun, and then the second sunrise . . .

Ah, but you coward, I thought, you could have found some way to stay above the surface for that second day! Or could you?

"Well, thank God you chose to come back."

I turned and saw David coming down the hall. He had only just returned home, his dark heavy coat was wet from the snow, and he hadn't even removed his boots.

He came to an abrupt halt and inspected me from head to toe, straining to see in the shadows. "Ah, the clothes will do," he said. "Good Lord, you look like one of those beachcombers, those surf people, those young men who live eternally in resorts."

I smiled.

He reached out, rather bravely, I thought, and took my hand and led me into the library, where the fire was quite vigorously burning by now. He studied me once again.

"There's no more pain," he said tentatively.

"There is sensation, but it's not exactly what we call pain. I'm going out for a little while. Oh, don't worry. I'll be back. I'm thirsting. I have to hunt."

His face went blank, but not so blank that I didn't see the blood in his cheeks, or all the tiny vessels in his eyes.

"Well, what did you think?" I asked. "That I'd given it up?"

"No, of course not."

"Well, then, care to come and watch?"

He said nothing, but I could see I'd frightened him.

"You must remember what I am," I said. "When you help me, you help the devil." I made a little gesture to his copy of *Faust*, still lying on the table. And there was that Lovecraft story. Hmmm.

"You don't have to take life to do it, do you?" he asked quite seriously.

But what a crude question.

I made a short derisive noise. "I like to take life," I said. I gestured to the tiger. "I'm a hunter as you were once. I think it's fun."

He looked at me for a long moment, his face full of a sort of troubled wonder and then he nodded slowly as if accepting this. But he was very far from accepting it.

"Have your supper while I'm gone," I said. "I can tell you're hungry. I can smell meat cooking somewhere in this house. And you can be certain that I intend to have my supper before I come back."

"You're quite determined that I'm to know *you*, aren't you?" he asked. "That there's to be no sentimentality or mistake."

"Exactly." I drew back my lips and showed him my fangs for a second. They are very small, actually, nothing compared to the leopard and the tiger, with which he kept company so obviously by choice. But this grimace always frightens mortals. It does more than frighten them. It actually shocks them. I think it sends some primal message of alarm through the organism which has little to do with its conscious courage or sophistication.

He blanched. He stood quite motionless, looking at me, and then gradually the warmth and the expression returned to his face.

"Very well," he said. "I'll be here when you come back. If you don't come back, I'll be furious! I won't speak to you again, I swear it. You vanish on me tonight, you'll never get another nod from me. It will be a crime against hospitality. You understand?"

"All right, all right!" I said with a shrug, though I was secretly touched that he wanted me here. I hadn't really been so sure, and I'd been so rude to him. "I'll come back. Besides, I want to know."

"What?"

"Why you aren't afraid of dying."

"Well, *you* aren't afraid of it, are you?"

I didn't answer. I saw the sun again, the great fiery ball becoming earth and sky, and I shuddered. Then I saw that oil lamp in my dream.

"What is it?" he asked.

"I *am* afraid of dying," I said with a nod for emphasis. "All my illusions are being shattered."

"You have illusions?" he asked quite honestly.

"Of course I do. One of my illusions was that no one could really refuse the Dark Gift, not knowingly . . ."

"Lestat, must I remind you that you refused it yourself?"

"David, I was a boy. I was being forced. I fought instinctively. But that had nothing to do with knowing."

"Don't sell yourself short. I think you would have refused even if you had fully understood."

"Now we're speaking about your illusions," I said. "I'm hungry. Get out of my way or I'll kill you."

"I don't believe you. You had better come back."

"I will. This time I'll keep the promise I made in my letter. You can say all you have to say."

I HUNTED the back streets of London. I was wandering near Charing Cross Station, looking for some petty cutthroat that would yield a mouthful even if his narrow little ambitions did sour my soul. But it didn't quite turn out that way.

There was an old woman walking there, shuffling along in a soiled coat, her feet bound with rags. Mad and bitter cold she was, and almost certain to die before morning, having stolen out of the back door of some place where they'd tried to lock her up, or so she bawled to the world in general, determined never to be caught again.

We made grand lovers! She had a name for me and a great warm cluster of memories, and there we were dancing in the gutter together, she and I, and I held her a long time in my arms. She was very well nourished, as so many beggars are in this century where food is so plentiful in the Western countries, and I drank slowly, oh, so slowly, savoring it, and feeling a rush all through my burnt skin.

When it was finished, I realized that I was experiencing the cold very keenly and had been all along. I was feeling all fluctuations of temperature with greater acuity. Interesting.

The wind was lashing me and I hated it. Maybe something of my flesh had actually been burnt off. I didn't know. I felt the wet cold in my feet, and my hands hurt so much I had to bury them in my pockets. I caught those memories again of the French winter of my last year at home, of the young mortal country lord with a bed of hay, and only the dogs for companions. All the blood in the world seemed not enough suddenly. Time to feed again, and again.

They were derelicts, all of them, lured into the icy darkness from their shacks of trash and cardboard, and doomed, or so I told myself, moaning and feasting amid the stench of rancid sweat and urine, and phlegm. But the blood was blood.

When the clocks struck ten, I was still thirsting, and victims were still plentiful, but I was tired of it, and it didn't matter anymore.

I traveled for many blocks, into the fashionable West End, and there entered a dark little shop, full of smart, finely cut garments for gentlemen—ah, the ready-made wealth of these years—and outfitted myself to my taste in gray tweed pants and belted coat, with a thick white wool sweater, and even a pair of very pale green tinted glasses with delicate gold frames. Then off I wandered, back into the chill night full of swirling snowflakes, singing to myself and doing a little tap dance under the street lamp just as I used to do for Claudia and—

Slam! Bang! Up stepped this fierce and beautiful young tough with wine on his breath, divinely sleazy, who drew a knife on me, all set to murder me for the money I didn't have, which reminded me that I was a miserable thief for having just stolen a wardrobe of fine Irish clothes. Hmmm. But I was lost again in the tight hot embrace, crushing the bastard's ribs, sucking him dry as a dead rat in a summer attic, and he went down in amazement and ecstasy, one hand clutching painfully, to the very last, at my hair.

He did have some money in his pockets. What luck. I put that in the clothier's for the garments I'd taken, which seemed more than adequate when I did my arithmetic, at which I am not so good, preternatural powers or no. Then I wrote a little note of thanks, unsigned, of course. And I locked up the shop door tight with a few little telepathic twists, and off I went again.

FIVE

IT WAS striking midnight when I reached Talbot Manor. It was as if I had never seen the place before. I had time now to roam the maze in the snow, and to study the pattern of clipped shrubbery, and imagine what the garden would be come spring. Beautiful old place.

Then there were the close dark little rooms themselves, built to hold out the cold English winters, and the little lead-mullioned windows, many of which were full of light now, and most inviting in the snowy dark.

David had finished his supper, obviously, and the servants—an old man and woman—were at work still in the kitchen belowstairs while the lord changed his clothes in his bedroom on the second floor.

I watched him as he put on, over his pajamas, a long black dressing gown with black velvet lapels and sash that made him look very much like a cleric, though it was far too ornately patterned to be a cassock, especially with the white silk scarf tucked in at the neck.

Then he made his way down the stairs.

I entered by my favorite door at the end of the passage and came up beside him in the library as he bent to rake the fire.

"Ah, you did come back," he said, trying to conceal his delight. "Good Lord, but you come and go so quietly!"

"Yes, it's very annoying, isn't it?" I looked at the Bible on the table, the copy of *Faust*, and the little short story by Lovecraft, still stapled, but smoothed out. There was David's decanter of Scotch also and a pretty thick-bottomed crystal glass.

I stared at the short story, the memory of the anxious young man coming back to me. So odd the way he moved. A vague tremor passed through me at the thought of his having spotted me in three distinctly different places. I'd probably never lay eyes on him again. On the other hand . . . But there was time to deal with this pest of a mortal. David was on my mind now, and the delicious awareness that we had the night to talk to each other.

"Wherever did you get those handsome clothes?" David asked. His eyes passed over me slowly, lingeringly, and he seemed not to notice my attention to his books.

"Oh, a little shop somewhere. I never steal the garments of my victims, if that's what you mean. And besides, I'm too addicted to lowlife and they don't dress well enough for that sort of thing."

I settled in the chair opposite his, which was my chair now, I supposed. Deep, pliant leather, creaking springs, but very comfortable, with a high winged back and broad substantial arms. His own chair did not match it but was just as good, and a little more creased and worn.

He stood before the flames, still studying me. Then he sat down too. He took the glass stopper from the crystal decanter, filled his glass, and lifted it in a little salute.

He took a deep swallow and winced slightly as the liquid obviously warmed his throat.

Suddenly, vividly, I remembered that particular sensation. I remembered being in the loft of the barn on my land in France, and drinking cognac just like that, and even making that grimace, and my mortal friend and lover, Nicki, snatching the bottle greedily from my hand.

"I see you are yourself again," David said with sudden warmth, lowering his voice slightly as he peered at me. He sat back, with the glass resting on the right arm of his chair. He looked very dignified, though far more at ease than I had ever seen him. His hair was thick and wavy, and had become a beautiful shade of dark gray.

"Do I seem myself?" I asked.

"You have that mischievous look in your eye," he answered under his breath, still scanning me intently. "There's a little smile on your lips. Won't leave for more than a second when you speak. And the skin—it makes a remarkable difference. I pray you're not in pain. You aren't, are you?"

I made a small dismissive gesture. I could hear his heartbeat. It was ever so slightly weaker than it had been in Amsterdam. Now and then it was irregular as well.

"How long will your skin stay dark like this?" he asked.

"Years, perhaps, seems one of the ancient ones told me so. Didn't I write about it in *The Queen of the Damned?*" I thought of Marius and how angry he was with me in general. How disapproving he would be of what I'd done.

"It was Maharet, your ancient red-haired one," David said. "In your book, she claimed to have done the very thing merely to darken her skin."

"What courage," I whispered. "And you don't believe in her existence, do you? Though I am sitting right here with you now."

"Oh, I do believe in her. Of course I do. I believe everything you've written. But I *know* you! Tell me—what actually happened in the desert? Did you really believe you would die?"

"You would ask that question, David, and right off the bat." I sighed. "Well, I can't claim that I did really believe it. I was probably playing my usual games. I swear to God I don't tell lies to others. But I lie to myself. I don't think I can die now, at least not in any way that I myself could contrive."

He let out a long sigh.

"So why aren't *you* afraid of dying, David? I don't mean to torment you with the old offer. I honestly can't quite figure it out. You're really, truly not afraid to die, and that I simply do not understand. Because you *can* die, of course."

Was he having doubts? He didn't answer immediately. Yet he seemed powerfully stimulated, I could see that. I could all but hear his brain working, though of course I couldn't hear his thoughts.

"Why the *Faust* play, David? Am I Mephistopheles?" I asked. "Are you Faust?"

He shook his head. "I may be Faust," he said finally, taking another drink of the Scotch, "but you're not the devil, that's perfectly clear." He gave a sigh.

"I have wrecked things for you, though, haven't I? I knew it in Amsterdam. You don't stay in the Motherhouse unless you have to. I'm not driving you mad, but I've had a very bad effect, have I not?"

Again, he didn't answer right away. He was looking at me with his large prominent black eyes, and obviously considering the question from all angles. The deep lines of his face—the creases in his forehead, the lines at the corners of his eyes and around the edges of his mouth—reinforced his genial and open expression. There was not a sour note to this being, but there was unhappiness beneath the surface, and it was tangled with deep considerations, going back through a long life.

"Would have happened anyway, Lestat," he said finally. "There are reasons why I'm no longer so good at being the Superior General. Would have happened anyway, I'm relatively certain of that."

"Explain it to me. I thought you were in the very womb of the order, that it was your life."

He shook his head. "I was always an unlikely candidate for the Talamasca. I've mentioned how I spent my youth in India. I could have lived my life that way. I'm no scholar in the conventional sense, never was. Nevertheless I *am* like Faust in the play. I'm old, and I haven't cracked the secrets of the universe. Not at all. I thought I had when I was young. The first time I saw . . . a vision. The first time I knew a witch, the first time I heard the voice of a spirit, the first time I called up a spirit and made it do my bidding. I thought I had! But that was nothing. Those are earthbound things . . . earthbound mysteries. Or mysteries I'll never solve, at any rate."

He paused, as if he wanted to say something more, something in particular. But then he merely lifted the glass and drank almost absently, and this time without the grimace, for that obviously had been for the first drink of the night. He stared at the glass, and refilled it from the decanter.

I hated it that I couldn't read his thoughts, that I caught not the slightest flickering emanations behind his words.

"You know why I became a member of the Talamasca?" he asked. "It had nothing to do with scholarship at all. Never dreamed I'd be confined to the Motherhouse, wading through papers, and typing files into the computer, and sending faxes off all over the world. Nothing like that at all. It started with another hunting expedition, a new frontier, so to speak, a trip to far-off Brazil. That's where I discovered the occult, you might say, in the little crooked streets of old Rio, and it seemed every bit as exciting and dangerous as my old tiger hunts had ever been. That's what drew me—the danger. And how I came to be so far from it, I don't know."

I didn't reply, but something came clear to me, that there was obviously a danger in his knowing me. He must have liked the danger. I had thought he was possessed of a scholar's naïveté about it, but now this didn't seem to be the case.

"Yes," he said at once, his eyes growing wide as he smiled. "Exactly. Although I can't honestly believe you'd ever harm me."

"Don't deceive yourself," I said suddenly. "And you do, you know. You commit the old sin. You believe in what you see. I am not what you see."

"How so?"

"Ah, come now. I look like an angel, but I'm not. The old rules of nature encompass many creatures like me. We're beautiful like the diamond-backed snake, or the striped tiger, yet we're merciless killers. You do let your eyes deceive you. But I don't want to quarrel with you. Tell me this story. What happened in Rio? I'm eager to know."

A little sadness came over me as I spoke these words. I wanted to say, if I cannot have you as my vampire companion, then let me know you as a mortal. It thrilled me, softly and palpably, that we sat there together, as we did.

"All right," he said, "you've made your point and I acknowledge it. Drawing close to you years ago in the auditorium where you were singing, seeing you the very first time you came to me—it did have the dark lure of danger. And that you tempt me with your offer—that, too, is dangerous, for I am only human, as we both know."

I sat back, a little happier, lifting my leg and digging my heel into the leather seat of the old chair. "I like people to be a little afraid of me," I said with a shrug. "But what happened in Rio?"

"I came full in the face of the religion of the spirits," he said. "Candomble. You know the word?"

Again I gave a little shrug. "Heard it once or twice," I said. "I'll go there sometime, maybe soon." I thought in a flash of the big cities of South America, of her rain forests, and of the Amazon. Yes, I had quite an appetite for such an adventure, and the despair that had carried me down into the Gobi seemed very far away. I was glad I was still alive, and quietly I refused to be ashamed.

"Oh, if I could see Rio again," he said softly, more to himself than to me. "Of course, she isn't what she was in those days. She's a world of skyscrapers now and big luxury hotels. But I would love to see that curving shoreline again, to see Sugar Loaf Mountain, and the statue of Christ atop Corcovado. I don't believe there is a more dazzling piece of geography on earth. Why did I let so many years go by without returning to Rio?"

"Why can't you go anytime that you wish?" I asked. I felt a strong protectiveness for him suddenly. "Surely that bunch of monks in London can't keep you from going. Besides, you're the boss."

He laughed in the most gentlemanly manner. "No, they wouldn't stop me," he said. "It's whether or not I have the stamina, both mental and physical. But that's quite beside the point here, I wanted to tell you what happened. Or perhaps it is the point, I don't know."

"You have the means to go to Brazil if you want to?"

"Oh, yes, that has never been an issue. My father was a clever man when it came to money. As a consequence I've never had to give it much thought."

"I'd put the money in your hands if you didn't have it."

He gave me one of his warmest, most tolerant smiles. "I'm old," he said, "I'm lonely, and something of a fool, as any man must be if he has any wisdom at all. But I'm not poor, thank heaven."

"So what happened to you in Brazil? How did it begin?"

He started to speak, then fell silent.

"You really mean to remain here? To listen to what I have to say?"

"Yes," I said immediately. "Please." I realized I wanted nothing more in all the world. I had not a single plan or ambition in my heart, not a thought for anything else but being here with him. The simplicity of it stunned me somewhat.

Still he seemed reluctant to confide in me. Then a subtle change came over him, a sort of relaxation, a yielding perhaps.

Finally he began.

"It was after the Second World War," he said. "The India of my boyhood was gone, simply gone. And besides, I was hungry for new places. I got up a hunting expedition with my friends for the Amazon jungles. I was obsessed with the prospect of the Amazon jungles. We were after the great South American jaguar—" He gestured to the spotted skin of a cat I had not noticed before, mounted upon a stand in a corner of the room. "How I wanted to track that cat."

"Seems that you did."

"Not immediately," he said with a short ironic laugh. "We decided to preface our expedition with a nice luxurious holiday in Rio, a couple of weeks to roam Copacabana Beach, and all the old colonial sites—the monasteries, churches, and so forth. And understand, the center of the city was different in that time, a warren of little narrow streets, and wonderful old architecture! I was so eager for it, for the sheer alien quality of it! That's what sends us Englishmen into the tropics. We have to get away from all this propriety, this tradition—and immerse ourselves in some seemingly savage culture which we can never tame or really understand."

His whole manner was changing as he spoke; he was becoming even more vigorous and energetic, eyes brightening and words flowing more quickly in that crisp British accent, which I so loved.

"Well, the city itself surpassed all expectations, of course. Yet it was nothing as entrancing as the people. The people in Brazil are like no people I've ever seen. For one thing, they're exceptionally beautiful, and though everyone agrees on this point, no one knows why. No, I'm quite serious," he said, when he saw me smile. "Perhaps it's the blending of Portuguese and African, and then toss in the Indian blood. I honestly can't say. The fact is, they are extraordinarily attractive and they have extremely sensuous voices. Why, you could fall in love with their voices, you could end up kissing their voices; and the music, the bossa nova, that's their language all right."

"You should have stayed there."

"Oh, no!" he said, taking another quick sip of the Scotch. "Well, to continue. I developed a passion, shall we say, for this boy, Carlos, the very first week. I was absolutely swept away; all we did was drink and make love for days and nights on end in my suite in the Palace Hotel. Quite truly obscene."

"Your friends waited?"

"No, laid down the law. Come with us now, or we leave you. But it was perfectly fine with them if Carlos came along." He made a little gesture with his right hand. "Ah, these were all sophisticated gentlemen, of course."

"Of course."

"But the decision to take Carlos proved to be a dreadful mistake. His mother was a Candomble priestess, though I hadn't the slightest idea of it. She didn't want her boy going off into the Amazon jungles. She wanted him going to school. She sent the spirits after me."

He paused, looking at me, perhaps trying to gauge my reaction.

"That must have been wonderful fun," I said.

"They pummeled me in the darkness. They picked up the bed off the floor and dumped me out! They turned the taps in the shower so that I was nearly scalded. They filled my teacups with urine. After a full seven days, I thought I was going out of my mind. I'd gone from annoyance and incredulity to sheer terror. Dishes flew off the table in front of me. Bells rang in my ears. Bottles went crashing from the shelves. Wherever I went, I saw dark-faced individuals watching me."

"You knew it was this woman?"

"Not at first. But Carlos finally broke down and confessed everything. His mother didn't intend to remove the curse until I left. Well, I left that very night.

"I came back to London, exhausted and half mad. But it didn't do any good. They came with me. Same things started to happen right here in Talbot Manor. Doors slamming, furniture moving, the bells ringing all the time in the servants' pantry belowstairs. Everyone was going mad. And my mother—my mother had been more or less of a spiritualist, always running to various mediums all over London. She brought in the Talamasca. I told them the whole story, and they started explaining Candomble and spiritism to me."

"They exorcised the demons?"

"No. But after about a week's intense study in the library of the Motherhouse and extensive interviews with the few members who had been to Rio, I was able to get the demons under control myself. Everyone was quite surprised. Then when I decided to go back to Brazil, I astonished them. They warned me this priestess was plenty powerful enough to kill me.

" 'That's exactly it,' I said to them. 'I want that sort of power myself. I'm going to become her pupil. She's going to teach me.' They begged me not to go. I told them I'd give them a written report on my return. You can understand how I felt. I'd seen the work of these invisible entities. I'd felt them touch me. I'd seen objects hurtling through the air. I thought the great world of the invisible was opening up to me. I *had* to go there. Why, nothing could have discouraged me from it. Nothing at all."

"Yes, I see," I said. "It *was* as exciting as hunting big game."

"Precisely." He shook his head. "Those were the days. I suppose I thought if the war hadn't killed me, nothing could kill me." He drifted off suddenly, into his memories, locking me out.

"You confronted the woman?"

He nodded.

"Confronted her and impressed her, and then bribed her beyond her wildest dreams. I told her I wanted to become her apprentice. I swore on my knees to her that I wanted to learn, that I wouldn't leave until I'd penetrated the mystery, and learned all that I could." He gave a little laugh. "I'm not sure this woman had ever encountered an anthropologist, even an amateur, and I suppose that is what I might have been called. Whatever, I stayed a year in Rio. And believe you me, that was the most remarkable year of my life. I only left Rio finally, because I knew if I didn't, I never would. David Talbot the Englishman would have been no more."

"You learned how to summon the spirits?"

He nodded. Again, he was remembering, seeing images I couldn't see. He was troubled, faintly sad. "I wrote it all down," he said finally. "It's in the files at the Motherhouse. Many, many have read the story over the years."

"Never tempted to publish it?"

"Can't do it. It's part of being in the Talamasca. We never publish outside."

"You're afraid you've wasted your life, aren't you?"

"No. I'm not, really . . . Though what I said earlier is true. I haven't cracked the secrets of the universe. I've never even passed the point I reached in Brazil. Oh, there were shocking revelations afterwards. I remember the first night I read the files on the vampires, how incredulous I was, and then those strange moments when I went down into the vaults and picked through the evidence. But in the end it was like Candomble. I only penetrated so far."

"Believe me, I know. David, the world is meant to remain a mystery. If there is any explanation, we are not meant to hit upon it, of that much I'm sure."

"I think you're right," he said sadly.

"And I think you're more afraid of death than you will admit.

You've taken a stubborn tack with me, a moral one, and I don't blame you. Maybe you're old enough and wise enough to really know you don't want to be one of us. But don't go talking about death as if it's going to give you answers. I suspect death is awful. You just stop and there's no more life, and no more chance to know anything at all."

"No. I can't agree with you there, Lestat," he said. "I simply can't." He was gazing at the tiger again, and then he said, "Somebody formed the fearful symmetry, Lestat. Somebody had to. The tiger and the lamb . . . it couldn't have happened all by itself."

I shook my head. "More intelligence went into the creation of that old poem, David, than ever went into the creation of the world. You sound like an Episcopalian. But I know what you're saying. I've thought it from time to time myself. Stupidly simple. There has to be something *to* all this. There has to be! So many missing pieces. The more you consider it, the more atheists begin to sound like religious fanatics. But I think it's a delusion. It is all process and nothing more."

"Missing pieces, Lestat. Of course! Imagine for a moment that I made a robot, a perfect replica of myself. Imagine I gave him all the encyclopedias of information that I could—you know, programmed it into his computer brain. Well, it would only be a matter of time before he'd come to me, and say, 'David, where's the rest of it? The explanation! How did it all start? Why did you leave out the explanation for why there was ever a big bang in the first place, or what precisely happened when the minerals and other inert compounds suddenly evolved into organic cells? What about the great gap in the fossil record?' "

I laughed delightedly.

"And I'd have to break it to the poor chap," he said, "that there was no explanation. That I didn't have the missing pieces."

"David, nobody has the missing pieces. Nobody ever will."

"Don't be so sure."

"That's your hope, then? That's why you're reading the Bible? You couldn't crack the occult secrets of the universe, and now you've gone back to God?"

"God *is* the occult secret of the universe," David said, thoughtfully, almost as if brooding upon it, face very relaxed and almost young. He was staring at the glass in his hand, maybe liking the way the light collected in the crystal. I didn't know. I had to wait for him to speak.

"I think the answer might be in Genesis," he said finally, "I really do."

"David, you amaze me. Talk about missing pieces. Genesis is a bunch of fragments."

"Yes, but telling fragments remain to us, Lestat. God created man in his own image and likeness. I suspect that that is the key. Nobody knows what it really means, you know. The Hebrews didn't think God was a man."

"And how can it be the key?"

"God is a creative force, Lestat. And so are we. He told Adam, 'Increase and multiply.' That's what the first organic cells did, Lestat, increased and multiplied. Not merely changed shape but replicated themselves. God is a creative force. He made the whole universe out of himself through cell division. That's why the devils are so full of envy—the bad angels, I mean. They are *not* creative creatures; they have no bodies, no cells, they're spirit. And I suspect it wasn't envy so much as a form of suspicion—that God was making a mistake in making another engine of creativity in Adam, so like Himself. I mean the angels probably felt the physical universe was bad enough, with all the replicating cells, but thinking, talking beings who could increase and multiply? They were probably outraged by the whole experiment. That was their sin."

"So you're saying God isn't pure spirit."

"That's right. God has a body. Always did. The secret of cell-dividing life lies within God. And all living cells have a tiny part of God's spirit in them, Lestat, that's the missing piece as to what makes life happen in the first place, what separates it from nonlife. It's exactly like your vampiric genesis. You told us that the spirit of Amel—one evil entity—infused the bodies of all the vampires . . . Well, men share in the spirit of God in the same way."

"Good Lord, David, you're going out of your mind. We're a mutation."

"Ah, yes, but you exist in our universe, and your mutation mirrors the mutation that we are. Besides, others have struck upon the same theory. God is the fire, and we are all tiny flames; and when we die, those tiny flames go back into the fire of God. But the important thing is to realize that God Himself is Body *and* Soul! Absolutely.

"Western civilization has been founded upon an inversion. But it is my honest belief that in our daily deeds we know and honor the truth. It is only when we talk religion that we say God is pure spirit and always was and always will be, and that the flesh is evil. The truth is in Genesis, it's there. I'll tell you what the big bang was, Lestat. It was when the cells of God began to divide."

"This really is a lovely theory, David. Was God surprised?"

"No, but the angels were. I'm quite serious. I'll tell you the superstitious part—the religious belief that God is perfect. He's obviously not."

"What a relief," I said. "It explains so much."

"You're laughing at me now. I don't blame you. But you're absolutely right. It explains everything. God has made many mistakes. Many, many mistakes. As surely God Himself knows! And I suspect the angels tried to warn Him. The Devil became the Devil because he tried to warn God. God is love. But I'm not sure God is absolutely brilliant."

I was trying to suppress my laughter, but I couldn't do it entirely. "David, if you keep this up, you'll be struck by lightning."

"Nonsense. God does want us to figure it out."

"No. That I can't accept."

"You mean you accept the rest?" he said with another little laugh. "No, but I'm quite serious. Religion is primitive in its illogical conclusions. Imagine a perfect God allowing for the Devil to come into existence. No, that's simply never made sense.

"The entire flaw in the Bible is the notion that God is perfect. It represents a failure of imagination on the part of the early scholars. It's responsible for every impossible theological question as to good and evil with which we've been wrestling through the centuries. God is good, however, wondrously good. Yes, God is love. But no creative force is perfect. That's clear."

"And the Devil? Is there any new intelligence about him?"

He regarded me for a moment with just a touch of impatience. "You are such a cynical being," he whispered.

"No, I'm not," I said. "I honestly want to know. I have a particular interest in the Devil, obviously. I speak of him much more often than I speak of God. I can't figure out really why mortals love him so much, I mean, why they love the idea of him. But they do."

"Because they don't believe in him," David said. "Because a perfectly evil Devil makes even less sense than a perfect God. Imagine, the Devil never learning anything during all this time, never changing his mind about being the Devil. It's an insult to our intellect, such an idea."

"So what's your truth behind the lie?"

"He's not purely unredeemable. He's merely part of God's plan. He's a spirit allowed to tempt and try humans. He disapproves of humans, of the entire experiment. See, that was the nature of the Devil's Fall, as I see it. The Devil didn't think the idea would work. But the key, Lestat, is understanding that God is matter! God is physical, God is the Lord of Cell Division, and the Devil abhors the excess of letting all this cell division run wild."

Again, he went into one of his maddening pauses, eyes widening again with wonder, and then he said:

"I have another theory about the Devil."

"Tell me."

"There's more than one of them. And nobody appointed much likes the job." This he said almost in a murmur. He was distracted, as if he wanted to say more, but didn't.

I laughed outright.

"Now *that* I can understand," I said. "Who would like the job of being the Devil? And to think that one can't possibly win. And especially considering that the Devil was an angel at the start of it all, and supposed to be very smart."

"Exactly." He pointed his finger at me. "Your little story about Rembrandt. The Devil, if he had a brain, should have acknowledged the genius of Rembrandt."

"And the goodness of Faust."

"Ah, yes, you saw me reading *Faust* in Amsterdam, didn't you? And you purchased your own copy as a consequence."

"How did you know that?"

"The proprietor of the bookstore told me the next afternoon. A strange blond-haired young Frenchman came in moments after I'd left, bought the very same book, and stood in the street reading it for half an hour without moving. Whitest skin the man had ever seen. Had to be you, of course."

I shook my head and smiled. "I do these clumsy things. It's a wonder some scientist hasn't scooped me up in a net."

"That's no joke, my friend. You were very careless in Miami several nights ago. Two victims drained entirely of blood."

This created such instant confusion in me that at first I said nothing, then only that it was a wonder the news had reached him on this side of the sea. I felt the old despair touch me with its black wing.

"Bizarre killings make international headlines," he answered. "Besides, the Talamasca receives reports of all sorts of things. We have people who clip for us in cities everywhere, sending in items on all aspects of the paranormal for our files. 'Vampire Killer Strikes Twice in Miami.' Several sources sent it along."

"But they don't really believe it was a vampire, you know they don't."

"No, but you keep it up and they might come to believe it. That's what you wanted to happen before with your little rock music career. You wanted them to catch on. It's not inconceivable. And this sport of yours with the serial killers! You're leaving quite a trail of those."

This truly astonished me. My hunting of the killers had taken me back and forth across continents. I had never thought anyone would connect these widely scattered deaths, except Marius, of course.

"How did you come to figure it out?"

"I told you. Such stories always come into our hands. Satanism, vampirism, voodoo, witchcraft, sightings of werewolves; it all comes across my desk. Most of it goes into the trash, obviously. But I know the grain of truth when I see it. And your killings are very easy to spot.

"You've been going after these mass murderers for some time now. You leave their bodies in the open. You left this last one in a hotel, where he was found only an hour after his death. As for the old woman, you were equally careless! Her son found her the following day. No wounds for the coroner to find on either victim. You're a nameless celebrity in Miami, quite overshadowing the notoriety of the poor dead man in the hotel."

"I don't give a damn," I said angrily. But I did, of course. I deplored my own carelessness, yet I did nothing to correct it. Well, this must surely change. Tonight, had I done any better? It seemed cowardly to plead excuses for such things.

David was watching me carefully. If there was one dominant characteristic to David, it was his alertness. "It's not inconceivable," he said, "that you could be caught."

I gave a scornful, dismissive laugh.

"They *could* lock you up in a laboratory, study you in a cage of space-age glass."

"That's impossible. But what an interesting thought."

"I knew it! You want it to happen."

I shrugged. "Might be fun for a little while. Look, it's a sheer impossibility. The night of my one appearance as a rock singer, all manner of bizarre things happened. The mortal world merely swept up afterwards and closed its files. As for the old woman in Miami, that was a terrible mishap. Should never have happened—" I stopped. What about those who died in London this very night?

"But you enjoy taking life," he said. "You said it was fun."

I felt such pain suddenly I wanted to leave. But I'd promised I wouldn't. I just sat there, staring into the fire, thinking about the Gobi Desert, and the bones of the big lizards and the way the light of the sun had filled up the entire world. I thought of Claudia. I smelled the wick of the lamp.

"I'm sorry, I don't mean to be cruel to you," he said.

"Well, why the hell not? I can't think of a finer choice for cruelty. Besides, I'm not always so kind to you."

"What do you really want? What is your overriding passion?"

I thought of Marius, and Louis, who had both asked me that same question many a time.

"What could redeem what I've done?" I asked. "I meant to put an end to the killer. He was a man-eating tiger, my brother. I lay in wait for him. But the old woman—she was a child in the forest, nothing more. But what does it matter?" I thought of those wretched creatures whom I'd taken earlier this evening. I'd left such carnage in the back alleys of London. "I wish I could remember that it doesn't matter," I said. "I meant to save her. But what good would one act of mercy be in the face of all I've done? I'm damned if there is a God or a Devil. Now why don't you go on with your religious talk? The odd thing is, I find talk of God and the Devil remarkably soothing. Tell me more about the Devil. He's changeable, surely. He's smart. He must feel. Why ever would he remain static?"

"Exactly. You know what it says in the Book of Job."

"Remind me."

"Well, Satan is there in heaven, with God. God says, where have you been? And Satan says, roaming around the earth! It's a regular conversation. And they begin arguing about Job. Satan believes Job's goodness is founded entirely upon his good fortune. And God agrees to let Satan torment Job. This is the most nearly true picture of the situation which we possess. God doesn't know everything. The Devil is a good friend of his. And the whole thing is an experiment. And this Satan is a far cry from being *the* Devil as we know him now, world-wide."

"You're really speaking of these ideas as if they were real beings . . ."

"I think they are real," he said, his voice trailing off slightly as he fell into his thoughts. Then he roused himself. "I want to tell you something. Actually I should have confessed it before now. In a way, I'm as superstitious and religious as the next man. Because all this is based on a vision of sorts—you know, the sort of revelation that affects one's reason."

"No, I don't know. I have dreams but without revelation," I said. "Explain, please."

He sank back into reverie again, looking at the fire.

"Don't shut me out," I said softly.

"Hmmm. Right. I was thinking how to describe it. Well, you know I am a Candomble priest still. I mean I can summon invisible forces: the pest spirits, the astral tramps, whatever one wants to call them . . . the poltergeist, the little haunts. That means I must have always had a latent ability to see spirits."

"Yes. I suppose . . ."

"Well, I did see something once, something inexplicable, before I ever went to Brazil."

"Yes?"

"Before Brazil, I'd pretty much discounted it. In fact, it was so disturbing, so perfectly unaccountable, that I'd put it out of my mind by the time I went to Rio. Yet now, I think of it all the time. I can't stop myself from thinking of it. And that's why I've turned to the Bible, as if I'll find some wisdom there."

"Tell me."

"Happened in Paris right before the war. I was there with my mother. I was in a café on the Left Bank, and I don't even remember now which café it was, only that it was a lovely spring day and a simply grand time to be in Paris, as all the songs say. I was drinking a beer, reading the English papers, and I realized I was overhearing a conversation." He drifted away again. "I wish I knew what really happened," he murmured under his breath.

He sat forward, gathered up the poker in his right hand, and jabbed at the logs, sending a plume of fiery sparks up the dark bricks.

I wanted desperately to pull him back, but I waited. At last he went on.

"I was in this café, as I said."

"Yes."

"And I realized I was overhearing this strange conversation . . . and it wasn't in English and it wasn't in French . . . and gradually I came to know that it wasn't in any language really, and yet it was fully understandable to me. I put down my paper, and began to concentrate. On and on it went. It was a sort of argument. And suddenly I didn't know whether or not the voices were audible in any conventional sense. I wasn't sure anyone else could actually hear this! I looked up and slowly turned around.

"And there they were . . . two beings, seated at the table talking to each other, and just for a moment, it seemed normal—two men in conversation. I looked back at my paper, and this swimming feeling came over me. I had to anchor myself to something, to fix on the paper for a moment and then the tabletop, and make the swimming cease. The noise of the café came back like a full orchestra. And I knew I'd just turned and looked at two individuals who weren't human beings.

"I turned around again, forcing myself to focus tightly, to be aware of things, keenly aware. And there they were still, and it was painfully clear they were illusory. They simply weren't of the same fabric as everything else. Do you know what I'm saying? I can break it down into parts. They weren't being illuminated by the same light, for instance, they existed in some realm where the light was from another source."

"Like the light in Rembrandt."

"Yes, rather like that. Their clothes and their faces were smoother than those of human beings. Why, the whole vision was of a different texture, and that texture was uniform in all its details."

"Did they see you?"

"No. I mean to say, they didn't look at me, or acknowledge me. They looked at each other, they went on talking, and I picked up the thread again instantly. It was God talking to the Devil and telling the Devil that he must go on doing the job. And the Devil didn't want to do it. He explained that his term had already been too long. The same thing was happening to him that had happened to all the others. God said that He understood, but the Devil ought to know how important he was, he couldn't simply shirk his duties, it wasn't that simple, God needed him, and needed him to be strong. And all this was very amicable."

"What did they look like?"

"That's the worst part of it. I don't know. At the time I saw two vague shapes, large, definitely male, or assuming male form, shall we say, and pleasant-looking—nothing monstrous, nothing out of the ordinary really. I wasn't aware of any absence of particulars—you know, hair color, facial features, that sort of thing. The two figures seemed quite complete. But when I tried to reconstruct the event afterwards, I couldn't recall any details! I don't think the illusion *was* that nearly complete. I think I was satisfied by it, but the sense of completeness sprang from something else."

"From what?"

"The content, the meaning, of course."

"They never saw you, never knew you were there."

"My dear boy, they had to know I was there. They must have known. They must have been doing it for my benefit! How else could I have been allowed to see it?"

"I don't know, David. Maybe they didn't mean for you to see. Maybe it's that some people can see, and some people can't. Maybe it was a little rip in the other fabric, the fabric of everything else in the café."

"That could be true. But I fear it wasn't. I fear I was meant to see it and it was meant to have some effect on me. And that's the horror, Lestat. It didn't have a very great effect."

"You didn't change your life on account of it."

"Oh, no, not at all. Why, two days later I doubted I'd even seen it. And with each telling to another person, with each little verbal confrontation—'David, you've gone crackers'—it became ever more uncertain and vague. No, I never did anything about it."

"But what was there to do? What can anybody do on account of any revelation but live a good life? David, surely you told your brethren in the Talamasca about the vision."

"Yes, yes, I told them. But that was much later, after Brazil, when I filed my long memoirs, as a good member should do. I told them the whole story, such as it was, of course."

"And what did they say?"

"Lestat, the Talamasca never says much of anything, that's what one has to face. 'We watch and we are always there.' To tell the truth, it wasn't a very popular vision to go talking about with the other members. Speak of spirits in Brazil and you have an audience. But the Christian God and His Devil? No, I fear the Talamasca is subject somewhat to prejudices and even fads, like any other institution. The story raised a few eyebrows. I don't recall much else. But then when you're talking to gentlemen who have seen werewolves, and been seduced by vampires, and fought witches, and talked to ghosts, well, what do you expect?"

"But God and the Devil," I said, laughing. "David, that's the big time. Maybe the other members envied you more than you realized."

"No, they didn't take it seriously," he said, acknowledging my humor with a little laugh of his own. "I'm surprised that you've taken it seriously, to be quite frank."

He rose suddenly, excitedly, and walked across the room to the window, and pushed back the drape with his hand. He stood trying to see out into the snow-filled night.

"David, what could these apparitions have meant for you to do?"

"I don't know," he said, in a bitter discouraged voice. "That's my point. I'm seventy-four, and I don't know. I'll die without knowing. And if there is no illumination, then so be it. That in itself is an answer, whether I am conscious enough to know it or not."

"Come back and sit down, if you will. I like to see your face when you talk."

He obeyed, almost automatically, seating himself and reaching for the empty glass, eyes shifting to the fire again.

"What do you think, Lestat, really? Inside of you? Is there a God or a Devil? I mean truly, what do you believe?"

I thought for a long time before I answered. Then:

"I do think God exists. I don't like to say so. But I do. And probably some form of Devil exists as well. I admit—it's a matter of the missing pieces, as we've said. And you might well have seen the Supreme Being and his Adversary in that Paris café. But it's part of their maddening game that we can never figure it out for certain. You want a likely explanation for their behavior? Why they let you have a little glimpse? They wanted to get you embroiled in some sort of religious response! They play with us that way. They throw out visions and miracles and bits and pieces of divine revelation. And we go off full of zeal and found a church. It's all part of their game, part of their ongoing and endless talk. And you know? I think your view of them—an imperfect God and a learning Devil—is just about as good as anyone else's interpretation. I think you've hit on it."

He was staring at me intently, but he didn't reply.

"No," I continued. "We aren't meant to know the answers. We aren't meant to know if our souls travel from body to body through reincarnation. We aren't meant to know if God made the world. If He's Allah or Yahweh or Shiva or Christ. He plants the doubts as He plants the revelations. We're all His fools."

Still he didn't answer.

"Quit the Talamasca, David," I said. "Go to Brazil before you're too old. Go back to India. See the places you want to see."

"Yes, I think I should do that," he said softly. "And they'll probably take care of it all for me. The elders have already met to discuss the entire question of David and his recent absences from the Motherhouse. They'll retire me with a nice pension, of course."

"Do they know that you've seen me?"

"Oh, yes. That's part of the problem. The elders have forbidden contact. Very amusing really, since they are so desperate to lay eyes upon you themselves. They know when you come round the Motherhouse, of course."

"I know they do," I said. "What do you mean, they've forbidden contact?"

"Oh, just the standard admonition," he said, eyes still on the burning log. "All very medieval, really, and based upon an old directive: 'You are not to encourage this being, not to engage in or prolong conversation; if he persists in his visits, you are to do your best to lure him to some populated place. It is well known that these creatures are loath to attack when surrounded by mortals. And never, never are you to attempt to learn secrets from this being, or to believe for one moment that any emotions evinced by him are genuine, for these creatures dissemble with remarkable ability, and have been known, for reasons that cannot be analyzed, to drive mortals mad. This has befallen sophisticated investigators as well as hapless innocents with whom the vampires come in contact. You are warned to report any and all meetings, sightings, etc., to the elders without delay.' "

"Do you really know this by heart?"

"I wrote the directive myself," he said, with a little smile. "I've given it to many other members over the years."

"They know I'm here now?"

"No, of course not. I stopped reporting our meetings to them a long time ago." He fell into his thoughts again, and then: "Do you search for God?" he asked.

"Certainly not," I answered. "I can't imagine a bigger waste of time, even if one has centuries to waste. I'm finished with all such quests. I look to the world around me now for truths, truths mired in the physical and in the aesthetic, truths I can fully embrace. I care about your vision because you saw it, and you told me, and I love you. But that's all."

He sat back, gazing off again into the shadows of the room.

"Won't matter, David. In time, you'll die. And probably so shall I."

His smile was warm again as though he could not accept this except as a sort of joke.

There was a long silence, during which he poured a little more Scotch and drank it more slowly than he had before. He wasn't even close to being intoxicated. I saw that he planned it that way. When I was mortal I always drank to get drunk. But then I'd been very young, and very poor, castle or no castle, and most of the brew was bad.

"You search for God," he said, with a little nod.

"The hell I do. You're too full of your own authority. You know perfectly well that I am not the boy you see here."

"Ah, I must be reminded of that, you're correct. But you could never abide evil. If you've told the truth half the time in your books, it's plain that you were sick of evil from the beginning. You'd give anything to discover what God wants of you and to do what He wants."

"You're in your dotage already. Make your will."

"Oooh, so cruel," he said with his bright smile.

I was going to say something else to him, when I was distracted. There was a little pulling somewhere in my consciousness. Sounds. A car passing very slowly on the narrow road through the distant village, in a blinding snow.

I scanned, caught nothing, merely the snow falling, and the car edging its way along. Poor sad mortal to be driving through the country at this hour. It was four of the clock.

"It's very late," I said. "I have to leave now. I don't want to spend another night here, though you've been most kind. It's nothing to do with anyone knowing. I simply prefer . . ."

"I understand. When will I see you again?"

"Perhaps sooner than you think," I said. "David, tell me. The other night, when I left here, hell-bent on burning myself to a crisp in the Gobi, why did you say that I was your only friend?"

"You are."

We sat there in silence for a moment.

"You are my only friend as well, David," I said.

"Where are you going?"

"I don't know. Back to London, perhaps. I'll tell you when I go back across the Atlantic. Is that all right?"

"Yes, do tell me. Don't . . . don't ever believe that I don't want to see you, don't ever abandon me again."

"If I thought I was good for you, if I thought your leaving the order and traveling again was good for you . . ."

"Oh, but it is. I don't belong anymore in the Talamasca. I'm not even sure I trust it any longer, or believe in its aims."

I wanted to say more—to tell him how much I loved him, that I'd sought shelter under his roof and he'd protected me and that I would never forget this, and that I would do anything he wished of me, anything at all.

But it seemed pointless to say so. I don't know whether he would have believed it, or what the value would have been. I was still convinced that it was not good for him to see me. And there wasn't very much left to him in this life.

"I know all this," he said quietly, gracing me with that smile again.

"David," I said, "the report you made of your adventures in Brazil. Is there a copy here? Could I read this report?"

He stood up and went to the glass-doored bookshelf nearest his desk. He looked through the many materials there for a long moment, then removed two large leather folders from the shelf.

"This is my life in Brazil—what I wrote in the jungles after, on a little rattletrap portable typewriter at a camp table, before I came home to England. I did go after the jaguar, of course. Had to do it. But the hunt was nothing compared to my experiences in Rio, absolutely nothing. That was the turning point, you see. I believe the very writing of this was some desperate attempt to become an Englishman again, to distance myself from the Candomble people, from the life I'd been living with them. My report for the Talamasca was based upon the material here."

I took it from him gratefully.

"And this," he said, holding the other folder, "is a brief summary of my days in India and Africa."

"I would like to read that too."

"Old hunting stories mostly. I was young when I wrote this. It's all big guns and action! It was before the war."

I took this second folder as well. I stood up, in slow gentlemanly fashion.

"I've talked the night away," he said suddenly. "That was rude of me. Perhaps you had things to say."

"No, not at all. It was exactly what I wanted." I offered my hand and he took it. Amazing the sensation of his touch against the burnt flesh.

"Lestat," he said, "the little short story here . . . the Lovecraft piece. Do you want it back, or shall I save it for you?"

"Ah, that, now that's a rather interesting tale—I mean how I came in possession of *that.* "

I took the story from him and shoved it in my coat. Perhaps I'd read it again. My curiosity returned, and along with it a sort of fearful suspicion. Venice, Hong Kong, Miami. How had that strange mortal spotted me in all three places, and managed to see that I had spotted him!

"Do you care to tell me about it?" David asked gently.

"When there's more time," I said, "I shall tell you." Especially if I ever see that guy again, I thought. How ever did he do it?

I went out in a civilized manner, actually making a little bit of deliberate noise as I closed the side door of the house.

IT WAS close to dawn when I reached London. And for the first time in many a night, I was actually glad of my immense powers, and the great feeling of security which they conveyed. I needed no coffins, no dark hiding places, merely a room completely isolated from the rays of the sun. A fashionable hotel with heavy curtains would provide both the peace and the comfort.

And I had a little time to settle in the warm light of a lamp and begin David's Brazilian adventure, which I looked forward to, with inordinate delight.

I had almost no money with me, thanks to my recklessness and madness, so I used my considerable powers of persuasion with the clerks of venerable old Claridge's so that they accepted the number of my credit account, though I had no card to verify it, and upon my signature—Sebastian Melmoth, one of my favorite aliases—I was shown to a lovely upper suite crowded with charming Queen Anne furniture and fitted with every convenience I could wish.

I put out the polite little printed notice that I wasn't to be disturbed, left word with the desk I must not be bothered until well after sunset, then latched all the doors from the inside.

There really wasn't time to read. The morning was coming behind the heavy gray sky and the snow drifting down still in large soft wet flakes. I closed all the draperies, save one, so that I might look at the sky, and I stood there, at the front of the hotel, waiting for the spectacle of the light to come, and still a little afraid of its fury, and the pain in my skin growing a little worse from that fear, more than anything else.

David was much on my mind; I hadn't ceased to think about our conversation for a second since I'd left him. I kept hearing his voice and trying to imagine his fragmentary vision of God and the Devil in the café. But my position on all this was simple and predictable. I thought David in possession of the most comforting delusions. And soon he'd be gone from me. Death would have him. And all I would have would be these manuscripts of his life. I couldn't force myself to believe he would know anything more at all when he was dead.

Nevertheless it was all very surprising, really, the turn the conversation had taken, and his energy, and the peculiar things he'd said.

I was comfortable in these thoughts, watching the leaden sky and the snow piling on the sidewalks far below, when I suddenly experienced a bout of dizziness—in fact, a complete moment of disorientation, as though I were falling asleep. It was very pleasurable, actually, the subtle vibratory sensation, accompanied by a weightlessness, as though I were indeed floating out of the physical and into my dreams. Then came that pressure again which I'd felt so fleetingly in Miami— of my limbs constricting, indeed of my whole form pressing inwards upon me, narrowing me and compressing me, and the sudden frightening image of myself being forced through the very top of my head!

Why was this happening? I shuddered as I had done on that lonely dark Florida beach when it happened before. And at once the feeling was dissipated. I was myself again and vaguely annoyed.

Was something going wrong with my handsome, godlike anatomy? Impossible. I didn't need the old ones to assure me of such a truth. And I had not made up my mind whether I should worry about this or forget it, or indeed, try to induce it again myself, when I was brought out of my preoccupation by a knock at the door.

Most irritating.

"A message for you, sir. The gentleman requested I put it in your hands."

Had to be some mistake. Nevertheless I opened the door.

The young man gave me an envelope. Fat, bulky. For one second I could only stare at it. I had a one-pound note still in my pocket, from the little thief I'd chomped on earlier, and I gave this to the boy, and locked the door again.

This was exactly the same kind of envelope I'd been given in Miami by that lunatic mortal who'd come running towards me across the sand. And the sensation! I'd experienced that bizarre sensation right at the moment my eyes had fallen on that creature. Oh, but this was not possible . . .

I tore open the envelope. My hands were suddenly shaking. It was another little printed short story, clipped out of a book exactly as the first one had been, and stapled at the upper-left-hand corner in precisely the same way!

I was dumbfounded! How in the hell had this being tracked me here? No one knew I was here! David didn't even know I was here! Oh, there were the credit card numbers involved, but dear God, it would have taken hours for any mortal to locate me that way, even if such a thing were possible, which it really was not.

And what had the sensation to do with it—the curious vibratory feeling and the pressure which seemed to be inside my own limbs?

But there was no time to consider any of this. It was almost morning!

The danger in the situation made itself immediately apparent to me. Why the hell hadn't I seen it before? This being did most definitely have some means of knowing where I was—even where I chose to conceal myself during daylight! I had to get out of these rooms. How perfectly outrageous!

Trembling with annoyance, I forced myself to scan this story, which was only a few pages in length. "Eyes of the Mummy" was the title, author Robert Bloch. A clever little tale, but what could it possibly mean to me? I thought of the Lovecraft, which had been much longer and seemed wholly different. What on earth could all this signify? The seeming idiocy of it further maddened me.

But it was too late to think about it anymore. I gathered up David's manuscripts, and left the rooms, rushing out of a fire exit and going up to the roof. I scanned the night in all directions. I couldn't find the little bastard! Lucky for him. I would surely have destroyed him on sight. When it comes to protecting my daylight lair, I have little patience or restraint.

I moved upwards, covering the miles with the greatest speed I could attain. At last I descended in a snow-covered wood far, far north of London and there I dug my own grave in the frozen earth as I had done so many times before.

I was in a fury for having to do so. A positive fury. I'm going to kill this son of a bitch, I thought, whoever the hell he is. How dare he come stalking me, and shoving these stories in my face! Yes, I shall do that, kill him as soon as I catch him.

But then the drowsiness came, the numbness, and very soon nothing mattered . . .

Once again I was dreaming, and she was there, lighting the oil lamp, and saying, "Ah, the flame doesn't frighten you anymore . . ."

"You're mocking me," I said, miserably. I'd been weeping.

"Ah, but, Lestat, you do have a way of recovering from these cosmic fits of despair awfully fast. There you were dancing under the street lamps in London. Really!"

I wanted to protest, but I was crying, and I couldn't talk . . .

In one last jolt of consciousness, I saw that mortal in Venice— under the arches of San Marco—where I'd first noticed him—saw his brown eyes and smooth youthful mouth.

What do you want? I demanded.

Ah, but it is what you *want,* he seemed to reply.

SIX

I WASN'T so angry with the little fiend when I woke up. Actually, I was powerfully intrigued. But then the sun had set and I had the upper hand.

I decided upon a little experiment. I went to Paris, making the crossing very quickly and on my own.

Now let me digress here for a moment, only to explain that in recent years I had avoided Paris utterly, and indeed, I knew nothing of it as a twentieth-century city at all. The reasons for this are probably obvious. I had suffered much there in ages past, and I guarded myself against the visions of modern buildings rising around *Père-Lachaise* cemetery or electrically lighted Ferris wheels turning in the Tuileries. But I had always secretly longed to return to Paris, naturally. How could I not?

And this little experiment gave me courage and a perfect excuse. It deflected the inevitable pain of my observations, for I had a purpose. But within moments of my arrival, I realized that I was very truly in Paris—that this could be no place else—and I was overwhelmed with happiness as I walked on the grand boulevards, and inevitably past the place where the Theatre of the Vampires had once stood.

Indeed a few theatres of that period had survived into modern times, and there they were—imposing and ornate and still drawing in their audiences, amid the more modern structures on all sides.

I realized as I wandered the brilliantly lighted Champs Élysées—which was jammed with tiny speeding cars, as well as thousands of pedestrians—that this was no museum city, like Venice. It was as alive now as it had ever been in the last two centuries. A capital. A place of innovation still and courageous change.

I marveled at the stark splendour of the Georges Pompidou Center, rising so boldly within sight of the venerable flying buttresses of Notre Dame. Oh, I was glad I had come.

But I had a task, did I not?

I didn't tell a soul, mortal or immortal, that I was there. I did not call my Paris lawyer, though it was most inconvenient. Rather I acquired a great deal of money in the old familiar manner of taking it from a couple of thoroughly unsavory and well-heeled criminal victims in the dark streets.

Then I headed for the snow-covered Place Vendôme, which contained the very same palaces which it had in my day, and under the alias of Baron Van Kindergarten, ensconced myself in a lavish suite at the Ritz.

There for two nights, I avoided the city, enveloped in a luxury and style that was truly worthy of Marie Antoinette's Versailles. Indeed it brought tears to my eyes to see the excessive Parisian decoration all around me, the gorgeous Louis XVI chairs, and the lovely embossed paneling of the walls. Ah, Paris. Where else can wood be painted gold and still look beautiful!

Sprawled on a tapestried directoire daybed, I set at once to reading David's manuscripts, only now and then breaking off to walk about the silent parlour and bedroom, or to open a real French window, with its encrusted oval knob, and gaze out at the back garden of the hotel, so very formal and quiet and proud.

David's writing captivated me. I soon felt closer to him than ever before.

What was plain was that David had been wholly a man of action in his youth, and drawn into the realm of books only when they spoke of action, and that he'd always found his greatest pleasure in the hunt. He taken down his first game when he was only ten years old. His descriptions of shooting the big Bengal tigers were infused with the excitement of the pursuit itself and the risks he ultimately endured. Always drawing very close to the beast before he fired his gun, he had almost been killed more than once.

He had loved Africa as well as India, hunting elephants in the days when no one ever dreamed the species would be in danger of dying out. Again, he had been charged innumerable times by the big bulls before he had brought them down. And in hunting the lions of the Serengeti Plain he had courted similar risks.

Indeed, he had gone out of his way to hike arduous mountain trails, to swim in dangerous rivers, to lay his hand upon the tough hide of the crocodile, to overcome his inveterate revulsion for snakes. He had loved to sleep in the open; to scribble entries in his diary by the light of oil lanterns or candles; to eat only the meat of the animals he killed, even when there was very little of it; and to skin his kills without aid.

His power of description was not so very great. He was not patient with written words, especially not when he was young. Yet one could feel the heat of the tropics in this memoir; one heard the buzz of the gnats. It seemed inconceivable that such a man had ever enjoyed the wintry comforts of Talbot Manor, or the luxury of the mother-houses of the order, to which he was somewhat addicted now.

But many another British gentleman had known such choices and done what he thought appropriate to his position and his age.

As for the adventure in Brazil, it might as well have been written by a different man. There was the same sparse and precise vocabulary, and there was the same lust for danger, naturally, but with the turning to the supernatural, a far more clever and cerebral individual had come to the fore. Indeed, the vocabulary itself changed, incorporating many baffling Portuguese and African words for concepts and physical feelings which David felt plainly at a loss to describe.

But the gist was that the deep telepathic powers of David's brain had been developed through a series of primitive and terrifying encounters with Brazilian priestesses, and spirits as well. And the body of David had become a mere instrument for this psychic power, thereby paving the way for the scholar who had emerged in the years that followed.

There was much physical description in this Brazilian memoir. It told of small wooden rooms in the country where the Candomble believers gathered, lighting candles before their plaster statues of Catholic saints and Candomble gods. It told of the drums and the dancing; and the inevitable trances as various members of the group became unconscious hosts to the spirits and took on the attributes of a certain deity for long spells of unremembered time.

But the emphasis was now entirely upon the invisible—upon the perception of inner strength and the battle with the forces outside. The adventurous young man who had sought truth purely in the physical—the smell of the beast, the jungle path, the crack of the gun, the fall of the prey—was gone.

By the time David had left the city of Rio de Janeiro he was a different being. For though his narrative had been tightened and polished later, and undoubtedly edited, it nevertheless included much of his diary written at the very time. There was no doubt that he had been on the verge of madness in the conventional sense. He no longer saw streets and buildings and people everywhere he looked; he saw spirits, gods, invisible powers emanating from others, and various levels of spiritual resistance upon the part of humans, both conscious and unconscious, to all such things. Indeed, if he had not gone into the jungles of the Amazon, if he had not forced himself to become the British game hunter again, he might have been lost forever from his old world.

For months, he had been a gaunt, sunburnt creature in shirtsleeves and soiled pants, wandering Rio in search of ever greater spiritual experience, having no contact whatsoever with his countrymen no matter how they badgered him for such contact. And then he'd outfitted himself in his proper khaki, taken up his big guns, laid up a store of the best British provisions for a camping trip, and gone off to recover himself as he brought down the spotted jaguar, and skinned and gutted the carcass of the beast with his own knife.

Body and soul!

It really wasn't so incredible that in all these years he had never returned to Rio de Janeiro, for if he had ever made the journey back there, perhaps he could not have left.

Yet obviously, the life of the Candomble adept was not enough for him. Heroes seek adventure, but the adventure itself does not swallow them whole.

How it sharpened my love for him to know of these experiences, and how it saddened me to think that he had spent his life in the Talamasca ever since. It did not seem worthy of him, or no, it did not seem the best thing to make him happy, no matter how he insisted that he had wanted it. It seemed the very wrong thing.

And of course, this deepening knowledge of him made me ache for him all the more. I considered again that in my dark preternatural youth, I had made companions for myself who could never really be companions—Gabrielle, who had no need of me; Nicolas, who had gone mad; Louis, who could not forgive me for having seduced him into the realm of the undead, even though he had wanted it himself.

Only Claudia had been the exception—my intrepid little Claudia, companion hunter and slayer of random victims—vampire par excellence. And it had been her alluring strength which caused her ultimately to turn upon her maker. Yes, she had been the only one who had been like me really—as they say in this day and age. And that might have been the reason that she was haunting me now.

Surely there was some connection to my love of David! And I had failed to see it before. How I loved him; and how deep had been the emptiness when Claudia turned against me, and was my companion no more.

These manuscripts more fully illuminated another point for me as well. David was the very man to refuse the Dark Gift, and to the bitter end. This man feared nothing really. He didn't like death, but he didn't fear it. He never had.

But I had not come to Paris merely to read this memoir. I had another purpose in mind. I left the blessed and timeless isolation of the hotel and began to wander—slowly, visibly—about.

In the Rue Madeleine, I purchased fine clothes for myself, including a dark blue double-breasted coat of cashmere wool. Then I spent hours on the Left Bank, visiting its bright and inviting cafés, and thinking of David's story of God and the Devil, and wondering what on earth he had really seen. Of course, Paris would be a fine place for God and the Devil but . . .

I traveled the underground Metro for some time, studying the other passengers, trying to determine what was so different about Parisians. Was it their alertness, their energy? The way they avoided eye contact with others? I could not determine it. But they were very different from Americans—I had seen it everywhere—and I realized I understood them. I liked them.

That Paris was such a rich city, so filled with expensive fur coats and jewels and boutiques beyond counting, left me faintly amazed. It seemed richer even than the cities of America. It had seemed no less rich perhaps in my time with its glass coaches and white-wigged ladies and gentlemen. But the poor had been there too, everywhere, even dying in the very streets. And now I saw only the rich, and at moments, the entire city with its millions of motorcars and countless stone town houses, hotels and mansions seemed almost beyond belief.

Of course I hunted. I fed.

At twilight the next night, I stood on the top floor of the Pompidou under a sky as purely violet as any in my beloved New Orleans, watching all the lights of the great sprawling city come to life. I gazed at the distant Eiffel Tower, rising so sharply in the divine gloom.

Ah, Paris, I knew I would come back here, yes, and soon. Some night in the future I would make a lair for myself on the Île St. Louis, which I had always loved. To hell with the big houses of the Avenue Foch. I would find the building where once Gabrielle and I had worked the Dark Magic together, mother leading her son to make her his daughter, and mortal life had released her as if it were a mere hand I'd grabbed by the wrist.

I would bring Louis back with me—Louis, who had loved this city so much before he lost Claudia. Yes, he must be invited to love it again.

Meantime I'd walk slowly over to the Café de la Paix in the great hotel where Louis and Claudia had lodged during that tragic year in the reign of Napoleon III, and I would sit there with my glass of wine, untouched, forcing myself to think calmly of all that—and that it was done.

Well, I had been strengthened by my ordeal in the desert, that was plain. And I was ready for something to happen . . .

. . . And finally in the early hours of the morning, when I had become a bit melancholy and was grieving a little for the old tumble-down buildings of the 1780s, and when the mists were hanging over the half-frozen river, and I was leaning on the high stone ledge of the bank very near the bridge to the Île de la Cité, I saw my man.

First came that sensation, and this time I recognized it right off for what it was. I studied it as it was happening to me—the faint disorientation which I allowed without ever losing control; and soft delicious ripples of vibration; and then the deep constriction which included my entire form—fingers, toes, arms, legs, trunk—as before. Yes, as if my entire body, while retaining its exact proportions, was growing smaller and smaller, and I was being forced out of this dwindling shape! At the very moment when it seemed damned nigh impossible to remain within myself, my head cleared, and the sensations came to a halt.

This was precisely what had happened both times before. I stood at the bridge, considering this, and memorizing the details.

Then I beheld a battered little car jerking to a stop on the far side of the river, and out he climbed—the young brown-haired one—awkwardly as before, and rising to his full height tentatively and fixing me with his ecstatic and glittering eyes.

He'd left the motor of his little machine running. I smelled his fear as I had before. Of course he knew that I had seen him, there could be no mistake of that. I'd been here a full two hours, waiting for him to find me, and I suppose he realized this as well.

Finally he screwed up his courage and came across the bridge through the fog, an immediately impressive figure in a long greatcoat, with a white scarf about the neck, half walking, half running, and stopping a few feet away from me, as I stood there with my elbow on the rail, staring at him coldly. He thrust at me another little envelope. I grabbed his hand.

"Don't be hasty, Monsieur de Lioncourt!" he whispered desperately. British accent, upper-class, very like David's, and he'd got the French syllables very close to perfect. He was near perishing with fear.

"Who the hell are you!" I demanded.

"I have a proposition for you! You'd be a fool if you didn't listen. It's something you'll want very much. And no one else in this world can offer it to you, be assured!"

I let him go and he sprang back, nearly toppling over, hand flung out to catch the stone rail. What was it about this man's gestures? He was powerfully built, but he moved as if he were a thin, tentative creature. I couldn't figure it out.

"Explain this proposition now!" I said, and I could hear his heart come to a stop inside his broad chest.

"No," he said. "But we shall talk very soon." Such a cultured voice, a polished voice.

Far too refined and careful for the large glazed brown eyes, and the smooth robust young face. Was he some hothouse plant grown to prodigious proportions in the company of elderly people, never having seen a person his own age?

"Don't be hasty!" he shouted again, and off he ran, stumbling, then catching himself, and then forcing his tall, clumsy body into the small car, and driving off through the frozen snow.

Indeed, he was going so fast as he disappeared into St. Germain, I thought he would have a wreck and kill himself.

I looked down at the envelope. Another damned short story, no doubt. I tore it open angrily, not sure I should have let him go, and yet somehow enjoying this little game, and even enjoying my own indignation at his cleverness and capacity for tracking me.

I saw that, indeed, it was a video tape of a recent film. *Vice Versa* was the title. What on earth . . . ? I flipped it over, and scanned the advertisement. A comic piece.

I returned to the hotel. There was yet another package waiting for me. Another video tape. *All of Me* was the name of it, and once again, the description on the back of the plastic case gave a fair idea of what it was about.

I went to my rooms. No video player! Not even in the Ritz. I rang David, though it was now very near dawn.

"Would you come to Paris? I'll have everything arranged for you. See you at dinner, eight o'clock tomorrow in the dining room downstairs."

Then I did call my mortal agent, rousing him from bed and instructing him to arrange David's ticket, limousine, suite, and whatever else he should need. There should be cash waiting for David; there should be flowers; and chilled champagne. Then I went out to find a safe place to sleep.

But an hour later—as I stood in the dark dank cellar of an old abandoned house—I wondered if the little mortal bastard couldn't see me even now, if he didn't know where I slept by day, and couldn't come bring in the sun upon me, like some cheap vampire-hunter in a bad movie, with no respect for the mysterious at all.

I dug deep beneath the cellar. No mortal alone could have found me there. And even in my sleep, I might have strangled him if he had, without my ever knowing it.

"So WHAT do you think it all means?" I said to David. The dining room was exquisitely decorated and half empty. I sat there in the candlelight, in black dinner jacket and boiled shirt, with my arms folded before me, enjoying the fact that I needed only the pale-violet tinted glasses now to hide my eyes. How well I could see the tapestried portieres, and the dim garden beyond the windows.

David was eating lustily. He'd been utterly delighted to come to Paris, loved his suite over the Place Vendôme, with its velvet carpets and gilded furnishings, and had spent all afternoon in the Louvre.

"Well, you can see the theme, can't you?" he replied.

"I'm not sure," I said. "I do see common elements, of course, but these little stories are all different."

"How so?"

"Well, in the Lovecraft piece, Asenath, this diabolical woman, switches bodies with her husband. She runs about the town using his male body, while he is stuck at home in her body, miserable and confused. I thought it was a hoot, actually. Just wonderfully clever, and of course Asenath isn't Asenath, as I recall, but her father, who has switched bodies with her. And then it all becomes very Lovecraftian, with slimy half-human demons and such."

"That may be the irrelevant part. And the Egyptian story?"

"Completely different. The moldering dead, which still possess life, you know . . ."

"Yes, but the plot."

"Well, the soul of the mummy manages to get possession of the body of the archaeologist, and he, the poor devil, is put in the rotted body of the mummy—"

"Yes?"

"Good Lord, I see what you're saying. And then the film *Vice Versa*. It's about the soul of a boy and the soul of a man who switch bodies! All hell breaks loose until they are able to switch back. And the film *All of Me*, it's about body switching as well. You're absolutely right. All four stories are about the same thing."

"Exactly."

"Christ, David. It's all coming clear. I don't know why I didn't see it. But . . ."

"This man is trying to get you to believe that he knows something about this body switching. He's trying to entice you with the suggestion that such a thing can be done."

"Good Lord. Of course. That explains it, the way he moves, walks, runs."

"What?"

I sat there stunned, reenvisioning the little beast before I answered, bringing up to mind every image of him from every conceivable angle which memory would allow. Yes, even in Venice, he'd had that obvious awkwardness about him.

"David, he *can* do it."

"Lestat, don't jump to such a mad conclusion! He may think that he can do it. He may want to try it. He may be living entirely in a world of delusions—"

"No. That's his proposition, David, the proposition he says that I will want to hear! He *can* switch bodies with people!"

"Lestat, you can't believe—"

"David, that's what's wrong with him! I've been trying to figure it since I saw him on the beach in Miami. That isn't his body! That's why he can't use its musculature or its . . . its height. That's why he almost falls when he runs. He can't control those long powerful legs. Good God, that man is in someone else's body. And the voice, David, I told you about his voice. It's not the voice of a young man. Oh, that explains it! And you know what I think? I think he chose that particular body because I'd notice it. And I'll tell you something else. He's already tried this switching trick with me and it's failed."

I couldn't continue. I was too dazzled by the possibility.

"How do you mean, tried?"

I described the peculiar sensations—the vibration and the constriction, the sense that I was being forced quite literally out of my physical self.

He didn't reply to what I'd said, but I could see the effect this had upon him. He sat motionless, his eyes narrow, his right hand half closed and resting idly beside his plate.

"It was an assault upon me, wasn't it? He tried to get me out of my body! Maybe so that he could get in. And of course he couldn't do it. But why would he risk mortally offending me with such an attempt?"

"Has he mortally offended you?" David asked.

"No, he's merely made me all the more curious, powerfully curious!"

"There you have your answer. I think he knows you too well."

"What?" I heard what he said but I couldn't reply just now. I drifted into remembering the sensations. "That feeling was so strong. Oh, don't you see what he's doing? He's suggesting that he can switch with me. He's offering me that handsome young mortal frame."

"Yes," David said coldly. "I think you're right."

"Why else would he stay in that body?" I said. "He's clearly very uncomfortable in it. He wants to switch. He's saying that he can switch! That's why he's taken this risk. He must know it would be easy for me to kill him, squash him like a little bug. I don't even like him—the manner, I mean. The body is excellent. No, that's it. He can do it, David, he knows how."

"Snap out of it! You can't put it to the test."

"What? Why not? You're telling me it can't be done? In all those archives you have no records . . . ? David, I know he's done it. He just can't force me into it. But he's switched with another mortal, that I know."

"Lestat, when it happens we call it possession. It's a psychic accident! The soul of a dead person takes over a living body; a spirit possessing a human being; it has to be persuaded to let go. Living people don't go around doing it deliberately and in concerted agreement. No, I don't think it *is* possible. I don't think we do have any such cases! I . . ." He broke off, clearly in doubt.

"You know you have such cases," I said. "You must."

"Lestat, this is very dangerous, too dangerous for any sort of trial."

"Look, if it can happen by accident, it can happen this way too. If a dead soul can do it, why not a living soul? I know what it means to travel outside my body. You know. You learned it in Brazil. You described it in fine detail. Many, many human beings know. Why, it was part of the ancient religions. It's not inconceivable that one could return to another body and hold on to it while the other soul struggles in vain to recapture it."

"What an awful thought."

I explained again about the sensations and how powerful they had been. "David, it's possible he stole that body!"

"Oh, that's just lovely."

Again, I was remembering the feeling of constriction, the terrific and strangely pleasurable feeling that I was being squeezed out of myself through the top of my head. How strong it had been! Why, if he could make me feel that, surely he could make a mortal man rise out of himself, especially if that mortal man did not have the slightest idea of what was being done.

"Calm yourself, Lestat," David said a little disgustedly. He laid his heavy fork upon the half-empty plate. "Now think this through. Perhaps such a switch could be achieved for a few minutes. But anchoring in the new body, remaining inside it, and functioning day in and day out? No. This would mean functioning when you are asleep as well as awake. You're talking about something entirely different and obviously dangerous. You can't experiment with this. What if it worked?"

"That's the whole point. If it works, then I can get into that body." I paused. I could scarcely speak it and then I did. I said it. "David, I can be a mortal man."

It took my breath away. A moment of silence passed as we stared at each other. The look of vague dread in his eyes did nothing to still my excitement.

"I'd know how to use that body," I said, half in a whisper. "I'd know how to use those muscles and those long legs. Oh, yes, he chose that body because he knew I would consider it a possibility, a real possibility—"

"Lestat, you can't pursue this! He's speaking of trading here, switching! You can't let this suspect individual have your body in return! The idea's monstrous. You inside that body is quite enough!"

I fell into stunned silence.

"Look," he said, trying to bring me back to him. "Forgive me for sounding like the Superior General of a religious order, but this is something you simply cannot do! First off, where *did* he get that body? What if he did, in fact, steal it? Surely no handsome young man cheerfully gave it over without so much as a qualm! This is a sinister being, and must be recognized as such. You can't deliver to him a body as powerful as your own."

I heard all this, I understood it, but I couldn't absorb it. "Think of it, David," I said, knowing that I sounded mad and only barely coherent. "David, I could be a mortal man."

"Would you kindly wake up and pay attention to me, please! This is not a matter of comical stories and Lovecraftian pieces of gothic romance." He wiped his mouth with his napkin, and crossly slugged down a swallow of wine, and then reached across the table and took hold of my wrist.

I should have let him lift it and clasp it. But I didn't yield and he realized within a second that he could no more move my wrist away from the table than he could move that of a statue made of granite.

"That's it, right there!" he declared. "You can't play with this. You can't take the risk that it will work, and this fiend, whoever he is, will have possession of your strength."

I shook my head. "I know what you're saying, but, David, think of it. I have to talk to him! I have to find him and find out whether this can be done. He himself is unimportant. It's the process that's important. Can it be done?"

"Lestat, I'm begging you. Don't explore this any further. You're going to make another ghastly mistake!"

"What do you mean?" It was so hard to pay attention to what he was saying. Where was that wily fiend right now? I thought of his eyes, how beautiful they would be if *he* were not looking out of them. Yes, it was a fine body for this experiment! Wherever *did* he get it? I had to find out.

"David, I'm going to leave you now."

"No, you're not! Stay right where you are, or so help me God I'll send a legion of hobgoblins after you, every filthy little spirit I trafficked with in Rio de Janeiro! Now listen to me."

I laughed. "Keep your voice down," I said. "We'll be thrown out of the Ritz."

"Very well, we'll strike a bargain. I'll go back to London and hit the computer. I'll boot up every case of body switching in our files. Who knows what we'll discover? Lestat, maybe he's in that body and it's deteriorating around him, and he can't get out or stop the deterioration. Did you think of that?"

I shook my head. "It's not deteriorating. I would have caught the scent. There's nothing wrong with that body."

"Except maybe he stole it from its rightful owner and that poor soul is stumbling around in *his* body, and what that looks like, we haven't a clue."

"Calm down, David, please. You go on back to London, and hit the files, as you described. I'm going to find this little bastard. I'm going to hear what he has to say. Don't worry! I won't proceed without consulting you. And if I do decide—"

"You won't decide! Not until you talk to me."

"All right."

"This is a pledge?"

"On my honor as a bloodthirsty murderer, yes."

"I want a phone number in New Orleans."

I stared at him hard for a moment. "All right. I've never done this before. But here it is." I gave him the phone number of my French Quarter rooftop rooms. "Aren't you going to write it down?"

"I've memorized it."

"Then farewell!"

I rose from the table, struggling, in my excitement, to move like a human. Ah, move like a human. Think of it, to be inside a human body. To see the sun, really see it, a tiny blazing ball in a blue sky! "Oh, and, David, I almost forgot, everything's covered here. Call my man. He'll arrange for your flight . . ."

"I don't care about that, Lestat. Listen to me. Set an appointment to speak with me about this, right now! You dare vanish on me, I'll never—"

I stood there smiling down at him. I could tell I was charming him. Of course he wouldn't threaten never to speak to me again. How absurd. "Ghastly mistakes," I said, unable to stop smiling. "Yes, I do make them, don't I?"

"What will they do to you—the others? Your precious Marius, the older ones, if you do such a thing?"

"They might surprise you, David. Maybe all they want is to be human again. Maybe that's all any of us want. Another chance." I thought of Louis in his house in New Orleans. Dear God, what would Louis think when I told him about all this?

David muttered something under his breath, angry and impatient, yet his face was full of affection and concern.

I blew him a little kiss and was gone.

SCARCELY an hour had passed before I realized I couldn't find the wily fiend. If he was in Paris, he was cloaked so that I couldn't pick up the faintest shimmer of his presence. And nowhere did I catch an image of him in anyone else's mind.

This didn't mean he wasn't in Paris. Telepathy is extremely hit or miss; and Paris was a vast city, teeming with citizens of all the countries of the world.

At last I came back to the hotel, discovered David had already checked out, leaving all his various phone numbers with me for fax, computer, and regular calls.

"Please contact me tomorrow evening," he'd written. "I shall have some information for you by then."

I went upstairs to prepare for the journey home. I couldn't wait to see this lunatic mortal again. And Louis—I had to lay it all before Louis. Of course he wouldn't believe it was possible, that would be the first thing he'd say. But he would understand the lure. Oh, yes, he would.

I hadn't been in the room a minute, trying to determine if there was anything here I needed to take with me—ah, yes, David's manuscripts—when I saw a plain envelope lying on the table beside the bed. It was propped against a great vase of flowers. "Count van Kindergarten" was written on it in a firm, rather masculine script.

I knew the minute I saw it that it was a note from him. The message inside was handwritten, in the same firm, heavily engraved style.

Don't be hasty. And don't listen to your fool friend from the Talamasca either. I shall see you in New Orleans tomorrow night. Don't disappoint me. Jackson Square. We shall then make an appointment to work a little alchemy of our own. I think you understand now what's at stake.

Yours sincerely,

Raglan James

"Raglan James." I whispered the name aloud. Raglan James. I didn't like the name. The name was like him.

I dialed the concierge.

"This fax system which has just been invented," I said in French, "you have it here? Explain it to me, please."

It was as I suspected, a complete facsimile of this little note could be sent from the hotel office over a telephone wire to David's London machine. Then David would not only have this information, he would have the handwriting, for what it was worth.

I arranged to have this done, picked up the manuscripts, stopped by the desk with the note of Raglan James, had it faxed, took it back, and then went to Notre Dame to say good-bye to Paris with a little prayer.

I was mad. Absolutely mad. When had I ever known such pure happiness! I stood in the dark cathedral, which was now locked on account of the hour, and I thought of the first time I'd ever stepped into it so many, many decades ago. There had been no great square before the church doors, only the little Place de Grève hemmed in with crooked buildings; and there had been no great boulevards in Paris such as there are now, only broad mud streets, which we thought so very grand.

I thought of all those blue skies, and what it had felt like to be hungry, truly hungry for bread and for meat, and to be drunk on good wine. I thought of Nicolas, my mortal friend, whom I'd loved so much, and how cold it had been in our little attic room. Nicki and I arguing the way that David and I had argued! Oh, yes.

It seemed my great long existence had been a nightmare since those days, a sweeping nightmare full of giants and monsters and horrid ghastly masks covering the faces of beings who menaced me in the eternal dark. I was trembling. I was weeping. To be human, I thought. To be human again. I think I said the words aloud.

Then a sudden whispered laugh startled me. It was a child some-where in the darkness, a little girl.

I turned around. I was almost certain I could see her—a small gray form darting up the far aisle towards a side altar, and then out of sight. Her footsteps had been barely audible. But surely this was some mis-take. No scent. No real presence. Just illusion.

Nevertheless I cried out: "Claudia!"

And my voice came tumbling back to me in a harsh echo. No one there, of course.

I thought of David: "You're going to make another ghastly mistake!"

Yes, I have made ghastly mistakes. How can I deny it? Terrible, terrible errors. The atmosphere of my recent dreams came back to me, but it wouldn't deepen, and there remained only a evanescent sense of being with her. Something about an oil lamp and her laughing at me.

I thought again of her execution—the brick-walled air well, the approaching sun, how small she had been; and then the remembered pain of the Gobi Desert mingled with it and I couldn't bear it any longer. I realized I had folded my arms around my chest, and was trembling, my body rigid, as though being tormented with an electric shock. Ah, but surely she hadn't suffered. Surely it had been instanta-neous for one so tender and little. Ashes to ashes . . .

This was pure anguish. It wasn't those times I wanted to remem-ber, no matter how long I'd lingered in the Café de la Paix earlier, or how strong I imagined I had become. It was my Paris, before the Theatre of the Vampires, when I'd been innocent and alive.

I stayed a while longer in the dark, merely looking at the great branching arches above me. What a marvelous and majestic church this was—even now with the pop and rattle of motorcars beyond. It was like a forest made of stone.

I blew a kiss to it, as I had to David. And I went off to undertake the long journey home.

SEVEN

NEW ORLEANS.

I arrived quite early in the evening for I had gone backwards in time against the turning of the world. It was cold and crisp, but not cruelly so, though a bad norther was on its way. The sky was without a cloud and full of small and very distinct stars.

I went at once to my little rooftop apartment in the French Quarter, which for all its glamour is not very high at all, being on the top of a four-storey building, erected long before the Civil War, and having a rather intimate view of the river and its beautiful twin bridges, and which catches, when the windows are open, the noises of the happily crowded Café du Monde and of the busy shops and streets around Jackson Square.

It was not until tomorrow night that Mr. Raglan James meant to meet me. And impatient as I was for this meeting, I found the schedule comfortable, as I wanted to find Louis right away.

But first I indulged in the mortal comfort of a hot shower, and put on a fresh suit of black velvet, very trim and plain, rather like the clothes I'd worn in Miami, and a pair of new black boots. And ignoring my general weariness—I would have been asleep in the earth by now, had I been still in Europe—I went off, walking like a mortal, through the town.

For reasons of which I wasn't too certain, I took a turn past the old address in the Rue Royale where Claudia and Louis and I had once lived. Actually I did this rather often, never allowing myself to think about it, until I was halfway there.

Our coven had endured for over fifty years in that lovely upstairs apartment. And surely this factor ought to be considered when I'm being condemned, either by myself or by someone else, for my errors. Louis and Claudia had both been made by me, and for me, I admit that. Nevertheless, ours had been a curiously incandescent and satisfying existence before Claudia decided I should pay for my creations with my life.

The rooms themselves had been crammed with every conceivable ornament and luxury which the times could provide. We'd kept a carriage, and a team of horses at the nearby stables, and servants had lived beyond the courtyard in back. But the old brick buildings were now somewhat faded, and neglected, the flat unoccupied of late, except for ghosts, perhaps, who knows, and the shop below was rented to a bookseller who never bothered to dust the volumes in the window, or those on his shelves. Now and then he procured books for me—volumes on the nature of evil by the historian Jeffrey Burton Russell, or the marvelous philosophical works of Mircea Eliade, as well as vintage copies of the novels I loved.

The old man was in there reading, in fact, and I watched him for a few minutes through the glass. How different were the citizens of New Orleans from all the rest of the American world. Profit meant nothing to this old gray-haired being at all.

I stood back and looked up at the cast-iron railings above. I thought of those disturbing dreams—the oil lamp, her voice. Why was she haunting me so much more relentlessly than ever before?

When I closed my eyes, I could hear her again, talking to me, but the substance of her words was gone. I found myself thinking back once more on her life and her death.

Gone now without a trace was the little hovel in which I'd first seen her in Louis's arms. A plague house it had been. Only a vampire would have entered. No thief had dared even to steal the gold chain from her dead mother's throat. And how ashamed Louis has been that he had chosen a tiny child as his victim. But I had understood. No trace remained, either, of the old hospital where they'd taken her afterwards. What narrow mud street had I passed through with that warm mortal bundle in my arms, and Louis rushing after me, begging to know what I meant to do.

A gust of cold wind startled me suddenly.

I could hear the dull raucous music from the taverns of the Rue Bourbon only a block away; and people walking before the cathedral—laughter from a woman nearby. A car horn blasting in the dark. The tiny electronic throb of a modern phone.

Inside the bookstore, the old man played the radio, twisting the dial from Dixieland to classical and finally to a mournful voice singing poetry to the music of an English composer . . .

Why had I come to this old building, which stood forlorn and indifferent as a tombstone with all its dates and letters worn away?

I wanted no more delay, finally.

I'd been playing with my own mad excitement at what had only just happened in Paris, and I headed uptown to find Louis and lay it all before him.

Again, I chose to walk. I chose to feel the earth, to measure it with my feet.

IN OUR time—at the end of the eighteenth century—the uptown of the city didn't really exist. It was country upriver; there were plantations still, and the roads were narrow and hard to travel, being paved only with dredged shells.

Later in the nineteenth century, after our little coven had been destroyed, and I was wounded and broken, and gone to Paris to search for Claudia and Louis, the uptown with all its small towns was merged with the great city, and many fine wooden houses in the Victorian style were built.

Some of these ornate wooden structures are vast, every bit as grand in their own cluttered fashion as the great antebellum Greek Revival houses of the Garden District, which always put me in mind of temples, or the imposing town houses of the French Quarter itself.

But much of uptown with its small clapboard cottages, as well as big houses, still retains for me the aspect of the country, what with the enormous oaks and magnolias sprouting up everywhere to tower over the little roofs, and so many streets without sidewalks, along which the gutters are no more than ditches, full of wildflowers flourishing in spite of the winter cold.

Even the little commercial streets—a sudden stretch here and there of attached buildings—remind one not of the French Quarter with its stone facades and old-world sophistication, but rather of the quaint "main streets" of rural American towns.

This is a great place for walking in the evening; you can hear the birds sing as you will never hear them in the Vieux Carré; and the twilight lasts forever over the roofs of the warehouses along the ever-curving river, shining through the great heavy branches of the trees. One can happen upon splendid mansions with rambling galleries and gingerbread decoration, houses with turrets and gables, and widow's walks. There are big wooden porch swings hanging behind freshly painted wooden railings. There are white picket fences. Broad avenues of clean well-clipped lawns.

The little cottages display an endless variation; some are neatly painted in deep brilliant colors according to the current fashion; others, more derelict but no less beautiful, have the lovely gray tone of driftwood, a condition into which a house can fall easily in this tropical place.

Here and there one finds a stretch of street so overgrown one can scarce believe one is still within a city. Wild four-o'clocks and blue plumbago obscure the fences that mark property; the limbs of the oak bend so low they force the passerby to bow his head. Even in its coldest winters, New Orleans is always green. The frost can't kill the camellias, though it does sometimes bruise them. The wild yellow Carolina jasmine and the purple bougainvillea cover fences and walls.

It is in one such stretch of soft leafy darkness, beyond a great row of huge magnolia trees, that Louis made his secret home.

The old Victorian mansion behind the rusted gates was unoccupied, its yellow paint almost all peeled away. Only now and then did Louis roam through it, a candle in his hand. It was a cottage in back—covered with a great shapeless mountain of tangled pink Queen's Wreath—which was his true dwelling, full of his books and miscellaneous objects he'd collected over the years. Its windows were quite hidden from the street. In fact, it's doubtful anyone knew this house existed. The neighbors could not see it for the high brick walls, the dense old trees, and oleander growing wild around it. And there was no real path through the high grass.

When I came upon him, all the windows and doors were open to the few simple rooms. He was at his desk, reading by the light of a single candle flame.

For a long moment, I spied upon him. I loved to do this. Often I followed him when he went hunting, simply to watch him feed. The modern world doesn't mean anything to Louis. He walks the streets like a phantom, soundlessly, drawn slowly to those who welcome death, or seem to welcome it. (I'm not sure people really ever welcome death.) And when he feeds, it is painless and delicate and swift. He must take life when he feeds. He does not know how to spare the victim. He was never strong enough for the "little drink" which carries me through so many nights; or did before I became the ravenous god.

His clothes are old-fashioned always. As so many of us do, he finds garments which resemble the styles of his time in mortal life.

Big loose shirts with gathered sleeves and long cuffs please him, and tight-fitting pants. When he wears a coat, which is seldom, it is fitted like the ones I choose—a rider's jacket, very long and full at the hem.

I bring him these garments sometimes as presents, so that he doesn't wear his few acquisitions right to rags. I had been tempted to straighten up his house, hang the pictures, fill the place with finery, sweep him up into heady luxury the way I had in the past.

I think he wanted me to do this, but he wouldn't admit it. He existed without electricity, or modern heat, wandering in chaos, pretending to be wholly content.

Some of the windows of this house were without glass, and only now and then did he bolt the old-fashioned louvered shutters. He did not seem to care if the rain came in on his possessions because they weren't really possessions. Just junk heaped here and there.

But again, I think he wanted me to do something about it. It's amazing how often he came to visit me in my overheated and brilliantly illuminated rooms downtown. There he watched my giant television screen for hours. Sometimes he brought his own films for it on disk or tape. *The Company of Wolves*, that was one which he watched over and over. *Beauty and the Beast*, a French film by Jean Cocteau, also pleased him mightily. Then there was *The Dead*, a film made by John Huston from a story by James Joyce. And please understand this film has nothing to do with our kind whatsoever; it is about a fairly ordinary group of mortals in Ireland in the early part of this century who gather for a convivial supper on Little Christmas night. There were many other films which delighted him. But these visits could never be commanded by me, and they never lasted very long. He often deplored the "rank materialism" in which I "wallowed" and turned his back on my velvet cushions and thickly carpeted floor, and lavish marble bath. He drifted off again, to his forlorn and vine-covered shack.

Tonight, he sat there in all his dusty glory, an ink smudge on his white cheek, poring over a large cumbersome biography of Dickens, recently written by an English novelist, turning the pages slowly, for he is no faster at reading than most mortals. Indeed of all of us survivors he is the most nearly human. And he remains so by choice.

Many times I've offered him my more powerful blood. Always, he has refused it. The sun over the Gobi Desert would have burnt him to ashes. His senses are finely tuned and vampiric, but not like those of a Child of the Millennia. He cannot read anyone's thoughts with much success. When he puts a mortal into a trance, it's always a mistake.

And of course I cannot read his thoughts because I made him, and the thoughts of the fledgling and master are always closed to each other, though why, no one of us knows. My suspicion is that we know a great deal of each other's feelings and longings; only the amplification is too loud for any distinct image to come clear. Theory. Someday perhaps they *will* study us in laboratories. We will beg for live victims through the thick glass walls of our prisons as they ply us with questions, and extract samples of blood from our veins. Ah, but how do that to Lestat who can burn another to cinders with one decisive thought?

Louis didn't hear me in the high grass outside his little house.

I slipped into the room, a great glancing shadow, and was already seated in my favorite red velvet bergère—I'd long ago brought it there for myself—opposite him when he looked up.

"Ah, you!" he said at once, and slammed the book shut.

His face, quite thin and finely drawn by nature, an exquisitely delicate face for all its obvious strength, was gorgeously flushed. He had hunted early, I'd missed it. I was for one second completely crushed.

Nevertheless it was tantalizing to see him so enlivened by the low throb of human blood. I could smell the blood too, which gave a curious dimension to being near him. His beauty has always maddened me. I think I idealize him in my mind when I'm not with him; but then when I see him again I'm overcome.

Of course it was his beauty which drew me to him, in my first nights here in Louisiana, when it was a savage, lawless colony, and he was a reckless, drunken fool, gambling and picking fights in taverns, and doing what he could to bring about his own death. Well, he got what he thought he wanted, more or less.

For a moment, I couldn't understand the expression of horror on his face as he stared at me, or why he suddenly rose and came towards me and bent down and touched my face. Then I remembered. My sun-darkened skin.

"What have you done?" he whispered. He knelt down and looked up at me, resting his hand lightly on my shoulder. Lovely intimacy, but I wasn't going to admit it. I remained composed in the chair.

"It's nothing," I said, "it's finished. I went into a desert place, I wanted to see what would happen . . ."

"You wanted to see what would happen?" He stood up, took a step back, and glared at me. "You meant to destroy yourself, didn't you?"

"Not really," I said. "I lay in the light for a full day. The second morning, somehow or other I must have dug down into the sand."

He stared at me for a long moment, as if he would explode with disapproval, and then he retreated to his desk, sat down a bit noisily for such a graceful being, composed his hands over the closed book, and looked wickedly and furiously at me.

"Why did you do it?"

"Louis, I have something more important to tell you," I said. "Forget about all this." I made a gesture to include my face. "Something very remarkable has happened, and I have to tell you the whole tale." I stood up, because I couldn't contain myself. I began to pace, careful not to trip over all the heaps of disgusting trash lying about, and maddened slightly by the dim candlelight, not because I couldn't see in it, but because it was so weak and partial and I like light.

I told him everything—how I'd seen this creature, Raglan James, in Venice and in Hong Kong, and then in Miami, and how he'd sent me the message in London and then followed me to Paris as I supposed he would. Now we were to meet near the square tomorrow night. I explained the short stories and their meaning. I explained the strangeness of the young man himself, that he was not in his body, that I believed he could effect such a switch.

"You're out of your mind," Louis said.

"Don't be so hasty," I answered.

"You quote this idiot's words to me? Destroy him. Put an end to him. Find him tonight if you can and do away with him."

"Louis, for the love of heaven . . ."

"Lestat, this creature can find you at will? That means he knows where you lie. You've led him here now. He knows where I lie. He's the worst conceivable enemy! Mon Dieu, why do you go looking for adversity? Nothing on earth can destroy you now, not even the Children of the Millennia have the combined strength to do it, and not even the sun at midday in the Gobi Desert—so you court the one enemy who has power over you. A mortal man who can walk in the light of day. A man who can achieve complete dominion over you when you yourself are without a spark of consciousness or will. No, destroy him. He's far too dangerous. If I see him, I'll destroy him."

"Louis, this man can give me a human body. Have you listened to anything that I've said."

"Human body! Lestat, you can't become human by simply taking over a human body! You weren't human when you were alive! You were born a monster, and you know it. How the hell can you delude yourself like this."

"I'm going to weep if you don't stop."

"Weep. I'd like to see you weep. I've read a great deal about your weeping in the pages of your books but I've never seen you weep with my own eyes."

"Ah, that makes you out to be a perfect liar," I said furiously. "You described my weeping in your miserable memoir in a scene which we both know did not take place!"

"Lestat, kill this creature! You're mad if you let him come close enough to you to speak three words."

I was confounded, utterly confounded. I dropped down in the chair again and stared into space. The night seemed to breathe with a soft lovely rhythm outside, the fragrance of the Queen's Wreath just barely touching the moist cool air. A faint incandescence seemed to come from Louis's face, from his hands folded on the desk. He was veiled in stillness, waiting for my response, I presumed, though why, I had no idea.

"I never expected this from you," I said, crestfallen. "I expected some long philosophical diatribe, like the trash you wrote in your memoir, but this?"

He sat there, silent, peering at me steadily, the light sparking for an instant in his brooding green eyes. He seemed tormented in some deep way, as if my words had caused him pain. Certainly it wasn't my insult to his writing. I insulted his writing all the time. That was a joke. Well, sort of a joke.

I couldn't figure what to say or do. He was working on my nerves. When he spoke his voice was very soft.

"You don't really want to be human," he said. "You don't believe that, do you?"

"Yes, I believe it!" I answered, humiliated by the feeling in my voice. "How could *you* not believe it?" I stood up and commenced my pacing again. I made a circuit of the little house, and wandered out into the jungle garden, pushing the thick springy vines out of my way. I was in such a state of confusion I couldn't speak to him anymore.

I was thinking of my mortal life, vainly trying not to mythologize it, but I could not drive away from me those memories—the last wolf hunt, my dogs dying in the snow. Paris. The boulevard theatre. Unfinished! *You don't really want to be human.* How could he say such a thing?

It seemed an age I was out in the garden, but finally, for better or worse, I wandered back inside. I found him still at his desk, looking at me in the most forlorn, almost heartbroken way.

"Look," I said, "there are only two things which I believe—the first is that no mortal can refuse the Dark Gift once he really knows what it is. And don't speak to me about David Talbot refusing me. David is not an ordinary man. The second thing I believe is that all of us would be human again if we could. Those are my tenets. There's nothing else."

He made a little weary accepting gesture and sat back in his chair. The wood creaked softly beneath his weight, and he lifted his right hand languidly, wholly unconscious of the seductive quality of this simple gesture, and ran his fingers back through his loose dark hair.

The memory pierced me suddenly of the night I had given him the blood, of how he had argued with me at the last moment that I must not do it, and then he'd given in. I had explained it all to him beforehand—while he was still the drunken feverish young planter in the sickbed with the rosary wound around the bedpost. But how can such a thing be explained! And he'd been so convinced that he wanted to come with me, so certain that mortal life held nothing for him—so bitter and burnt out and so young!

What had he known then? Had he ever read a poem by Milton, or listened to a sonata by Mozart? Would the name Marcus Aurelius have meant anything to him? In all probability, he would have thought it a fancy name for a black slave. Ah, those savage and swaggering plantation lords with their rapiers and their pearl-handled pistols! They did appreciate excess; I shall, in retrospect, give them that.

But he was far from those days now, wasn't he? The author of *Interview with the Vampire,* of all preposterous titles! I tried to quiet myself. I loved him too much not to be patient, not to wait until he spoke again. I'd fashioned him of human flesh and blood to be my preternatural tormentor, had I not?

"It can't be undone that easily," he said now, rousing me from memory, dragging me back into this dusty room. His voice was deliberately gentle, almost conciliatory or imploring. "It can't be that simple. You can't change bodies with a mortal man. To be candid, I don't even think it's possible, but even if it were—"

I didn't answer. I wanted to say, But what if it can be done! What if I can know again what it means to be alive.

"And then what about your body," he said, pleading with me, holding his anger and outrage in check so skillfully. "Surely you can't place all your powers at the disposal of this creature, this sorcerer or whatever he is. The others have told me that they cannot even calculate the limits of your power. Ah, no. It's an appalling idea. Tell me, how does he know how to find you! That's the most significant part."

"That's the least significant part," I replied. "But clearly, if this man can switch bodies, then he can leave his body. He can navigate as a spirit for long enough to track me and find me. I must be very visible to him when he's in this state, given what I am. This is no miracle in itself, you understand."

"I know," he said. "Or so I read and so I hear. I think you've found a truly dangerous being. This is worse than what we are."

"How so worse?"

"It implies another desperate attempt at immortality, switching bodies! Do you think this mortal, whoever he is, plans to grow old in this or any other body, and allow himself to die!"

I had to confess I followed his meaning. Then I told him about the man's voice, the sharp British accent, the cultured sound of it, and how it didn't seem the voice of a young man.

He shuddered. "He probably comes from the Talamasca," he said. "That's probably where he found out about you."

"All he had to do was buy a paperback novel to find out about me."

"Ah, but not to *believe*, Lestat, not to believe it was true."

I told him that I had spoken to David. David would know if this man was from his own order, but as for myself I didn't believe it. Those scholars would never have done such a thing. And there was something sinister about this mortal. The members of the Talamasca were almost tiresome in their wholesomeness. Besides, it didn't matter. I would talk to this man and discover everything for myself.

He grew reflective again and very sad. It almost hurt me to look at him. I wanted to grab him by the shoulders and shake him, but that would only have made him furious.

"I love you," he said softly.

I was amazed.

"You're always looking for a way to triumph," he continued. "You never give in. But there is no way to triumph. This is purgatory we're in, you and I. All we can be is thankful that it isn't actually hell."

"No, I don't believe it," I said. "Look, it doesn't matter what you say or what David said. I'm going to talk to Raglan James. I want to know what this is about! Nothing's going to prevent that."

"Ah, so David Talbot has also warned you against him."

"Don't choose your allies among my friends!"

"Lestat, if this human comes near me, if I believe that I am in danger from him, I will destroy him. Understand."

"Of course, I do. He wouldn't approach you. He's picked me, and with reason."

"He's picked you because you are careless and flamboyant and vain. Oh, I don't say this to hurt you. Truly I don't. You long to be seen and approached and understood and to get into mischief, to stir everything up and see if it won't boil over and if God won't come down and grab you by the hair. Well, there is no God. You might as well be God."

"You and David . . . the same song, the same admonitions, though he claims to have seen God and you don't believe He exists."

"David has seen God?" he asked respectfully.

"Not really," I murmured with a scornful gesture. "But you both scold in the same way. Marius scolds in the same way."

"Well, of course, you pick the voices that scold you. You always have, in the same manner in which you pick those who will turn on you and stick the knife right into your heart."

He meant Claudia, but he couldn't bear to speak her name. I knew I could hurt him if I said it, like flinging a curse in his face. I wanted to say, You had a hand in it! You were there when I made her, and there when she lifted the knife!

"I don't want to hear any more!" I said. "You'll sing the song of limitations all your long dreary years on this earth, won't you? Well, I am not God. And I am not the Devil from hell, though I sometimes pretend to be. I am not the crafty cunning Iago. I don't plot ghastly scenarios of evil. And I can't quash my curiosity or my spirit. Yes, I want to know if this man can really do it. I want to know what will happen. And I won't give up."

"And you'll sing the song of victory eternally though there is none to be had."

"Ah, but there is. There must be."

"No. The more we learn, the more we know there are no victories. Can't we fall back on nature, do what we must to endure and nothing more?"

"That is the most paltry definition of nature I have ever heard. Take a hard look at it—not in poetry but in the world outside. What do you see in nature? What made the spiders that creep beneath the damp floorboards, what made the moths with their multicolored wings that look like great evil flowers in the dark? The shark in the sea, why does it exist?" I came towards him, planted my hands on his desk and looked into his face. "I was so sure you would understand this. And by the way, I wasn't born a monster! I was a born a mortal child, the same as you. Stronger than you! More will to live than you! That was cruel of you to say."

"I know. It was wrong. Sometimes you frighten me so badly I hurl sticks and stones at you. It's foolish. I'm glad to see you, though I dread admitting it. I shiver at the thought that you might have really brought an end to yourself in the desert! I can't bear the thought of existence now without you! You infuriate me! Why don't you laugh at me? You've done it before."

I drew myself up and turned my back on him. I was looking out at the grass blowing gently in the river wind, and the tendrils of the Queen's Wreath reaching down to veil the open door.

"I'm not laughing," I said. "But I'm going to pursue this, no sense in lying about that to you. Lord God, don't you see? If I'm in a mortal body for five minutes only, what I might learn?"

"All right," he said despairingly. "I hope you discover the man's seduced you with a pack of lies, that all he wants is the Dark Blood, and that you send him straight to hell. Once more, let me warn you, if I see him, if he threatens me, I shall kill him. I haven't your strength. I depend upon my anonymity, that my little memoir, as you always call it, was so very far removed from the world of this century that no one took it as fact."

"I won't let him harm you, Louis," I said. I turned and threw an

evil glance at him. "I would never ever have let anyone harm you."
And with this I left.

OF COURSE, this was an accusation, and he felt the keen edge of it, I'd
seen that to my satisfaction, before I turned again and went out.

The night Claudia rose up against me, he had stood there, the
helpless witness, abhorring but not thinking to interfere, even as I
called his name.

He had taken what he thought to be my lifeless body and dumped
it in the swamp. Ah, naive little fledglings, to think you could so easily
get rid of me.

But why think of it now? He had loved me then whether or not
he knew it; of my love for him and for that wretched angry child, I
had never the slightest doubt.

He had grieved for me, I'll give him that much. But then he is so
good at grieving! He wears woe as others wear velvet; sorrow flatters
him like the light of candles; tears become him like jewels.

Well, none of that trash works with me.

I WENT back to my rooftop quarters, lighted all my fine electric lamps,
and lay about wallowing in rank materialism for a couple of hours,
watching an endless parade of video images on the giant screen, and
then slept for a little while on my soft couch before going out to hunt.

I was weary, off my clock from wandering. I was thirsty too.

IT WAS quiet beyond the lights of the Quarter, and the eternally illuminated skyscrapers of downtown. New Orleans sinks very fast into
dimness, either in the pastoral streets I've already described or amid the
more forlorn brick buildings and houses of the central town.

It was through these deserted commercial areas, with their shut-
up factories and warehouses and bleak little shotgun cottages, that I
wandered to a wondrous place near the river, which perhaps held no
significance for any other being than myself.

It was an empty field close to the wharves, stretching beneath the
giant pylons of the freeways which led to the high twin river bridges

which I have always called, since the first moment I beheld them, the Dixie Gates.

I must confess these bridges have been given some other, less charming name by the official world. But I pay very little attention to the official world. To me these bridges will always be the Dixie Gates, and I never wait too long after returning home before I go to walk near them and admire them, with all their thousands of tiny twinkling lights.

Understand they are not fine aesthetic creations such as the Brooklyn Bridge, which incited the devotion of the poet Hart Crane. They do not have the solemn grandeur of San Francisco's Golden Gate.

But they are bridges, nevertheless, and all bridges are beautiful and thought-provoking; and when they are fully illuminated as these bridges are, their many ribs and girders take on a grand mystique.

Let me add here that the same great miracle of light occurs in the black southern nighttime countryside with the vast oil refineries and electric power stations, which rise in startling splendour from the flat invisible land. And these have the added glories of smoking chimneys and ever-burning gas flames. The Eiffel Tower is now no mere scaffold of iron but a sculpture of dazzling electric light.

But we are speaking of New Orleans, and I wandered now to this riverfront wasteland, bounded on one side by dark drab cottages, and on the other by the deserted warehouses, and at the northern end by the marvelous junkyards of derelict machinery and chain-link fences overgrown with the inevitable copious and beautiful flowering vines.

Ah, fields of thought and fields of despair. I loved to walk here, on the soft barren earth, amid the clumps of high weeds, and scattered bits of broken glass, to listen to the low pulse of the river, though I could not see it, to gaze at the distant rosy glow of downtown.

It seemed the essence of the modern world, this awful horrid forgotten place, this great gap amid picturesque old buildings, where only now and then did a car creep by, on the deserted and supposedly dangerous streets.

And let me not fail to mention that this area, in spite of the dark paths which led up to it, was itself never really dark. A deep steady flood of illumination poured down from the lamps of the freeways, and came forth from the few street lights, creating an even and seemingly sourceless modern gloom.

Makes you want to rush there, doesn't it? Aren't you just dying to go prowl around there in the dirt?

Seriously, it is divinely sad to stand there, a tiny figure in the cosmos, shivering at the muffled noises of the city, of awesome machines groaning in faraway industrial compounds, or occasional trucks rumbling by overhead.

From there it was a stone's throw to a boarded-up tenement, where in the garbage-strewn rooms I found a pair of killers, their feverish brains dulled by narcotics, upon whom I fed slowly and quietly, leaving them both unconscious but alive.

Then I went back to the lonely empty field, roaming with my hands in my pockets, kicking the tin cans I found, and circling for a long time beneath the freeways proper, then leaping up and walking out on the northern arm of the nearer Dixie Gate itself.

How deep and dark my river. The air was always cool above it; and in spite of the dismal haze hanging over all, I could still see a wealth of cruel and tiny stars.

For a long time I lingered, pondering everything Louis had said to me, everything David had said to me, and still wild with excitement to meet the strange Raglan James the following night.

At last I became bored even with the great river. I scanned the city for the crazy mortal spy, and couldn't find him. I scanned uptown and could not find him. But still I was unsure.

As the night wore away, I made my way back to Louis's house—which was dark and deserted now—and I wandered the narrow little streets, more or less still searching for the mortal spy, and standing guard. Surely Louis was safe in his secret sanctuary, safe within the coffin to which he retreated well before every dawn.

Then I walked back down to the field again, singing to myself, and thought how the Dixie Gates with all their lights reminded me of the pretty steamboats of the nineteenth century, which had looked like great wedding cakes decked with candles, gliding by. Is that a mixed metaphor? I don't care. I heard the music of the steamboats in my head.

I tried to conceive of the next century, and what forms it would bring down upon us, and how it would shuffle ugliness and beauty with new violence, as each century must. I studied the pylons of the freeways, graceful soaring arches of steel and concrete, smooth as sculpture, simple and monstrous, gently bending blades of colorless grass.

And here came the train finally, rattling along the distant track before the warehouses, with its tedious string of dingy boxcars, disruptive and hideous and striking deep alarms with its shrieking whistle, within my all too human soul.

The night snapped back with utter emptiness after the last boom and clatter had died away. No visible cars moved on the bridges, and a heavy mist traveled silently over the breadth of the river, obscuring the fading stars.

I was weeping again. I was thinking of Louis, and of his warnings. But what could I do? I knew nothing of resignation. I never would. If that miserable Raglan James did not come tomorrow night, I'd search the world for him. I didn't want to talk to David anymore, didn't want to hear his warnings, couldn't listen. I knew I would follow this through.

I kept staring at the Dixie Gates. I couldn't get the beauty of the twinkling lights out of my head. I wanted to see a church with candles—lots of small flickering candles like the candles I'd seen in Notre Dame. Fumes rising from their wicks like prayers.

An hour till sunrise. Enough time. I headed slowly downtown.

The St. Louis Cathedral had been locked all night, but these locks were nothing to me.

I stood in the very front of the church, in the dark foyer, staring at the bank of candles burning beneath the statue of the Virgin. The faithful made their offerings in the brass coin box before lighting these candles. Vigil lights, they called them.

Often I'd sat in the square in the early evening, listening to these people come and go. I liked the smell of the wax; I liked the small shadowy church which seemed to have changed not one whit in over a century. I sucked in my breath and then I reached into my pockets, drew out a couple of crumpled dollars, and put them through the brass slot.

I lifted the long wax wick, dipped it into an old flame, and carried the fire to a fresh candle, watched the little tongue grow orange and bright.

What a miracle, I thought. One tiny flame could make so many other flames; one tiny flame could set afire a whole world. Why, I had, with this simple gesture, actually increased the sum total of light in the universe, had I not?

Such a miracle, and for this there will never be an explanation, and there are no Devil and God speaking together in a Paris café. Yet David's crazed theories soothed me when I thought of them in reverie. "Increase and multiply," said the Lord, the great Lord, Yahweh—from the flesh of the two a multitude of children, like a great fire from only two little flames . . .

There was a noise suddenly, sharp, distinct, ringing through the church like a deliberate footfall. I froze, quite astonished that I hadn't known someone was there. Then I remembered Notre Dame, and the sound of the child's steps on the stone floor. A sudden fear swept over me. She was there, wasn't she? If I looked around the corner, I would see her this time, maybe with her bonnet on, and her curls straggling from the wind, and her hands wrapped in woolen mittens, and she'd be looking up at me with those immense eyes. Golden hair and beautiful eyes.

There came a sound again. I hated this fear!

Very slowly I turned, and I saw Louis's unmistakable form emerging from the shadows. Only Louis. The light of the candles slowly revealed his placid and slightly gaunt face.

He had on a dusty sad coat, and his worn shirt was open at the collar, and he looked faintly cold. He approached me slowly and clasped my shoulder with a firm hand.

"Something dreadful's going to happen to you again," he said, the light of the candles playing exquisitely in his dark green eyes. "You're going to see to it. I know."

"I'll win out," I said with a little uneasy laugh, a tiny giddy happiness at seeing him. Then a shrug. "Don't you know that by now? I always do."

But I was amazed that he'd found me here, that he had come so close to dawn. And I was trembling still from all my mad imaginings, that she had come, come as she had in my dreams, and I had wanted to know why.

I was worried for him suddenly; he seemed so fragile with his pallid skin and long delicate hands. And yet I could feel the cool strength emanating from him as I always had, the strength of the thoughtful one who does nothing on impulse, the one who sees from all angles, who chooses his words with care. The one who never plays with the coming sun.

He drifted back away from me, abruptly, and he slipped silently out the door. I went after him, failing to lock the door behind me, which was unforgivable, I suppose, for the peace of churches should never be disturbed, and I watched him walk through the cold black morning, along the sidewalk near the Pontalba Apartments, across from the square.

He was hurrying in his subtle graceful way, with long easy strides. The light was coming, gray and lethal, giving a dull gleam to the shopwindows beneath the overhanging roof. I could stand it for another half hour, perhaps. He could not.

I realized I didn't know where his coffin was hidden, and how far he had to go to reach it. I had not the slightest idea.

Before he reached the corner nearest the river, he turned around. He gave a little wave to me, and in that gesture there was more affection than in anything he had said.

I went back to close up the church.

EIGHT

THE next night, I went at once to Jackson Square.

The terrible norther had finally come down into New Orleans, bringing with it a freezing wind. This sort of thing can happen at any time during the winter months, though some years it happens not at all. I'd stopped at my rooftop flat to put on a heavy wool overcoat, delighted as before that I had such feeling now in my newly bronzed skin.

A few tourists braved the weather to visit the cafés and bakeries still open near the cathedral; and the evening traffic was noisy and hurried. The greasy old Café du Monde was crowded behind its closed doors.

I saw him immediately. What luck.

They had chained the gates of the square, as they always did now at sunset, a dreadful annoyance, and he was outside, facing the cathedral, looking anxiously about.

I had a moment to study him before he realized I was there. He was a little taller than I am, six feet two, I figured, and he was extremely well built, as I'd seen before. I'd been right about the age. The body couldn't have been more than twenty-five years old. He was clad in very expensive clothes—a fur-lined raincoat, very well tailored, and a thick scarlet cashmere scarf.

When he saw me, a spasm passed through him, of pure anxiety and mad delight. That awful glittering smile came over him and vainly trying to conceal his panic, he fixed his eyes upon me as I made a slow, humanlike approach.

"Ah, but you do look like an angel, Monsieur de Lioncourt," he whispered breathlessly, "and how splendid your darkened skin. What a lovely enhancement. Forgive me for not saying so before."

"So you're here, Mr. James," I said, raising my eyebrows. "What's the proposition? I don't like you. Talk fast."

"Don't be so rude, Monsieur de Lioncourt," he said. "It would be a dreadful mistake to offend me, really it would." Yes, a voice exactly like David's voice. Same generation, most likely. And something of India in it, no doubt.

"You're quite right on that," he said. "I spent many years in India too. And a little time in Australia and Africa as well."

"Ah, so you can read my thoughts very easily," I said.

"No, not as easily as you might think, and now probably not at all."

"I'm going to kill you," I said, "if you don't tell me how you've managed to follow me and what you want."

"You know what I want," he said, laughing mirthlessly and anxiously under his breath, his eyes fixing on me and then veering away. "I told you through the stories, but I can't talk here in the freezing cold. This is worse than Georgetown, which is where I live, by the way. I was hoping to escape this sort of weather. And why ever did you drag me to London and Paris at this time of year?" More dry anxious spasms of laughter. Obviously he couldn't stare at me for more than a minute before glancing away as if I were a blinding light. "It was bitter cold in London. I hate cold. This is the tropics, is it not? Ah, you with your sentimental dreams of winter snow."

This last remark stunned me before I could conceal it. I was enraged for one silent instant, and then I regained my control.

"Come, the café," I said, pointing to the old French Market at the other side of the square. I hurried ahead along the pavement. I was too confused and excited to risk another word.

The café was extremely noisy but warm. I led the way to a table in the farthest corner from the door, ordered the famous café au lait for both of us, and sat there in rigid silence, faintly distracted by the stickiness of the little table, and grimly fascinated by him, as he shivered, unwound his red scarf anxiously, then put it on again, and finally pulled off his fine leather gloves, and stuffed them in his pockets, and then took them out again, and put on one of them, and laid the other one on the table and then snatched it up again, and put it on as well.

There was something positively horrible about him, about the way this alluringly splendid body was pumped up with his devious, jittery spirit, and cynical fits of laughter. Yet I couldn't take my eyes off him. In some devilish way I enjoyed watching him. And I think he knew it.

There was a provocative intelligence lurking behind this flawless, beautiful face. He made me realize how intolerant I had become of anyone truly young.

Suddenly the coffee was set down before us, and I wrapped my naked hands around the warm cup. I let the steam rise in my face. He watched this, with his large clear brown eyes, as if he were the one who was fascinated, and now he tried to hold my gaze steadily and calmly, which he found very hard. Delicious mouth, pretty eyelashes, perfect teeth.

"What the hell's the matter with you?" I asked.

"You know. You've figured it out. I'm not fond of this body, Monsieur de Lioncourt. A body thief has his little difficulties, you know."

"Is that what you are?"

"Yes, a body thief of the first rank. But then you knew that when you agreed to see me, did you not? You must forgive me my occasional clumsiness. I have been for most of my life a lean if not emaciated man. Never in such good health." He gave a sigh, the youthful face for a moment sad.

"But those chapters are closed now," he said with sudden discomfort. "Let me come to the point immediately, out of respect for your enormous preternatural intellect and vast experience—"

"Don't mock me, you little pissant!" I said under my breath. "You play with me, I'll tear you apart slowly. I told you I don't like you. Even your little title for yourself I don't like."

That shut him up. He calmed down altogether. Perhaps he lost his temper, or was frozen with terror. I think it was simply that he stopped being so fearful and became coldly angry instead.

"All right," he said softly, and soberly, without all the frenzy. "I want to trade bodies with you. I want yours for a week. I'll see to it that you have this body. It's young, it's in perfect health. You like the look of it, obviously. I shall show you various certificates of health if you wish. The body was quite thoroughly tested and examined right before I took possession of it. Or stole it. It's quite strong; you can see that. Obviously, it's strong, quite remarkably strong—"

"How can you do it?"

"We do it together, Monsieur de Lioncourt," he said very politely, his tone becoming more civil and courteous with each sentence he spoke. "There can be no question of body theft when I'm dealing with a creature such as you."

"But you've tried, haven't you?"

He studied me for a moment, clearly unsure as to how he should answer. "Well, you can't blame me for that now, can you?" he said imploringly. "Any more than I can blame you for drinking blood." He smiled as he said the word "blood." "But really I was simply trying to get your attention, which isn't an easy thing to do." He seemed thoughtful, utterly sincere. "Besides, cooperation is always involved on some level, no matter how submerged that level may be."

"Yes," I said, "but what are the actual mechanics, if that isn't too crude a word. How do we cooperate with each other! Be specific with me. I don't believe this can be done."

"Oh, come now, of course you do," he suggested gently, as if he were a patient teacher. It seemed almost an impersonation of David, without David's vigor. "How else would I have managed to take ownership of this body?" He made a little illustrative gesture as he continued. "We will meet at an appropriate place. Then we will rise out of our bodies, which you know very well how to do and have so eloquently described in your writing, and then we will take possession of each other's bodies. There's nothing to it really, except complete courage and an act of will." He lifted the cup, his hand trembling violently, and he drank a mouthful of the hot coffee. "For you, the test will be the courage, nothing more."

"What will keep me anchored in the new body?"

"There'll be no one in there, Monsieur de Lioncourt, to push you out. This is entirely different from possession, you understand. Oh, possession is a battle. When you enter into this body, there will be not the slightest resistance from it. You can remain until you choose to disengage."

"It's too puzzling!" I said, with obvious annoyance. "I know reams have been written on these questions, but something doesn't quite . . ."

"Let me try to put it in perspective," he said, voice hushed and almost exquisitely accommodating. "We're dealing here with science, but it is science which has not yet been fully codified by scientific minds. What we have are the memoirs of poets and occult adventurers, quite incapable of anatomizing what takes place."

"Exactly. As you pointed out, I've done it myself, traveled out of the body. Yet I don't know what takes place. Why doesn't the body die when one leaves it? I don't understand."

"The soul has more than one part, as does the brain. Surely you know that a child can be born without a cerebellum, yet the body can live if it has what is called the brain stem."

"Dreadful thought."

"Happens all the time, I assure you. Victims of accidents in which the brain is damaged irretrievably can still breathe and even yawn in their slumber, as the lower brain carries on."

"And you can possess such bodies?"

"Oh, no, I need a healthy brain in order to take full possession, absolutely must have all those cells in good working order and able to lock into the invading *mind*. Mark my words, Monsieur de Lioncourt. Brain is not mind. But again, we are not talking of possession, but of something infinitely finer than that. Allow me to continue, please."

"Go ahead."

"As I was saying, the soul has more than one part, in the same manner as the brain. The larger part of it—identity, personality, consciousness, if you will—this is what springs loose and travels; but a small residual soul remains. It keeps the vacant body animate, so to speak, for otherwise vacancy would mean death, of course."

"I see. The residual soul animates the brain stem; that is what you mean."

"Yes. When you rise out of your body, you will leave a residual soul there. And when you come into this body, you will find the residual soul there as well. It's the very same residual soul I found when I took possession. And that soul will lock with any higher soul eagerly and automatically; it wants to embrace that higher soul. Without it, it feels incomplete."

"And when death occurs both souls leave?"

"Precisely. Both souls go together, the residual soul and the larger soul, in a violent evacuation, and then the body is a mere lifeless shell and begins its decay." He waited, observing me with the same seemingly sincere patience, and then he said: "Believe me, the force of actual death is much stronger. There's no danger at all in what we propose to do."

"But if this little residual soul is so damned receptive, why can't I, with all my power, jolt some little mortal soul right out of its skin, and move in?"

"Because the larger soul would try to reclaim its body, Monsieur de Lioncourt, even if there were no understanding of the process, it would try again and again. Souls do not want to be without a body. And even though the residual soul welcomes the invader, something in it always recognizes the particular soul of which it was once a part. It will choose that soul if there is a battle. And even a bewildered soul can make a powerful attempt to reclaim its mortal frame."

I said nothing, but much as I suspected him, indeed reminded myself to be on guard, I found a continuity in all he said.

"Possession is always a bloody struggle," he reiterated. "Look what happens with evil spirits, ghosts, that sort of thing. They're always driven out eventually, even if the victor never knows what took place. When the priest comes with his incense and his holy-water mumbo jumbo, he is calling on that residual soul to oust the intruder and draw the old soul back in."

"But with the cooperative switch, both souls have new bodies."

"Precisely. Believe me, if you think you can hop into a human body without my assistance, well, give it a try, and you'll see what I mean. You'll never really experience the five senses of a mortal as long as the battle's raging inside."

His manner became even more careful, confidential. "Look at this body again, Monsieur de Lioncourt," he said with beguiling softness. "It can be yours, absolutely and truly yours." His pause seemed as precise suddenly as his words. "It was a year ago you first saw it in Venice. It's been host to an intruder without interruption for all of that time. It will play host to you."

"Where did you get it?"

"Stole it, I told you," he said. "The former owner is dead."

"You have to be more specific."

"Oh, must I, really? I do so hate to incriminate myself."

"I'm not a mortal officer of the law, Mr. James. I'm a vampire. Speak in words I can understand."

He gave a soft faintly ironic laugh. "The body was carefully chosen," he said. "The former owner had no mind left. Oh, there was nothing organically wrong with him, absolutely nothing. As I told you, he'd been quite thoroughly tested. He'd become a great quiet laboratory animal of sorts. He never moved. Never spoke. His reason had been hopelessly shattered, no matter how the healthy cells of the brain continued to pop and crackle along, as they are wont to do. I accomplished the switch in stages. Jolting him out of his body was simple. It was luring him down into my old body and leaving him there which took the skill."

"Where is your old body now?"

"Monsieur de Lioncourt, there is simply no way that the old soul will ever come knocking; that I guarantee."

"I want to see a picture of your old body."

"Whatever for?"

"Because it will tell me things about you, more perhaps than you yourself are telling me. I demand it. I won't proceed without it."

"You won't?" He retained the polite smile. "What if I get up and leave here?"

"I'll kill your splendid new body as soon as you try. No one in this café will even notice. They'll think you're drunk and that you've tumbled into my arms. I do that sort of thing all the time."

He fell silent, but I could see that he was calculating fiercely, and then I realized how much he was savoring all this, that he had been all along. He was like a great actor, deeply immersed in the most challenging part of his career.

He smiled at me, with startling seductiveness, and then, carefully removing his right glove, he drew a little item out of his pocket and put it in my hand. An old photograph of a gaunt man with thick white wavy hair. I judged him to be perhaps fifty. He wore some sort of white uniform with a little black bow tie.

He was a very nice looking man, actually, much more delicate in appearance than David, but he had the same sort of British elegance about him, and his smile was not unpleasant. He was leaning on the railing of what might have been the deck of a ship. Yes, it was a ship.

"You knew I'd ask for this, didn't you?"

"Sooner or later," he said.

"When was this taken?"

"That's of no importance. Why on earth do you want to know?" He betrayed just a little annoyance, but then he covered at once. "It was ten years ago," he said with a slight sinking of the voice. "Will it do?"

"And so that makes you . . . what? Mid-sixties, perhaps?"

"I'll settle for that," he said with a very broad and intimate smile.

"How did you learn all this? Why haven't others perfected this trick?"

He looked me up and down and a little coldly, and I thought his composure might snap. Then he retreated into his polite manner again. "Many people have done it," he said, his voice assuming a tone of special confidence. "Your friend David Talbot could have told you that. He didn't want to. He lies, like all those wizards in the Talamasca. They're religious. They think they can control people; they use their knowledge for control."

"How do you know about them?"

"I was a member of their order," he said, his eyes brightening playfully, as he smiled again. "They kicked me out of it. They accused me of using my powers for gain. What else is there, Monsieur de Lioncourt? What do you use your powers for, if not for gain?"

So, Louis had been right. I didn't speak. I tried to scan him but it was useless. Instead, I received a strong sense of his physical presence, of the heat emanating from him, of the hot fount of his blood. Succulent, that was the word for this body, no matter what one thought of his soul. I disliked the feeling because it made me want to kill him now.

"I found out about you through the Talamasca," he said, assuming the same confidential tone as before. "Of course I was familiar with your little fictions. I read all that sort of thing. That's why I used those short stories to communicate with you. But it was in the archives of the Talamasca that I discovered that your fictions weren't fictions at all."

I was silently enraged that Louis had figured it right.

"All right," I said. "I understand all this about the divided brain and the divided soul, but what if you don't want to give my body back to me after we've made this little switch, and I'm not strong enough to reclaim it; what's to keep you from making off with my body for good?"

He was quite still for a moment, and then said with slow measured words: "A very large bribe."

"Ah."

"Ten million dollars in a bank account waiting for me when I repossess this body." He reached into his coat pocket again and drew out a small plastic card with a thumbnail picture of his new face on it. There was also a clear fingerprint, and his name, Raglan James, and a Washington address.

"You can arrange it, surely. A fortune that can only be claimed by the man with this face and this fingerprint? You don't think I'd forfeit a fortune of that size, do you? Besides, I don't want your body forever. *You* don't even want it forever, do you? You've been far too eloquent on the subject of your agonies, your angst, your extended and noisy descent into hell, etcetera. No. I only want your body for a little while. There are many bodies out there, waiting for me to take possession of them, many kinds of adventure."

I studied the little card.

"Ten million," I said. "That's quite a price."

"It's nothing to you and you know it. You have billions squirreled away in international banks under all your colorful aliases. A creature with your formidable powers can acquire all the riches of the world. It's only the tawdry vampires of second-rate motion pictures who tramp through eternity living hand to mouth, as we both know."

He blotted his lips fastidiously with a linen handkerchief, then drank a gulp of his coffee.

"I was powerfully intrigued," he said, "by your descriptions of the vampire Armand in *The Queen of the Damned*—how he used his precious powers to acquire wealth, and built his great enterprise, the Night Island, such a lovely name. It rather took my breath away." He smiled, and then went on, the voice amiable and smooth as before. "It wasn't very difficult for me to document and annotate your assertions, you realize, though as we both know, your mysterious comrade has long ago abandoned the Night Island, and has vanished from the realm of computer records—at least as far as I can ascertain."

I didn't say anything.

"Besides, for what I offer, ten million is a bargain. Who else has made you such an offer? There isn't anyone else—at the moment, that is—who can or will."

"And suppose *I* don't want to switch back at the end of the week?" I asked. "Suppose I want to be human forever."

"That's perfectly fine with me," he said graciously. "I can get rid of your body anytime I want. There are lots of others who'll take it off my hands." He gave me a respectful and admiring smile.

"What are you going to do with my body?"

"Enjoy it. Enjoy the strength, the power! I've had everything the human body has to offer—youth, beauty, resilience. I've even been in the body of a woman, you know. And by the way, I don't recommend that at all. Now I want what *you* have to offer." He narrowed his eyes and cocked his head. "If there were any corporeal angels hanging about, well, I might approach one of them."

"The Talamasca has no record of angels?"

He hesitated, then gave a small contained laugh. "Angels are pure spirit, Monsieur de Lioncourt," he said. "We are talking bodies, no? I am addicted to the pleasures of the flesh. And vampires are fleshly monsters, are they not? They thrive on blood." Again, a light came into his eyes when he said the word "blood."

"What's your game?" I asked. "I mean really. What's your passion? It can't be the money. What's the money for? What will you buy with it? Experiences you haven't had?"

"Yes, I would say that's it. Experiences I haven't had. I'm obviously a sensualist, for want of a better word, but if you must know the truth—and I don't see why there should be any lies between us—I'm a thief in every respect. I don't enjoy something unless I bargain for it, trick someone out of it, or steal it. It's my way of making something out of nothing, you might say, which makes me like God!"

He stopped as if he were so impressed with what he had just said that he had to catch his breath. His eyes were dancing, and then he looked down at the half-empty coffee cup and gave a long secretive private smile.

"You do follow my drift, don't you?" he asked. "I stole these clothes," he said. "Everything in my house in Georgetown is stolen— every piece of furniture, every painting, every little objet d'art. Even the house itself is stolen, or shall we say, it was signed over to me amid a morass of false impressions and false hopes. I believe they call it swindling? All the same thing." He smiled proudly again, and with such seeming depth of feeling that I was amazed. "All the money I possess is stolen. So is the car I drive in Georgetown. So are the airline tickets I used to chase you around the world."

I didn't respond. How strange he was, I thought, intrigued by him and yet still repelled by him, for all his graciousness and seeming honesty. It was an act, but what a nearly perfect act. And then the bewitching face, which seemed with every new revelation to be more mobile and expressive and pliant. I roused myself. There was more I had to know.

"How did you accomplish that, following me about? How did you know where I was?"

"Two ways, to be perfectly frank with you. The first is obvious. I can leave my body for short periods, and during those periods I can search for you over vast distances. But I don't like that sort of bodiless travel at all. And of course you are not easy to find. You cloak yourself for long periods; then you blaze away in careless visibility; and of course you move about with no discernible pattern. Often by the time I'd located you, and brought my body to the location, you were gone.

"Then there's another way, almost as magical—computer systems. You use many aliases. I've been able to discover four of them. I'm often not quick enough to catch up with you through the computer. But I can study your tracks. And when you double back again, I know where to close in."

I said nothing, merely marveling again at how much he was enjoying all of this.

"I like your taste in cities," he said. "I like your taste in hotels—the Hassler in Rome, the Ritz in Paris, the Stanhope in New York. And of course the Park Central in Miami, lovely little hotel. Oh, don't get so suspicious. There's nothing to chasing people through computer systems. There's nothing to bribing clerks to show you a credit card receipt, or bullying bank employees to reveal things they've been told not to reveal. Tricks usually handle it perfectly well. You don't have to be a preternatural killer to do it. No, not at all."

"You steal through the computer systems?"

"When I can," he said with a little twist to his mouth. "I steal in any fashion. Nothing's beneath my dignity. But I'm not capable of stealing ten million dollars through any means. If I were, I wouldn't be here, now, would I? I'm not that clever. I've been caught twice. I've been in prison. That's where I perfected the means of traveling out of body, since there wasn't any other way." He made a weary bitter sarcastic smile.

"Why are you telling me all this?"

"Because your friend David Talbot is going to tell you. And because I think we should understand each other. I'm weary of taking risks. This is the big score, your body—and ten million dollars when I give it up."

"What is it with you?" I asked. "This all sounds so petty, so mundane."

"Ten million is mundane?"

"Yes. You've swapped an old body for a new one. You're young again! And the next step, if I consent, will be my body, my powers. But it's the money that matters to you. It's really just the money and nothing else."

"It's both!" he said sourly and defiantly. "They're very similar." With conscious effort he regained his composure. "You don't realize it because you acquired your wealth and your power simultaneously," he said. "Immortality and a great casket full of gold and jewels. Wasn't that the story? You walked out of Magnus's tower an immortal with a king's ransom. Or is the story a lie? You're real enough, that's plain. But I don't know about all those things you wrote. But you ought to understand what I'm saying. You're a thief yourself."

I felt an immediate flush of anger. Suddenly he was more consummately distasteful than he'd been in that anxious jittering state when we first sat down.

"I'm not a thief," I said quietly.

"Yes, you are," he answered with amazing sympathy. "You always steal from your victims. You know you do."

"No, I never do unless . . . I have to."

"Have it your way. I think you're a thief." He leant forward, eyes glittering again, as the soothing measured words continued: "You steal the blood you drink, you can't argue with that."

"What actually happened with you and the Talamasca?" I asked.

"I told you," he said. "The Talamasca threw me out. I was accused of using my gifts to gain information for personal use. I was accused of deception. And of stealing, of course. They were very foolish and shortsighted, your friends in the Talamasca. They underestimated me completely. They should have valued me. They should have studied me. They should have begged me to teach them the things I know.

"Instead they gave me the boot. Six months' severance. A pittance. And they refused my last request . . . for first-class passage to America on the *Queen Elizabeth 2*. It would have been so simple for them to grant my wish. They owed me that much, after the things I'd revealed to them. They should have done it." He sighed, and glanced at me, and then at his coffee. "Little things like that matter in this world. They matter very much."

I didn't reply. I looked down at the picture again, at the figure on the deck of the ship, but I'm not sure he took notice of it. He was staring off into the noisy glare of the café, eyes dancing over walls and ceiling and occasional tourists and taking note of none.

"I tried to bargain with them," he said, voice soft and measured as before. "If they wanted a few items returned or a few questions answered—you know. But they wouldn't hear of it, not them! And money means nothing to them, no more than it means to you. They were too mean-spirited to even consider it. They gave me a tourist-class plane ticket, and a check for six months' pay. Six months' pay! Oh, I am so very weary of all the little ups and downs!"

"What made you think you could outwit them?"

"I *did* outwit them," he said, eyes flashing with a little smile. "They're not very careful with their inventories. They have no idea really how many of their little treasures I managed to appropriate. They'll never guess. Of course you were the real theft—the secret that you existed. Ah, discovering that little vault full of relics was such a stroke of good luck. Understand, I didn't take anything of your old possessions—rotted frock coats from your very closets in New Orleans, parchments with your fancy signature, why, there was even a locket with a painted miniature of that accursed little child—"

"Watch your tongue," I whispered.

He went quiet. "I'm sorry. I meant no offense, truly."

"What locket?" I asked. Could he hear the sudden racing of my heart? I tried to still it, to keep the warmth from rising again in my face.

How meek he looked as he answered. "A gold locket on a chain, little oval miniature inside. Oh, I didn't steal it. I swear to you. I left it there. Ask your friend Talbot. It's still in the vault."

I waited, commanding my heart to be still, and banishing all

images of that locket from my mind. Then: "The point is, the Talamasca caught you and they put you out."

"You don't have to continue insulting me," he said humbly. "It's
entirely possible for us to make our little bargain without any unpleas-
antness. I'm very sorry that I mentioned this locket, I didn't—"

"I want to think over your proposition," I said.

"That might be a mistake."

"Why?"

"Give it a chance! Act quickly. Act now. And remember, please,
if you harm me, you'll throw away this opportunity forever. I'm the
only key to this experience; use me or you'll never know what it's like
to be a human being again." He drew close to me, so close I could feel
his breath on my cheek. "You'll never know what it's like to walk in
the sunlight, to enjoy a full meal of real food, to make love to a woman
or a man."

"I want you to leave here now. Get out of this city and never
come back. I'll come to you at this address in Georgetown when I'm
ready. And it won't be for a week this switch. Not the first time at any
rate. It will be . . ."

"May I suggest two days?"

I didn't answer.

"What if we start with one day?" he asked. "If you like it, then
we can arrange for a longer time?"

"One day," I said, my voice sounding very strange to me. "One
period of twenty-four hours . . . for the first time."

"One day and two nights," he said quietly. "Let me suggest this
coming Wednesday, as soon after sunset as you like. We shall make
the second switch early on Friday, before dawn."

I didn't reply.

"You have this evening and tomorrow evening to make your
preparations," he said coaxingly. "After the switch you will have all
of Wednesday night and the full day Thursday. Of course you'll have
Thursday night as well up until . . . shall we say, two hours before
Friday's sunrise? That ought to be comfortable enough."

He studied me keenly, then became more anxious: "Oh, and bring
one of your passports with you. I don't care which one. But I want
a passport, and a bit of credit plastic, and money in my pockets over
and above the ten million. You understand?"

I didn't say anything.

"You know this will work."

Again, I didn't answer.

"Believe me, all I've told you is true. Ask Talbot. I wasn't born this handsome individual you see before you. And this body is waiting right now this very minute for you."

I was quiet.

"Come to me Wednesday," he said. "You'll be very glad that you did." He paused, and then his manner became even softer. "Look, I . . . feel that I know you," he said, his voice dropping to a whisper. "I know what you want! It's dreadful to want something and not to have it. Ah, but then to know that it's within your grasp."

I looked up slowly into his eyes. The handsome face was tranquil, devoid of any stamp of expression, and the eyes seemed rather miraculous in their fragility and their precision. The skin itself seemed supple and as if it would feel like satin to my touch. And then came the voice again, in a seductive half whisper, the words touched with sadness.

"This is something only you and I can do," he said. "In a way, it is a miracle which only you and I can understand."

The face appeared monstrous suddenly in its tranquil beauty; even the voice seemed monstrous in its lovely timbre and eloquence, so expressive of empathy and even affection, perhaps even love.

I had the urge to grab the creature by the throat; I had the urge to shake it until it lost its composure and its semblance of deep feeling, but I would not have dreamed of doing so really. I was mesmerized by the eyes and the voice. I was allowing myself to be mesmerized, the way I had allowed those earlier physical sensations of assault to sweep over me. And it occurred to me that I allowed this simply because this being seemed so very fragile and foolish and I was sure of my own strength.

But that was a lie. I wanted to do this thing! I wanted to make this switch.

Only after a long while, he broke away, and let his gaze move over the café. Was he biding his time? What went on inside his clever conniving, and thoroughly concealed soul! A being who could steal bodies! Who could live inside another's flesh.

Slowly, he took a pen from his pocket, tore loose one of the paper napkins, and wrote down the name and address of a bank. He gave this to me and I took it and slipped it into my pocket. I didn't speak.

"Before we switch, I'll give you my passport," he said, studying me with every word. "The one with the correct face on it, of course. I'll leave you comfortable in my house. I assume you'll have money in your pockets. You always do. You'll find it quite cozy, my house. You'll like Georgetown." His words were like soft fingers tapping the back of my hand, annoying yet vaguely thrilling. "It's quite a civilized place, an old place. Of course it is snowing there. You realize it. It's very cold. If you really don't want to do it in a cold climate—"

"I don't mind about the snow," I said under my breath.

"Yes, of course. Well, I'll be sure to leave you quite a few winter garments," he said in the same conciliatory manner.

"None of those details matter," I said. What a fool he was to think that they did. I could feel my heart skipping beats.

"Oh, I don't know about that," he said. "When you're human you might find that a lot of things matter."

To you, perhaps, I thought. All that matters to me is to be in that body, and to be alive. In my mind's eye, I saw the snow of that last winter in the Auvergne. I saw the sun spilling down on the mountains . . . I saw the little priest from the village church, shivering in the great hall as he complained to me about the wolves coming down into the village at night. Of course I would hunt down the wolves. It was my duty.

I didn't care whether he'd read these thoughts or not.

"Ah, but don't you want to taste good food? Don't you want to drink good wine? What about a woman, or a man, for that matter? You'll need money and pleasant accommodations, of course."

I didn't reply. I saw the sun on the snow. I let my eyes move slowly to his face. I thought how curiously graceful he seemed in this new mode of persuasiveness, how very like David, indeed.

He was about to go on with his talk of luxuries when I gestured for silence.

"All right," I said. "I think you'll see me on Wednesday. Shall we say an hour after dark? Oh, and I must warn you. This fortune of ten million dollars. It will only be available to you for two hours on Friday morning. You'll have to appear in person to claim it." And here I touched his shoulder lightly. "This person, of course."

"Of course. I'm looking forward to it."

"And you'll need a code word to complete the transaction. And you'll only learn the code word from me when you return my body as agreed."

"No. No code words. The transfer of funds must be complete and irrevocable before the bank closes on Wednesday afternoon. All I have to do the following Friday is appear before the representative, allow him to take my fingerprint if you insist upon it, and then he will sign the money over to me."

I was quiet, thinking it over.

"After all, my handsome friend," he said, "what if you don't like your day as a human being? What if you don't feel you've gotten your money's worth?"

"I'll get my money's worth," I whispered, more to myself than to him.

"No," he said patiently but insistently. "No code words."

I studied him. He smiled at me, and he appeared almost innocent and truly young. Good Lord, it must have meant *something* to him, this youthful vigor. How could it not have dazzled him, at least for a while? In the beginning, perhaps, he must have thought he'd attained everything that he could ever want.

"Not by a long shot!" he said suddenly, as if he couldn't stop the words from slipping out of his mouth.

I couldn't help but laugh.

"Let me tell you a little secret about youth," he said with sudden coldness. "Bernard Shaw said it was wasted on the young, you remember that clever overrated little remark?"

"Yes."

"Well, it isn't. The young know how difficult and truly dreadful youth can be. Their youth is wasted on everyone else, that's the horror. The young have no authority, no respect."

"You're mad," I said. "I don't think you use what you steal very well. How could you not thrill to the sheer stamina? Glory in the beauty you see reflected in the eyes of those who look at you everywhere you go?"

He shook his head. "That's for you to enjoy," he said. "The body's young the way you've always been young. You will thrill to the stamina of it, as you say. You will glory in all those loving looks." He broke off. He took the final sip of his coffee and stared into the cup.

"No code words," he said politely.

"Very well."

"Ah, good," he said with a full warm smile of amazing brightness. "Remember I offered you a week for this sum," he said. "It's your decision to take one full day. Perhaps after you've had a taste you'll want a much longer time."

"Perhaps so," I said. Again, I was distracted by the sight of him, by the sight of the large warm hand which he covered now with the glove.

"And another switch will cost you another handsome sum," he said merrily, all smiles now, as he arranged his scarf within his lapels.

"Yes, of course."

"Money really *doesn't* mean anything to you, does it?" he asked, thoughtfully.

"Nothing at all." How tragic for you, I thought, that it means so much.

"Well, perhaps I should take my leave now, and allow you to make your preparations. I shall see you Wednesday as planned."

"Don't try to run out on me," I said in a low voice, leaning forward slightly, and then lifting my hand and touching his face.

The gesture clearly startled him; he became motionless, like an animal in the wood who suddenly sensed danger where there had been none before. But his expression remained calm, and I let my fingers rest against his smoothly shaven skin.

Then I moved them down slowly, feeling the firmness of his jawbone, and then I placed my hand on his neck. Here, too, the razor had passed, leaving its faint dark shadow; the skin was firm, surprisingly muscular, and a clean, youthful scent rose from it as I saw the sweat break out on his forehead, as I saw his lips move in a surprisingly graceful smile.

"Surely you enjoyed being young just a little," I said under my breath.

He smiled, as if he knew just how radiant and seductive the smile could be.

"I dream the dreams of the young," he said. "And they are always dreams of being older, and richer, and wiser, and stronger, don't you think?"

I gave a little laugh.

"I'll be there Wednesday night," he said with the same silver-tongued sincerity. "You can be certain of it. Come. It will happen, I promise you." He leant forward and whispered. "You will be inside this body!" And once again, he smiled in the most charming and ingratiating fashion. "You'll see."

"I want you to leave New Orleans now."

"Ah, yes, immediately," he said. And without another word, he stood up, moving back away from me, and then tried to conceal his sudden fear. "I have my ticket already," he said. "I don't like your filthy little Caribbean backwater." He made a little self-deprecating laugh, an almost pretty laugh. Then he went on as if he were a wise teacher scolding a student. "We'll talk more when you come to Georgetown. And don't try to spy on me in the meantime. I'll know it if you do. I'm too good at picking up that sort of thing. Even the Talamasca was amazed at my powers. They should have kept me in the fold! They should have studied me!" He broke off.

"I'll spy on you anyway," I said, echoing his low key and careful tone. "I don't really care whether or not you know."

He laughed again, in a low, subdued, and slightly smoldering fashion, and then gave me a little nod and rushed towards the door. He was once again the awkward, ungainly being, full of crazed excitement. And how tragic it seemed, for surely that body could move like a panther with another soul inside.

I caught him on the sidewalk, startling him, indeed scaring him half out of his powerful little psychic mind. We were almost eye-to-eye.

"What do you want to do with my body?" I asked. "I mean, besides flee from the sun every morning as if you were a nocturnal insect or a giant slug?"

"What do you think?" he said, once again playing the charming English gentleman with utter sincerity. "I want to drink blood." His eyes grew very wide, and he leaned closer. "I want to take life when I drink it. That's the point, isn't it? It's not merely the blood you steal from them, it's their lives. I've never stolen anything that valuable from anyone." He gave me a knowing smile. "The body, yes, but not the blood and the life."

I let him go, backing away from him as sharply as he'd backed away from me only a moment before. My heart was pounding, and I could feel a tremor passing through me as I stared at him, at his handsome and seemingly innocent face.

He continued to smile. "You are a thief par excellence," he said. "Every breath you take is stolen! Oh, yes, I must have your body. I must experience this. To invade the vampire files of the Talamasca was a triumph, but to possess your body, and to steal blood whilst in it! Ah, that is beyond all my finest accomplishments! You are the ultimate thief."

"Get away from me," I whispered.

"Oh, come now, don't be so fastidious," he said. "You hate it when other people do it to you. You're quite privileged, Lestat de Lioncourt. You've found what Diogenes was searching for. An honest man!" Another broad smile, and then a low volley of simmering laughter, as if he couldn't contain it any longer. "I shall see you Wednesday. And you must come early. I want as much of the night as I can have."

He turned and hurried into the street, waving frantically for a taxi, and then bolting against the traffic to force his way into a cab which had just come to a stop, quite obviously, for someone else. A little argument ensued, but he won out immediately, slamming the door in the other fellow's face as the cab sped off. I saw him wink at me through the dirty window, and wave. And then he and his taxi were gone.

I was sick with confusion. I stood there unable to move. The night for all its coldness was busy and full of the mingled voices of the passing tourists, of cars slowing as they passed the square. Without intent, without words, I tried to see it as it might be in the sunshine; I tried to imagine the heavens over this spot that shocking vague blue.

Then slowly I turned up the collar of my coat.

I walked for hours. I kept hearing that beautiful cultured voice in my ears.

It's not merely the blood you steal from them, it's their lives. I've never stolen anything that valuable from anyone. The body, yes, but not the blood and the life.

I couldn't have faced Louis. I couldn't bear the thought of talking to David. And if Marius learned of this, I was finished before I'd begun. Who knew what Marius would do to me for even entertaining such an idea? And yet Marius, with all his vast experience, would know if this was truth or fancy! Ye gods, had Marius never wanted to do it himself?

At last, I went back to my apartment, and turned out the lights and sat sprawled on the soft velvet sofa, before the darkened glass wall, peering out at the city below.

Remember, please, if you harm me, you'll throw away this opportu-

nity forever . . . Use me or you'll never know what it's like to be a human being again . . . You'll never know what it's like to walk in the sunlight, to enjoy a full meal of real food, to make love to a woman or a man.

I thought about the power of rising out of one's material form. I didn't like this power, and it did not happen to me spontaneously, this astral projection, as it was called, this spirit traveling. Indeed, I had used it so few times I could have counted them on one hand.

And in all my suffering in the Gobi, I had not tried to leave my material form, nor had I been propelled out of it, nor had I even thought of such a possibility.

Indeed, the idea of being disconnected from my body—of floating about, earthbound, and unable to find a door to heaven or hell—was absolutely terrifying to me. And that such a traveling, disembodied soul could not pass through the gates of death at will had been plain to me the very first time I'd ever experimented with this little trick. But to go into the body of a mortal! To anchor there, to walk, to feel, to see, as a mortal, ah, I could not contain my excitement. It was becoming pure pain.

After the switch you will have all of Wednesday night and the full day Thursday. The full day Thursday, the full day . . .

Finally, sometime before morning, I called my agent in New York. This man had no knowledge of my Paris agent at all. He knew me under two names only. And I had not used either of these in many a moon. It was very unlikely Raglan James had any knowledge of these identities and their various resources. It seemed the simplest route to pursue.

"I have some work for you, very complicated work. And it must be done immediately."

"Yes, sir, always, sir."

"All right, this is the name and address of a bank in the District of Columbia. I want you to write it down . . ."

NINE

THE following evening I completed all the necessary papers for this transfer of ten million in American dollars, and sent these papers by messenger to the bank in Washington, along with Mr. Raglan James's photo-identification card, and a full reiteration of instructions in my own hand, and with the signature of Lestan Gregor, which for various reasons, was the best name to be used for the entire affair.

My New York agent also knew me by another alias, as I have indicated, and we agreed that this other name would in no way figure in this transaction, and that should I need to contact my agent, this other name, and a couple of new code words, would empower him to make transfers of money on verbal instructions alone.

As for the name Lestan Gregor, it was to disappear utterly from record as soon as this ten million went into the possession of Mr. James. All the remaining assets of Mr. Gregor were now transferred to my other name—which by the way was Stanford Wilde, for all that it matters now.

All of my agents are used to such bizarre instructions—shifts of funds, collapsing of identities, and the authority to wire funds to me anywhere I might be in the world on the basis of a telephone call. But I tightened the system. I gave bizarre and difficult-to-pronounce code words. I did everything I could, in short, to improve security surrounding my identities, and to fix the terms of the transfer of the ten million as firmly as I could.

As of Wednesday noon, the money would be in a trust account at the Washington bank, from which it could only be claimed by Mr. Raglan James, and only between the hours of ten and twelve on the following Friday. Mr. James would verify his identity by physical conformity to his picture, and by fingerprint, and by signature, before the money would be placed in his account. At one minute after twelve noon, the entire transaction would be null and void, and the money would be sent back to New York. Mr. James was to be presented with all these terms on Wednesday afternoon at the very latest, and with the assurance that nothing could prevent this transfer if all the instructions were followed as laid out.

It seemed an ironclad arrangement, as far as I could figure, but then I wasn't a thief, contrary to what Mr. James believed. And knowing that he was, I examined all aspects of the deal over and over, rather compulsively, in order to deny him the upper hand.

But why was I still deceiving myself, I wondered, that I would not go through with this experiment? For surely I intended to do exactly that.

Meantime, the phone in my apartment was ringing over and over again, as David tried desperately to reach me, and I sat there in the dark, thinking things over, and refusing to answer, vaguely annoyed by the ringing, and finally unplugging the cord.

This was despicable, what I meant to do. This varmint would use my body, no doubt, for the most sinister and cruel crimes. And I was going to allow this to happen, merely so that I could be human? How impossible to justify, in any light whatever, to anyone whom I knew.

Every time I thought of the others discovering the truth—*any* of them—I shuddered, and put the thought completely from my mind. Pray they were busy throughout the vast hostile world, with their own inevitable pursuits.

How much better to think about the entire proposition with pounding excitement. And Mr. James was right about the matter of money, of course. Ten million meant absolutely nothing to me. I had carried through the centuries a great fortune, increasing it by various offhand means until even I myself did not know its true size.

And much as I understood how very different the world was for a mortal being, I still could not quite comprehend why the money was so important to James. After all, we were dealing with questions of potent magic, of vast preternatural power, of potentially devastating spiritual insights, and demonic, if not heroic, deeds. But the money was clearly what the little bastard wanted. The little bastard, for all his insults, did not really see past the money. And perhaps that was just as well.

Think how very dangerous he might be had he truly grand ambitions. But he did not.

And I *wanted* that human body. And that was the bottom line.

The rest was rationalization at best. And as the hours passed, I did quite a bit of that.

For example, was the surrender of my powerful body really so despicable? The little creep couldn't even use the human body he had. He'd turned into the perfect gentleman for half an hour at the café table, then blown it with his awkward graceless gestures, as soon as he'd stood up. He'd never be able to use my physical strength. He wouldn't be able to direct my telekinetic powers either, no matter how psychic he claimed to be. He might do all right with the telepathy, but when it came to entrancing or spellbinding, I suspected he would not even begin to use those gifts. I doubted he would be able to move very fast. Indeed, he'd be clumsy and slow and ineffective. Actual flight probably wouldn't be a possibility for him. And he might even get himself into a terrible scrape.

Yes, it was all well and good that he was such a small-souled miserable little schemer. Better that than a god on a rampage, certainly. As for me, what did I plan to do?

The house in Georgetown, the car, these things meant nothing! I'd told him the truth. I wanted to be alive! Of course I would need some money for food and drink. But seeing the light of day cost nothing. Indeed, the experience need not involve any great material comfort or luxury. I wanted the spiritual and physical experience of being mortal flesh again. I saw myself as wholly unlike the miserable Body Thief!

But I had one remaining doubt. What if ten million wasn't enough to bring this man back with my body? Perhaps I should double the amount. To such a small-minded person, a fortune of twenty million would truly be an enticement. And in the past, I had always found it effective to double the sums which people charged for their services, thereby commanding a loyalty from them of which they had not even conceived.

I called New York again. Double the sum. My agent, naturally enough, thought I was losing my mind. We used our new code words to confirm the authority of the transaction. Then I hung up.

It was time now to talk to David or go to Georgetown. I had made a promise to David. I sat very still, waiting for the phone to ring, and when it did, I picked it up.

"Thank God you're there."

"What is it?" I asked.

"I recognized the name Raglan James immediately, and you're absolutely right. The man is not inside his own body! The person you're dealing with is sixty-seven years old. He was born in India, grew up in London, and has been in prison five times. He's a thief known to every law enforcement agency in Europe, and what they call in America a confidence man. He's also a powerful psychic, a black magician—one of the most crafty we've ever known."

"So he told me. He worked his way into the order."

"Yes, he did. And this was one of the worst mistakes we've ever made. But Lestat, this man could seduce the Blessed Virgin, and steal a pocket watch from the Living Lord. Yet he was his own undoing within a matter of months. That's the crux of what I'm trying to tell you. Now, please do listen. This sort of black witch or sorcerer always brings evil upon himself! With his gifts he should have been able to deceive us forever; instead he used his skill to fleece the other members, and to steal from the vaults!"

"He told me that. What about this whole question of body switching? Can there be any doubt?"

"Describe the man as you've seen him."

I did. I emphasized the height and the robust nature of the physical frame. The thick glossy hair, the uncommonly smooth and satinlike skin. The exceptional beauty.

"Ah, I'm looking at a picture of this man right now."

"Explain."

"He was confined briefly in a London hospital for the criminally insane. Mother an Anglo-Indian, which may explain the exceptionally beautiful complexion you're describing, and which I can see here plainly enough. Father a London cabbie who died in jail. The fellow himself worked in a garage in London, specializing in extremely expensive cars. Dealt in drugs as a sideline so that he could afford the cars himself. One night he murdered his entire family—wife, two children, brother-in-law and mother—and then gave himself up to the police. A frightening mix of hallucinogenic drugs was found in his blood, along with a great deal of alcohol. These were the very same drugs he often sold to the neighborhood youths."

"Derangement of the senses but nothing wrong with the brain."

"Precisely, the entire murderous tantrum was drug induced as far as the authorities could see. The man himself never spoke a word after the incident. He remained steadfastly immune to any stimulus until three weeks after his commitment to hospital, at which time he mysteriously escaped, leaving the body of a slain orderly in his room. Can you guess who this slain orderly turned out to be?"

"James."

"Exactly. Positive identification made postmortem through fingerprints, and confirmed through Interpol and Scotland Yard. James had been working in the hospital under an assumed name for a month before the incident, no doubt waiting for just such a body to arrive!"

"And then he cheerfully murdered his own body. Steely little son of a bitch to do that."

"Well, it was a very sick body—dying of cancer to be precise. The autopsy revealed he wouldn't have survived another six months. Lestat, for all we know, James may have contributed to the commission of the crimes which placed the young man's body at his disposal. If he hadn't stolen this body, he would have hit upon another in a similar state. And once he'd dealt the death blow to his old body, it went into the grave, don't you see, carrying James's entire criminal record with it."

"Why did he give me his real name, David? Why did he tell me he'd belonged to the Talamasca?"

"So I could verify his story, Lestat. Everything he does is calculated. You don't understand how clever this creature is. He wants you to know that he can do what he says he can do! And that the former owner of that young body is quite unable to interfere."

"But, David, there are still aspects to this which are baffling. The soul of the other man. Did it die in that old body? Why didn't it . . . get out!"

"Lestat, the poor being probably never knew such a thing was possible. Undoubtedly James manipulated the switch. Look, I have a file here of testimony from other members of the order pertaining to how this character jolted them right out of the physical and took possession of their bodies for short periods of time.

"All the sensations you experienced—the vibration, the constriction—were reported by these people as well. But we are speaking here of educated members of the Order of the Talamasca. This garage mechanic had no training in such things.

"His entire experience with the preternatural had to do with drugs. And God knows what ideas were mixed up with it. And throughout, James was dealing with a man in a severe state of shock."

"What if it's all some sort of clever ruse," I said. "Describe James to me, the man you knew."

"Slender, almost emaciated, very vibrant eyes, and thick white hair. Not a bad-looking man. Beautiful voice, as I recall."

"That's our man."

"Lestat, the note you faxed to me from Paris—it leaves no doubt. It's James's writing. It's his signature. Don't you realize that he found out about you through the order, Lestat! That is the most disturbing aspect of this to me, that he located our files."

"So he said."

"He entered the order to gain access to such secrets. He cracked the computer system. There's no telling what he might have discovered. Yet he couldn't resist stealing a silver wristwatch from one of the members, and a diamond necklace from the vaults. He played reckless games with the others. He robbed their rooms. You can't entertain any further communication with this person! It's out of the question."

"You sound like the Superior General, now, David."

"Lestat, we're speaking of switching here! That means putting your body, with all its gifts, at the disposal of this man."

"I know."

"You cannot do it. And let me make a shocking suggestion. If you do enjoy taking life, Lestat, as you've told me, why not murder this revolting individual as soon as you can?"

"David, this is wounded pride talking. And I *am* shocked."

"Don't play with me. There's no time for it here. You realize that this character is plenty clever enough to be counting upon your volatile nature in this little game? He has picked you for this switch just as he picked the poor mechanic in London. He has studied the evidence of your impulsiveness, your curiosity, your general fearlessness. And he can fairly well assume that you won't listen to a word of warning from me."

"Interesting."

"Speak up; I can't hear you."

"What else can you tell me?"

"What else do you require!"

"I want to understand this."

"Why?"

"David, I see your point about the poor befuddled mechanic;

nevertheless, why didn't his soul pop loose from the cancer-riddled body when James dealt it one fine blow to the head?"

"Lestat, you said it yourself. The blow was to the head. The soul was already enmeshed with the new brain. There was no moment of clarity or will in which it could have sprung free. Even with a clever sorcerer like James, if you damage the tissues of the brain severely before the soul has a chance to disengage, it cannot do it, and physical death will follow, taking the entire soul with it out of this world. If you do decide to put an end to this miserable monster, by all means take him by surprise, and see to it that you smash his cranium as you might a raw egg."

I laughed. "David, I've never heard you so incensed."

"That's because I know you, and I think you mean to do this switch, and you must not!"

"Answer a few more of my questions. I want to think this through."

"No."

"Near-death experiences, David. You know, those poor souls that suffer a heart attack, go up through a tunnel, see a light, and then come back to life. What's happening with them?"

"Your guess is as good as mine."

"I don't believe you." I reported James's talk of the brain stem and the residual soul, as best I could. "In these near-death experiences, has a little bit of the soul remained behind?"

"Perhaps, or maybe these individuals do confront death—they actually do cross over—and yet the soul, whole and entire, is sent back. I don't know."

"But whatever the case, you can't simply die by going out of your body, can you? If in the Gobi Desert, I had gone up and out of my body, I couldn't have found the gateway, could I? It wouldn't have been there. It opens only for the whole soul."

"Yes. As far as I know, yes." He paused. Then: "Why do you ask me this? Do you still dream of dying? I don't believe it. You're too desperately fond of being alive."

"I've been dead for two centuries, David. What about ghosts? The earthbound spirits?"

"They've failed to find that gateway, even though it opened. Or they refused to go through. Look, we can talk about all this some night in the future, roaming the alleyways of Rio, or wherever you like. The important thing is, you must swear to me not to deal with this sorcerer any longer, if you won't go so far as to follow my suggestion that you put an end to him as soon as you can."

"Why are you so afraid of him!"

"Lestat, you must understand how destructive and vicious this individual can be. You can't give your body over to him! And that is just what you mean to do. Look, if you meant to possess a mortal body for a while, I'd be dead against it, for that is diabolical and unnatural enough! But to give your body to this madman! Ye gods, will you please come here to London? Let me talk you out of this. Don't you owe me as much!"

"David, you investigated him before he became a member of the order, did you not? What sort of man is he . . . I mean how did he become this wizard of sorts?"

"He deceived us with elaborate fabrications and counterfeit records on a scale you wouldn't believe. He loves that sort of connivance. And he's something of a computer genius. Our real investigation took place after he'd gone."

"So? Where did it all start?"

"Family was rich, merchant class. Lost its money before the war. Mother was a famous medium, apparently quite legitimate and dedicated, and charged a pittance for her services. Everybody in London knew her. I remember hearing of her, long before I was ever interested in that sort of thing. The Talamasca pronounced her genuine on more than one occasion, but she refused to be studied. She was a fragile creature, and very much loved her only son."

"Raglan," I said.

"Yes. She died of cancer. Terrible pain. Her only daughter became a seamstress, still works for a bridal shop in London. Simply exquisite work. She's deeply grieved over the death of her troublesome brother, but relieved he's gone. I talked to her this morning. She said her brother had been destroyed when he was quite young, by their mother's death."

"Understandable," I said.

"Father worked almost all his life for Cunard shipping, spending his last years as a cabin steward in first class on the *Queen Elizabeth 2*. Very proud of his record. Great scandal and disgrace not so many years ago, when James was also hired, thanks to the influence of his father, and promptly robbed one of the passengers of four hundred pounds in cash. Father disowned him, was reinstated by Cunard before he died. Never spoke to his son again."

"Ah, the photograph on the ship," I said.

"What?"

"And when you expelled him, he had wanted to sail on that very vessel back to America . . . first class, of course."

"He told you that? It's possible. I didn't really handle the particulars myself."

"Not important, go on. How did he get into the occult?"

"He was highly educated, spent years at Oxford, though at times he had to live like a pauper. Started dabbling in mediumship even before his mother died. Didn't come into his own until the fifties, in Paris, where he soon acquired an enormous following, then started bilking his clients in the most crude and obvious ways imaginable, and went to jail.

"Same thing happened later in Oslo, more or less. After a series of odd jobs, including very menial work, he started some sort of a spiritualist church, swindled a widow out of her life savings, and was deported. Then Vienna, where he worked as a waiter in a first-class hotel until he became a psychic counselor to the rich within a matter of weeks. Soon a hasty departure. He barely escaped arrest. In Milan, he bilked a member of the old aristocracy out of thousands before he was discovered, and had to leave the city in the middle of the night. His next stop was Berlin, where he was arrested but talked himself out of custody, and then back to London, where he went to jail again."

"Ups and downs," I said, remembering his words.

"That's always the pattern. He rises from the lowest employment to living in extravagant luxury, running up ludicrous accounts for fine clothing, motorcars, jet excursions here and there, and then it all collapses in the face of his petty crimes, treachery, and betrayal. He can't break the cycle. It *always* brings him down."

"So it seems."

"Lestat, there is something positively stupid about this creature. He speaks eight languages, can invade any computer network, and possess other people's bodies long enough to loot their wall safes—he is obsessed with wall safes, by the way, in an almost erotic fashion!— and yet he plays silly tricks on people and ends up with handcuffs on his wrists! The objects he took from our vaults were nearly impossible for him to sell. He ended up dumping them on the black market for a pittance. He's really something of an arch fool."

I laughed under my breath. "The thefts are symbolic, David. This is a creature of compulsion and obsession. It's a game. That's why he cannot hang on to what he steals. It's the process that counts with him, more than anything else."

"But, Lestat, it's an endlessly destructive game."

"I understand, David. Thank you for this information. I'll call you soon."

"Wait just a minute, you can't ring off, I won't allow it, don't you realize—"

"Of course I do, David."

"Lestat, there is a saying in the world of the occult. Like attracts like. Do you know what it means?"

"What would I know about the occult, David? That's your territory, not mine."

"This is no time for sarcasm."

"I'm sorry. What does it mean?"

"When a sorcerer uses his powers in a petty and selfish fashion, the magic always rebounds upon him."

"Now you're talking superstition."

"I am talking a principle which is as old as magic itself."

"He isn't a magician, David, he's merely a creature with certain measurable and definable psychic powers. He can possess other people. In one case of which we know, he effected an actual switch."

"It's the same thing! Use those powers to try to harm others and the harm comes back to oneself."

"David, I am the extant proof that such a concept is false. Next you will explain the concept of karma to me and I will slowly drop off to sleep."

"James is the quintessential evil sorcerer! He's already defeated death once at the expense of another human being; he must be stopped."

"Why didn't you try to stop *me*, David, when you had the opportunity? I was at your mercy at Talbot Manor. You could have found some way."

"Don't push me away with your accusations!"

. "I love you, David. I will contact you soon." I was about to put down the phone, when I thought of something. "David," I said. "There's something else I'd like to know."

"Yes, what?" Such relief that I hadn't hung up.

"You have these relics of ours—old possessions in your vaults."

"Yes." Discomfort. This was an embarrassment to him, it seemed.

"A locket," I said, "a locket with a picture of Claudia, you have seen such a thing?"

"I believe I have," he said. "I verified the inventory of all of those items after you first came to me. I believe there was a locket. I'm almost certain, in fact. I should have told you this, shouldn't I, before now?"

"No. Doesn't matter. Was it a locket on a chain, such as women wear?"

"Yes. Do you want me to look for this locket? If I find it, I shall give it to you, of course."

"No, don't look for it now. Perhaps sometime in the future. Good-bye, David. I'll come to you soon."

I hung up, and removed the small phone plug from the wall. So there had been a locket, a woman's locket. But for whom had such a thing been made? And why did I see it in my dreams? Claudia would not have carried her own image with her in a locket. And surely I would remember it if she had. As I tried to envision it, or remember it, I was filled with a peculiar combination of sadness and dread. It seemed I was very near a dark place, a place full of actual death. And as so often happens with my memories, I heard laughter. Only it wasn't Claudia's laughter this time. It was mine. I had a sense of preternatural youth and endless possibility. In other words I was remembering the young vampire I'd been in the old days of the eighteenth century before time had dealt its blows.

Well, what did I care about this damned locket? Maybe I'd picked up the image from James's brain as he pursued me. It had been for him merely a tool to ensnare me. And the fact was, I'd never even seen such a locket. He would have done better to pick some other trinket that had once belonged to me.

No, that last explanation seemed too simple. The image was too vivid. And I'd seen it in my dreams before James had made his way into my adventures. I grew angry suddenly. I had other things to consider just now, did I not? Get thee behind me, Claudia. Take your locket, please, ma chérie, and go.

. . .

FOR a very long time, I sat still in the shadows, conscious that the clock was ticking on the mantel, and listening to the occasional noise of traffic from the street.

I tried to consider the points David had made to me. I tried. But all I was thinking was . . . so James can do it, really do it. He is the white-haired man in the photograph, and he did switch with the mechanic in the hospital in London. It can be done!

Now and then I saw the locket in my mind's eye—I saw the miniature of Claudia painted so artfully in oils. But no emotion came to me, no sorrow, no anger, no grief.

It was James upon whom my entire heart was fastened. James can do it! James isn't lying. I can live and breathe in that body! And when the sun rises over Georgetown on that morning, I shall see it with those eyes.

IT WAS an hour after midnight when I reached Georgetown. A heavy snow had been falling all evening long, and the streets were filled with deep white drifts of it, clean and beautiful; and it was banked against the doors of the houses, and etching in white the fancy black iron railings and the deep window ledges here and there.

The town itself was immaculate and very charming—made up of graceful Federal-style buildings, mostly of wood, which had the clean lines of the eighteenth century, with its penchant for order and balance, though many had been built in the early decades of the nineteenth. I roamed for a long time along deserted M Street, with its many commercial establishments, and then through the silent campus of the nearby university, and then through the cheerfully lighted hillside streets.

The town house of Raglan James was a particularly fine structure, made of red brick and built right on the street. It had a pretty center doorway and a hefty brass knocker, and two cheerful flickering gas lamps. Old-fashioned solid shutters graced the windows, and there was a lovely fanlight over the door.

The windows were clean, in spite of the snow on the sills, and I could see into the bright and orderly rooms. There was a smart look to the interior—trim white leather furnishings of extreme modern severity and obvious expense. Numerous paintings on the walls— Picasso, de Kooning, Jasper Johns, Andy Warhol—and intermingled with these multimillion dollar canvases, several large expensively mounted photographs of modern ships. Indeed there were several replicas of large ocean liners in glass cases in the lower hall. The floors gleamed with plastic lacquer. Small dark Oriental rugs of geometric design were everywhere, and the many ornaments gracing glass tables and inlaid teak cabinets were almost exclusively Chinese.

Meticulous, fashionable, costly, and highly individual—that was the personality of the place. It looked to me the way the dwellings of mortals always did—like a series of pristine stage sets. Quite impossible to believe I could be mortal, and belong in such a house, even for an hour or more.

Indeed, the small rooms were so polished it seemed impossible that anyone actually inhabited them at all. The kitchen was full of gleaming copper pots, and black glass-doored appliances, cabinets without visible handles to open them, and bright red ceramic plates.

In spite of the hour, James himself was nowhere to be found.

I entered the house.

A second storey held the bedroom, with a low modern bed, no more than a wooden frame with a mattress inside it, and covered with a quilt of bright geometric pattern, and numerous white pillows—as austere and elegant as all the rest. The closet was crammed with expensive garments, and so were the drawers of the Chinese bureau and another small hand-carved chest by the bed.

Other rooms lay empty, but nowhere was there evidence of neglect. I saw no computers here either. No doubt he kept these someplace else.

In one of these rooms, I concealed a great deal of money for my later use, hiding it inside the chimney of the unused fireplace.

I also concealed some money in an unused bathroom, behind a mirror on the wall.

These were simple precautions. I really couldn't conceive of what it would be like to be human. I might feel quite helpless. Just didn't know.

After I made these little arrangements, I went up on the roof. I could see James at the base of the hill, just turning the corner from M

Street, a load of parcels in his arms. He'd been up to thievery, no doubt, for there was no place to shop in these slow hours before dawn. I lost sight of him as he started his ascent.

But another strange visitor appeared, without making the slightest sound that a mortal could hear. It was a great dog, seeming to materialize out of nowhere, which made its way back the alleyway and to the rear yard.

I'd caught its scent as soon as it approached, but I did not see the animal until I came over the roof to the back of the house. I'd expected to hear from it before this time, for surely it would pick up my scent, know instinctively that I wasn't human, and then begin to sound its natural alarm of growls and barks.

Dogs had done that enough to me over the centuries, though they don't always. Sometimes I can entrance them and command them. But I feared the instinctive rejection and it always sent a pain through my heart.

This dog had not barked or given any clue that he knew I was there. He was staring intently at the rear door of the house and the butter-yellow squares of light falling from the window of the door onto the deep snow.

I had a good chance to study him in undisturbed silence, and he was, very simply, one of the most handsome dogs I had ever beheld.

He was covered in deep, plush fur, beautifully golden and gray in places, and overlaid with a faint saddle of longer black hairs. His overall shape was that of a wolf, but he was far too big to be a wolf, and there was nothing furtive and sly about him, as is the case with wolves. On the contrary, he was wholly majestic in the way that he sat staring motionless at the door.

On closer inspection, I saw that he most truly resembled a giant German shepherd, with the characteristic black muzzle and alert face.

Indeed, when I drew close to the edge of the roof, and he at last looked up at me, I found myself vaguely thrilled by the fierce intelligence gleaming in his dark almond-shaped eyes.

Still he gave no bark, no growl. There seemed a near-human comprehension in him. But how could that explain his silence? I had done nothing to enthrall him, to lure or befuddle his dog mind. No. No instinctive aversion at all.

I dropped down into the snow in front of him, and he merely continued to look at me, with those uncanny and expressive eyes.

Indeed, so large was he and so calm and sure of himself, that I laughed to myself with delight as I looked at him. I couldn't resist reaching out to touch the soft fur between his ears.

He cocked his head to one side as he continued to look at me, and I found this very endearing, and then to my further amazement he lifted his immense paw and stroked my coat. His bones were so big and heavy he put me in mind of my mastiffs of long ago. He had their slow heavy grace as he moved. I reached out to embrace him, loving his strength and his heaviness, and he reared back on his hind legs and threw his huge paws up on my shoulders, and ran his great ham-pink tongue over my face.

This produced in me a wonderful happiness, really near to weeping, and then some giddy laughter. I nuzzled him, and held him, and stroked him, loving his clean furry smell, and kissing him all over his black muzzle, and then looking him in the eye.

Ah, this is what Little Red Riding Hood saw, I thought, when she beheld the wolf in her grandmother's nightcap and gown. It was too funny, really, the extraordinary and keen expression in his dark face.

"Why don't you know me for what I am?" I asked. And then as he sank back down to a majestic sitting position, and looked up at me almost obediently, it struck me that this was an omen, this dog.

No, "omen" is not the proper word. This did not come from anyone, this gift. It was merely something which put me more in mind of what I meant to do and why I meant to do it, and how little I really cared about the risks involved.

I stood beside the dog, petting him and stroking him and moments passed. It was a small garden, and the snow was falling again, deepening around us, and the cold pain in my skin was growing deeper too. The trees were bare and black in the silent storm. Whatever flowers or grass there might have been was of course not visible; but a few garden statues of darkened concrete and a sharp, thick shrubbery— now nothing but bare twigs and snow—marked a clear rectangular pattern to the whole.

I must have been there with the dog perhaps three minutes before my hand discovered the round silver disk dangling from his chain-link collar, and finally I gathered this up and held it to the light.

Mojo. Ah, I knew this word. Mojo. It had to do with voodoo, gris-gris, charms. Mojo was a good charm, a protective charm. I approved of it as a name for a dog; it was splendid, in fact, and when I called him Mojo he became faintly excited and once again stroked me slowly with his big eager paw.

"Mojo, is it?" I said again. "That's very beautiful." I kissed him and felt the leathery black tip of his nose. There was something else written on the disk, however. It was the address of this house.

Very suddenly the dog stiffened; it moved slowly and gracefully out of the sitting position and into an alert stance. James was coming. I heard his crunching steps in the snow. I heard the sound of his key in the lock of his front door. I sensed him realize suddenly that I was very near.

The dog gave a deep fierce growl and moved slowly closer to the rear door of the house. There came the sound of the boards inside creaking under James's heavy feet.

The dog gave a deep angry bark. James opened the door, fixed his fierce crazy eyes on me, smiled, and then hurled something heavy at the animal which it easily dodged.

"Glad to see you! But you're early," he said.

I didn't answer him. The dog was growling at him in the same menacing fashion and he gave his attention to the animal again, with great annoyance.

"Get rid of it!" he said, purely furious. "Kill it!"

"You're talking to me?" I asked coldly. I laid my hand on the animal's head again, stroking it, and whispering to it to be still. It drew closer to me, rubbing its heavy flank against me and then seated itself beside me.

James was tense and shivering as he watched all this. Suddenly he pushed up his collar against the wind, and folded his arms. The snow was blowing all over him, like white powder, clinging to his brown eyebrows and his hair.

"It belongs to this house, doesn't it?" I said coldly. "This house which you stole."

He regarded me with obvious hatred, and then flashed one of those awful evil smiles. I truly wished he'd lapse back into being the English gentleman. It was so much easier for me when he did. It crossed my mind that it was absolutely base to have to deal with him. I wondered if Saul had found the Witch of Endor so distasteful. But the body, ah, the body, how splendid it was.

Even in his resentment, with his eyes fixed upon the dog, he could not wholly disfigure the beauty of the body.

"Well, it seems you've stolen the dog too," I said.

"I'll get rid of it," he whispered, looking at it again with fierce contempt. "And you, where do things stand with you? I won't give you forever to make up your mind. You've given me no certain answer. I want an answer now."

"Go to your bank tomorrow morning," I said. "I'll see you after dark. Ah, but there is one more condition."

"What is it!" he asked between his clenched teeth.

"Feed the animal. Give it some meat."

Then I made my exit so swiftly he couldn't see it, and when I glanced back, I could see Mojo gazing up at me, through the snowy darkness, and I smiled to think that the dog had seen my movement, fast as it was. The last sound I heard was James cursing to himself ungracefully as he slammed the back door.

An hour later, I lay in the dark waiting for the sun above, and thinking again of my youth in France, of the dogs lying beside me, of riding out on that last hunt with those two huge mastiffs, picking their way slowly through the deep snow.

And the face of the vampire peering at me from the darkness in Paris, calling me "Wolfkiller" with such reverence, such crazed reverence, before he sank his fangs into my neck.

Mojo, an omen.

So we reach into the raging chaos, and we pluck some small glittering thing, and we cling to it, and tell ourselves it has meaning, and that the world is good, and we are not evil, and we will all go home in the end.

Tomorrow night, I thought, if that bastard has been lying, I shall split open his chest and tear out his beating heart, and feed it to that big beautiful dog.

Whatever happens, I shall keep this dog.

And I did.

And before this story moves any further, let me say something about this dog. He isn't going to do anything in this book.

He won't save a drowning baby, or rush into a burning building to rouse the inhabitants from near-fatal sleep. He isn't possessed by an evil spirit; he isn't a vampire dog. He's in this narrative simply because I found him in the snow behind that town house in Georgetown, and I loved him, and from that first moment, he seemed somehow to love me. It was all too true to the blind and merciless laws I believe in—the laws of nature, as men say; or the laws of the Savage Garden, as I call them myself. Mojo loved my strength; I loved his beauty. And nothing else ever really mattered at all.

TEN

"I WANT the details," I said, "of how you pushed him out of his body, and how you managed to force him into yours."

Wednesday at last. Not a half hour had passed since the sun had set. I had startled him when I appeared on the back steps.

We were sitting now in the immaculate white kitchen, a room curiously devoid of mystery for such an esoteric meeting. A single bulb in a handsome copper fixture flooded the table between us with a soft rosy illumination, which lent a deceiving coziness to the scene.

The snowfall continued, and beneath the house the furnace gave a low continuous roar. I'd brought the dog in with me, much to the annoyance of the lord of the house, and after some reassurance, the beast lay quietly now like an Egyptian sphinx, looking up at us, front legs stretched straight before him on the waxed floor. Now and then James glanced at him uneasily, and with reason. The dog looked as if he had the devil inside him and the devil knew the whole tale.

James was far more relaxed now than he had been in New Orleans. He was entirely the English gentleman, which set off the tall, youthful body to powerful advantage. He wore a gray sweater, stretched fetchingly tight over his big chest, and a pair of dark pants.

There were silver rings on his fingers. And a cheap watch on his wrist. I hadn't remembered these items. He was studying me with a little twinkle in his eye, much easier to endure than those horrid glaring smiles. I couldn't take my eyes off him, off this body which might soon become mine.

I could smell the blood in the body, of course, and this ignited some low smoldering passion in me. The more I looked at him, the more I wondered what it would be like to drink his blood and be done with it here and now. Would he try to escape the body and leave me holding a mere breathing shell?

I looked at his eyes, and thought, *sorcerer,* and a rare and unfamiliar excitement completely obliterated the common hunger. I'm not sure I believed he could do it, however. I thought that the evening might end in a tasty feast and no more.

I clarified my question for him. "How did you find this body? How did you get the soul to go into yours?"

"I'd been searching for just such a specimen—a man psychologically shocked out of all will and capacity for reason, yet sound of limb and brain. Telepathy is quite an aid in such matters, for only a telepath could have reached the remnants of intelligence still buried within him. I had to convince him on the deepest unconscious level, so to speak, that I had come to be of help, that I knew he was a good person, that I was on his side. And once I'd reached that rudimentary core, it was fairly easy to plunder his memories and manipulate him into obedience." He gave a little shrug. "The poor chap. His responses were entirely superstitious. I suspect he thought I was his guardian angel at the end."

"And you lured him out of his body?"

"Yes, by a series of bizarre and rather ornate suggestions, that's exactly what I did. Again telepathy is a powerful ally. One has to be psychic, really, to manipulate others in such a way. The first time he rose perhaps a foot or two, then slam, back into the flesh he went. More of a reflex than a decision. But I was patient, oh, very patient. And when I finally lured him out for the space of several seconds, that was sufficient for me to pop inside of him, and at once focus my intense energy upon shoving him down into what was left of the old me."

"How nicely you put it."

"Well, we are body and soul, you know," he said with a placid smile. "But why go all through this now? You know how to rise out of your body. This isn't going to be difficult for *you*."

"I might surprise you. What happened to him after he was in your body? Did he realize what had taken place?"

"Not at all. You must understand the man was deeply psychologically crippled. And, of course, he was an ignorant fool."

"And you didn't give him even a moment's time, did you? You killed him."

"Monsieur de Lioncourt, what I did was a mercy to him! How dreadful to have left him in that body, confused as he was! He wasn't going to recover, you realize, no matter what body he was inhabiting. He'd murdered his entire family. Even the baby in the crib."

"Were you part of that?"

"What a low opinion you have of me! Not at all. I was watching the hospitals for such a specimen. I knew one would come along. But why these last questions? Didn't David Talbot tell you there are numerous documented cases of switching in the Talamasca files."

David had not told me this. But then I could scarcely blame him.

"Did they all involve murder?" I asked.

"No. Some involved bargains such as you and I have struck."

"I wonder. We are oddly paired, you and I."

"Yes, but well paired, you must admit. This is a very nice body I have for you," he said of himself, placing an open hand on his broad chest. "Not as beautiful as yours, of course. But very nice! And exactly what you ought to require. As for your body, what more can I say? I hope you didn't listen to David Talbot about me. He's made so many tragic mistakes."

"What do you mean?"

"He's a slave to that wretched organization," he said sincerely. "They completely control him. If only I could have spoken to him at the end, he would have seen the significance of what I had to offer, what I could teach. Did he tell you of his escapades in old Rio? Yes, an exceptional person, a person I should like to have known. But I can tell you, he's no one to cross."

"What's to stop you from killing me as soon as we switch bodies? That's just what you did to this creature you lured into your old body, with one swift blow to the head."

"Ah, so you have talked to Talbot," he said, refusing to be rattled. "Or did you merely do the research on your own? Twenty million dollars will stop me from killing you. I need the body to go to the bank, remember? Absolutely marvelous of you to double the sum. But I would have kept the bargain for ten. Ah, you've liberated me, Monsieur de Lioncourt. As of this Friday, at the very hour when Christ was nailed to the cross, I shall never have to steal again."

He took a sip of his warm tea. Whatever his facade, he was becoming increasingly anxious. And something similar and more enervating was building in me. *What if this does work?*

"Oh, but it will work," he said in that grave heartfelt manner. "And there are other excellent reasons why I wouldn't attempt to harm you. Let's talk them through."

"By all means."

"Well, you could get out of the mortal body if I attacked it. I've already explained you must cooperate."

"What if you were too fast?"

"It's academic. I wouldn't try to harm you. Your friends would know if I did. As long as you, Lestat, are here, inside a healthy human body, your companions wouldn't think of destroying your preternatural body, even if I'm at the controls. They wouldn't do that to you, now, would they? But if I killed you—you know, smashed your face or whatever before you could disentangle yourself . . . and God knows, this is a possibility, I myself am keenly aware of it, I assure you!—your companions would find me sooner or later for an impostor, and do away with me very quickly, indeed. Why, they would probably feel your death when it happened. Don't you think?"

"I don't know. But they would discover everything eventually."

"Of course!"

"It's imperative that you stay away from them while you're in my body, that you don't go near New Orleans, that you keep clear of any and all blood drinkers, even the very weak. Your skill at cloaking yourself, you must use it, you realize . . ."

"Yes, certainly. I've considered the entire enterprise, please be assured. If I were to burn up your beautiful Louis de Pointe du Lac, the others would know immediately, wouldn't they? And I might be the next torch burning brightly in the dead of night myself."

I didn't answer. I felt anger moving through me as if it were a cold liquid, driving out all anticipation and courage. But I wanted this! I wanted it, and it was near at hand!

"Don't go troubling yourself about such nonsense," he pleaded. His manner was so like David Talbot's. Perhaps it was deliberate. Maybe David was the model. But I thought it more a matter of similar breeding, and some instinct for persuasiveness which even David did not possess. "I'm not really a murderer, you know," he said with sudden intensity. "It's acquisition that means everything. I want comfort, beauty around me, every conceivable luxury, the power to go and live where I please."

"You want any instructions?"

"As to what?"

"What to do when you're inside my body."

"You've already given me my instruction, dear boy. I have read your books." He flashed me a broad smile, dipping his head slightly and looking up at me as if he were trying to lure me into his bed. "I've read all the documents in the Talamasca archives as well."

"What sort of documents?"

"Oh, detailed descriptions of vampire anatomy—your obvious limits, that sort of thing. You ought to read them for yourself. Perhaps you'd laugh. The earliest chapters were penned in the Dark Ages and are filled with fanciful nonsense that would have made even Aristotle weep. But the more recent files are quite scientific and precise."

I didn't like this line of discussion. I didn't like anything that was happening. I was tempted to finish it now. And then quite suddenly, I knew I was going to go through with this. I knew.

A curious calm descended on me. Yes, we were going to do this in a matter of minutes. And it was going to work. I felt the color drain from my face—an imperceptible cooling of the skin, which was still hurting from its terrible ordeal in the sun.

I doubt he noted this change, or any hardening of my expression, for he went right on talking as before.

"The observations written in the 1970s after the publication of *Interview with the Vampire* are most interesting. And then the very recent chapters, inspired by your fractured and fanciful history of the species—my word! No, I know all about your body. I know more about it perhaps than you do. Do you know what the Talamasca really wants? A sample of your tissue, a specimen of your vampiric cells! You'd be wise to see that they never acquire such a specimen. You've been too free with Talbot, really. Perhaps he pared your fingernails or cut off a lock of your hair while you slept beneath his roof."

Lock of hair. Wasn't there a lock of blond hair in that locket? It had to be vampire hair! Claudia's hair. I shuddered, drawing deeper into myself and shutting him away. Centuries ago there had been a dreadful night when Gabrielle, my mortal mother and newborn fledgling, had cut off her vampire hair. Through the long hours of the day, as she lay in the coffin, it had all grown back. I did not want to remember her screams when she discovered it—those magnificent tresses once again luxuriant and long over her shoulders. I did not want to think of her and what she might say to me now about what I meant to do. It had been years since I had laid eyes upon her. It might be centuries before I saw her again.

I looked again at James, as he sat there radiant with expectation, straining to appear patient, face glowing in the warm light.

"Forget the Talamasca," I said under my breath. "Why do you have such a hard time with this body? You're clumsy. You're only comfortable when you're sitting in a chair and you can leave matters entirely to your voice and your face."

"Very perceptive," he said, with unshakable decorum.

"I don't think so. It's rather obvious."

"It's simply too big a body," he said calmly. "It's too muscular, too . . . shall we say, athletic? But it's perfect for you."

He paused, looked at the teacup thoughtfully and then up at me again. The eyes seemed so wide, so innocent.

"Lestat, come now," he said. "Why are we wasting time with this conversation? I don't intend to dance with the Royal Ballet once I'm inside you. I simply mean to enjoy the whole experience, to experiment, to see the world through your eyes." He glanced at his watch. "Well, I'd offer you a little drink to screw up your courage, but that would be self-defeating in the long run, wouldn't it? Oh, and by the way, the passport. Were you able to obtain it? You remember I asked you to provide me with a passport. I do hope you remembered, and of course I have a passport for you. I fear you won't be going anywhere, on account of this blizzard—"

I laid my passport on the table before him. He reached up under his sweater, and withdrew his own from his shirt pocket and put it in my hand.

I examined it. It was American and a fake. Even the issue date of two years ago was fake. Raglan James. Age twenty-six. Correct picture. Good picture. This Georgetown address.

He was studying the American passport—also a fake—which I had given him.

"Ah, your tanned skin! You had this prepared specially . . . Must have been last night."

I didn't bother to answer.

"How very clever of you," he said, "and what a good picture." He studied it. "Clarence Oddbody. Wherever did you come up with a name like that?"

"A little private joke. What does it matter? You'll have it only tonight and tomorrow night." I shrugged.

"True. Very true."

"I'll expect you back here early Friday morning, between the hours of three and four."

"Excellent." He started to put the passport into his pocket and then caught himself with a sharp laugh. Then his eyes fixed on me and a look of pure delight passed over him. "Are you ready?"

"Not quite." I took a wallet of money out of my pocket, opened it, and slipped out about half of the bills inside and gave them to him.

"Ah, yes, the petty cash, how considerate of you to remember," he said. "I'm forgetting all the important details in my excitement. Inexcusable and you are such a gentleman."

He gathered up the bills and once again caught himself before he could stuff them in his pockets. He put them back on the table and smiled.

I laid my hand on the wallet. "The rest is for me, once we make the switch. I trust you're comfortable with the amount I've given you? The little thief in you won't be tempted to scoop up what's left?"

"I'll do my best to behave myself," he said good-naturedly. "Now, do you want me to change clothes? I stole these garments especially for you."

"They're fine."

"Should I empty my bladder, perhaps? Or would you like the privilege?"

"I would."

He nodded. "I'm hungry. I thought you'd like it that way. There's an excellent restaurant down the street. Paolo's. Good spaghetti carbonara. Even in the snow you can walk it."

"Marvelous. I'm not hungry. I thought that would be easier for you. You spoke of a car. Where is the car?"

"Oh, yes, the car. Outside, to the left of the front steps. Red Porsche roadster, thought you'd like that. Here are the keys. But be careful . . ."

"Of what?"

"Well, the snow obviously, you might not be able to move it at all."

"Thanks for the warning."

"Don't want you to be hurt. It could cost me twenty million if you're not here Friday as planned. Nevertheless the driver's license with the correct picture is in the desk in the living room. What's the matter?"

"Clothes for you," I said. "I forgot to provide them, other than what I have on."

"Oh, I thought of that a long time ago, when I was snooping about in your hotel room in New York. I have my wardrobe, you needn't worry, and I like that black velvet suit. You do dress beautifully. Always did, didn't you? But then you come from a time of such lavish costumes. This age must seem awfully dreary to you. Are those antique buttons? Ah, well, I'll have time to examine them."

"Where will you be going?"

"Where I want to go, of course. Are you losing your nerve?"

"No."

"Know how to drive the car?"

"Yes. If I didn't, I'd figure it out."

"Think so? Think you'll have your preternatural intelligence when you're in this body? I wonder. I'm not sure you will. The little synapses in the mortal brain might not fire off so fast."

"I don't know anything about synapses," I said.

"All right. Let's begin, then," he said.

"Yes, now, I think." My heart turned to a small, tight knot inside me, but his manner became completely authoritative and commanding at once.

"Listen closely," he said. "I want you to rise out of your body, but not till I'm finished speaking. You'll move up. You've done it before. When you are close to the ceiling and looking directly down on both of us at this table, you will make a concentrated effort to move into this body. You must not think of anything else. You must not let fear interrupt your concentration. You must not wonder as to how this is being done. You want to descend into this body, you want to connect completely and instantaneously with every fiber and cell. Picture it as you do it! Imagine yourself already inside."

"Yes, I follow you."

"As I've told you, there is something invisible in it, something left from the original occupant, and that something is hungry to be complete again—with your soul."

I nodded. He went on.

"You may be prey to a variety of unpleasant sensations. This body will feel very dense to you, and constricting as you slide in. Don't waver. Imagine your spirit invading the fingers of each hand, the toes of each foot. Look through the eyes. That is most important. Because the eyes are part of the brain. When you look through them, you are anchoring within the brain. Now you won't shake loose, you can be sure of it. Once you're in, it will take quite a bit of effort to get out."

"Will I see you in spirit form while we're changing?"

"No, you won't. You could, but that would take a great deal of concentration away from your immediate goal. You don't want to see anything but this body; you want to get in it and start moving it and breathing through it, and seeing through it, as I've said."

"Yes."

"Now, one thing which will frighten you is the sight of your own body, lifeless, or inhabited finally by me. Don't allow this to get the better of you. Here a certain trust and humility must play a part. Believe me when I say that I shall accomplish the possession without injury to your body, and then I shall leave immediately, so as to relieve you of that constant reminder of what we've done. You won't see me again until Friday morning, as we've agreed. I won't speak to you, because the sound of my voice coming out of your mouth would upset you, distract you. You understand?"

"How will your voice sound? How will my voice sound?"

Once more he looked at his watch, then back at me. "There'll be differences," he said. "The size of the voice box is different. This man, for example, gave a slight depth to my voice which I don't ordinarily possess. But you'll keep your rhythm, your accent, your patterns of speech, of course. Only the timbre will be different. Yes, that's the word."

I took a long careful look at him.

"Is it important that I believe this can be done?"

"No," he said with a broad smile. "This isn't a séance. You needn't stoke the fire for the medium with your faith. You'll see in an instant. Now what else is there to say?" He tensed, coming forward in the chair.

The dog gave a sudden deep growl.

I quieted him with my outstretched hand.

"Go on!" said James sharply, voice dropping to a whisper. "Go out of your body now!"

I sat back, gesturing again for the dog to be still. Then I willed myself to rise, and felt a sudden total vibration through my entire frame. Then came the marvelous realization that I was indeed rising, a spirit form, weightless and free, my manly shape still visible to me with its arms and legs, stretching out just below the white ceiling, so that I did indeed look down and see the astounding spectacle of my own body seated still in the chair. Oh, what a glorious feeling, as if I could go anywhere in an instant! As if I had no need of the body, and my link to it had been a deception from the moment of birth.

The physical body of James slumped forward ever so slightly, and his fingers began to move outward on the white tabletop. I mustn't become distracted. The switch was the thing!

"Down, down into that body!" I said aloud, but there was no voice audible, and then without words I forced myself to plummet and merge with that new flesh, that physical form.

A loud rushing filled my ears, and then a sense of constriction, as if my entire self were being forced through a narrow, slippery tube. Excruciating! I wanted freedom. But I could feel myself filling the empty arms and legs, the flesh heavy and tingling as it closed over me, as a mask of similar sensations closed over my face.

I struggled to open my eyes before I even realized what I was doing, that I was flexing the lids of this mortal body, that indeed, I was blinking, staring through mortal eyes into the dimly lighted room, staring at my old body exactly opposite, at my old blue eyes peering back at me through the violet-colored glasses, staring at my old tanned skin.

I felt I would suffocate—I had to escape this!—but it hit me, I was in! I was in the body! The switch had been done. Irresistibly I took a deep hoarse heavy breath, moving this monstrous encasement of flesh as I did so, and then I slapped my hand to my chest, appalled at its thickness, and heard the heavy wet sloshing of the blood through my heart.

"Dear God, I'm in it," I cried out, struggling to clear away the darkness that surrounded me, the shadowy veil which stopped me from seeing more clearly the brilliant form opposite, which now sprang to life.

My old body jerked upward, arms thrown up as if in horror, one hand crashing into the overhead light and exploding the bulb, as the chair below clattered to the floor. The dog leapt to his feet and gave out a loud, menacing riff of deep-throated barks.

"No, Mojo, down, boy," I heard myself crying from this thick tight mortal throat, still straining to see in the darkness, and unable to do it, and realizing that it was *my* hand grabbing for the dog's collar and jerking him backwards before he could attack the old vampire body, which stared down at the dog in utter amazement, blue eyes glittering fiercely, and very wide and blank.

"Ah, yes, kill it!" came the voice of James, roaring at horrific volume out of my old preternatural mouth.

My hands shot to my ears to protect me from the sound. The dog rushed forward again, and once again, I grabbed him by the collar, fingers curling painfully around the chain links, appalled at his strength and how little there seemed to be in my mortal arms. Ye gods, I had to make this body work! This was only a dog, and I was a strong mortal man!

"Stop, Mojo!" I pleaded with him as he dragged me right out of the chair and painfully onto my knees. "And you, get out of here!" I bellowed. The pain in my knees was dreadful. The voice was puny and opaque. "Get out!" I yelled again.

The creature that had been me danced past me, arms flailing still, and crashed into the back door, shattering the windowpanes, and letting in a cold gust of wind. The dog was maddened and now almost impossible for me to control.

"Get out!" I screamed again, and watched in consternation as the creature backed straight through the door now, shattering wood and all remaining glass, and rose off the porch boards into the snow-filled night.

I saw him for one last instant, suspended in midair above the back steps, a hideous apparition, the snow swirling about him, his limbs moving now in concert as though he were a swimmer in an invisible sea. His blue eyes were still wide and senseless, as if he couldn't work the preternatural flesh around them into an expression, and glittering like two incandescent gems. His mouth—my old mouth—was spread wide in a meaningless grin.

Then he was gone.

The breath went out of me. The room was freezing as the wind gusted into every corner, knocking about the copper pots on their fancy rack and pushing against the dining room door. And suddenly the dog became quiet.

I realized I was sitting on the floor beside him, and that my right arm was locked around his neck, and my left around his furry chest. Each breath I took hurt me, I was squinting against the snow, which flew right into my eyes, and I was trapped in this strange body padded with lead weights and mattress ticking, and the cold air was stinging my face and my hands.

"Good God, Mojo," I whispered in his soft pink ear. "Good God, it's happened. I'm a mortal man."

ELEVEN

ALL right," I said stupidly, again amazed at the weak, contained sound of it, low as the voice was. "It's begun, now get ahold of yourself." And that idea made me laugh.

The cold wind was the worst part. My teeth were chattering. The stinging pain in my skin was wholly different from the pain I felt as a vampire. Had to repair this door, but I had no idea whatsoever how to do it.

Was there anything left of the door? I couldn't tell. It was like trying to see through a cloud of noxious smoke. Slowly I climbed to my feet, at once aware of the increase in height and feeling very top-heavy and unsteady.

Every bit of warmth had fled the room. Indeed, I could hear the whole house rattling with the wind that was pouring in. Slowly and carefully, I stepped out on the porch. Ice. My feet went sliding to the right of me, flinging me back against the doorframe. Panic seized me, but I managed to grab hold of the moist wood with these large trembling fingers, and keep myself from going down the steps. Again I strained to see through the darkness, and couldn't make out anything clearly at all.

"Just calm down," I said to myself, aware that my fingers were sweating and growing numb at the same time, and that my feet were becoming painfully numb also. "There's no artificial light here, that's all, and you're looking through mortal eyes. Now do something intelligent about all this!" And stepping very carefully, and nearly slipping again, I moved back inside.

I could see the dim outline of Mojo seated there, watching me, panting noisily, and there was a tiny splinter of light in one of his dark eyes. I spoke to him gently.

"It's me, Mojo Man, okay? It's me!" And I stroked the soft hair between his ears gently. I reached for the table, and sat down in the chair very awkwardly, astonished again at the sheer thickness of my new flesh, and the sloshiness of it, and I clamped my hand over my mouth.

It really has happened, you fool, I thought. There's no doubt of it. It's a lovely miracle, that's what it is. You are actually free of that preternatural body! You are a human being. You are a human man. Now be done with this panic. Think like the hero you pride yourself on being! There are practical matters at hand. The snow's coming in on you. This mortal body is freezing, for the love of heaven. Now attend to things as you must!

Yet all I did was open my eyes wider, and stare at what seemed to be the snow piling up in little sparkling crystals on the white surface of the table, expecting every moment that this vision would become more distinct, when of course it would not.

That was spilt tea, wasn't it? And broken glass. Don't cut yourself on the broken glass, you won't heal! Mojo moved closer to me, big warm furry flank welcome against my trembling leg. But why did the feeling seem so distant, as if I were wrapped in layers of flannel? Why could I not smell his wondrous clean woolly smell? All right, senses are limited. You should have expected that.

Now, go look in a mirror; see the miracle. Yes, and just close off this entire room.

"Come on, boy," I said to the dog, and we went out of the kitchen into the dining room—each step I took feeling awkward and slow and lumbering—and with fumbling, very inexact fingers, I closed the door. The wind banged against it, and seeped around the edges of it, but the door held.

I turned around, off balance for a second, then righting myself. Shouldn't be so hard to get the knack of this, for the love of heaven! I settled back on my feet, and then looked down at them, amazed at how very large they were, and then at my hands, which were quite big too. But not bad-looking, no, not bad-looking. Don't panic! The watch was uncomfortable, but I needed it. All right, keep the watch. But the rings? Definitely didn't want them on my fingers. Itching. Wanted to pull them off. Couldn't! They wouldn't come. Lord God.

Now, stop. You're going to go mad because you can't pull these rings off your fingers. That's foolish. Just slow down. There's such a thing as soap, you know. Soap your hands, these big dark freezing-cold hands, and off the rings will come.

I crossed my arms and eased my hands around my sides, appalled at the feeling of the slippery human sweat beneath my shirt, nothing like blood sweat, and then I took a slow deep breath, ignoring the heavy ponderous feeling of my chest, the raw feeling of the very act of inhaling and exhaling, and I forced myself to look at the room.

This was not the time to scream in terror. Now, just look at the room.

It was very dim. One floor lamp burned, in a far corner, and another tiny lamp on the mantel, but it was still terribly dim. It seemed I was under water and the water was murky, maybe even clouded with ink.

This is normal. This is mortal. This is how they see. But how grim it all looked, how partial, having nothing of the open spatial qualities of the rooms through which a vampire moved.

How hideously gloomy, the dark gleaming chairs, the table barely visible, the dull gold light creeping up into the corners, the plaster moldings at the tops of the walls vanishing into shadow, impenetrable shadow, and how frightening the empty blackness of the hall.

Anything could have been hiding in these shadows—a rat, anything. There might have been another human being in that hall. I looked down at Mojo and was amazed again at how very indistinct he looked, how mysterious in a wholly different way. That was it, things lost their contours in this sort of dimness. Impossible really to gauge their full texture or size.

Ah, but there was the mirror above the mantel.

I went to it, frustrated by the heaviness of my limbs and by a sudden fear of stumbling, and a need to look more than once at my feet. I moved the little lamp under the mirror, and then I looked at my face.

Ah, yes. I was behind it now, and how amazingly different it looked. Gone were the tightness, and the awful nervous glitter of the eyes. There was a young man staring at me, and he looked more than a little afraid.

I lifted my hand and felt of the mouth and the eyebrows, of the forehead, which was a little higher than mine, and then of the soft hair. The face was very pleasing, infinitely more pleasing than I had realized, being square and without any heavy lines, and very well proportioned, and with dramatic eyes. But I didn't like the look of fear in the eyes. No, not at all. I tried to see a different expression, to claim the features from within and let them express the wonder I felt. But this wasn't easy. And I'm not sure I was feeling any wonder. Hmmm. I couldn't see anything in this face that was coming from inside.

Slowly I opened my mouth and spoke. I said in French that I was Lestat de Lioncourt in this body, and that everything was fine. The experiment had worked! I was in the very first hour of it, and the fiend James was gone, and everything had worked! Now something of my own fierceness showed in the eyes; and when I smiled I saw my own mischievous nature at least for a few seconds before the smile faded and I looked blank and amazed.

I turned and looked at the dog, who was right beside me, and gazing up at me, as was his habit, perfectly content.

"How do you know I'm in here?" I asked. "Instead of James?"

He cocked his head, and one ear gave a tiny movement.

"All right," I said. "Enough of all this weakness and craziness, let's go!" I started forward towards the dark hallway, and suddenly my right leg went out from under me, and I slid down heavily, left hand skidding along the floor to break my fall, my head slamming against the marble fireplace, and my elbow striking the marble hearth with a sudden violent explosion of pain. With a clatter, the fireplace tools came down upon me, but that was nothing. I'd struck the nerve in the elbow, and the pain was like a fire rushing up my arm.

I turned over on my face, and just held still for a moment waiting for the pain to pass. Only then did I realize my head was throbbing from being slammed against the marble. I reached up, and felt the wetness of blood in my hair. Blood!

Ah, beautiful. Louis would be so amused by this, I thought. I climbed up, the pain shifting and moving to the right behind my forehead, as if it were a weight which had slipped to the front of my head, and I steadied myself as I held the mantel shelf.

One of those many fancy little rugs lay snagged on the floor before me. The culprit. I kicked it out of the way, and turned and very slowly and carefully walked into the hall.

But where was I going? What did I mean to do? The answer came to me all of a sudden. My bladder was full, and the discomfort had grown worse when I'd fallen. I had to take a piss.

Wasn't there a bathroom down here somewhere? I found the hall light switch and turned on the overhead chandelier. For a long moment I stared at all the tiny bulbs—and there must have been twenty of them—realizing that this was quite a bit of light, no matter what I thought of it, but no one had said I couldn't turn on every lamp in the house.

I set out to do this. I went through the living room, the little library, and the back hall. Again and again, the light disappointed me, the sense of murkiness would not leave me, the indistinctness of things left me faintly alarmed and confused.

Finally, I made my way carefully and slowly up the stairs, fearful every moment of losing my balance, or tripping, and annoyed at the faint ache in my legs. Such long legs.

When I looked back down the stairway, I was stunned. You could fall and kill yourself here, I said to myself.

I turned and entered the cramped little bathroom, quickly finding the light. I had to piss, I simply had to, and I had not done this in over two hundred years.

I unzipped these modern pants, and removed my organ, which immediately astonished me by its limpness and size. The size was fine, of course. Who doesn't want these organs to be large? And it was circumcised, which was a nice touch. But this limpness, it felt remarkably repulsive to me, and I didn't want to touch the thing. I had to remind myself, this organ happens to be mine. Jolly!

And what about the smell coming from it, and the smell rising from the hair around it? Ah, that's yours too, baby! Now make it work.

I closed my eyes, exerted pressure very inexactly and perhaps too forcefully, and a great arc of stinking urine shot out from the thing, missing the toilet bowl altogether and splashing on the white seat.

Revolting. I backed up, correcting the aim, and watched with sickened fascination as the urine filled the bowl, as bubbles formed on the surface, and as the smell grew stronger and stronger and more nauseating until I couldn't bear it anymore. At last the bladder was empty. I shoved this flaccid, disgusting thing back in my pants, zipped them up, and slammed down the toilet lid. I pulled on the handle. Away went the urine, except for all the splatters which had struck the toilet seat and floor.

I tried to take a deep breath but the disgusting smell was all around me. I lifted my hands and realized that it was on my fingers as well.

At once, I turned on the water in the lavatory, snatched up the soap, and went to work. I lathered my hands over and over, but could reach no assurance that they were actually clean. The skin was far more porous than my preternatural skin; it felt dirty, I realized; and then I started to pull on the ugly silver rings.

Even amid all these soapsuds, the rings wouldn't come off. I thought back. Yes, the bastard had been wearing them in New Orleans. He probably couldn't get them off either, and now I was stuck with them! Past all patience, but there was nothing to be done until I could find a jeweler who knew how to remove them with some tiny saw or pliers or some other instrument. Just thinking about it made me so anxious that all my muscles were tensing and then releasing with painful spasms. I commanded myself to stop.

I rinsed my hands, over and over, ridiculously, and then I snatched up the towel and dried them, repulsed again by their absorbent texture, and by bits of dirt around the nails. Good God, why didn't this fool properly clean his hands?

Then I looked in the mirrored wall at the end of the bathroom and saw reflected in it a truly disgusting sight. A great patch of moisture on the front of my pants. That stupid organ hadn't been dry when I shoved it inside!

Well, in the old days, I'd never worried about that, had I? But then I'd been a filthy country lord who bathed in summer, or when he took it in his head to plunge into a mountain spring.

This patch of urine on my pants was out of the question! I went out of the bathroom, passing the patient Mojo with only a little pat on the head, and went into the master bedroom, tore open the closet and found another pair of pants, a better pair, in fact, of gray wool, and at once slipped off my shoes, and made the change.

Now, what should I do? Well, go get something to eat, I thought. And then I realized I was hungry! Yes, that was the precise nature of the discomfort I'd been feeling, along with the full bladder, and a general overall heaviness, since this little saga commenced.

Eat. But if you eat, you know what will happen? You'll have to go back in that bathroom again, or some bathroom, and relieve yourself of all the digested food. The thought almost made me gag.

In fact, I grew so nauseated even picturing human excrement coming from my body that for a moment I thought I would indeed vomit. I sat still, on the foot of the low modern bed, and tried to get my emotions under control.

I told myself that these were the simplest aspects of being human; I must not allow them to obscure the larger questions. And that, further, I was behaving like a perfect coward, and not the dark hero whom I claimed to be. Now, understand, I don't really believe I *am* a hero to the world. But I long ago decided that I must live as if I were a hero—that I must pass through all the difficulties which confront me, because they are only my inevitable circles of fire.

All right, this was a small and ignominious circle of fire. And I must stop the cowardice at once. Eat, taste, feel, see—that was the name of this trial! Oh, but what a trial this was going to be.

At last I climbed to my feet, taking a slightly longer stride to accommodate these new legs, and I went back to the closet and found to my amazement that there really weren't very many clothes here. A couple of pairs of wool pants, two fairly light wool jackets, both new, and a stack of perhaps three shirts on a shelf.

Hmmm. What had happened to all the rest? I opened the top drawer of the bureau. Empty. Indeed all of the drawers were empty. And so was the little chest by the bed.

What could this mean? He'd taken these clothes with him, or sent them on to someplace where he'd gone? But why? They wouldn't fit his new body, and he claimed to have taken care of all that. I was deeply troubled. *Could this mean that he wasn't planning to come back?*

That was absurd. He wouldn't pass up the sum of twenty million. And I could not spend my precious time as a mortal worrying hour by hour about such a thing!

I proceeded down the perilous staircase, Mojo padding softly beside me. I was controlling the new body fairly effortlessly now, heavy and uncomfortable though it was. I opened the hall closet. An old coat remained on a hanger. A pair of galoshes. Nothing else.

I went to the desk in the living room. He had told me that I might find the driver's license here. Slowly I opened the top drawer. Empty. Everything was empty. Ah, but there were some papers in one of the drawers. Seemed to have something to do with this house, and nowhere did the name Raglan James appear. I struggled to understand what these papers were. But the official lingo baffled me. I wasn't receiving an immediate impression of meaning, as I did when I had looked at things with my vampire eyes.

I recalled what James had said about synapses. Yes, my thinking was slower. Yes, it had been difficult to read each word.

Ah, well, what did it matter? There was no driver's license here. And what I needed was money. Ah, yes, money. I'd left the money on the table. Good Lord, it might have blown out into the yard.

At once I went back to the kitchen. It was now freezing cold in the room, and indeed the table and the stove and the hanging copper pots were covered with a thin layer of white frost. The wallet with the money was not on the table. The car keys were not on the table. And the light, of course, had been smashed.

I got down on my knees in the dark and began to feel about on the floor. I found the passport. But no wallet. No keys. Only bits of glass from the exploded light bulb, which stung my hands, and cut through the skin in two places. Tiny specks of blood on my hands. No fragrance. No real taste. I tried to see without feeling. No wallet. I went out on the step again, careful not to slip this time. No wallet. I couldn't see in the deep snow of the yard.

Ah, but it was useless, wasn't it? The wallet and the keys were far too heavy to have blown away. He'd taken them! Possibly he'd even come back for them! The petty little monster, and when I realized that he'd been in my body, my splendid powerful preternatural body, when he did this, I was absolutely paralyzed with rage.

All right, you thought this might happen, didn't you? It was in his nature. And you're freezing again, you're shivering. Get back into the dining room and close the door.

I did just that, though I had to wait on Mojo, who took his time, as if he were utterly indifferent to the snowy wind. Now the dining room was cold from my having left the door open. Indeed, as I hurried back upstairs, I realized that the temperature of the entire house had been lowered by this little trip to the kitchen. I had to remember to shut doors.

I went into the first of the unused rooms, where I'd hidden the money in the chimney, and as I reached up, I felt not the envelope which I'd lodged there, but a single sheet of paper. I removed it, already in a fury, before I even turned on the light so that I could see the words:

You really are a silly fool to think that a man of my abilities wouldn't find your little stash. One does not have to be a vampire to detect a bit of telltale moisture on the floor and on the wall. Have a pleasant adventure. I shall see you Friday. Take care of yourself! Raglan James.

I was too angry for a moment to move. I was positively fuming. My hands were knotted into fists. "You petty little miscreant!" I said in this miserable, heavy, opaque, brittle voice.

I went into the bathroom. Of course the second stash of money wasn't behind the mirror. There was only another note.

What is human life without difficulty? You must realize I cannot resist such little discoveries. It's like leaving bottles of wine around for an alcoholic. I shall see you Friday. Please walk carefully on the icy sidewalks. Wouldn't want you to break a leg.

Before I could stop myself I slammed my fist into the mirror! Ah, well. There was a blessing for you. Not a great gaping hole in the wall, as it would have been if Lestat le Vampire had done it; just a lot of broken glass. And bad luck, bad luck for seven years!

I turned around, went downstairs, and back into the kitchen, bolting the door behind me this time, and opened the refrigerator. Nothing inside! Nothing!

Ah, this little devil, what I was going to do to him! How could he think he would get away with this? Did he think I was incapable of giving him twenty million dollars and then wringing his neck? What in the world was he thinking . . .

Hmmm.

Was it as hard to figure out as all that? He wasn't coming back, was he? Of course he wasn't.

I went back into the dining room. There was no silver or china in the glass-doored cabinet. But certainly there had been silver and china last night. I went into the hallway. There were no paintings on the walls. I checked the living room. No Picasso, Jasper Johns, de Kooning, or Warhol. All gone. Even the photographs of the ships were gone.

The Chinese sculptures were gone. The bookshelves were half

empty. And the rugs. There were precious few of them left—one in the dining room, which had almost caused me to kill myself! And one at the foot of the steps.

This house had been emptied out of all its true valuables! Why, half the furniture was missing! The little bastard wasn't going to return! It was never part of his plan.

I sat down in the armchair nearest the door. Mojo, who'd been following me faithfully, took the opportunity to stretch out at my feet. I dug my hand into his fur and tugged at it, and smoothed it, and thought what a comfort it was that the dog was there.

Of course James was a fool to pull this. Did he think I couldn't call on the others?

Hmmm. Call on the others for help—what a perfectly gruesome idea. It did not take any great feat of imagination to guess what Marius would say to me if I told him what I'd done. In all probability he knew, and was smoldering with disapproval. As for the older ones, I shuddered to think on it at all. My best hope from any standpoint was that the body switch would go unnoticed. I'd realized that from the start.

The salient point here was that James didn't know how angry the others would be with me on account of this experiment. He couldn't know. And James didn't know, either, the limits of the power he now possessed.

Ah, but all this was premature. The theft of my money, the looting of the house—this was James's idea of an evil joke, no more, no less. He couldn't leave the clothes and money here for me. His thieving petty nature wouldn't allow it. He had to cheat a little, that was all. Of course he planned to come back and claim his twenty million. And he was counting on the fact that I wouldn't hurt him because I'd want to try this experiment again, because I would value him as the only being who could successfully pull it off.

Yes, that was his ace in the hole, I figured—that I wouldn't harm the one mortal who could effect the switch when I wanted to do it again.

Do this again! I had to laugh. I did laugh, and what a strange and alien sound it was. I shut my eyes tight, and sat there for a moment, hating the sweat clinging to my ribs, hating the ache in my belly and in my head, hating the heavy padded feeling of my hands and feet. And when I opened my eyes again all I beheld was this bleary world of indistinct edges and pallid colors . . .

Do this again? Oooh! Get a grip on yourself, Lestat. You've clenched your teeth so hard that you've hurt yourself! You've cut your tongue! You are making your own mouth bleed! And the blood tastes like water and salt, nothing but water and salt, water and salt! For the love of hell, get a grip on yourself. Stop!

After a quiet few moments, I stood up and went on a systematic search for a phone.

There was none in the entire house.

Beautiful.

How foolish I'd been not to plan sufficiently for this entire experience. I'd been so carried away with the larger spiritual issues, I'd made no sensible provisions for myself at all! I should have had a suite at the Willard, and money in the hotel safe! I should have arranged for a car.

The car. What about the car?

I went to the hall closet, removed the overcoat, noted a rip in the lining—probably the reason he didn't sell it—put it on, despairing that there were no gloves in the pockets, and went out the back way, after carefully securing the dining room door. I asked Mojo if he wanted to join me or stay there. Naturally he wanted to come along.

The snow in the alley was about a foot deep. I had to slosh my way through it and when I reached the street, I realized it was deeper still.

No red Porsche, of course. Not to the left of the front steps, nor anywhere on this block. Just to be certain, I made my way to the corner and then turned around and came back. My feet were freezing and so were my hands, and the skin of my face positively ached.

All right, I must set out on foot, at least until I located a public phone. The snow was blowing away from me, which was something of a blessing, but then I didn't know where I was going, did I?

As for Mojo he appeared to love this sort of weather, plowing ahead steadily, the snow tumbling and glistening in tiny flakes from his long plush gray coat. I should have switched bodies with the dog, I thought. And then the thought of Mojo inside my vampiric body started me to laughing. I went into one of my regular fits. I laughed and laughed and laughed, turning in circles, and then finally stopped because I was truly freezing to death.

But all this was terribly funny. Here I was a human being, the priceless event I'd dreamed of since my death, and I hated it to the marrow of these human bones! I felt a hunger pang in my noisy, churning stomach. And then another, which I could only call a hunger cramp.

"Paolo's, I have to find Paolo's but how am I going to get any food? I *need* food too, don't I? I can't simply go without food. I'll get weak if I don't have food."

When I came to the corner of Wisconsin Avenue, I saw lights and people down the hill. The street had been cleared of snow, and was definitely open to traffic. I could see the people moving busily back and forth under the street lamps, but all this was maddeningly dim, of course.

I hurried on, my feet painfully numb now, which is not a contradiction in terms, as you well know if you have ever walked in snow, and finally I saw the lighted window of a café. Martini's. All right. Forget Paolo's. Martini's will have to do. A car had stopped out front; a handsome young couple climbed out of the back and hurried to the door of the place and went inside. I drew up slowly to the door, and saw a fairly pretty young woman at the high wooden desk gathering up a pair of menus for the young couple, whom she then led into the shadows beyond. I glimpsed candles, checkered tablecloths. And I realized suddenly that the awful, nauseating smell that was filling my nostrils was the smell of burnt cheese.

I would not have liked this smell as a vampire, no, not in the least; but it wouldn't have sickened me quite this much. It would have been outside of me. But now it seemed connected to the hunger in me; it seemed to tug on the muscles inside my throat. In fact, the smell seemed suddenly to be inside my guts and to be nauseating me with a pressure, rather than a mere smell.

Curious. Yes, have to note all these things. This is being alive.

The pretty young woman had come back. I saw her pale profile as she looked down at the paper on her little wooden desk, and lifted her pen to make a mark. She had long wavy dark hair, and very pale skin. I wished I could see her better. I struggled to pick up her scent, but I couldn't. I only caught the scent of the burnt cheese.

I opened the door, ignoring the heavy stench that hit me, and moved through it, until I was standing in front of the young woman, and the blessed warmth of the place was wrapping itself around me, smells and all. She was painfully young, with rather small sharp features, and long narrow black eyes. Her mouth was large, exquisitely rouged, and she had a long beautifully shaped neck. The body was twentieth century—all bones beneath her black dress.

"Mademoiselle," I said, deliberately thickening my French accent, "I am very hungry, and it's very cold outside. Is there anything I can do to earn a plate of food? I shall wash the floors if you wish, scrub the pots and pans, do whatever I must."

She stared at me blankly for a moment. Then she stood back, tossed her long wavy hair, and rolled her eyes, and looked at me again coldly, and said: "Get out." Her voice sounded tinny and flat. It wasn't, of course, it was merely my mortal hearing. The resonance detected by a vampire could not be detected by me.

"May I have a piece of bread?" I asked. "A single piece of bread." The smells of food, bad as they were, tormented me. I couldn't actually remember what food tasted like. I couldn't remember texture and nourishment together, but something purely human was taking over. I was desperate for food.

"I'm going to call the police," she said, her voice quavering slightly, "if you don't get out."

I tried to scan her. Nothing. I looked around, squinting in the dark. Tried to scan the other humans. Nothing. Didn't have the power in this body. Oh, but that's not possible. I looked at her again. Nothing. Not even a glimmer of her thoughts. Not even an instinct really as to what sort of human she was.

"Ah, very well," I said, giving her the gentlest smile I could manage, with no idea of how it appeared or what its effect might be. "I hope you burn in hell for your lack of charity. But God knows, I don't deserve any more than this." I turned and was about to leave when she touched my sleeve.

"Look," she said, trembling slightly in her anger and discomfort, "you can't come here and expect people to give you food!" The blood was pulsing in her white cheeks. I couldn't smell it. But I could smell a sort of musky perfume rising from her, part human, part commercial scent. And suddenly I saw two tiny nipples sticking against the fabric of the dress. How amazing. Again, I tried to read her thoughts. I told myself I must be able to do this, it was an innate power. But it was no good.

"I told you I'd work for the food," I said, trying not to look at her breasts. "I'd do anything you asked. Look, I'm sorry. I don't want you to burn in hell. What a dreadful thing to say. It's only that I'm down on my luck now. Bad things have happened to me. Look, that's my dog there. How am I to feed him?"

"That dog!" She looked through the glass at Mojo, who sat majestically in the snow. "You must be joking," she said. What a shrill voice she had. Utterly without character. So many sounds coming at me had that very quality. Metallic and thin.

"No, he is my dog," I said with faint indignation. "I love him very much."

She laughed. "That dog eats here every night at the back kitchen door!"

"Ah, well, marvelous. One of us will eat. I'm so happy to hear it, mademoiselle. Maybe I should go to the back kitchen door. Perhaps the dog will leave something for me."

She gave a little chilly and false laugh. She was observing me, quite obviously, looking with interest at my face and my clothes. Whatever did I look like to her? I didn't know. The black overcoat was not a cheap garment, but neither was it stylish. The brown hair of this head of mine was full of snow.

She herself had a sort of scrawny, fine-toned sensuality. Very narrow nose, very finely shaped eyes. Very beautiful bones.

"All right," she said, "sit down up there at the counter. I'll have them bring you something. What do you want?"

"Anything, I don't care. I thank you for your kindness."

"All right, sit down." She opened the door, and shouted to the dog: "Go around to the back." She made a quick gesture.

Mojo did nothing but sit there, a patient mountain of fur. I went back out into the freezing wind, and told him to go to the kitchen door. I gestured to the side alley. He looked at me for a long moment and then he rose and moved slowly down the alley and disappeared.

I went back inside, grateful for a second time to be out of the cold, though I realized that my shoes were full of melted snow. I moved into the darkness of the interior of the restaurant, stumbling on a wooden stool that I didn't see, and nearly falling, and then seating myself on the stool. A place had already been set on the wooden counter, with a blue cloth mat and a heavy steel fork and knife. The smell of cheese was stifling. There were other smells—cooked onions, garlic, burnt grease. All revolting.

I was most uncomfortable sitting on this stool. The round hard edge of the wooden seat cut into my legs, and once again, I was bothered that I couldn't see in the dark. The restaurant appeared very deep, indeed to have several more rooms in a long chain. But I couldn't see all the way back there. I could hear frightful noises, like big pots being banged on metal, and they hurt my ears just a little, or more truly I resented them.

The young woman reappeared, smiling prettily as she set down a big glass of red wine. The smell was sour and potentially sickening.

I thanked her. And then I picked up the glass, and took a mouthful of the wine, holding it and then swallowing. At once I began to choke. I couldn't figure what had happened—whether I had swallowed in some wrong way, or it was irritating my throat for some reason, or what. I only knew I was coughing furiously, and I snatched up a cloth napkin from beside the fork and put it over my mouth. Some of the wine was actually caught in the back of my nose. As for the taste, it was weak and acidic. A terrible frustration rose in me.

I shut my eyes, and leaned my head against my left hand, the hand itself closed around the napkin in a fist.

"Here, try it again," she said. I opened my eyes and saw her filling the glass once more from a large carafe.

"All right," I said, "thank you." I was thirsty, powerfully thirsty. In fact, the mere taste of the wine had greatly increased this thirst. But this time, I reasoned, I wouldn't swallow so hard. I lifted the glass, took a small mouthful, tried to savor it, though there seemed almost nothing there to savor, and then I swallowed, slowly, and it went down the correct way. Thin, so thin, so totally different from a luscious filling swallow of blood. I must get the hang of this. I drank the rest of the contents of the glass. Then I lifted the carafe and filled it again, and drank that down too.

For a moment, I felt only frustration. Then gradually I began to feel a little sick. Food will come, I thought. Ah, there is food—a canister of bread sticks, or so they appear to be.

I lifted one, smelled it carefully, ascertaining that it was bread, and then I nibbled at it very fast until it was gone. It was like sand to the last tiny bit. Just like the sand of the Gobi Desert which had gotten into my mouth. Sand.

"How do mortals eat this?" I asked.

"More slowly," said the pretty woman and she let out a little laugh. "You're not mortal? Which planet are you from?"

"Venus," I answered, smiling at her again. "The planet of love."

She was studying me unreservedly, and a little flush came back to her sharp white little cheeks. "Well, stick around until I get off, why don't you? You can walk me home."

"I shall definitely do that," I said. And then the realization of what this could mean settled over me, with the most curious effect. I could bed this woman, perhaps. Ah, yes, that was definitely a possibility as far as she was concerned. My eyes drifted down to the two tiny nipples, protruding so enticingly through the black silk of the dress. Yes, bed her, I thought, and how smooth was the flesh of her neck.

The organ was stirring between my legs. Well, something is working, I mused. But how curiously local was this feeling, this hardening and swelling, and the odd way that it consumed all my thoughts. The need for blood was never local. I stared blankly before me. I did not look down when a plate of Italian spaghetti and meat sauce was set down at my place. The hot fragrance went up my nostrils—moldering cheese, burnt meat, and fat.

Go down, I was saying to the organ. This is not the time yet for that.

Finally I lowered my gaze to the plate. The hunger ground in me as if someone had my intestines in both hands and was wringing them out. Did I remember such a feeling? God knows I had been hungry enough in my mortal life. Hunger was like life itself. But the memory seemed so distant, so unimportant. Slowly I picked up the fork, which I had never used in those times, for we had none—only spoons and knives in our crude world—and I shoved the tines under the mess of wet spaghetti and lifted a heap of it to my mouth.

I knew it was too hot before it touched my tongue, but I didn't stop quickly enough. I was badly burnt and let the fork drop. Now, this is plain stupidity, I thought, and it was perhaps my fifteenth act of plain stupidity. What must I do to approach things with more intelligence, and patience and calm?

I sat back on the uncomfortable stool, as well as one can do such a thing without tumbling to the floor, and I tried to think.

I was trying to run this new body, which was full of uncommon weakness and sensation—painfully cold feet, for instance, wet feet in a draught running along the floor—and I was making understandable but stupid mistakes. Should have taken the galoshes. Should have found a phone before coming in here and called my agent in Paris. Not reasoning, behaving stubbornly as if I were a vampire when I was not.

Nothing of the temperature of this steaming food would have burnt me in my vampire skin, obviously. But I wasn't in my vampire skin. That's why I should have taken the galoshes. Think!

But how far was this experience from what I had expected. Oh, ye gods. Here I was talking about thinking when I'd thought I would be enjoying! Ah, I'd thought I would be immersed in sensations, immersed in memories, immersed in discoveries; and now all I could do was think how to hold back!

The truth was, I'd envisioned pleasure, a variety of pleasures— eating, drinking, a woman in my bed, then a man. But none of what I'd experienced was even vaguely pleasurable so far.

Well, I was to blame for this shameful situation, and I could make it change. I wiped my mouth now with my napkin, a coarse bit of artificial fiber, no more absorbent than a bit of oilcloth might have been, and then I picked up the wineglass and emptied it once more. A wave of sickness passed over me. My throat tightened and then I even felt dizzy. Good God, three glasses and I was getting drunk?

Once again, I lifted the fork. The sticky goo was cooler now, and I shoveled a heap of it into my mouth. Again, I almost choked! My throat locked convulsively, as if to prevent this mass of slop from smothering me. I had to stop, breathe slowly through my nostrils, tell myself this wasn't poison, I wasn't a vampire, and then chew the mess carefully so as not to bite my tongue.

But I'd bit my tongue earlier, and now that patch of sore skin began to hurt. The hurt filled my mouth, and was far more perceptible than the food. Nevertheless I continued to chew the spaghetti, and began to reflect on its tastelessness, its sourness, its saltiness, and its general awful consistency and then I swallowed it, feeling a painful tightening again, and then a hard knot lower in my chest.

Now, if Louis were going through this—if you were your old smug vampire self, sitting opposite, watching him, you would condemn him for everything that he was doing and thinking, you would abhor him for his timidity, and his wasting of this experience, for his failure to perceive.

Again, I lifted the fork. I chewed another mouthful, swallowed it. Well, there was a sort of taste. It simply wasn't the pungent delicious taste of blood. It was much tamer, and grainier, and stickier. Okay, another mouthful. You can get to like this. And besides, maybe this just isn't very good food. Another mouthful.

"Hey, slow down," said the pretty woman. She was leaning against me but I couldn't feel her juicy softness through the coat. I turned and looked up into her eyes again, marveling at her long curving black lashes, and how sweet her mouth looked as she smiled. "You're bolting your food."

"I know. Very hungry," I said. "Listen to me, I know this sounds dreadfully ungrateful. But do you have something that is not a great coagulated mass such as this? You know, something tougher—meat, perhaps?"

She laughed. "You are the strangest man," she said. "Really where are you from?"

"France, the countryside," I said.

"All right, I'll bring you something else."

As soon as she'd gone, I drank another glass of the wine. I was definitely getting dizzy, but I also felt a warmth that was sort of nice. I also felt like laughing suddenly, and I knew that I was partially intoxicated, at least.

I decided to study the other humans in the room. It was so weird not being able to pick up their scents, so weird not being able to hear their thoughts. I couldn't even really hear their voices, only a lot of racket and noise. And it was so weird to be both cold and hot here, my head swimming in the overheated air, and my feet freezing in the draught that ran along the floor.

The young woman set a plate of meat before me—veal, she called it. I picked up some small sliver, which seemed to amaze her—I should have used the knife and fork—and bit into it and found it to be rather tasteless like the spaghetti; but it was better. Cleaner, it seemed. I chewed it fairly lustily.

"Thank you, you've been kind to me," I said. "You are really lovely, and I regret my harsh words earlier, I really do."

She seemed fascinated, and of course I was playacting somewhat. I was pretending to be gentle, which I am not.

She left me so that she might take the payment from a couple who were leaving, and I returned to my meal—my first meal of sand and glue and bits of leather full of salt. I laughed to myself. More wine, I thought, it's like drinking nothing, but it's having an effect.

After she'd cleared the plate, she gave me another carafe. And I sat there, in my wet shoes and socks, cold and uncomfortable on the wooden stool, straining to see in the dark, and getting drunker and drunker as an hour passed, and then she was ready to go home.

I was no more comfortable at that point than I'd been when this all began. And as soon as I stood up off the stool, I realized I could hardly walk. There was no sensation in my legs at all. I had to look down to be certain they were there.

The pretty woman thought it very funny. I wasn't so sure. She helped me along the snowy sidewalk, calling to Mojo, whom she addressed simply as "Dog," with great respectful emphasis, and assured me that she lived only "a few steps up the street." The only good aspect of all this was that the cold did bother me less.

I was really off balance. My limbs were now totally leaden. Even the most brightly illuminated objects were out of focus. My head was aching. I thought sure I was going to fall. Indeed the fear of falling was becoming a panic.

But mercifully we reached her door, and she led me up a narrow carpeted flight of steps—a climb which left me so exhausted that my heart was pounding and my face was veiled with sweat. I could see almost nothing! It was madness. I heard her putting her key in the door.

A new dreadful stench assaulted my nostrils. The grim little apartment appeared to be a warren of pasteboard and plywood, with undistinguished printed posters covering the walls. But what could account for this smell? I realized suddenly that it came from the cats she kept in this place, which were allowed to relieve themselves in a box of earth. I saw the box of earth, full of cat excrement, sitting on the floor of a small open bathroom, and I really thought it was all over, I was going to die! I stood still, straining to keep myself from vomiting. There was a grinding pain in my stomach again, not hunger this time, and my belt felt painfully tight.

The pain grew sharper. I realized I had to perform a similar duty to that already performed by the cats. Indeed, I had to do it now or disgrace myself. And I had to go into that very same chamber. My heart came up in my throat.

"What's wrong?" she said. "Are you sick?"

"May I use this room?" I asked, gesturing to the open door.

"Of course," she said. "Go ahead."

Ten minutes, perhaps more, passed before I emerged. I was so powerfully disgusted by the simple process of elimination—by the smell of it, and the feel of doing it, and the sight of it—that I couldn't speak. But it was finished, done. Only the drunkenness remained now, the graceless experience of reaching for the light switch and missing it, of trying to turn the knob and having my hand—this big dark hand—miss.

I found the bedroom, very warm, and crowded with mediocre modern furniture of cheap laminate and no particular design.

The young woman was now entirely naked and sitting on the side of the bed. I tried to see her clearly in spite of the distortions created by the nearby lamp. But her face was a mass of ugly shadows, and her skin looked sallow. The stale smell of the bed surrounded her.

All I could conclude about her was that she was foolishly thin, as women tend to be in these times, and all the bones of her ribs showed through the milky skin, and that her breasts were almost freakishly small with tiny delicate pink nipples, and her hips weren't there. She was like a wraith. And yet she sat there smiling, as if this was normal, with all her pretty wavy hair hanging down her back, and hiding the small shadow of her pubis beneath one limp hand.

Well, it was perfectly obvious which marvelous human experience was meant to come now. But I could feel nothing for her. Nothing. I smiled, and I began to take off my clothes. I peeled off the overcoat, and was immediately cold. Why wasn't she cold? I then took off the sweater and was immediately horrified by the smell of my own sweat. *Lord God, was it really like this before?* And this body of mine had looked so clean.

She didn't seem to notice. I was grateful for that. I then removed my shirt and my shoes and my socks and my pants. My feet were still cold. Indeed, I was cold and naked, very naked. I didn't know whether or not I liked this at all. I suddenly saw myself in the mirror over her dressing table, and I realized that this organ was of course utterly drunk and asleep.

Again, she didn't seem surprised.

"Come here," she said. "Sit down."

I obeyed. I was shivering all over. Then I began to cough. The first cough was a spasm, catching me completely by surprise. Then a whole series of coughs followed, uncontrollably, and the last was so violent that it made a circle of pain around my ribs.

"I'm sorry," I said to her.

"I love your French accent," she whispered. She stroked my hair, and let her nails lightly scratch my cheek.

Now, this was a pleasant sensation. I bent my head and kissed her throat. Yes, this was nice also. It was nothing as exciting as closing on a victim, but it was nice. I tried to remember what it had been like two hundred years ago when I was the terror of the village girls. Seems some farmer was always at the castle gates, cursing me and swinging his fist at me and telling me that if his daughter was with child by me, I'd have to do something about it! It had all seemed such wonderful fun at the time. And the girls, oh the lovely girls.

"What is it?" she asked.

"Nothing," I said. I kissed her throat again. I could smell sweat on her body too. I didn't like it. But why? These smells were nothing as sharp, any of them, as they were to me in my other body. But they connected with something in this body—that was the ugly part. I felt no protection against these smells; they seemed not artifacts but something which could invade me and contaminate me. For instance, the sweat from her neck was now on my lips. I knew it was, I could taste it and I wanted to be away from her.

Ah, but this is madness. She was a human being, and I was a human being. Thank God this would be over Friday. But what right had I to thank God!

Her little nipples brushed against my chest, very hot and nubby and the flesh behind them was squashy and tender. I slipped my arm around her small back.

"You're hot, I think you have a fever," she said in my ear. She kissed my neck the way I'd been kissing hers.

"No, I'm all right," I said. But I didn't have the slightest idea of whether or not this was true. This was hard work!

Suddenly her hand touched my organ, startling me, and then bringing about an immediate excitement. I felt the organ lengthen and grow hard. The sensation was entirely concentrated, and yet it galvanized me. When I looked at her breasts now, and down at the small fur triangle between her legs, my organ grew even more hard. Yes, I remember this all right; my eyes are connected to it, and nothing else matters now, hmmm, all right. Just get her down on the bed.

"Whoa!" she whispered. "Now that's a piece of equipment!"

"Is it?" I looked down. The monstrous thing had doubled in size.

It did seem grossly out of proportion to everything else. "Yes, I suppose it is. Should have known James would have checked it out."

"Who's James?"

"No, doesn't matter," I mumbled. I turned her face towards me and kissed her wet little mouth this time, feeling her teeth through her thin lips. She opened her mouth for my tongue. This was good, even if her mouth was bad tasting. Didn't matter. But then my mind raced ahead to blood. Drink her blood.

Where was the pounding intensity of drawing near the victim, of the moment right before my teeth pierced the skin and the blood spilled all over my tongue?

No, it's not going to be that easy, or that consuming. It's going to be between the legs and more like a shiver, but this is some shiver, I'll say that.

Merely thinking of the blood had heightened the passion, and I shoved her roughly down on the bed. I wanted to finish, nothing else mattered but finishing.

"Wait a minute," she said.

"Wait for what?" I mounted her, and kissed her again, pushing my tongue deeper into her. No blood. Ah, so pale. No blood. My organ slid between her hot thighs, and I almost spurted then. But it wasn't enough.

"I said wait!" she screamed, her cheeks coloring. "You can't do it without a condom."

"What the hell are you saying?" I murmured. I knew the meaning of these words, yet they didn't make much sense. I pushed my hand down, felt the hairy opening, and then the juicy wet crack, which seemed deliciously small.

She screamed at me to get off of her, and she shoved at me with the heels of her hands. She looked very flushed and beautiful to me suddenly in her heat and rage, and when she nudged me with her knee, I slammed down against her, then drew up only long enough to ram the organ into her, and feel that sweet hot tight envelope of flesh close around me, making me gasp.

"Don't! Stop it! I said stop it!" she screamed.

But I couldn't wait. What the hell made her think this was the time to discuss such a thing, I wondered, in some vague crazed fashion. Then, in a moment of blinding spasmodic excitement I came. Semen came roaring out of the organ!

One moment it was eternal; the next it was finished, as if it had never begun. I lay exhausted on top of her, drenched with sweat, of course, and faintly annoyed by the stickiness of the whole event, and her panic-stricken screams.

At last I fell over onto my back. My head was aching, and all the evil smells of the room thickened—a soiled smell from the bed itself, with its sagging, lumpy mattress; the nauseating smell of the cats.

She leapt out of the bed. She appeared to have gone mad. She was crying and shivering, and she snatched up a blanket from the chair and covered herself with it and began screaming at me to get out, get out, get out.

"Whatever is the matter with you?" I asked.

She let loose with a volley of modern curses. "You bum, you miserable stupid bum, you idiot, you jerk!" That sort of thing. I could have given her a disease, she said. Indeed she rattled off the names of several; I could have gotten her pregnant. I was a creep, a prick, a putz! I was to clear out of here at once. How dare I do this to her? Get out before she called the police.

A wave of sleepiness passed over me. I tried to focus upon her, in spite of the darkness. Then came a sudden nausea sharper than I'd ever felt. I struggled to keep it under control, and only by a severe act of will managed not to vomit then and there.

Finally, I sat up and then climbed to my feet. I looked down at her as she stood there, crying, and screaming at me, and I saw suddenly that she was wretched, that I had really hurt her, and indeed there was an ugly bruise on her face.

Very slowly it came clear to me what had happened. She had wanted me to use some form of prophylactic, and I'd virtually forced her. No pleasure in it for her, only fear. I saw her again at the moment of my climax, fighting me, and I realized it was utterly inconceivable to her that I could have enjoyed the struggle, enjoyed her rage and her protests, enjoyed conquering her. But in a paltry and common way, I think I had.

The whole thing seemed overwhelmingly dismal. It filled me with despair. The pleasure itself had been nothing! I can't bear this, I thought, not a moment longer. If I could have reached James, I would have offered him another fortune, just to return at once. Reached James . . . I'd forgotten altogether about finding a phone.

"Listen to me, ma chère," I said. "I'm so sorry. Things simply went wrong. I know. I'm sorry."

She moved to slap me but I caught her wrist easily and brought her hand down, hurting her a little.

"Get out," she said again. "Get out or I'll call the police."

"I understand what you're saying to me. It's been forever since I did it. I was clumsy. I was bad."

"You're worse than bad!" she said in a deep raw voice.

And this time she did slap me. I wasn't quick enough. I was astonished by the force of the slap, how it stung. I felt of my face where she'd hit me. What an annoying little pain. It was an insulting pain.

"Go!" she screamed again.

I put on my clothes, but it was like lifting sacks of bricks to do it. A dull shame had come over me, a feeling of such awkwardness and discomfort in the slightest gesture I made or smallest word I spoke that I wanted simply to sink into the earth.

Finally, I had everything buttoned and zipped properly, and I had the miserable wet socks on my feet again, and the thin shoes, and I was ready to go.

She sat on the bed crying, her shoulders very thin, with the tender bones in her back poking at her pale flesh, and her hair dripping down in thick wavy clumps over the blanket she held to her breast. How fragile she looked—how sadly unbeautiful and repulsive.

I tried to see her as if I were really Lestat. But I couldn't do it. She appeared a common thing, utterly worthless, not even interesting. I was vaguely horrified. Had it been that way in my boyhood village? I tried to remember those girls, those girls dead and gone for centuries, but I couldn't see their faces. What I remembered was happiness, mischief, a great exuberance that had made me forget for intermittent periods the deprivation and hopelessness of my life.

What did that mean in this moment? How could this whole experience have been so unpleasant, so seemingly pointless? Had I been myself I would have found her fascinating as an insect is fascinating; even her little rooms would have appeared quaint to me, in their worst, most uninspiring details! Ah, the affection I always felt for all sad little mortal habitats. But why was that so!

And she, the poor being, she would have been beautiful to me simply because she was alive! I could not have been sullied by her had I fed on her for an hour. As it was, I felt filthy for having been with her, and filthy for being cruel to her. I understood her fear of disease! I, too, felt contaminated! But where lay the perspective of truth?

"I am so sorry," I said again. "You must believe me. It wasn't what I wanted. I don't know what I wanted."

"You're crazy," she whispered bitterly without looking up.

"Some night I'll come to you, soon, and I'll bring you a present, something beautiful that you really want. I'll give it to you and perhaps you'll forgive me."

She didn't answer.

"Tell me, what is it you really want? Money doesn't matter. What is it you want that you cannot have?"

She looked up, rather sullenly, her face blotched and red and swollen, and then she wiped at her nose with the back of her hand.

"You know what I wanted," she said in a harsh, disagreeable voice, which was almost sexless it was so low.

"No, I don't. Tell me what."

Her face was so disfigured and her voice so strange that she frightened me. I was still woozy from the wine I'd drunk earlier, yet my mind was unaffected by the intoxication. It seemed a lovely situation. This body drunk, but not me.

"Who are you?" she asked. She looked very hard now, hard and bitter. "You're somebody, aren't you . . . you're not just . . ." But her voice trailed off.

"You wouldn't believe me if I told you."

She turned her head even more sharply to the side, studying me as if it was all going to come to her suddenly. She'd have it figured out. I couldn't imagine what was going on in her mind. I knew only that I felt sorry for her, and I did not like her. I didn't like this dirty messy room with its low plaster ceiling, and the nasty bed, and the ugly tan carpet and the dim light and the cat box reeking in the other room.

"I'll remember you," I said miserably yet tenderly. "I'll surprise you. I'll come back and I'll bring something wonderful for you, something you could never get for yourself. A gift as if from another world. But right now, I have to leave you."

"Yes," she said, "you'd better go."

I turned to do exactly that. I thought of the cold outside, of Mojo waiting in the hallway, and of the town house with its back door shattered off the hinges, and no money and no phone.

Ah, the phone.

She had a phone. I'd spied it on the dresser.

As I turned and went towards it, she screamed at me, and hurled something at me. I think that it was a shoe. It struck my shoulder, but caused no pain. I picked up the receiver and punched the zero twice for long distance, and called my New York agent collect.

On and on it rang. No one there. Not even his machine. Most strange, and damned inconvenient.

I could see her in the mirror, staring at me in stiff and silent outrage, the blanket pulled around her like a sleek modern dress. How pathetic was all of this, down to the last jot.

I called Paris. Again it rang and rang, but finally there came the familiar voice—my agent roused from sleep. Quickly in French I told him I was in Georgetown, that I needed twenty thousand dollars, no, best send thirty, and I must have it now.

He explained that it was just sunrise in Paris. He would have to wait until the banks opened, but he would wire the money as soon as he could. It might be noon in Georgetown before it reached me. I memorized the name of the agency where I was to collect it, and I implored him to be prompt and see that he did not fail. This was an emergency, I was penniless. I had obligations. He gave me assurance that all would be handled at once. I put down the phone.

She was staring at me. I don't think she had understood the phone call. She could not speak French.

"I'll remember you," I said. "Please, forgive me. I'll go now. I've caused trouble enough."

She didn't answer. I stared at her, trying for the last time to fathom it, why she seemed so coarse and uninteresting. What had been my vantage point before that all life seemed so beautiful to me, all creatures but variations on the same magnificent theme? Even James had had a horrid glittering beauty like a great palmetto bug or a fly.

"Good-bye, ma chère," I said, "I'm very sorry—truly I am."

I found Mojo sitting patiently outside the apartment, and I hurried past him, snapping my fingers for him to come, which he did. And down the steps we went and out in the cold night.

IN SPITE of the wind gusting into the kitchen, and creeping around the dining room door, the other rooms of the town house were still quite warm. A stream of heated air came from the little brass grilles in the floors. How kind of James not to have turned off the heat, I thought. But then he plans to leave this place immediately that he has the twenty million. The bill will never be paid.

I went upstairs and through the master bedroom into the master bath. A pleasant room of new white tile and clean mirrors and a deep shower stall with doors of shining glass. I tried the water. Hot and strong. Quite deliciously hot. I peeled off all the damp and smelly clothes, laying the socks on the furnace grille and neatly folding the sweater for it was the only one I had, and then I stood in the hot shower for a long time.

With my head back against the tile, I might have actually fallen asleep standing up. But then I began to weep, and then just as spontaneously, to cough. I felt an intense burning in my chest, and the same burning deep inside my nose.

Finally I got out, toweled off, and looked again at this body in the mirror. I could not see a scar or a flaw anywhere in it. The arms were powerful but smoothly muscled, as was the chest. The legs were well formed. The face was truly beautiful, the dark skin quite nearly perfect, though there was nothing of the boy left in the structure of it, as there was in my own face. It was very much the face of a man— rectangular, a little hard, but pretty, very pretty, perhaps on account of the large eyes. It was also slightly rough. Beard coming in. Have to shave. Nuisance.

"But really, this ought to be splendid," I said aloud. "You've the body of a twenty-six-year-old male in perfect condition. But it's been a nightmare. You've made one stupid error after another. Why can't you meet this challenge? Where is your will and your strength?"

I felt chilled all over. Mojo had gone to sleep on the floor at the foot of the bed. I shall do that, sleep, I thought. Sleep like a mortal, and when I wake, the light of day will be coming into this room. Even if the sky is gray, it will be wondrous. It will be day. You will see the world of day as you've longed to see it all these years. Forget all this abysmal struggle and trivia and fear.

But a dreadful suspicion was coming over me. Hadn't my mortal life been nothing but abysmal struggle and trivia and fear? Wasn't that the way it was for most mortals? Wasn't that the message of a score of modern writers and poets—that we wasted our lives in foolish preoccupation? *Wasn't this all a miserable cliché?*

I was bitterly shaken. I tried to argue with myself once more, the way I'd been doing all along. But what was the use?

It felt terrible to be in this sluggish human body! It felt terrible not to have my preternatural powers. And the world, look at it, it was dingy and shabby, frayed at the edges and full of accidents. Why, I couldn't even see most of it. What world?

Ah, but tomorrow! Oh, Lord, another miserable cliché! I started laughing and another fit of coughing caught me. This time the pain was in my throat and quite considerable, and my eyes were watering. Best to sleep, best to rest, better to prepare for my one precious day.

I snapped off the lamp, and pulled back the covers of the bed. It was clean, I was thankful for that. I laid my head on the down pillow, brought up my knees close to my chest, drew the covers up to my chin, and went to sleep. I was vaguely sensible that if the house burned, I would die. If gas fumes came up out of the furnace grilles, I would die. Indeed, someone might come in the open back door to kill me. Indeed, all kinds of disasters were possible. But Mojo was there, wasn't he? And I was tired, so tired!

Hours later, I woke.

I was coughing violently and bitterly cold. I needed a handkerchief, found a box of paper tissue that would do well enough, and blew my nose perhaps a hundred times. Then, able to breathe again, I fell back into a strange feverish exhaustion, and the deceptive feeling that I was floating as I lay firmly on the bed.

Just a mortal cold, I thought. The result of letting myself become so miserably chilled. It will mar things, but it is also an experience, an experience I must explore.

The next time I woke up, the dog was standing beside the bed, and he was licking my face. I put out my hand, felt his furry nose, and laughed at him, then coughed again, throat burning, and realized I'd been coughing for some time.

The light was awfully bright. Wonderfully bright. Thank God, a bright lamp in this murky world at last. I sat up. For a moment, I was too dazed to rationally acknowledge what I saw.

The sky in the tops of the windows was perfectly blue, vibrantly blue, and the sunlight was pouring in on the polished floor, and all the world appeared glorious in the brightness—the bare tree branches with their white trimming of snow, and the snow-covered roof opposite, and the room itself, full of whiteness and lustrous color, light glancing off the mirror, and the crystal glass on the dresser, off the brass knob of the bathroom door.

"Mon Dieu, look at it, Mojo," I whispered, throwing back the covers and rushing to the window and shoving it all the way up. The cold air hit me, but what did it matter? Look at the deep color of the sky, look at the high white clouds traveling to the west, look at the rich and beautiful green of the tall pine tree in the neighboring yard.

Suddenly I was weeping uncontrollably, and coughing painfully once more.

"This is the miracle," I whispered. Mojo nudged me, giving a little high-pitched moan. The mortal aches and pains didn't matter. This was the biblical promise which had gone unfulfilled for two hundred years.

TWELVE

WITHIN moments of leaving the town house, of stepping out into the glorious daylight, I knew that this experience would be worth all of the trials and the pain. And no mortal chill, with all its debilitating symptoms would keep me from frolicking in the morning sun.

Never mind that my overall physical weakness was driving me mad: that I seemed to be made of stone as I plodded along with Mojo, that I couldn't jump two feet in the air when I tried, or that pushing open the door of the butcher shop took a colossal effort; or that my cold was growing steadily worse.

Once Mojo had devoured his breakfast of scraps, begged from the butcher, we were off together to revel in the light everywhere, and I felt myself becoming drunk on the vision of the sunlight falling upon windows and wet pavements, on the gleaming tops of brightly enameled automobiles, on the glassy puddles where the snow had melted, upon the plate-glass shopwindows, and upon the people—the thousands and thousands of happy people, scurrying busily about the business of the day.

How different they were from the people of the night, for obviously, they felt safe in the daylight, and walked and talked in a wholly unguarded fashion, carrying on the many transactions of daytime, which are seldom performed with such vigor after dark.

Ah, to see the busy mothers with their radiant little children in tow, piling fruit into their grocery baskets, to watch the big noisy delivery trucks park in the slushy streets as powerfully built men lugged great cartons and cases of merchandise through back doors! To see men shoveling snow and cleaning off windows, to see the cafés filled with pleasantly distracted creatures consuming great quantities of coffee and odoriferous fried breakfasts as they pored over the morning newspapers or fretted over the weather or discussed the day's work. Enchanting to watch gangs of schoolchildren, in crisp uniforms, braving the icy wind to organize their games in a sun-drenched asphalt yard.

A great optimistic energy bound all these beings together; one could feel it emanating from the students rushing between buildings on the university campus, or gathered together in close, warm restaurants to take lunch.

Like flowers to the light, these humans opened themselves, accelerating their pace, and their speech. And when I felt the heat of the sun itself upon my face and hands, I, too, opened as if I were a flower. I could feel the chemistry of this mortal body responding, despite the congestion in my head and the tiresome pain in my freezing hands and feet.

Ignoring the cough, which was growing worse by the hour, and a new blurriness of vision, which was a real nuisance, I took Mojo with me along noisy M Street into Washington, the capital of the nation proper, wandering about the marble memorials and monuments, the vast and impressive official buildings and residences, and up through the soft sad beauty of Arlington Cemetery with its thousands of tiny identical headstones, and to the handsome and dusty little mansion of the great Confederate general Robert E. Lee.

I was delirious by this time. And very possibly all my physical discomfort added to my happiness—giving me a drowsy, frenzied attitude rather like that of a person drunk or drugged. I don't know. I only know I was happy, very happy, and the world by light was not the world by dark.

Many, many tourists braved the cold as I did to see the famous sights. I reveled silently in their enthusiasm, realizing that all of these beings were affected by the broad open vistas of the capital city as I was affected by them—that it gladdened them and transformed them to see the vast blue sky overhead, and the many spectacular stone memorials to the accomplishments of humankind.

"I'm one of them!" I realized suddenly—not Cain forever seeking the blood of his brother. I looked about me in a daze. "I'm one of you!"

For a long moment I gazed down upon the city from the heights of Arlington, shivering with cold, and even crying a little at the astonishing spectacle of it—so orderly, so representative of the principles of the great Age of Reason—wishing that Louis were with me, or that David were here, and aching in my heart that they would so surely disapprove of what I had done.

But, oh, this was the true planet I beheld, the living earth born of sunshine and warmth, even under its shimmering mantle of winter snow.

I went down the hill finally, Mojo now and then running ahead and then circling back to accompany me, and I walked along the bank of the frozen Potomac, wondering at the sun reflected in the ice and melting snow. It was fun even to watch the melting snow.

Sometime in midafternoon I ended up once more in the great marble Jefferson Memorial, an elegant and spacious Greek pavilion with the most solemn and moving words engraved on its walls. My heart was bursting as I realized that for these precious hours I wasn't cut off from the sentiments expressed here. Indeed, for this little while I mingled with the human crowd, quite indistinguishable from anyone else.

But this was a lie, wasn't it? I carried my guilt within me—in the continuity of my memory, in my irreducible individual soul: Lestat the killer, Lestat the prowler of the night. I thought of Louis's warning: "You can't become human by simply taking over a human body!" I saw the stricken and tragic look on his face.

But Lord God, what if the Vampire Lestat hadn't ever existed, what if he were merely the literary creation, the pure invention, of the man in whose body I now lived and breathed! What a beautiful idea!

I remained for a long time on the steps of the memorial, my head bowed, the wind tearing at my clothes. A kind woman told me I was ill and must button up my coat. I stared into her eyes, realizing that she saw only a young man there before her. She was neither dazzled nor afraid. No hunger lurked in me to end her life so that I might better enjoy mine. Poor lovely creature of pale blue eyes and fading hair!

Very suddenly I caught her small wrinkled hand and kissed it, and I told her in French that I loved her, and I watched the smile spread over her narrow withered face. How lovely she appeared to me, as lovely as any human I'd ever gazed upon with my vampire eyes.

All the sordid shabbiness of last night was erased in these daylight hours. I think my greatest dreams of this adventure had been fulfilled.

But the winter was heavy and hard all around me. Even cheered by the blue sky, people spoke to one another of a worse storm yet to come. Shops were closing early, streets would again become impassable, the airport had been shut down. Passersby warned me to lay in candles, as the city might lose electric power. And an old gentleman, with a thick wool cap pulled down over his head, scolded me for not wearing a hat. A young woman told me that I looked sick and should hurry home.

Only a cold, I answered. A good cough tonic or whatever they call it now would be perfectly fine. Raglan James would know what to do when he reclaimed this body. He wouldn't be too happy about it, but he could console himself with his twenty million. Besides I had hours still to dose myself with commercial remedies and rest.

For the time being, I was too relentlessly uncomfortable overall to worry about such a thing. I'd wasted enough time upon such petty distractions. And of course help for all the petty annoyances of life— ah, real life—was at hand.

Indeed, I'd forgotten all about the time, hadn't I? My money should be at the agency, waiting for me. I caught a glimpse of a clock in a store window. Half past two. The big cheap watch on my wrist said the same thing. Why, I had only about thirteen hours left.

Thirteen hours in this awful body, with a throbbing head and sore limbs! My happiness vanished in a sudden cold thrill of fear. Oh, but this day was too fine to be ruined by cowardice! I simply put that out of my mind.

Bits of remembered poetry had come to me . . . and now and then a very dim memory of that last mortal winter, of crouching by the hearth in the great hall of my father's house, and trying desperately to warm my hands by a waning fire. But in general, I had been locked to the moment in a way that was entirely unfamiliar to my feverish, calculating, and mischievous little mind. So enchanted had I been by what was going on around me, that for hours I had experienced no preoccupation or distraction of any kind.

This was extraordinary, absolutely extraordinary. And in my euphoria, I was certain that I would carry with me forever the memory of this simple day.

The walk back to Georgetown seemed at times an impossible feat. Even before I'd left the Jefferson Memorial, the sky had begun to cloud over and was fast becoming the color of dull tin. The light was drying up as if it were liquid.

Yet I was loving it in its more melancholy manifestations. I was mesmerized by the sight of anxious mortals locking up storefronts and hurrying against the wind with sacks of groceries, of lighted headlamps flashing brightly and almost cheerily in the deepening gloom.

There would be no twilight, I realized that. Ah, very sad indeed. But as a vampire I often beheld the twilight. So why should I complain? Nevertheless, just for one second I regretted that I had spent my precious time in the teeth of the bitter winter. But for reasons I could scarce explain to myself, it had been just what I wanted. Winter bitter as the winters of my childhood. Bitter as that time in Paris when Magnus had carried me to his lair. I was satisfied. I was content.

By the time I reached the agency, even I knew that the fever and chills were getting the best of me and I must seek shelter and food. I was happy to discover that my money had arrived. A new credit card had been imprinted for me under one of my Paris aliases, Lionel Potter, and a wallet of traveler's checks had been prepared. I shoved all these in my pockets, and as the horrified clerk watched in silence, I shoved the thirty thousand dollars into my pockets as well.

"Somebody's going to rob you!" he whispered, leaning towards me across the counter. He said something I could scarce follow about getting to the bank with the money before it closed. And then I should go to the emergency room, immediately before the blizzard came in. Lots of people with the flu out there, practically an epidemic every winter it seemed.

For the sake of simplicity I agreed to everything, but I hadn't the slightest intention of spending my remaining mortal hours in the clutches of doctors. Besides, such a step wasn't required. All I needed was hot food, I thought, and some hot beverage, and the peace of a soft hotel bed. Then I could return this body to James in tolerable condition, and shoot cleanly back into my own.

But first I must have a change of clothes. It was only three-fifteen, and I had some twelve hours to go and could not bear for a moment longer these dirty and miserable rags!

I reached the great fancy Georgetown Mall just as it was closing so that people could flee the blizzard, but I managed to talk my way into a fancy clothier's, where I quickly made a pile for the impatient clerk of everything I thought I would need. A wave of dizziness caught me as I gave him the small plastic card. It amused me that he had now lost all impatience and was trying to sell me random scarves and ties. I could scarce understand what he was saying to me. Ah, yes, ring it up. We'll give all this to Mr. James at three a.m. Mr. James likes to get things for nothing. Sure, the other sweater, and why not, the scarf too.

As I managed to escape with my heavy load of shiny boxes and sacks, another wave of dizziness hit me. Indeed a blackness was rising all around me; it would have been very easy to sink to my knees and pass out on the floor. A lovely young woman came to my rescue. "You look like you're going to faint!" I was sweating profusely now, and even in the warmth of the mall I was cold.

What I needed was a taxi, I explained to her, but none was to be found. Indeed the crowds were very thin on M Street, and the snow had begun to fall once more.

I had spied a handsome brick hotel only a few blocks away, with the lovely romantic name The Four Seasons, and to that point I hurried, waving good-bye to the beautiful and kind young creature, and bowing my head as I burrowed into the fierce wind. I'd be warm and safe in The Four Seasons, I thought merrily, loving to speak the meaningful name aloud. I could dine there, and need not go back to the awful town house until the hour for the exchange drew near.

When I finally reached the lobby of the place, I found it more than satisfactory, and laid down a large deposit in guarantee that Mojo would be as clean and gentlemanly during our stay as I would be myself. The suite was sumptuous, with large windows over the Potomac, seemingly endless stretches of pale carpet, bathrooms fit for a Roman emperor, television sets and refrigerators concealed in handsome wood cabinets, and other little contraptions galore.

At once I ordered a feast for myself and Mojo, then I opened the small bar, which was stuffed with candies and other tasty tidbits as well as spirits, and helped myself to the best Scotch. Absolutely ghastly taste! How the hell could David drink this? The chocolate bar was better. Damned fantastic! I gobbled all of it, then called back the restaurant and added every chocolate dessert on the menu to my order of only moments ago.

David, I must call David, I thought. But it seemed an impossibility to climb out of the chair and move to the phone on the desk. And there was so much I wanted to consider, to fix in my mind. Discomforts be damned, this had been a hell of an experience! I was even getting used to these enormous hands hanging an inch below where they ought to be, and this porous dark skin. Mustn't fall asleep. What a waste . . .

Then the bell startled me! I had been sleeping. A full half hour of mortal time had passed. I struggled to my feet, as if I were hefting bricks with every step, and managed somehow to open the door for the room service attendant, an attractive older female with light yellow hair, who wheeled a linen-draped table, laden with food, into the living room of the suite.

I gave the steak to Mojo, having already laid down a bath towel for a dog tablecloth, and he set about to chewing lustily, lying down as he did so, which only the very large dogs do, and which made him look all the more monstrous, like a lion lazily gnawing upon a Christian pinned helplessly between his huge paws.

I at once drank the hot soup, unable to taste anything much in it, but that was to be expected with such a miserable cold. The wine was marvelous, much better than the vin ordinaire of the last night, and though it still tasted very thin compared to blood, I downed two glasses of it, and was about to devour the pasta, as they called it here, when I looked up and realized that the fretful female attendant was still there.

"You're sick," she said, "you're very, very sick."

"Nonsense, ma chère," I said, "I have a cold, a mortal cold, no more and no less." I fished in my shirt pocket for my wad of bills, gave her several twenties, and told her to go. She was very reluctant.

"That's quite a cough," she said. "I think you're really sick. You've been outside a long time, haven't you?"

I stared at her, absolutely weakened by her concern, and realizing that I was in true danger of bursting stupidly into tears. I wanted to warn her that I was a monster, that this body was merely stolen. How tender she was, how obviously habitually kind.

"We're all connected," I said to her, "all humankind. We must

care for each other, mustn't we?" I figured she would be horrified by
these sloppy sentiments, issued with such thick drunken emotion, and
that she would now take her leave. But she did not.

"Yes, we are," she said. "Let me call a doctor for you before the
storm gets any worse."

"No, dearest, go now," I said.

And with one last worried look at me, she did at last go out.

After I'd consumed the plate of fancy cheese-sauced noodles,
another bit of salt and tastelessness, I began to wonder if she wasn't
right. I went into the bathroom and switched on the lights. The man
in the mirror did look dreadful, his eyes bloodshot, his entire body
shivering, and his naturally dark skin rather yellowish if not downright
pale.

I felt of my forehead, but what good did that do? Surely I can't
die of this, I thought. But then I wasn't so sure. I remembered the
expression on the face of the attendant, and the concern of the people
who'd spoken to me in the street. Another fit of coughing over-
came me.

I must take action, I thought. But what action? What if the doctors gave me some powerful sedative which so numbed me that I
couldn't return to the town house? And what if their drugs affected
my concentration so that the switch could not be made? Good Lord,
I had not even tried to rise up out of this human body, a trick I knew
so well in my other form.

I didn't want to try it either. What if I couldn't get back! No, wait
for James for such experiments, and stay away from doctors with
needles!

The bell sounded. It was the tenderhearted female attendant, and
this time she had a sackful of medicines—bottles of bright red and
green liquids, and plastic containers of pills. "You really ought to call
a doctor," she said, as she placed all of these on the marble dresser in
a row. "Do you want for us to call a doctor?"

"Absolutely not," I said, pushing more money at her, and guiding
her out the door. But wait, she said. Would I let her take the dog out,
please, as he had just eaten?

Ah, yes, that was a marvelous idea. I pushed more bank notes into
her hand. I told Mojo to go with her, and do whatever she said. She
seemed fascinated by Mojo. She murmured something to the effect that
his head was larger than her own.

I returned to the bathroom and stared at the little bottles which she had brought. I was leery of these medicines! But then it wasn't very gentlemanly of me to return a sick body to James. Indeed, what if James didn't want it. No, not likely. He'd take the twenty million *and* the cough and the chills.

I drank a revolting gulp of the green medicine, fighting a convulsion of nausea, and then forced myself into the living room, where I collapsed at the desk.

There was hotel stationery there and a ballpoint pen which worked fairly well, in that slippery skittery fashion of ballpoint pens. I began to write, discovering that it was very difficult for me with these big fingers, but persevering, describing in hurried detail all that I had felt and seen.

On and on I wrote, though I could scarce keep my head up, and scarce breathe for the thickening of the cold. Finally, when there was no more paper and I could not read my own scrawl any longer, I stuffed these pages into an envelope, licked it and sealed it, and addressed it to myself care of my apartment in New Orleans, and then stuffed it into my shirt pocket, secure beneath my sweater, where it would not be lost.

Finally I stretched out on the floor. Sleep must take me now. It must cover many of the mortal hours remaining to me, for I had no strength for anything more.

But I did not sleep very deeply. I was too feverish, and too full of fear. I remember the gentle female attendant coming with Mojo, and telling me again that I was ill.

I remember a night maid wandering in, who seemed to fuss about for hours. I remember Mojo lying down beside me, and how warm he felt, and how I snuggled against him, loving the smell of him, the good woolly wonderful smell of his coat, even if it was nothing as strong as it would have been to me in my old body, and I did for one moment think I was back in France, in those old days.

But the memory of those old days had been in some way obliterated by this experience. Now and then I opened my eyes, saw an aureole about the burning lamp, saw the black windows reflecting the furnishings, and fancied I could hear the snow outside.

At some point, I climbed to my feet, and made for the bathroom, striking my head hard upon the doorframe, and falling to my knees. Mon Dieu, these little torments! How do mortals endure it? How did

I ever endure it? What a pain! Like liquid spreading under the skin.

But there were worse trials ahead. Sheer desperation forced me to use the toilet, as was required of me, to clean myself carefully afterwards, disgusting! And to wash my hands. Over and over, shivering with disgust, I washed my hands! When I discovered that the face of this body was now covered with a really thick shadow of rough beard, I laughed. What a crust it was over my upper lip and chin and even down into the collar of my shirt. What did I look like? A madman; a derelict. But I couldn't shave all this hair. I didn't have a razor and I'd surely cut my own throat if I did.

What a soiled shirt. I'd forgotten to put on any of the clothes I'd purchased, but wasn't it too late now for such a thing? With a dull woozy amazement, I saw by my watch that it was two o'clock. Good Lord, the hour of transformation was almost at hand.

"Come, Mojo," I said, and we sought the stairs rather than the elevator, which was no great feat as we were only one floor above the ground, and we slipped out through the quiet and near-deserted lobby and into the night.

Deep drifts of snow lay everywhere. The streets were clearly impassable to traffic, and there were times when I fell on my knees again, arms going deep into the snow, and Mojo licked my face as though he were trying to keep me warm. But I continued, struggling uphill, whatever my state of mind and body, until at last I turned the corner, and saw the lights of the familiar town house ahead.

The darkened kitchen was now quite filled with deep, soft snow. It seemed a simple matter to plow through it until I realized that a frozen layer—from the storm of the night before—lay beneath it, which was quite slick.

Nevertheless I managed to reach the living room safely, and lay down shivering on the floor. Only then did I realize I'd forgotten my overcoat, and all the money stuffed in its pockets. Only a few bills were left in my shirt. But no matter. The Body Thief would soon be here. I would have my own form back again, all my powers! And then how sweet it would be to reflect on everything, safe and sound in my digs in New Orleans, when illness and cold would mean nothing, when aches and pains would exist no more, when I was the Vampire Lestat again, soaring over the rooftops, reaching with outstretched hands for the distant stars.

The place seemed chilly compared to the hotel. I turned over once, peering at the little fireplace, and tried to light the logs with my mind. Then I laughed as I remembered I wasn't Lestat yet, but that James would soon arrive.

"Mojo, I can't endure this body a moment longer," I whispered. The dog sat before the front window, panting as he looked out into the night, his breath making steam on the dim glass.

I tried to stay awake, but I couldn't. The colder I became, the drowsier I became. And then a most frightening thought took hold of me. What if I couldn't rise out of this body at the appointed moment? If I couldn't make fire, if I couldn't read minds, if I couldn't . . .

Half wrapped in dreams, I tried the little psychic trick. I let my mind sink almost to the edge of dreams. I felt the low delicious vibratory warning that often precedes the rise of the spirit body. But nothing of an unusual nature happened. Again, I tried. "Go up," I said. I tried to picture the ethereal shape of myself tearing loose and rising unfettered to the ceiling. No luck. Might as well try to sprout feathered wings. And I was so tired, so full of pain. Indeed, I lay anchored in these hopeless limbs, fastened to this aching chest, scarce able to take a breath without a struggle.

But James would soon be here. The sorcerer, the one who knew the trick. Yes, James, greedy for his twenty million, would surely guide the whole process.

WHEN I opened my eyes again, it was to the light of day.

I sat bolt upright, staring before me. There could be no mistake. The sun was high in the heavens and spilling in a riot of light through the front windows and onto the lacquered floor. I could hear the sounds of traffic outside.

"My God," I whispered in English, for *Mon Dieu* simply doesn't mean the same thing. "My God, my God, my God."

I lay back down again, chest heaving, and too stunned for the moment to form a coherent thought or attitude, or to decide whether it was rage I felt or blind fear. Then slowly I lifted my wrist so that I might read the watch. Eleven forty-seven in the a.m.

Within less than fifteen minutes the fortune of twenty million dollars, held in trust at the downtown bank, would revert once more to Lestan Gregor, my pseudonymous self, who had been left here in this body by Raglan James, who had obviously not returned to this town house before morning to effect the switch which was part of our bargain and now, having forfeited that immense fortune, was very likely never to come back.

"Oh, God help me," I said aloud, the phlegm at once coming up in my throat, and the coughs sending deep stabs of pain into my chest. "I knew it," I whispered. "I knew it." What a fool I'd been, what an extraordinary fool.

You miserable wretch, I thought, you despicable Body Thief, you will not get away with it, damn you! How dare you do this to me, how dare you! And this body! This body in which you've left me, which is all I have with which to hunt you down, is truly truly sick.

By the time I staggered out into the street, it was twelve noon on the dot. But what did it matter? I couldn't remember the name or the location of the bank. I couldn't have given a good reason for going there anyway. Why should I claim the twenty million which in forty-five seconds would revert to me anyway? Indeed where was I to take this shivering mass of flesh?

To the hotel to reclaim my money and my clothing?

To the hospital for the medicine of which I was sorely in need?

Or to New Orleans to Louis, Louis who had to help me, Louis who was perhaps the only one who really could. And how was I to locate that miserable conniving self-destructive Body Thief if I did not have the help of Louis! Oh, but what would Louis do when I approached him? What would his judgment be when he realized what I'd done?

I was falling. I'd lost my balance. I reached for the iron railing too late. A man was rushing towards me. Pain exploded in the back of my head as it struck the step. I closed my eyes, clenching my teeth not to cry out. Then opened them again, and I saw above me the most serene blue sky.

"Call an ambulance," said the man to another beside him. Just dark featureless shapes against the glaring sky, the bright and wholesome sky.

"No!" I struggled to shout, but it came out a hoarse whisper. "I have to get to New Orleans!" In a rush of words I tried to explain about the hotel, the money, the clothing, would someone help me up, would someone call a taxi, I had to leave Georgetown for New Orleans at once.

Then I was lying very quietly in the snow. And I thought how lovely was the sky overhead, with the thin white clouds racing across it, and even these dim shadows that surrounded me, these people who whispered to one another so softly and furtively that I couldn't hear. And Mojo barking, Mojo barking and barking. I tried, but I couldn't speak, not even to tell him that everything would be fine, just perfectly fine.

A little girl came up. I could make out her long hair, and her little puff sleeves and a bit of ribbon blowing in the wind. She was looking down at me like the others, her face all shadows and the sky behind her gleaming frightfully, dangerously.

"Good Lord, Claudia, the sunlight, get out of it!" I cried.

"Lie still, mister, they're coming for you."

"Just lie quiet, buddy."

Where was she? Where had she gone? I shut my eyes, listening for the click of her heels on the pavement. Was that laughter I heard?

The ambulance. Oxygen mask. Needle. And I *understood.*

I was going to die in this body, and it would be so simple! Like a billion other mortals, I was going to die. Ah, this was the reason for all of it, the reason the Body Thief had come to me, the Angel of Death to give me the means which I had sought with lies and pride and self-deception. I was going to die.

And I didn't want to die!

"God, please, not like this, not in this body." I closed my eyes as I whispered. "Not yet, not now. Oh, please, I don't want to! I don't want to die. Don't let me die." I was crying, I was broken and terrified and crying. Oh, but it was perfect, wasn't it? Lord God, had a more perfect pattern ever revealed itself to me—the craven monster who had gone into the Gobi not to seek the fire from heaven but for pride, for pride, for pride.

My eyes were squeezed shut. I could feel the tears running down my face. "Don't let me die, please, please, don't let me die. Not now, not like this, not in this body! Help me!"

A small hand touched me, struggling to slip into mine, and then it was done, holding tight to me, tender and warm. Ah, so soft. So very little. And you know whose hand it is, you know, but you're too scared to open your eyes.

If she's there, then you are really dying. I can't open my eyes. I'm afraid, oh, so afraid. Shivering and sobbing, I held her little hand so tight that surely I was crushing it, but I wouldn't open my eyes.

Louis, she's here. She's come for me. Help me, Louis, please. I can't look at her. I won't. I can't get my hand loose from her! And where are you? Asleep in the earth, deep beneath your wild and neglected garden, with the winter sun pouring down on the flowers, asleep until the night comes again.

"Marius, help me. Pandora, wherever you are, help me. Khayman, come and help me. Armand, no hatred between us now. I need you! Jesse, don't let this happen to me."

Oh, the low and sorry murmur of a demon's prayer beneath the wailing of the siren. Don't open your eyes. Don't look at her. If you do, it's finished.

Did you call out for help in the last moments, Claudia? Were you afraid? Did you see the light like the fire of hell filling the air well, or was it the great and beautiful light filling the entire world with love?

We stood in the graveyard together, in the warm fragrant evening, full of distant stars and soft purple light. Yes, all the many colors of darkness. Look at her shining skin, the dark blood bruise of her lips, and deep color of her eyes. She was holding her bouquet of yellow and white chrysanthemums. I shall never forget that fragrance.

"Is my mother buried here?"

"I don't know, petite chérie. I never even knew her name." She was all rotted and stinking when I came upon her, the ants were crawling all over her eyes and into her open mouth.

"You should have found out her name. You should have done that for me. I would like to know where she is buried."

"That was half a century ago, chérie. Hate me for the larger things. Hate me, if you will, because you don't lie now at her side. Would she keep you warm if you did? Blood is warm, chérie. Come with me, and drink blood, as you and I know how to do. We can drink blood together unto the end of the world."

"Ah, you have an answer for everything." How cold her smile. In these shadows one can almost see the woman in her, defying the permanent stamp of child sweetness, with the inevitable enticement to kiss, to hold, to love.

"We are death, ma chérie, death is the final answer." I gathered her up in my arms, felt her tucked against me, kissed her, kissed her, and kissed her vampire skin. "There are no questions after that."

Her hand touched my forehead.

The ambulance was speeding, as if the siren were chasing it, as if the siren were the force driving it on. Her hand touched my eyelids. *I won't look at you!*

Oh, please, help me . . . the dreary prayer of the devil to his cohorts, as he tumbles deeper and deeper towards hell.

THIRTEEN

YES, I know where we are. You've been trying to bring me back here from the beginning, to the little hospital." How forlorn it looked now, so crude with its clay walls, and wooden shuttered windows, and the little beds lashed together out of barely finished wood. Yet she was there in the bed, wasn't she? I know the nurse, yes, and the old round-shouldered doctor, and I see you there in the bed—that's you, the little one with the curls on the top of the blanket, and Louis there . . .

All right, why am I here? I know this is a dream. It's not death. Death has no particular regard for people.

"Are you sure?" she said. She sat on the straight-back chair, golden hair done up in a blue ribbon, and there were blue satin slippers on her small feet. So that meant she was there in the bed, and there on the chair, my little French doll, my beauty, with the high rounded insteps, and the perfectly shaped little hands.

"And you, you're here with us and you're in a bed in the Washington, D.C., emergency room. You know you're dying down there, don't you?"

"Severe hypothermia, very possibly pneumonia. But how do we know what infections we've got? Hit him with antibiotics. There's no way we can get this man on oxygen now. If we send him to University, he'd end up in the hall there too."

"Don't let me die. Please . . . I'm so afraid."

"We're here with you, we're taking care of you. Can you tell me your name? Is there some family whom we can notify?"

"Go ahead, tell them who you really are," she said with a little silvery laugh, her voice always so delicate, so very pretty. I can feel her tender little lips, just to look at them. I used to like to press my finger against her lower lip, playfully, when I kissed her eyelids, and her smooth forehead.

"Don't be such a little smarty!" I said between my teeth. "Besides, who am I down there?"

"Not a human being, if that's what you mean. Nothing could make you human."

"All right, I'll give you five minutes. Why did you bring me here? What do you want me to say—that I'm sorry about what I did, taking you out of that bed and making you a vampire? Well, do you want the truth, the rock-bottom deathbed truth? I don't know if I am. I'm sorry you suffered. I'm sorry anybody has to suffer. But I can't say for certain that I'm sorry for that little trick."

"Aren't you the least little bit afraid of standing by yourself like this?"

"If the truth can't save me, nothing can." How I hated the smell of sickness around me, of all those little bodies, feverish and wet beneath their drab coverings, the entire dingy and hopeless little hospital of so many decades ago.

"My father who art in hell, Lestat be your name."

"And you? After the sun burnt you up in the air well in the Theatre of the Vampires, did you go to hell?"

Laughter, such high pure laughter, like glittering coins shaken loose from a purse.

"I'll never tell!"

"Now, I know this is a dream. That's all it's been from the beginning. Why would someone come back from the dead to say such trivial and inane things."

"Happens all the time, Lestat. Don't get so worked up. I want you to pay attention now. Look at these little beds, look at these children suffering."

"I took you away from it," I said.

"Aye, the way that Magnus took you away from your life, and gave you something monstrous and evil in return. You made me a slayer of my brothers and my sisters. All my sins have their origin in that moment, when you reached for me and lifted me from that bed."

"No, you can't blame it all on me. I won't accept it. Is the father parent to the crimes of his child? All right, so what if it is true. Who is there to keep count? That's the problem, don't you see? There is no one."

"So is it right, therefore, that we kill?"

"I gave you *life*, Claudia. It wasn't for all time, no, but it was life, and even our life is better than death."

"How you lie, Lestat. 'Even our life,' you say. The truth is, you think our accursed life is *better* than life itself. Admit it. Look at you down there in your human body. How you've hated it."

"It's true. I do admit it. But now, let's hear you speak from your heart, my little beauty, my little enchantress. Would you really have chosen death in that tiny bed rather than the life I gave you? Come now, tell me. Or is this like a mortal courtroom, where the judge can lie and the lawyers can lie, and only those on the stand must tell the truth?"

So thoughtfully she looked at me, one chubby hand playing with the embroidered hem of her gown. When she lowered her gaze the light shone exquisitely on her cheeks, on her small dark mouth. Ah, such a creation. The vampire doll.

"What did I know of choices?" she said, staring forward, eyes big and glassy and full of light. "I hadn't reached the age of reason when you did your filthy work, and by the way, Father, I've always wanted to know: Did you enjoy letting me suck the blood from your wrist?"

"That doesn't matter," I whispered. I looked away from her to the dying waif beneath the blanket. I saw the nurse in a ragged dress, hair pinned to the back of her neck, moving listlessly from bed to bed. "Mortal children are conceived in pleasure," I said, but I didn't know anymore if she was listening. I didn't want to look at her. "I can't lie. It doesn't matter if there is a judge or jury. I . . ."

"Don't try to talk. I've given you a combination of drugs that will help you. Your fever's going down already. We're drying up the congestion in your lungs."

"Don't let me die, please don't. It's all unfinished and it's monstrous. I'll go to hell if there is one, but I don't think there is. If there is, it's a hospital like this one, only it's filled with sick children, dying children. But I think there's just death."

"A hospital full of children?"

"Ah, look at the way she's smiling at you, the way she puts her hand on your forehead. Women love you, Lestat. She loves you, even in that body, look at her. Such love."

"Why shouldn't she care about me? She's a nurse, isn't she? And I'm a dying man."

"And such a beautiful dying man. I should have known you

wouldn't do this switch unless someone offered you a beautiful body. What a vain, superficial being you are! Look at that face. Better looking than your own face."

"I wouldn't go that far!"

She gave me the most sly smile, her face glowing in the dim, dreary room.

"Don't worry, I'm with you. I'll sit right here with you until you're better."

"I've seen so many humans die. I've caused their deaths. It's so simple and treacherous, the moment when life goes out of the body. They simply slip away."

"You're saying crazy things."

"No, I'm telling you the truth, and you know it. I can't say I'll make amends if I live. I don't think it's possible. Yet I'm scared to death of dying. Don't let go my hand."

"Lestat, why are we here?"

Louis?

I looked up. He was standing in the door of the crude little hospital, confused, faintly disheveled, the way he'd looked from the night I'd made him, not the wrathful blinded young mortal anymore, but the dark gentleman with the quiet in his eyes, with the infinite patience of a saint in his soul.

"Help me up," I said, "I have to get her from the little bed."

He put out his hand, but he was so confused. Didn't he share in that sin? No, of course not, because he was forever blundering and suffering, atoning for it all even as he did it. I was the devil. I was the only one who could gather her from the little bed.

Time now to lie to the doctor. "The child there, that is my child."

And he'd be oh, so glad to have one less burden.

"Take her, monsieur, and thank you." He looked gratefully at the gold coins as I tossed them on the bed. Surely I did that. Surely I didn't fail to help them. "Yes, thank you. God bless you."

I'm sure he will. He always has. I bless him too.

"Sleep now. As soon as there's a room available, we'll move you into it, you'll be more comfortable."

"Why are there so many here? Please don't leave me."

"No, I'll stay with you. I'll sit right here."

Eight o'clock. I was lying on the gurney, with the needle in my arm, and the plastic sack of fluid catching the light so beautifully, and I could see the clock perfectly. Slowly I turned my head.

A woman was there. She wore her coat now, very black against her white stockings and her thick soft white shoes. Her hair was in a thick coil on the back of her head, and she was reading. She had a broad face, of very strong bones and clear skin, and large hazel eyes. Her eyebrows were dark and perfectly drawn, and when she looked up at me, I loved her expression. She closed the book soundlessly and smiled.

"You're better," she said. A rich, soft voice. A bit of bluish shadow beneath her eyes.

"Am I?" The noise hurt my ears. So many people. Doors swooshing open and shut.

She stood up and came across the corridor, and took my hand in hers.

"Oh, yes, much better."

"Then I'll live?"

"Yes," she said. But she wasn't sure. Did she mean for me to see that she wasn't sure?

"Don't let me die in this body," I said, moistening my lips with my tongue. They felt so dry! Lord God, how I hated this body, hated the heave of the chest, hated even the voice coming from my lips, and the pain behind my eyes was unbearable.

"There you go again," she said, her smile brightening.

"Sit with me."

"I am. I told you I wouldn't leave. I'll stay here with you."

"Help me and you help the devil," I whispered.

"So you told me," she said.

"Want to hear the whole tale?"

"Only if you stay calm as you tell me, if you take your time."

"What a lovely face you have. What is your name?"

"Gretchen."

"You're a nun, aren't you, Gretchen?"

"How did you know that?"

"I could tell. Your hands, for one thing, the little silver wedding band, and something about your face, a radiance—the radiance of those who believe. And the fact that you stayed with me, Gretchen, when the others told you to go on. I know nuns when I see them. I'm the devil and when I behold goodness I know it."

Were those tears hovering in her eyes?

"You're teasing me," she said kindly. "There's a little tag here on my pocket. It says I'm a nun, doesn't it? Sister Marguerite."

"I didn't see it, Gretchen. I didn't mean to make you cry."

"You're better. Much better. I think you're going to be all right."

"I'm the devil, Gretchen. Oh, not Satan himself, Son of Morning, ben Sharar. But bad, very bad. Demon of the first rank, certainly."

"You're dreaming. It's the fever."

"Wouldn't that be splendid? Yesterday I stood in the snow and tried to imagine just such a thing—that all my life of evil was but the dream of a mortal man. No such luck, Gretchen. The devil needs you. The devil's crying. He wants you to hold his hand. You're not afraid of the devil, are you?"

"Not if he requires an act of mercy. Sleep now. They're coming to give you another shot. I'm not leaving. Here, I'll bring the chair to the side of the bed so you can hold my hand."

"What are you doing, Lestat?"

We were in our hotel suite now, much better place than that stinking hospital—I'll take a good hotel suite over a stinking hospital anytime—and Louis had drunk her blood, poor helpless Louis.

"Claudia, Claudia, listen to me. Come round, Claudia . . . You're ill, do you hear me? You must do as I tell you to get well." I bit through the flesh of my own wrist, and when the blood began to spill, I put it to her lips. "That's it, dear, more . . ."

"Try to drink a little of this." She slipped her hand behind my neck. Ah, the pain when I lifted my head.

"It tastes so thin. It's not like blood at all."

Her lids were heavy and smooth over her downcast eyes. Like a Grecian woman painted by Picasso, so simple she seemed, large-boned and fine and strong. Had anybody ever kissed her nun's mouth?

"People are dying here, aren't they? That's why the corridors are crowded. I hear people crying. It's an epidemic, isn't it?"

"It's a bad time," she said, her virginal lips barely moving. "But you'll be all right. I'm here."

Louis was so angry.

"But why, Lestat?"

Because she was beautiful, because she was dying, because I wanted to see if it would work. Because nobody wanted her and she was there, and I picked her up and held her in my arms. Because it was something I could accomplish, like the little candle flame in the church making another flame and still retaining its own light—my way of creating, my only way, don't you see? One moment there were two of us, and then we were three.

He was so heartbroken, standing there in his long black cloak, yet he could not stop looking at her, at her polished ivory cheeks, her tiny wrists. Imagine it, a child vampire! One of us.

"I understand."

Who spoke? I was startled, but it wasn't Louis, it was David, David standing near with his copy of the Bible. Louis looked up slowly. He didn't know who David was.

"Are we close to God when we create something out of nothing? When we pretend we are the tiny flame and we make other flames?"

David shook his head. "A bad mistake."

"And so is the whole world, then. She's our daughter—"

"I'm not your daughter. I'm my mama's daughter."

"No, dear, not anymore." I looked up at David. "Well, answer me."

"Why do you claim such high aims for what you did?" he asked, but he was so compassionate, so gentle. Louis was still horrified, staring at her, at her small white feet. Such seductive little feet.

"And then I decided to do it, I didn't care what he did with my body if he could put me into this human form for twenty-four hours so that I could see the sunlight, feel what mortals feel, know their weakness and their pain." I pressed her hand as I spoke.

She nodded, wiping my forehead again, feeling my pulse with her firm warm fingers.

". . . and I decided to do it, simply do it. Oh, I know it was wrong, wrong to let him go with all the power, but can you imagine, and now you see, I can't die in this body. The others won't even know what's happened to me. If they knew, they'd come . . ."

"The other vampires," she whispered.

"Yes." And then I was telling her all about them, about my search so long ago to find the others, thinking that if I only knew the history of things, it would explain the mystery . . . On and on I talked to her, explaining us, what we were, all about my trek through the centuries, and then the lure of the rock music, the perfect theatre for me, and what I'd wanted to do, about David and God and the Devil in the Paris café, and David by the fire with the Bible in his hand, saying God is not perfect. Sometimes my eyes were closed; sometimes they were open. She was holding my hand all the while.

People came and went. Doctors argued. A woman was crying.

Outside it was light again. I saw it when the door opened, and that cruel blast of cold air swept through the corridor. "How are we going to bathe all these patients?" a nurse asked. "That woman should be in isolation. Call the doctor. Tell him we have a case of meningitis on the floor."

"It's morning again, isn't it? You must be so tired, you've been with me all through the afternoon and the night. I'm so scared, but I know you have to go."

They were bringing in more sick people. The doctor came to her and told her they would have to turn all these gurneys so that their heads were against the wall.

The doctor told her she ought to go home. Several new nurses had just come on duty. She ought to rest.

Was I crying? The little needle hurt my arm, and how dry my throat was, how dry my lips.

"We can't even officially admit all these patients."

"Can you hear me, Gretchen?" I asked. "Can you follow what I'm saying?"

"You've asked me that over and over again," she said, "and each time I've told you that I can hear, that I can understand. I'm listening to you. I won't leave you."

"Sweet Gretchen. Sister Gretchen."

"I want to take you out of here with me."

"What did you say?"

"To my house, with me. You're much better now, your fever's way down. But if you stay here . . ." Confusion in her face. She put the cup to my lips again and I drank several gulps.

"I understand. Yes, please take me, please." I tried to sit up. "I'm afraid to stay."

"Not just yet," she said, coaxing me back down on the gurney. Then she pulled the tape off my arm and extracted that vicious little needle. Lord God, I had to piss! Was there no end to these revolting physical necessities? What in the hell was mortality? Shitting, pissing, eating, and then the same cycle all over again! Is this worth the vision of the sunshine? It wasn't enough to be dying. I had to piss. But I couldn't bear using that bottle again, even though I could scarce remember it.

"Why aren't you afraid of me?" I asked. "Don't you think I'm insane?"

"You only hurt people when you're a vampire," she said simply, "when you're in your rightful body. Isn't that true?"

"Yes," I said. "That's true. But you're like Claudia. You're not afraid of anything."

"You are playing her for a fool," said Claudia. "You're going to hurt her too."

"Nonsense, she doesn't believe it," I said. I sat down on the couch in the parlour of the little hotel, surveying the small fancy room, feeling very at home with these delicate old gilded furnishings. The eighteenth century, my century. Century of the rogue and the rational man. My most perfect time.

Petit-point flowers. Brocade. Gilded swords and the laughter of drunken men in the street below.

David was standing at the window, looking out over the low roofs of the colonial city. Had he ever been in this century before?

"No, never!" he said in awe. "Every surface is worked by hand, every measurement is irregular. How tenuous the hold of created things upon nature, as if it could slide back to the earth so easily."

"Leave, David," said Louis, "you don't belong here. We have to remain. There's nothing we can do."

"Now, that's a bit melodramatic," said Claudia. "Really." She wore that soiled little gown from the hospital. Well, I would soon fix that. I would sack the shops of laces and ribbons for her. I would buy silks for her, and tiny bracelets of silver, and rings set with pearls.

I put my arm around her. "Ah, how nice to hear someone speak the truth," I said. "Such fine hair, and now it will be fine forever."

I tried to sit up again, but it seemed impossible. They were rushing an emergency case through the corridor, two nurses on either side, and someone struck the gurney and the vibration moved through me. Then it was quiet, and the hands on the big clock moved with a little jerk. The man next to me moaned, and turned his head. There was a huge white bandage over his eyes. How naked his mouth looked.

"We have to get these people into isolation," said a voice.

"Come on, now, I'm taking you home."

And Mojo, what had become of Mojo? Suppose they'd come to take him away? This was a century in which they incarcerated dogs, simply for being dogs. I had to explain this to her. She was lifting me, or trying to do it, slipping her arm around my shoulders. Mojo barking in the town house. Was he trapped?

Louis was sad. "There's plague out there in the city."

"But that can't hurt you, David," I said.

"You're right," he said. "But there are other things . . ."

Claudia laughed. "She's in love with you, you know."

"You would have died of the plague," I said.

"Maybe it was not my time."

"Do you believe that, that we have our time?"

"No, actually I don't," she said. "Maybe it was just easier to blame you for everything. I never really knew right from wrong, you see."

"You had time to learn," I said.

"So have you, much more time than I ever had."

"Thank God you're taking me," I whispered. I was standing on my feet. "I'm so afraid," I said. "Just plain ordinary afraid."

"One less burden to the hospital," Claudia said with a ringing laugh, her little feet bobbing over the edge of the chair. She had on the fancy dress again, with the embroidery. Now that was an improvement.

"Gretchen the beautiful," I said. "It makes a flame in your cheeks when I say that."

She smiled as she brought my left arm over her shoulder now, and kept her right arm locked around my waist. "I'll take care of you," she whispered in my ear. "It isn't very far."

Beside her little car, in the bitter wind, I stood holding that stinking organ, and watching the yellow arc of piss, steam rising from it as it struck the melting snow. "Lord God," I said. "That feels almost good! What are human beings that they can take pleasure in such dreadful things!"

FOURTEEN

AT SOME point I began drifting in and out of sleep, aware that we were in a little car, and that Mojo was with us, panting heavily by my ear, and that we were driving through wooded snow-covered hills. I was wrapped in a blanket, and feeling miserably sick from the motion of the car. I was also shivering. I scarcely remembered our return to the town house, and the finding of

Mojo, waiting there so patiently. I was vaguely sensible that I could die in this gasoline-driven vehicle if another vehicle collided with it. It seemed painfully real, real as the pain in my chest. And the Body Thief had tricked me.

Gretchen's eyes were set calmly on the winding road ahead, the dappled sunlight making a soft lovely aureole about her head of all the fine little hairs which had come loose from her thick coiled braid of hair, and the smooth pretty waves of hair growing back from her temples. A nun, a beautiful nun, I thought, my eyes closing and opening as if of their own volition.

But why is this nun being so good to me? Because she is a nun?

It was quiet all around us. There were houses in the trees, set upon knolls, and in little valleys, and very close to one another. A rich suburb, perhaps, with those small-scale wooden mansions rich mortals sometimes prefer to the truly palatial homes of the last century.

At last we entered a drive beside one of these dwellings, passing through a copse of bare-limbed trees, and came to a gentle halt beside a small gray-shingled cottage, obviously a servants' quarters or guest-house of sorts, at some remove from the main residence.

The rooms were cozy and warm. I wanted to sink down into the clean bed, but I was too soiled for that, and insisted that I be allowed to bathe this distasteful body. Gretchen strongly protested. I was sick, she said. I couldn't be bathed now. But I refused to listen. I found the bathroom and wouldn't leave it.

Then I fell asleep again, leaning against the tile as Gretchen filled the tub. The steam felt sweet to me. I could see Mojo lying by the bed, the wolflike sphinx, watching me through the open door. Did she think he looked like the devil?

I felt groggy and impossibly weak and yet I was talking to Gretchen, trying to explain to her how I had come to be in this predicament, and how I had to reach Louis in New Orleans so that he could give me the powerful blood.

In a low voice, I told her many things in English, only using French when for some reason I couldn't find the word I wanted, rambling on about the France of my time, and the crude little colony of New Orleans where I had existed after, and how wondrous this age was, and how I'd become a rock star for a brief time, because I thought that as a symbol of evil I'd do some good.

Was this human to want her understanding, this desperate fear that I would die in her arms, and no one would ever know who I'd been or what had taken place?

Ah, but the others, they knew, and they had not come to help me.

I told her all about this too. I described the ancients, and their disapproval. What was there that I did not tell her? But she must understand, exquisite nun that she was, how much I'd wanted as the rock singer to do good.

"That's the only way the literal Devil can do good," I said. "To play himself in a tableau to expose evil. Unless one believes that he is doing good when he is doing evil, but that would make a monster out of God, wouldn't it?—the Devil is simply part of the divine plan."

She seemed to hear these words with critical attention. But it didn't surprise me when she answered that the Devil had not been part of God's plan. Her voice was low and full of humility. She was taking my soiled clothes off me as she spoke, and I don't think she wanted to speak at all, but she was trying to calm me. The Devil had been the most powerful of the angels, she said, and he had rejected God out of pride. Evil could not be part of God's plan.

When I asked her if she knew all the arguments against this, and how illogical it was, how illogical all of Christianity was, she said calmly that it didn't matter. What mattered was doing good. That was all. It was simple.

"Ah, yes, then you understand."

"Perfectly," she said to me.

But I knew that she did not.

"You are good to me," I said. I kissed her gently on the cheek, as she helped me into the warm water.

I lay back in the tub, watching her bathe me and noting that it felt good to me, the warm water against my chest, the soft strokes of the sponge on my skin, perhaps better than anything I had endured so far. But how long the human body felt! How strangely long my arms. An image came back to me from an old film—of Frankenstein's monster lumbering about, swinging his hands as if they didn't belong at the ends of his arms. I felt as if I were that monster. In fact, to say that I felt entirely monstrous as a human is to hit the perfect truth.

Seems I said something about it. She cautioned me to be quiet. She said that my body was strong and fine, and not unnatural. She looked deeply worried. I felt a little ashamed, letting her wash my hair, and my face. She explained it was the sort of thing which a nurse did all the time.

She said she had spent her life in the foreign missions, nursing the sick, in places so soiled and ill equipped that even the overcrowded Washington hospital seemed like a dream compared to them.

I watched her eyes move over my body, and then I saw the flush in her cheeks, and the way that she looked at me, overcome with shame, and confusion. How curiously innocent she was.

I smiled to myself, but I feared she would be hurt by her own carnal feelings. What a cruel joke on us both that she found this body enticing. But there was no doubt that she did, and it stirred my blood, my human blood, even in my fever and exhaustion. Ah, this body was always struggling for something.

I could barely stand as she dried me all over with the towel, but I was determined to do it. I kissed the top of her head, and she looked up at me, in a slow vague way, intrigued and mystified. I wanted to kiss her again, but I hadn't the strength. She was very careful in drying my hair, and gentle as she dried my face. No one had touched me in this manner in a very long time. I told her I loved her for the sheer kindness of it.

"I hate this body so much; it's hell to be in it."

"It's that bad?" she asked. "To be human?"

"You don't have to humor me," I said. "I know you don't believe the things I've told you."

"Ah, but our fantasies are like our dreams," she said with a serious little frown. "They have meaning."

Suddenly, I saw my reflection in the mirror of the medicine cabinet—this tall caramel-skinned man with thick brown hair, and the large-boned soft-skinned woman beside him. The shock was so great, my heart stopped.

"Dear God, help me," I whispered. "I want my body back." I felt like weeping.

She urged me to lie down against the pillows of the bed. The warmth of the room felt good. She began to shave my face, thank God! I hated the feeling of the hair on it. I told her I'd been clean-shaven, as all men of fashion were, when I died, and once we were made vampires we remained the same forever. We grew whiter and whiter, that was true, and stronger and stronger; and our faces became smoother. But our hair was forever the same length, and so were our fingernails and whatever beard we had; and I had not had that much to begin with.

"Was this transformation a painful thing?" she asked.

"It was painful because I fought. I didn't want it to happen. I didn't really know what was being done to me. It seemed some monster out of the medieval past had captured me, and dragged me out of the civilized city. You must remember in those years that Paris was a wonderfully civilized place. Oh, you would think it barbaric beyond description if you were spirited there now, but to a country lord from a filthy castle, it was so exciting, what with the theatres, and the opera, and the balls at court. You can't imagine. And then this tragedy, this demon coming out of the dark and taking me to his tower. But the act itself, the Dark Trick? It isn't painful, it's ecstasy. And then your eyes are opened, and all humanity is beautiful to you in a way that you never realized before."

I put on the clean skivvy shirt which she gave to me, and climbed under the covers, and let her bring the covers up to my chin. I felt as if I were floating. Indeed, this was one of the most pleasant feelings I'd experienced since I'd become mortal—this feeling like drunkenness. She felt my pulse and my forehead. I could see the fear in her, but I didn't want to believe it.

I told her that the real pain for me as an evil being was that I understood goodness, and I respected it. I had never been without a conscience. But all my life—even as a mortal boy—I had always been required to go against my conscience to obtain anything of intensity or value.

"But how? What do you mean?" she asked.

I told her that I had run off with a band of actors when I was a boy, committing an obvious sin of disobedience. I had committed the sin of fornication with one of the young women of the troupe. Yet those days, acting on the village stage and making love, had seemed of inestimable value! "You see, that's when I was alive, merely alive. The trivial sins of a boy! After I was dead, every step I took in the world was a commitment to sin, and yet at every turn I saw the sensual and the beautiful."

How could this be, I asked her. When I'd made Claudia a child vampire, and Gabrielle, my mother, into a vampire beauty, I'd been reaching again for an intensity! I'd found it irresistible. And in those moments no concept of sin made sense.

I said more, speaking again of David and his vision of God and the Devil in the café, and of how David thought that God was not perfect, that God was learning all the time, and that, indeed, the Devil learned so much that he came to despise his job and beg to be let out of it. But I knew I had told her all these things before in the hospital when she'd been holding my hand.

There were moments when she stopped her fussing with the pillows, and with pills and glasses of water, and merely looked at me. How still her face was, how emphatic her expression, the dark thick lashes surrounding her paler eyes, her large soft mouth so eloquent of kindness.

"I know you are good," I said. "I love you for it. Yet I would give it to you, the Dark Blood, to make you immortal—to have you with me in eternity because you are so mysterious to me and so strong."

There was a layer of silence around me, a dull roaring in my ears, and a veil over my eyes. I watched motionless as she lifted a syringe, tested it apparently by squirting a tiny bit of silver liquid into the air, and then put the needle into my flesh. The faint burning sensation was very far away, very unimportant.

When she gave me a large glass of orange juice I drank this greedily. Hmmm. Now this was something to taste, thick like blood, but full of sweetness and strangely like devouring light itself.

"I'd forgotten all about such things," I said. "How good it tastes, better than wine, really. I should have drunk it before. And to think I would have gone back without knowing it." I sank down into the pillow and looked up at the bare rafters of the low sloping ceiling. Nice clean little room, very white. Very simple. Her nun's cell. Snow was falling gently outside the little window. I counted twelve little panes of glass.

I was slipping in and out of sleep. I vaguely recall her trying to make me drink soup and that I couldn't do it. I was shaking, and terrified that those dreams would come again. I didn't want Claudia to come. The light of the little room burnt my eyes. I told her about Claudia haunting me, and the little hospital.

"Full of children," she said. Hadn't she remarked on this before. How puzzled she looked. She spoke softly of her work in the missions . . . with children. In the jungles of Venezuela and in Peru.

"Don't speak anymore," she said.

I knew I was frightening her. I was floating again, in and out of darkness, aware of a cool cloth on my forehead, and laughing again at this weightless feeling. I told her that in my regular body I could fly through the air. I told her how I had gone into the light of the sun above the Gobi Desert.

Now and then, I opened my eyes with a start, shaken to discover myself here. Her small white room.

In the burnished light, I saw a crucifix on the wall, with a bleeding Christ; and a statue of the Virgin Mary atop a small bookcase—the old familiar image of the Mediatrix of All Graces, with her bowed head and outstretched hands. Was that Saint Rita there with the red wound in her forehead? Ah, all the old beliefs, and to think they were alive in this woman's heart.

I squinted, trying to read the larger titles on the books on her shelves: Aquinas, Maritain, Teilhard de Chardin. The sheer effort of interpreting these various names to mean Catholic philosophers exhausted me. Yet I read other titles, my mind feverish and unable to rest. There were books on tropical diseases, childhood diseases, on child psychology. I could make out a framed picture on the wall near the crucifix, of veiled and uniformed nuns together, perhaps at a ceremony. If she was one of them, I couldn't tell, not with these mortal eyes, and hurting the way they were. The nuns wore short blue robes, and blue and white veils.

She held my hand. I told her again I had to go to New Orleans. I had to live to reach my friend Louis, who would help me recover my body. I described Louis to her—how he existed beyond the reach of the modern world in a tiny unlighted house behind his ramshackle garden. I explained that he was weak, but he could give me the vampiric blood, and then I'd be a vampire again, and I'd hunt the Body Thief and have my old form restored to me. I told her how very human Louis was, that he would not give me much vampiric strength, but I could not find the Body Thief unless I had a preternatural body.

"So this body will die," I said, "when he gives the blood to me. You are saving it for death." I was weeping. I realized I was speaking French, but it seemed that she understood, because she told me in French that I must rest, that I was delirious.

"I am with you," she said in French, very slowly and carefully. "I will protect you." Her warm gentle hand was over mine. With such care, she brushed the hair back from my forehead.

Darkness fell around the little house.

There was a fire burning in the little hearth, and Gretchen was lying beside me. She had put on a long flannel gown, very thick and white; and her hair was loose, and she was holding me as I shivered. I liked the feel of her hair against my arm. I held on to her, frightened I'd hurt her. Over and over again, she wiped my face with a cool cloth. She forced me to drink the orange juice or cold water. The hours of the night were deepening and so was my panic.

"I won't let you die," she whispered in my ear. But I heard the fear which she couldn't disguise. Sleep rolled over me, thinly, so that the room retained its shape, its color, its light. I called upon the others again, begging Marius to help me. I began to think of terrible things— that they were all there as so many small white statues with the Virgin and with Saint Rita, watching me, and refusing to help.

Sometime before dawn, I heard voices. A doctor had come—a tired young man with sallow skin and red-rimmed eyes. Once again, a needle was put into my arm. I drank greedily when the ice water was given me. I could not follow the doctor's low murmuring, nor was I meant to understand it. But the cadences of the voice were calm and obviously reassuring. I caught the words "epidemic" and "blizzard" and "impossible conditions."

When the door shut, I begged her to come back. "Next to your beating heart," I whispered in her ear as she lay down at my side. How sweet this was, her tender heavy limbs, her large shapeless breasts against my chest, her smooth leg against mine. Was I too sick to be afraid?

"Sleep now," she said. "Try not to worry." At last a deep sleep was coming to me, deep as the snow outside, as the darkness.

"Don't you think it's time you made your confession?" asked Claudia. "You know you really are hanging by the proverbial thread." She was sitting in my lap, staring up at me, hands on my shoulders, her little upturned face not an inch from mine.

My heart shrank, exploding in pain, but there was no knife, only these little hands clutching me, and the perfume of crushed roses rising from her shimmering hair.

"No. I can't make my confession," I said to her. How my voice trembled. "Oh, Lord God, what do you want of me!"

"You're not sorry! You've never been sorry! Say it. Say the truth! You deserved the knife when I put it through your heart, and you know it, you've always known it!"

"No!"

Something in me broke as I stared down at her, at the exquisite face in its frame of fine-spun hair. I lifted her, and rose, placing her in the chair before me and I dropped to my knees at her feet.

"Claudia, listen to me. I didn't begin it. I didn't make the world! It was always there, this evil. It was in the shadows, and it caught me, and made me part of it, and I did what I felt I must. Don't laugh at me, please, don't turn your head away. I didn't make evil! I didn't make myself!"

How perplexed she was, staring at me, watching me, and then her small full mouth spread beautifully in a smile.

"It wasn't all anguish," I said, my fingers digging into her little shoulders. "It wasn't hell. Tell me it wasn't. Tell me there was happiness. Can devils be happy? Dear God, I don't understand."

"You don't understand, but you always *do* something, don't you?"

"Yes, and I'm not sorry. I'm not. I would roar it from the rooftops right up into the dome of heaven. Claudia, I would do it again!" A great sigh passed out of me. I repeated the words, my voice growing louder. "*I would do it again!*"

Stillness in the room.

Her calm remained unbroken. Was she enraged? Surprised? Impossible to know as I looked into her expressionless eyes.

"Oh you are evil, my father," she said in a soft voice. "How can you abide it?"

David turned from the window. He stood over her shoulder, looking down at me as I stayed there on my knees.

"I am the ideal of my kind," I said. "I am the perfect vampire. You are looking at the Vampire Lestat when you look at me. No one outshines this figure you see before you—no one!" Slowly I rose to my feet. "I am not time's fool, nor a god hardened by the millennia; I am not the trickster in the black cape, nor the sorrowful wanderer. I have a conscience. I know right from wrong. I know what I do, and yes, I do it. I am the Vampire Lestat. That's your answer. Do with it what you will."

. . .

DAWN. Colorless and bright over the snow. Gretchen slept, cradling me.

SHE didn't wake when I sat up and reached for the glass of water. Tasteless, but cool.

Then her eyes opened, and she sat up with a start, her dark blond hair tumbling down around her face, dry and clean and full of thin light.

I kissed her warm cheek, and felt her fingers on my neck, and then again across my forehead.

"You brought me through it," I said, my voice hoarse and shaky. Then I lay back down on the pillow, and I felt the tears once more on my cheeks, and closing my eyes, I whispered, "Good-bye, Claudia," hoping that Gretchen wouldn't hear.

WHEN I opened my eyes again, she had a big bowl of broth for me, which I drank, finding it almost good. There were apples and oranges cut open and glistening upon a plate. I ate these hungrily, amazed at the crispness of the apples, and the chewy fibrous quality of the oranges. Then came a hot brew of strong liquor and honey and sour lemon, which I loved so much that she hurried to make more of it for me.

I thought again how like the Grecian women of Picasso she was, large and fair. Her eyebrows were dark brown and her eyes light— almost a pale green—which gave her face a look of dedication and innocence. She was not young, this woman, and that, too, enhanced her beauty very much for me.

There was something selfless and distracted in her expression, in the way that she nodded and told me I was better when I asked.

She looked perpetually deep in thought. For a long moment, she remained, looking down at me as if I puzzled her, and then very slowly she bent and pressed her lips to mine. A raw vibration of excitement passed through me.

Once more I slept.

No dreams came to me.

It was as if I'd always been human, always in this body, and oh, so grateful for this soft clean bed.

Afternoon. Patches of blue beyond the trees.

In a trance, it seemed, I watched her build up the fire. I watched the glow on her smooth bare feet. Mojo's gray hair was covered with light powdery snow, as he ate quietly and steadily from a plate between his paws, now and then looking up at me.

My heavy human body was simmering still in its fever, but cooler, better, its aches less acute, its shivering gone now entirely. Ah, why has she done all this for me? Why? And what can I do for her, I thought. I wasn't afraid of dying anymore. But when I thought of what lay ahead—the Body Thief must be caught—I felt a stab of panic. And for another night I would be too ill to leave here.

Again, we lay wrapped in each other's arms, dozing, letting the light grow dim outside, the only sound that of Mojo's labored breathing. The little fire blazed. The room was warm and still. All the world seemed warm and still. The snow began to fall; and soon the soft merciless darkness of the night came down.

A wave of protectiveness passed over me when I looked at her sleeping face, when I thought of the soft distracted look I had seen in her eyes. Even her voice was tinged with a deep melancholy. There was something about her which suggested a profound resignation. Whatever happened, I would not leave her, I thought, until I knew what I could do to repay her. Also I liked her. I liked the darkness inside her, the concealed quality of her, and the simplicity of her speech and movements, the candor in her eyes.

When I woke next, the doctor was there again—the same young fellow with the sallow skin and tired face, though he did look somewhat rested, and his white coat was very clean and fresh. He had put a tiny bit of cold metal against my chest, and was obviously listening to my heart or lungs or some other noisy internal organ for a bit of significant information. His hands were covered with slick ugly plastic gloves. And he was speaking to Gretchen in a low voice, as if I weren't there, about the continuing troubles at the hospital.

Gretchen was dressed in a simple blue dress, rather like a nun's dress, I thought, except that it was short, and beneath it she wore black stockings. Her hair was beautifully mussed and straight and clean and made me think of the hay which the princess spun into gold in the tale of Rumpelstiltskin.

Again came the memory of Gabrielle, my mother, of the eerie and nightmarish time after I'd made her a vampire, and she had cut her yellow hair, and it had all grown back within the space of a day while she slept the deathlike sleep in the crypt, and she'd almost gone mad when she realized it. I remembered her screaming and screaming before she could be calmed. I didn't know why I thought of it, except that I loved this woman's hair. She was nothing like Gabrielle. Nothing.

At last the doctor was finished with his poking and prodding and listening, and went away to confer with her. Curse my mortal hearing. But I knew I was almost cured. And when he stood over me again, and told me I would now be "fine" and needed only a few more days' rest, I said quietly that it was Gretchen's nursing which had done it.

To this he gave an emphatic nod and a series of unintelligible murmurs, and then off he went into the snow, his car making a faint grinding noise outside as he passed through the driveway.

I felt so clearheaded and good that I wanted to cry. Instead I drank some more of the delicious orange juice, and I began to think of things . . . remember things.

"I need to leave you for only a little while," Gretchen said. "I have to get some food."

"Yes, and I shall pay for this food," I said. I laid my hand on her wrist. Though my voice was still weak and hoarse, I told her about the hotel, that my money was there in my coat. It was enough money for me to pay her for my care as well as for the food, and she must get it. The key must be in my clothes, I explained.

She had put my clothes on hangers, and now she did find the key in the shirt pocket.

"See?" I said with a little laugh. "I have been telling you the truth about everything."

She smiled, and her face was filled with warmth. She said she would go to the hotel and get my money for me, if I would agree to lie quiet. It wasn't such a good idea to leave money lying about, even in a fine hotel.

I wanted to answer, but I was so sleepy. Then, through the little window, I saw her walking through the snow, towards the little car. I saw her climb inside. What a strong figure she was, very sturdy of limb, but with fair skin and a softness to her that made her lovely to behold and most embraceable. I was frightened, however, on account of her leaving me.

When I opened my eyes again, she was standing there with my overcoat over her arm. Lots of money, she said. She'd brought it all back. She'd never seen so much money in packets and wads. What a strange person I was. There was something like twenty-eight thousand dollars there. She'd closed out my account at the hotel. They'd been worried about me. They had seen me run off in the snow. They had made her sign a receipt for everything. This bit of paper she gave to me, as if it was important. She had my other possessions with her, the clothing I had purchased, which was still in its sacks and boxes.

I wanted to thank her. But where were the words? I would thank her when I came back to her in my own body.

After she had put away all the clothing, she fixed us a simple supper of broth again and bread with butter. We ate this together, with a bottle of wine, of which I drank much more than she thought permissible. I must say that this bread and butter and wine was about the best human food I'd tasted so far. I told her so. And I wanted more of the wine, please, because this drunkenness was absolutely sublime.

"Why did you bring me here?" I asked her.

She sat down on the side of the bed, looking towards the fire, playing with her hair, not looking at me. She started to explain again about the overcrowding at the hospital, the epidemic.

"No, why did you do it? There were others there."

"Because you're not like anyone I've ever known," she said. "You make me think of a story I once read . . . about an angel forced to come down to earth in a human body."

With a flush of pain, I thought of Raglan James telling me that I looked like an angel. I thought of my other body roaming the world, powerful and under his loathsome charge.

She gave a sigh as she looked at me. She was puzzled.

"When this is finished, I'll come back to you in my real body," I said. "I'll reveal myself to you. It may mean something to you to know that you were not deceived; and you are so strong, I suspect the truth won't hurt you."

"The truth?"

I explained that often when we revealed ourselves to mortals we drove them mad—for we were unnatural beings, and yet we did not know anything about the existence of God or the Devil. In sum, we were like a religious vision without revelation. A mystic experience, but without a core of truth.

She was obviously enthralled. A subtle light came into her eyes. She asked me to explain how I appeared in the other form.

I described to her how I had been made a vampire at the age of twenty. I'd been tall for those times, blond, with light-colored eyes. I told her again about burning my skin in the Gobi. I feared the Body Thief intended to keep my body for good, that he was probably off someplace, hidden from the rest of the tribe, trying to perfect his use of my powers.

She asked me to describe flying to her.

"It's more like floating, simply rising at will—propelling yourself in this direction or that by decision. It's a defiance of gravity quite unlike the flight of natural creatures. It's frightening. It's the most frightening of all our powers; and I think it hurts us more than any other power; it fills us with despair. It is the final proof that we aren't human. We fear perhaps we will one night leave the earth and never touch it again."

I thought of the Body Thief using this power. I had seen him use it.

"I don't know how I could have been so foolish as to let him take a body as strong as mine," I said. "I was blinded by the desire to be human."

She was merely looking at me. Her hands were clasped in front of her and she was looking at me steadily and calmly with large hazel eyes.

"Do you believe in God?" I asked. I pointed to the crucifix on the wall. "Do you believe in these Catholic philosophers whose books are on the shelf?"

She thought for a long moment. "Not in the way you ask," she said.

I smiled. "How then?"

"My life has been one of self-sacrifice ever since I can remember. That is what I believe in. I believe that I must do everything I can to lessen misery. That is all I can do, and that is something enormous. It is a great power, like your power of flight."

I was mystified. I realized that I did not think of the work of a nurse as having to do with power. But I saw her point completely.

"To try to know God," she said, "this can be construed as a sin of pride, or a failure of imagination. But all of us know misery when we see it. We know sickness; hunger; deprivation. I try to lessen these things. It's the bulwark of my faith. But to answer you truly—yes, I do believe in God and in Christ. So do you."

"No, I don't," I said.

"When you were feverish you did. You spoke of God and the Devil the way I've never heard anyone else speak of them."

"I spoke of tiresome theological arguments," I said.

"No, you spoke of the irrelevance of them."

"You think so?"

"Yes. You know good when you see it. You said you did. So do I. I devote my life to trying to do it."

I sighed. "Yes, I see," I said. "Would I have died had you left me in the hospital?"

"You might have," she said. "I honestly don't know."

It was very pleasurable merely to look at her. Her face was large with few contours and nothing of elegant aristocratic beauty. But beauty she had in abundance. And the years had been gentle with her. She was not worn from care.

I sensed a tender brooding sensuality in her, a sensuality which she herself did not trust or nurture.

"Explain this to me again," she said. "You spoke of being a rock singer because you wanted to do good? You wanted to be good by being a symbol of evil? Talk of this some more."

I told her yes. I told her how I had done it, gathering the little band, Satan's Night Out, and making them professionals. I told her that I had failed; there had been a war among our kind, I myself had been taken away by force, and the entire debacle had happened without a rupture in the rational fabric of the mortal world. I had been forced back into invisibility and irrelevance.

"There's no place for us on earth," I said. "Perhaps there was once, I don't know. The fact that we exist is no justification. Hunters drove wolves from the world. I thought if I revealed our existence that hunters would drive us from the world too. But it wasn't to be. My brief career was a string of illusions. No one believes in us. And that's how it's meant to be. Perhaps we are to die of despair, to vanish from the world very slowly, and without a sound.

"Only I can't bear it. I can't bear to be quiet and be nothing, and to take life with pleasure, and to see the creations and accomplishments of mortals all around me, and not to be part of them, but to be Cain. The lonely Cain. That's the world to me, you see—what mortals do and have done. It isn't the great natural world at all. If it was the natural world, then maybe I would have had a better time of it being immortal than I did. It's the accomplishments of mortals. The paintings of Rembrandt, the memorials of the capital city in the snow, great cathedrals. And we are cut off eternally from such things, and rightfully so, and yet we see them with our vampire eyes."

"Why did you change bodies with a mortal man?" she asked.

"To walk in the sun again for one day. To think and feel and breathe like a mortal. Maybe to test a belief."

"What was the belief?"

"That being mortal again was what we all wanted, that we were sorry that we'd given it up, that immortality wasn't worth the loss of our human souls. But I know now I was wrong."

I thought of Claudia suddenly. I thought of my fever dreams. A leaden stillness came over me. When I spoke again, it was a quiet act of will.

"I'd much rather be a vampire," I said. "I don't like being mortal. I don't like being weak, or sick, or fragile, or feeling pain. It's perfectly awful. I want my body back as soon as I can get it from that thief."

She seemed mildly shocked by this. "Even though you kill when you are in your other body, even though you drink human blood, and you hate it and you hate yourself."

"I don't hate it. And I don't hate myself. Don't you see? That's the contradiction. I've never hated myself."

"You told me you were evil, you said when I helped you I was helping the devil. You wouldn't say those things if you didn't hate it."

I didn't answer. Then I said, "My greatest sin has always been that I have a wonderful time being myself. My guilt is always there; my moral abhorrence for myself is always there; but I have a good time. I'm strong; I'm a creature of great will and passion. You see, that's the core of the dilemma for me—how can I enjoy being a vampire so much, how can I enjoy it if it's evil? Ah, it's an old story. Men work it out when they go to war. They tell themselves there is a cause. Then they experience the thrill of killing, as if they were merely beasts. And beasts do know it, they really do. The wolves know it. They know the sheer thrill of tearing to pieces the prey. I know it."

She seemed lost in her thoughts for a long time. I reached out and touched her hand.

"Come, lie down and sleep," I said. "Lie beside me again. I won't hurt you. I can't. I'm too sick." I gave a little laugh. "You're very beautiful," I said. "I wouldn't think of hurting you. I only want to be near you. The late night's coming again, and I wish you would lie with me here."

"You mean everything you say, don't you?"

"Of course."

"You realize you are like a child, don't you? You have a great simplicity to you. The simplicity of a saint."

I laughed. "Dearest Gretchen, you're misunderstanding me in a crucial way. But then again, maybe you aren't. If I believed in God, if I believed in salvation, then I suppose I would have to be a saint."

She reflected for a long time, then she told me in a low voice that she had taken a leave of absence from the foreign missions only a month ago. She had come up from French Guiana to Georgetown to study at the university, and she worked only as a volunteer at the hospital. "Do you know the real reason why I took the leave of absence?" she asked me.

"No; tell me."

"I wanted to know a man. The warmth of being close to a man. Just once, I wanted to know it. I'm forty years old, and I've never known a man. You spoke of moral abhorrence. You used those words. I had an abhorrence for my virginity—of the sheer perfection of my chastity. It seemed, no matter what one believed, to be a cowardly thing."

"I understand," I said. "Surely to do good in the missions has nothing to do, finally, with chastity."

"No, they are connected," she said. "But only because hard work is possible when one is single-minded, and married to no one but Christ."

I confessed I knew what she meant. "But if the self-denial becomes an obstacle to work," I said, "then it's better to know the love of a man, isn't it?"

"That is what I thought," she said. "Yes. Know this experience, and then return to God's work."

"Exactly."

In a slow dreamy voice, she said: "I've been looking for the man. For the moment."

"That's the answer, then, as to why you brought me here."

"Perhaps," she said. "God knows, I was so frightened of everyone else. I'm not frightened of you." She looked at me as if her own words had left her surprised.

"Come, lie down and sleep. There's time for me to heal and for you to be certain it's what you really want. I wouldn't dream of forcing you, of doing anything cruel to you."

"But why, if you're the devil, can you speak with such kindness?"

"I told you, that's the mystery. Or it's the answer, one or the other. Come, come lie beside me."

I closed my eyes. I felt her climbing beneath the covers, the warm pressure of her body beside me, her arm slipping across my chest.

"You know," I said, "this is almost good, this aspect of being human."

I was half asleep when I heard her whisper:

"I think there's a reason you took *your* leave of absence," she said. "You may not know it."

"Surely you don't believe me," I murmured, the words running together sluggishly. How delicious it was to slip my arm around her again, to tuck her head against my neck. I was kissing her hair, loving the soft springiness of it against my lips.

"There is a secret reason you came down to earth," she said, "that you came into the body of a man. Same reason that Christ did it."

"And that is?"

"Redemption," she said.

"Ah, yes, to be saved. Now wouldn't that be lovely?"

I wanted to say more, how perfectly impossible it was to even consider such a thing, but I was sliding away, into a dream. And I knew that Claudia would not be there.

Maybe it wasn't a dream after all, only a memory. I was with David in the Rijksmuseum and we were looking at the great painting by Rembrandt.

To be saved. What a thought, what a lovely, extravagant, and impossible thought . . . How nice to have found the one mortal woman in all the world who would seriously think of such a thing.

And Claudia wasn't laughing anymore. Because Claudia was dead.

FIFTEEN

EARLY morning, just before the sun comes. The time when in the past I was often in meditation, tired, and half in love with the changing sky.

I bathed slowly and carefully, the small bathroom full of dim light and steam around me. My head was clear, and I felt happiness, as if the sheer respite from sickness was a form of joy. I shaved my face slowly, until it was perfectly smooth, and then, delving into the little cabinet behind the mirror, I found what I wanted—the little rubber sheaths that would keep her safe from me, from my planting a child within her, from this body giving her some other dark seed that might harm her in ways I could not foresee.

Curious little objects, these—gloves for the organ. I would love to have thrown them away, but I was determined that I would not make the mistakes I had made before.

Silently, I shut the little mirror door. And only then did I see a telegram message taped above it—a rectangle of yellowed paper with the words in pale indistinct print:

GRETCHEN, COME BACK, WE NEED YOU. NO QUESTIONS ASKED. WE ARE WAITING FOR YOU.

The date of the communication was very recent—only a few days before. And the origin was Caracas, Venezuela.

I approached the bed, careful not to make a sound, and I laid the small safety devices on the table in readiness, and I lay with her again, and began to kiss her tender sleeping mouth.

Slowly, I kissed her cheeks, and the flesh beneath her eyes. I wanted to feel her eyelashes through my lips. I wanted to feel the flesh of her throat. Not for killing, but for kissing; not for possession, but for this brief physical union that will take nothing from either one of us; yet bring us together in a pleasure so acute it is like pain.

She waked slowly under my touch.

"Trust in me," I whispered. "I won't hurt you."

"Oh, but I want you to hurt me," she said in my ear.

Gently, I pulled the flannel gown off her. She lay back looking up at me, her breasts as fair as the rest of her, the areolas of her nipples very small and pink and the nipples themselves hard. Her belly was smooth, her hips broad. A lovely dark shadow of brown hair lay between her legs, glistening in the light coming through the windows. I bent down and kissed this hair. I kissed her thighs, parting her legs with my hand, until the warm inside flesh was open to me, and my organ was stiff and ready. I looked at the secret place there, folded and demure and a dark pink in its soft veil of down. A coarse warm excitement went through me, further hardening the organ. I might have forced her, so urgent was the feeling.

But no, not this time.

I moved up, beside her, turning her face to me, and accepting her kisses now, slow and awkward and fumbling. I felt her leg pressed against mine, and her hands moving over me, seeking the warmth beneath my armpits, and the damp nether hair of this male body, thick and dark. It was my body, ready for her and waiting. This, my chest, which she touched, seeming to love its hardness. My arms, which she kissed as if she prized their strength.

The passion in me ebbed slightly, only to grow hot again instantly, and then to die down again, waiting, and then to rise once more.

No thoughts came to me of the blood drinking; no thought at all of the thunder of the life inside her which I might have consumed, a dark draught, at another time. Rather the moment was perfumed with the soft heat of her living flesh. And it seemed vile that anything could harm her, anything mar the common mystery of her—of her trust and her yearning and her deep and common fear.

I let my hand slip down to the little doorway; how sorry and sad that this union would be so partial, so brief.

Then, as my fingers gently tried the virgin passage, her body caught fire. Her breasts seemed to swell against me, and I felt her open, petal by petal, as her mouth grew harder against my mouth.

But what of the dangers: didn't she care about them? In her new passion, she seemed heedless, and completely under my command. I forced myself to stop, to remove the little sheath from its packet, and to roll it up and over the organ, as her passive eyes remained fixed on me, as if she no longer had a will of her own.

It was this surrender that she needed, it was what she required of herself. Once again, I fell to kissing her. She was moist and ready for me. I could keep it back no longer, and when I rode her now, it was hard. The little passage was snug and maddeningly heated as its juices flowed. I saw the blood come up into her face as the rhythm quickened; I bent my lips to lick at her nipples, to claim her mouth again. When the final moan came out of her, it was like the moan of pain. And there it was again, the mystery—that something could be so perfectly finished, and complete, and have lasted such a little while. Such a precious little while.

Had it been union? Were we one with each other in this clamorous silence?

I don't think that it was union. On the contrary, it seemed the most violent of separations: two contrary beings flung at each other in heat and clumsiness, in trust and in menace, the feelings of each unknowable and unfathomable to the other—its sweetness terrible as its brevity; its loneliness hurtful as its undeniable fire.

And never had she looked so frail to me as she did now, her eyes closed, her head turned into the pillow, her breasts no longer heaving but very still. It seemed an image to provoke violence—to beckon to the most wanton cruelty in a male heart.

Why was this so?

I didn't want any other mortal to touch her!

I didn't want her own guilt to touch her. I didn't want regret to hurt her, or for any of the evils of the human mind to come near her.

And only now did I think of the Dark Gift again, and not of Claudia, but of the sweet throbbing splendour in the making of Gabrielle. Gabrielle had never looked back from that long-ago moment. Clad in strength and certainty, she had begun her wandering, never suffering an hour's moral torment as the endless complexities of the great world drew her on.

But who could say what the Dark Blood would give to any one human soul? And this, a virtuous woman, a believer in old and merciless deities, drunk on the blood of martyrs and the heady suffering of a thousand saints. Surely she would never ask for the Dark Gift or accept it, any more than David would.

But what did such questions matter until she knew the words I spoke were true? And what if I could never prove their truth to her? What if I never had the Dark Blood again inside me to give anyone and I remained forever trapped in this mortal flesh? I lay quiet, watching the sunlight fill the room. I watched it strike the tiny body of the crucified Christ above her bookshelf; I watched it fall upon the Virgin with her bowed head.

Snuggled against each other, we slept again.

SIXTEEN

NOON. I was dressed in the clean new clothes which I had bought on that last fateful day of my wandering—soft white pullover shirt with long sleeves, fashionably faded denim pants.

We had made a picnic of sorts before the warm crackling little fire—a white blanket spread out on the carpet, on which we sat having our late breakfast together, as Mojo dined sloppily and greedily in his own fashion on the kitchen floor. It was French bread and butter again, and orange juice, and boiled eggs, and the fruit in big slices. I was eating hungrily, ignoring her warnings that I was not entirely well. I was plenty well enough. Even her little digital thermometer said so.

I ought to be off to New Orleans. If the airport was open, I could have been there by nightfall, perhaps. But I didn't want to leave her just now. I asked for some wine. I wanted to talk. I wanted to understand her, and I was also afraid to leave her, afraid of being alone without her. The plane journey struck a cowardly fear in my soul. And besides, I liked being with her . . .

She'd been talking easily about her life in the missions, of how she'd loved it from the very beginning. The first years she'd spent in Peru, then she'd gone on to the Yucatán. Her most recent assignment had been in the jungles of French Guiana—a place of primitive Indian tribes. The mission was St. Margaret Mary—six hours' journey up the Maroni River by motorized canoe from the town of St. Laurent. She and the other sisters had refurbished the concrete chapel, the little whitewashed schoolhouse, and the hospital. But often they had to leave the mission itself and go directly to the people in their villages. She loved this work, she said.

She laid out for me a great sweep of photographs—small rectangular colored pictures of the crude little mission buildings, and of her and her sisters, and of the priest who came through to say Mass. None of these sisters wore veils or habits out there; they were dressed in khaki or white cotton, and their hair was free—real working sisters, she explained. And there she was in these pictures—radiantly happy, none of the brooding melancholy evident in her. In one snapshot she stood surrounded by dark-faced Indians, before a curious little building with ornate carvings on its walls. In another she was giving an injection to a wraith of an old man who sat in a brightly painted straight-back chair.

Life in these jungle villages had been the same for centuries, she said. These people had existed long before the French or Spanish ever set foot on the soil of South America. It was difficult to get them to trust the sisters and the doctors and the priests. She herself did not care whether or not they learnt their prayers. She cared about inoculations, and the proper cleaning of infected wounds. She cared about setting broken limbs so that these people would not be crippled forever.

Of course they wanted her to come back. They'd been very patient with her little leave of absence. They needed her. The work was waiting for her. She showed me the telegram, which I had already seen, tacked to the wall above the bathroom mirror.

"You miss it, obviously you do," I said.

I was studying her, watching for signs of guilt over what we had done together. But I didn't see this in her. She did not seem racked with guilt over the telegram either.

"I'm going back, of course," she said simply. "This may sound absurd, but it was a difficult thing to leave in the first place. But this question of chastity; it had become a destructive obsession."

Of course I understood. She looked at me with large quiet eyes.

"And now you know," I said, "that it's not really so very important at all whether or not you sleep with a man. Isn't that what you found out?"

"Perhaps," she said, with a faint simple smile. How strong she seemed, sitting there on the blanket, her legs demurely folded to one side, her hair loose still, and more like a nun's veil here in this room than in any photograph of her.

"How did it begin for you?" I asked.

"Do you think that's important?" she asked. "I don't think you'll approve of my story if I tell you."

"I want to know," I answered.

She'd grown up, the daughter of a Catholic schoolteacher and an accountant in the Bridgeport section of Chicago, and very early on exhibited a great talent for playing the piano. The whole family had sacrificed for her lessons with a famous teacher.

"Self-sacrifice, you see," she said, smiling faintly again, "even from the beginning. Only it was music then, not medicine."

But even then, she had been deeply religious, reading the lives of the saints, and dreaming of being a saint—of working in the foreign missions when she grew up. Saint Rose de Lima, the mystic, held a special fascination for her. And so did Saint Martin de Porres, who had worked more in the world. And Saint Rita. She had wanted to work with lepers someday, to find a life of all-consuming and heroic work. She'd built a little oratory behind her house when she was a girl, and there she would kneel for hours before the crucifix, hoping that the wounds of Christ would open in her hands and feet—the stigmata.

"I took these stories very seriously," she said. "Saints are real to me. The possibility of heroism is real to me."

"Heroism," I said. My word. But how very different was my definition of it. I did not interrupt her.

"It seemed that the piano playing was at war with my spiritual soul. I wanted to give up everything for others, and that meant giving up the piano, above all, the piano."

This saddened me. I had the feeling she had not told this story often, and her voice was very subdued when she spoke.

"But what about the happiness you gave to people when you played?" I asked. "Wasn't that something of real value?"

"Now, I can say that it was," she said, her voice dropping even lower, and her words coming with painful slowness. "But then? I wasn't sure of it. I wasn't a likely person for such a talent. I didn't mind being heard; but I didn't like being seen." She flushed slightly as she looked at me. "Perhaps if I could have played in a choir loft, or behind a screen it would have been different."

"I see," I said. "There are many humans who feel this way, of course."

"But you don't, do you?"

I shook my head.

She explained how excruciating it was for her to be dressed in white lace, and made to play before an audience. She did it to please her parents and her teachers. Entering the various competitions was an agony. But almost invariably she won. Her career had become a family enterprise by the time she was sixteen.

"But what about the music itself. Did you enjoy it?"

She thought for a moment. Then: "It was absolute ecstasy," she answered. "When I played alone . . . with no one there to watch me, I lost myself in it completely. It was almost like being under the influence of a drug. It was . . . it was almost erotic. Sometimes melodies would obsess me. They'd run through my head continuously. I lost track of time when I played. I still cannot really listen to music without being swept up and carried away. You don't see any radio here or tape player. I can't have those things near me even now."

"But why deny yourself this?" I looked around. There was no piano in this room either.

She shook her head dismissively. "The effect is too engulfing, don't you see? I can forget everything else too easily. And nothing is accomplished when this happens. Life is on hold, so to speak."

"But, Gretchen, is that true?" I asked. "For some of us such intense feelings *are* life! We seek ecstasy. In those moments, we . . . we transcend all the pain and the pettiness and the struggle. That's how it was for me when I was alive. That's how it is for me now."

She considered this, her face very smooth and relaxed. When she spoke, it was with quiet conviction.

"I want more than that," she said. "I want something more palpably constructive. But to put it another way, I cannot enjoy such a pleasure when others are hungry or suffering or sick."

"But the world will always include such misery. And people need music, Gretchen, they need it as much as they need comfort or food."

"I'm not sure I agree with you. In fact, I'm fairly sure that I don't. I have to spend my life trying to alleviate misery. Believe me, I have been through all these arguments many times before."

"Ah, but to choose nursing over music," I said. "It's unfathomable to me. Of course nursing is good." I was too saddened and confused to continue. "How did you make the actual choice?" I asked. "Didn't the family try to stop you?"

She went on to explain. When she was sixteen, her mother took ill, and for months no one could determine the cause of her illness. Her mother was anemic; she ran a constant fever; finally it was obvious she was wasting away. Tests were made, but the doctors could find no explanation. Everyone felt certain that her mother was going to die. The atmosphere of the house had been poisoned with grief and even bitterness.

"I asked God for a miracle," she said. "I promised I would never touch the piano keys again as long as I lived, if God would only save my mother. I promised I would enter the convent as soon as I was allowed—that I would devote my life to nursing the sick and the dying."

"And your mother was cured."

"Yes. Within a month she was completely recovered. She's alive now. She's retired, she tutors children after school—in a storefront in a black section of Chicago. She has never been sick since, in any way."

"And you kept the promise?"

She nodded. "I went into the Missionary Sisters when I was seventeen and they sent me to college."

"And you kept this promise never to touch the piano again?"

She nodded. There was not a trace of regret in her, nor was there a great longing or need for my understanding or approval. In fact, I knew my sadness was obvious to her, and that, if anything, she felt a little concerned for me.

"Were you happy in the convent?"

"Oh, yes," she said with a little shrug. "Don't you see? An ordinary life is impossible for someone like me. I have to be doing something hard. I have to be taking risks. I entered this religious order because their missions were in the most remote and treacherous areas of South America. I can't tell you how I love those jungles!" Her voice became low and almost urgent. "They can't be hot enough or dangerous enough for me. There are moments when we're all overworked and tired, when the hospital's overcrowded and the sick children are bedded down outside under lean-tos and in hammocks and I feel so alive! I can't tell you. I stop maybe long enough to wipe the sweat off my face, to wash my hands, to perhaps drink a glass of water. And I think: I'm alive; I'm here. I'm doing what matters."

Again she smiled. "It's another kind of intensity," I said, "something wholly unlike the making of music. I see the crucial difference."

I thought of David's words to me about his early life—how he had sought the thrill in danger. She was seeking the thrill in utter self-sacrifice. He had sought the danger of the occult in Brazil. She sought the hard challenge of bringing health to thousands of the nameless, and the eternally poor. This troubled me deeply.

"There's a vanity in it too, of course," she said. "Vanity is always the enemy. That's what troubled me the most about my . . . my chastity," she explained, "the pride I felt in it. But you see, even coming back like this to the States was a risk. I was terrified when I got off the plane, when I realized I was here in Georgetown and nothing could stop me from being with a man if I wanted it. I think I went to work at the hospital out of fear. God knows, freedom isn't simple."

"This part I understand," I said. "But your family, how did they respond to this promise you made, to your giving up the music?"

"They didn't know at the time. I didn't tell them. I announced my vocation. I stuck to my guns. There was a lot of recrimination. After all, my sisters and brothers had worn secondhand clothes so I could have piano lessons. But this is often the case. Even in a good Catholic family, the news that a daughter wants to be a nun is not always greeted with cheers and accolades."

"They grieved for your talent," I said quietly.

"Yes, they did," she said with a slight lift of her eyebrows. How honest and tranquil she seemed. None of this was said with coldness or hardness. "But I had a vision of something vastly more important than a young woman on a concert stage, rising from the piano bench to collect a bouquet of roses. It was a long time before I told them about the promise."

"Years later?"

She nodded. "They understood. They saw the miracle. How could they help it? I told them I'd been more fortunate than anyone I knew who had ever gone into the convent. I'd had a clear sign from God. He had resolved all conflicts for all of us."

"You believe this."

"Yes. I do," she said. "But in a way, it doesn't matter whether it's true or not. And if anyone should understand, you should."

"Why is that?"

"Because you speak of religious truths and religious ideas and you know that they matter even if they are only metaphors. This is what I heard in you even when you were delirious."

I sighed. "Don't you ever want to play the piano again? Don't you ever want to find an empty auditorium, perhaps, with a piano on the stage, and just sit down and . . ."

"Of course I do. But I can't do it, and I won't do it." Her smile now was truly beautiful.

"Gretchen, in a way this is a terrible story," I said. "Why, as a good Catholic girl couldn't you have seen your musical talent as a gift from God, a gift not to be wasted?"

"It was from God, I knew it was. But don't you see? There was a fork in the road; the sacrifice of the piano was the opportunity that God gave me to serve Him in a special way. Lestat, what could the music have meant compared to the act of helping people, hundreds of people?"

I shook my head. "I think the music can be seen as equally important."

She thought for a long while before she answered. "I couldn't continue with it," she said. "Perhaps I used the crisis of my mother's illness, I don't know. I had to become a nurse. There was no other way for me. The simple truth is—I cannot live when I am faced with the misery in the world. I cannot justify comfort or pleasure when other people are suffering. I don't know how anyone can."

"Surely you don't think you can change it all, Gretchen."

"No, but I can spend my life affecting many, many individual lives. That's what counts."

This story so upset me that I couldn't remain seated there. I stood up, stretching my stiff legs, and I went to the window and looked out at the field of snow.

It would have been easy to dismiss it had she been a sorrowful or mentally crippled person, or a person of dire conflict and instability. But nothing seemed farther from the truth. I found her almost unfathomable.

She was as alien to me as my mortal friend Nicolas had been so many, many decades ago, not because she was like him. But because his cynicism and sneering and eternal rebellion had contained an abnegation of self which I couldn't really understand. My Nicki—so full of seeming eccentricity and excess, yet deriving satisfaction from what he did only because it pricked others.

Abnegation of self—that was the heart of it.

I turned around. She was merely watching me. I had the distinct feeling again that it didn't matter much to her what I said. She didn't require my understanding. In a way, she was one of the strongest people I'd encountered in all my long life.

It was no wonder she took me out of the hospital; another nurse might not have assumed such a burden at all.

"Gretchen," I asked, "you're never afraid that your life has been wasted—that sickness and suffering will simply go on long after you've left the earth, and what you've done will mean nothing in the larger scheme?"

"Lestat," she said, "it is the larger scheme which means nothing." Her eyes were wide and clear. "It is the small act which means all. Of course sickness and suffering will continue after I'm gone. But what's important is that I have done all I can. That's my triumph, and my vanity. That's my vocation and my sin of pride. That is my brand of heroism."

"But, chérie, it works that way only if someone is keeping score—if some Supreme Being will ratify your decision, or you'll be rewarded for what you've done, or at least upheld."

"No," she said, choosing her words thoughtfully as she proceeded. "Nothing could be farther from the truth. Think of what I've said. I'm telling you something that is obviously new to you. Maybe it's a religious secret."

"How so?"

"There are many nights when I lie awake, fully aware that there may be no personal God, and that the suffering of the children I see every day in our hospitals will never be balanced or redeemed. I think of those old arguments—you know, how can God justify the suffering of a child? Dostoevsky asked that question. So did the French writer Albert Camus. We ourselves are always asking it. But it doesn't ultimately matter.

"God may or may not exist. But misery is real. It is absolutely real, and utterly undeniable. And in that reality lies my commitment—the core of my faith. I have to do something about it!"

"And at the hour of your death, if there is no God . . ."

"So be it. I will know that I did what I could. The hour of my death could be now." She gave a little shrug. "I wouldn't feel any different."

"This is why you feel no guilt for our being there in the bed together."

She considered. "Guilt? I feel happiness when I think of it. Don't you know what you've done for me?" She waited, and slowly her eyes filled with tears. "I came here to meet you, to be with you," she said, her voice thickening. "And I can go back to the mission now."

She bowed her head, and slowly, silently regained her calm, her eyes clearing. Then she looked up and spoke again.

"When you spoke of making this child, Claudia . . . when you spoke of bringing your mother, Gabrielle, into your world . . . you spoke of reaching for something. Would you call it a transcendence? When I work until I drop in the mission hospital, I transcend. I transcend doubt and something . . . something perhaps hopeless and black inside myself. I don't know."

"Hopeless and black, yes, that's the key, isn't it? The music didn't make this go away."

"Yes, it did, but it was false."

"Why false? Why was doing that good—playing the piano—false?"

"Because it didn't do enough for others, that's why."

"Oh, but it did. It gave them pleasure, it had to."

"Pleasure?"

"Forgive me, I'm choosing the wrong tack. You've lost yourself in your vocation. When you played the piano, you were yourself—don't you see? You were the unique Gretchen! It was the very meaning of the word 'virtuoso.' And you wanted to lose yourself."

"I think you're right. The music simply wasn't my way."

"Oh, Gretchen, you frighten me!"

"But I shouldn't frighten you. I'm not saying the other way was wrong. If you did good with your music—your rock singing, this brief career you described—it was the good you could do. I do good my way, that's all."

"No, there's some fierce self-denial in you. You're hungry for love the way I starve night after night for blood. You punish yourself in your nursing, denying your carnal desires, and your love of music, and all the things of the world which are like music. You *are* a virtuoso, a virtuoso of your own pain."

"You're wrong, Lestat," she said with another little smile, and a shake of her head. "You know that's not true. It's what you want to believe about someone like me. Lestat, listen to me. If all you've told me is true, isn't it obvious in light of that truth that you were meant to meet me?"

"How so?"

"Come here, sit with me and talk to me."

I don't know why I hesitated, why I was afraid. Finally I came back to the blanket and sat down opposite, crossing my legs. I leaned back against the side of the bookcase.

"Don't you see?" she asked. "I represent a contrary way, a way you haven't ever considered, and one which might bring you the very consolation you seek."

"Gretchen, you don't believe for a moment that I've told the truth about myself. You can't. I don't expect you to."

"I do believe you! Every word you've said. And the literal truth is unimportant. You seek something that the saints sought when they renounced their normal lives, when they blundered into the service of Christ. And never mind that you don't believe in Christ. It's unimportant. What is important is that you have been miserable in the existence you've lived until now, miserable to the point of madness, and that my way would offer you an alternative."

"You're speaking of this for me?" I asked.

"Of course I am. Don't you see the pattern? You come down into this body; you fall into my hands; you give me the moment of love I require. But what have I given you? What is my meaning for you?"

She raised her hand for quiet.

"No, don't speak of larger schemes again. Don't ask if there is a literal God. Think on all I've said. I've said it for myself, but also for you. How many lives have you taken in this otherworldly existence of yours? How many lives have I saved—literally saved—in the missions?"

I was ready to deny the entire possibility, when suddenly it occurred to me to wait, to be silent, and merely to consider.

The chilling thought came to me again that I might never recover my preternatural body, that I might be trapped in this flesh all my life.

If I couldn't catch the Body Thief, if I couldn't get the others to help me, the death I said I wanted would indeed be mine in time. I had fallen back into time.

And what if there was a scheme to it? What if there was a destiny? And I spent that mortal life working as Gretchen worked, devoting my entire physical and spiritual being to others? What if I simply went with her back to her jungle outpost? Oh, not as her lover, of course. Such things as that were not meant for her, obviously. But what if I went as her assistant, her helper? What if I sank my mortal life into that very frame of self-sacrifice?

Again, I forced myself to remain quiet, to see it.

Of course there was an added capability of which she knew nothing—the wealth I could bestow upon her mission, upon missions like it. And though this wealth was so vast some men could not have calculated it, I could calculate it. I could see in a large incandescent vision its limits, its effects. Whole village populations fed and clothed, hospitals stocked with medicines, schools furnished with books and blackboards and radios and pianos. Yes, pianos. Oh, this was an old, old tale. This was an old, old dream.

I remained quiet as I considered it. I saw the moments of each day of my mortal life—my possible mortal life—spent along with every bit of my fortune upon this dream. I saw this as if it were sand sliding through the narrow center of an hourglass.

Why, at this very minute, as we sat here in this clean little room, people starved in the great slums of the Eastern world. They starved in Africa. Worldwide, they perished from disease and from disaster. Floods washed away their dwellings; drought shriveled their food and their hopes. The misery of even one country was more than the mind could endure, were it described in even vague detail.

But even if everything I possessed I gave to this endeavor, what would I have accomplished in the final analysis?

How could I even know that modern medicine in a jungle village was better than the old way? How could I know that the education given a jungle child spelt happiness for it? How could I know that any of this was worth the loss of myself? How could I make myself care whether it was or not! That was the horror.

I didn't care. I could weep for any individual soul who suffered, yes, but about sacrificing my life to the nameless millions of the world, I couldn't care! In fact, it filled me with dread, terrible dark dread. It was sad beyond sad. It seemed no life at all. It seemed the very opposite of transcendence.

I shook my head. In a low stammering voice I explained to her why this vision frightened me so much.

"Centuries ago, when I first stood on the little boulevard stage in Paris—when I saw the happy faces, when I heard applause—I felt as if my body and soul had found their destiny; I felt as if every promise in my birth and childhood had begun its fulfillment at last.

"Oh, there were other actors, worse and better; other singers; other clowns; there have been a million since and a million will come after this moment. But each of us shines with his own inimitable power; each of us comes alive in his own unique and dazzling moment; each of us has his chance to vanquish the others forever in the mind of the beholder, and that is the only kind of accomplishment I can really understand: the kind of accomplishment in which the self—this self, if you will—is utterly whole and triumphant.

"Yes, I could have been a saint, you are right, but I would have had to found a religious order or lead an army into battle; I would have had to work miracles of such scope that the whole world would have been brought to its knees. I am one who must dare even if I'm wrong—completely wrong. Gretchen, God gave me an individual soul and I cannot bury it."

I was amazed to see that she was still smiling at me, softly and unquestioningly, and that her face was full of calm wonder.

"Better to reign in hell," she asked carefully, "than to serve in heaven?"

"Oh, no. I would make heaven on earth if I could. But I must raise my voice; I must shine; and I must reach for the very ecstasy that you've denied—the very intensity from which you fled! That to me is transcendence! When I made Claudia, blundering error that it was—yes, it was transcendence. When I made Gabrielle, wicked as it seemed, yes, it was transcendence. It was a single, powerful, and horrifying act, which wrung from me all my unique power and daring. They shall not die, I said, yes, perhaps the very words you use to the village children.

"But it was to bring them into my unnatural world that I uttered these words. The goal was not merely to save, but to make of them what I was—a unique and terrible being. It was to confer upon them the very individuality I cherished. We shall live, even in this state called living death, we shall love, we shall feel, we shall defy those who would judge us and destroy us. That was my transcendence. And self-sacrifice and redemption had no part in it."

Oh, how frustrating it was that I could not communicate it to her, I could not make her believe it in literal terms. "Don't you see, I survived all that has happened to me because I am who I am. My strength, my will, my refusal to give up—those are the only components of my heart and soul which I can truly identify. This ego, if you wish to call it that, is my strength. I am the Vampire Lestat, and nothing . . . not even this mortal body . . . is going to defeat me."

I was amazed to see her nod, to see her totally accepting expression.

"And if you came with me," she said gently, "the Vampire Lestat would perish—wouldn't he?—in his own redemption."

"Yes, he would. He would die slowly and horribly among the small and thankless tasks, caring for the never-ending hordes of the nameless, the faceless, the eternally needy."

I felt so sad suddenly that I couldn't continue. I was tired in an awful mortal way, the mind having worked its chemistry upon this body. I thought of my dream and of my speech to Claudia, and now I had told it again to Gretchen, and I knew myself as never before.

I drew up my knees and rested my arms on them, and I put my forehead on my arms. "I can't do it," I said under my breath. "I can't bury myself alive in such a life as you have. And I don't want to, that's the awful part. I don't want to do it! I don't believe it would save my soul. I don't believe it would matter."

I felt her hands on my arms. She was stroking my hair again, drawing it back from my forehead.

"I understand you," she said, "even though you're wrong."

I gave a little laugh as I looked up at her. I took a napkin from our little picnic and I wiped my nose and my eyes.

"But I haven't shaken your faith, have I?"

"No," she said. And this time her smile was different, more warm and more truly radiant. "You've confirmed it," she said in a whisper. "How very strange you are, and how miraculous that you came to me. I can almost believe your way is right for you. Who else could be you? No one."

I sat back, and drank a little sip of wine. It was now warm from the fire, but still it tasted good, sending a ripple of pleasure through my sluggish limbs. I drank some more of it. I set down the glass and looked at her.

"I want to ask you a question," I said. "Answer me from your heart. If I win my battle—if I regain my body—do you want me to come to you? Do you want me to show you that I've been telling the truth? Think carefully before you answer.

"I want to do it. I really do. But I'm not sure that it's the best thing for you. Yours is almost a perfect life. Our little carnal episode couldn't possibly turn you away from it. I was right—wasn't I?—in what I said before. You know now that erotic pleasure really isn't important to you, and you're going to return to your work in the jungle very soon, if not immediately."

"That's true," she said. "But there's something else you should know, also. There was a moment this morning when I thought I could throw away everything—just to be with you."

"No, not you, Gretchen."

"Yes, me. I could feel it sweeping me away, the way the music once did. And if you were to say 'Come with me,' even now, I might go. If this world of yours really existed . . ." She broke off with another little shrug, tossing her hair a little and then smoothing it back behind her shoulder. "The meaning of chastity is not to fall in love," she said, her focus sharpening as she looked at me. "I could fall in love with you. I know I could."

She broke off, and then said in a low, troubled voice, "You could become my god. I know that's true."

This frightened me, yet I felt at once a shameless pleasure and satisfaction, a sad pride. I tried not to yield to the feeling of slow physical excitement. After all, she didn't know what she was saying. She couldn't know. But there was something powerfully convincing in her voice and in her manner.

"I'm going back," she said in the same voice, full of certitude and humility. "I'll probably leave within a matter of days. But yes, if you win this battle, if you recover your old form—for the love of God, come to me. I want to . . . I want to *know!*"

I didn't reply. I was too confused. Then I spoke the confusion.

"You know, in a horrible way, when I do come to you and reveal my true self, you may be disappointed."

"How could that be?"

"You think me a sublime human being for the spiritual content of all I've said to you. You see me as some sort of blessed lunatic spilling truth with error the way a mystic might. But I'm not human. And when you know it, maybe you'll hate it."

"No, I could never hate you. And to know that all you've said is true? That would be . . . a miracle."

"Perhaps, Gretchen. Perhaps. But remember what I said. We are a vision without revelation. We are a miracle without meaning. Do you really want that cross along with so many others?"

She didn't answer. She was weighing my words. I could not imagine what they meant to her. I reached for her hand, and she let me take it, folding her fingers gently around mine, her eyes still constant as she looked at me.

"There is no God, is there, Gretchen?"

"No, there isn't," she whispered.

I wanted to laugh and to weep. I sat back, laughing softly to myself and looking at her, at the calm, statuesque manner in which she sat there, the light of the fire caught in her hazel eyes.

"You don't know what you've done for me," she said. "You don't know how much it has meant. I am ready—ready to go back now."

I nodded.

"Then it won't matter, will it, my beautiful one, if we get into that bed together again. For surely we should do it."

"Yes, we should do that, I think," she answered.

It was almost dark when I left her quietly to take the phone by its long cord into the little bath and call my New York agent. Once again, the number rang and rang. I was just about to give up, and turn again to my man in Paris, when a voice came on the line, and slowly let me know in halting awkward terms that my New York representative was indeed no longer alive. He had died by violence several nights ago in his office high above Madison Avenue. Robbery had now been affirmed as the motive for the attack; his computer and all his files had been stolen.

I was so stunned that I could make no answer to the helpful voice on the phone. At last I managed to collect myself sufficiently to put a few questions.

On Wednesday night, about eight o'clock, the crime had occurred. No, no one knew the extent of damage done by the theft of the files. Yes, unfortunately the poor man had suffered.

"Awful, awful situation," said the voice. "If you were in New York, you couldn't avoid knowing about it. Every paper in town had the story. They were calling it a vampire killing. The man's body was entirely drained of blood."

I hung up the phone, and for a long moment sat there in rigid silence. Then I rang Paris. My man there answered after only a small delay.

Thank God I had called, said my man. But please, I must identify myself. No, the code words weren't enough. What about conversations which had taken place between us in the past? Ah, yes, yes, that was it. Talk, talk, he said. I at once poured out a litany of secrets known only to me and this man, and I could hear his great relief as he at last unburdened himself.

The strangest things had been happening, he said. He'd been contacted twice by someone claiming to be me, who obviously wasn't. This individual even knew two of our code words used in the past, and gave an elaborate story as to why he did not know the latest ones. Meantime, several electronic orders had come in for shifts of funds, but in every case, the codes were wrong. But not entirely wrong. Indeed, there was every indication that this person was in the process of cracking our system.

"But, Monsieur, let me tell you the simplest part. This man does not speak the same French that you do! I don't mean to insult you, Monsieur, but your French is rather . . . how shall I say, unusual? You speak old-fashioned words. And you put words in unusual order. I know when it is you."

"I understand exactly," I said. "Now believe me when I say this. You must not talk to this person anymore. He is capable of reading your mind. He is trying to get the code words from you telepathically. We are going to set up a system, you and I. You will make one transfer to me now . . . to my bank in New Orleans. But everything must be locked up tight after that. And when I contact you again, I shall use three old-fashioned words. We won't agree on them . . . but they will be words you've heard me use before and you will know them."

Of course this was risky. But the point was, this man knew me!

I went on to tell him that the thief in question was most dangerous, that he had done violence to my man in New York, and every conceivable personal protection must be taken. I should pay for all this—guards of any number, round the clock. He must err on the side of excess. "You'll hear from me again, very soon. Remember, old-fashioned words. You'll know me when you speak to me."

I put down the phone. I was trembling with rage, unsupportable rage! Ah, the little monster! It is not enough for him to have the body of the god, he must ransack the god's storehouses. The little fiend, the little imp! And I had been so foolish not to realize that this would happen!

"Oh, you are human all right," I said to myself. "You are a human idiot!" And oh, to think of the denunciations Louis would heap upon my head before he consented to help me!

And what if Marius knew! Oh, that was too awful to contemplate. Just reach Louis as fast as you can.

I had to obtain a valise, and get to the airport. Mojo would undoubtedly have to travel by crate, and this, too, must be obtained. My farewell to Gretchen would not be the graceful, slow leave-taking I had envisioned. But surely she would understand.

Much was happening within the complex delusionary world of her mysterious lover. It was time to part.

SEVENTEEN

THE trip south was a small nightmare. The airport, only just reopened after the repeated storms, had been jammed to overflowing with anxious mortals waiting for their long-delayed flights or come to find their arriving loved ones.

Gretchen gave way to tears, and so did I. A terrible fear had seized her that she would never see me again, and I could not reassure her sufficiently that I would come to her at the Mission of St. Margaret Mary in the jungles of French Guiana, up the Maroni River from St. Laurent. The written address was carefully placed in my pocket along with all numbers relevant to the motherhouse in Caracas, from which the sisters could direct me should I be unable to find the place on my own. She had already booked a midnight flight for the first leg of her return.

"One way or another, I must see you again!" she said to me in a voice that was breaking my heart.

"You will, ma chère," I said, "that I promise you. I'll find the mission. I'll find you."

The flight itself was hellish. I did little more than lie there in a stupor, waiting for the plane to explode and for my mortal body to be blown to pieces. Drinking large amounts of gin and tonic did not alleviate the fear; and when I did free my mind from it for a few moments at a time, it was only to become obsessed with difficulties facing me. My rooftop apartment, for example, was full of clothes which did not fit me. And I was used to going in through a door on the roof. I had no key now to the street stairway. Indeed, the key was in my nocturnal resting place beneath the Lafayette Cemetery, a secret chamber I could not possibly reach with only a mortal's strength, for it was blocked with doors at several points which not even a gang of mortal men might have opened.

And what if the Body Thief had been to New Orleans before me? What if he had sacked my rooftop rooms, and stolen all the money hidden there? Not likely. No, but if he had stolen all the files of my poor unfortunate mortal agent in New York . . . Ah, better to think about the plane exploding. And then there was Louis. What if Louis were not there? What if . . . And so on it went for the better part of two hours.

At last, we made our rattling, roaring, cumbersome, and terrifying descent, amid a rainstorm of biblical proportions. I collected Mojo, discarding his crate, and leading him boldly into the back of the taxi. And off we drove into the unabated storm, with the mortal driver taking every conceivable risk available to him, as Mojo and I were flung into each other's arms, more or less, over and over again.

It was near midnight when we finally reached the narrow tree-lined streets of uptown, the rain falling so heavily and steadily that the houses behind their iron fences were scarcely visible. When I saw the dismal, abandoned house of Louis's property, crowded by the dark trees, I paid the driver, snatched up the valise, and led Mojo out of the cab into the downpour.

It was cold, yes, very cold, but not as bad as the deep, freezing air of Georgetown. Indeed, even in this icy rain, the dark rich foliage of the giant magnolias and the evergreen oaks seemed to make the world more cheerful and bearable. On the other hand, I had never beheld with mortal eyes a dwelling as forlorn as the great massive abandoned house which stood before Louis's hidden shack.

For one moment as I shaded my eyes from the rain and looked up at those black and empty windows, I felt a terrible irrational fear that no being dwelt in this place, that I was mad, and destined to remain in this weak human body forever.

Mojo leapt the small iron fence just as I leapt it. And together we plowed through the high grass, around the ruins of the old porch, and back into the wet and overgrown garden. The night was full of the noise of the rain, thundering against my mortal ears, and I almost wept when I saw the small house, a great gleaming hulk of wet vines, standing there before me.

In a loud whisper I called Louis's name. I waited. No sound came from within. Indeed the place seemed on the verge of collapse in its decay. Slowly I approached the door. "Louis," I said again. "Louis, it is I, Lestat!"

Cautiously I stepped inside amid the heaps and stacks of dusty objects. Quite impossible to see! Yet I made out the desk, the whiteness of the paper, and the candle standing there, and a small book of matches beside it.

With trembling wet fingers, I struggled to strike a match, and only after several efforts succeeded. At last I touched it to the wick, and a thin bright light filled all the room, shining upon the red velvet chair which was mine, and the other worn and neglected objects.

A powerful relief coursed through me. I was here! I was almost safe! And I was not mad. This was my world, this awful cluttered unbearable little place! Louis would come. Louis would have to come before long; Louis was almost here. I all but collapsed in the chair in sheer exhaustion. I laid my hands on Mojo, scratching his head, and stroking his ears.

"We've made it, boy," I said. "And soon we'll be after that devil. We'll find a way to deal with him." I realized I was shivering again, indeed, I was feeling the old telltale congestion in my chest. "Good Lord, not again," I said. "Louis, come for the love of heaven, come! Wherever you are, come back here now. I need you."

I was just about to reach into my pocket for one of the many paper handkerchiefs Gretchen had forced upon me, when I realized that a figure was standing exactly at my left, only an inch from the arm of the chair, and that a very smooth white hand was reaching for me. In the same instant, Mojo leapt to his feet, giving forth his worst, most menacing growls, and then appeared to charge the figure.

I tried to cry out, to identify myself, but before my lips were even open, I'd been hurled against the floor, deafened by Mojo's barking, and I felt the sole of a leather boot pressed to my throat, indeed, to the very bones of my neck, crushing them with such force that surely they were about to be broken.

I couldn't speak, nor could I free myself. A great piercing cry came from the dog, and then he, too, fell silent, and I heard the muffled sounds of his large body sinking to the floor. Indeed I felt the weight of him on my legs, and I struggled frantically and helplessly in pure terror. All reason left me as I clawed at the foot pinning me down, as I pounded the powerful leg, as I gasped for breath, only hoarse inarticulate growls coming from me.

Louis, it's Lestat. I'm in the body, the human body.

Harder and harder the foot pressed. I was strangling as the bones were about to be crushed, yet I couldn't utter one syllable to save myself. And above me in the gloom, I saw his face—the subtle gleaming whiteness of the flesh that did not seem at all to be flesh, the exquisitely symmetrical bones, and the delicate half-closed hand, which hovered in the air, in a perfect attitude of indecision, as the deep-set eyes, fired with a subtle and incandescent green, looked down upon me without the slightest palpable emotion.

With all my soul I cried the words again, but when had he ever been able to divine the thoughts of his victims? I could have done that, but not he! Oh, God help me, Gretchen help me, I was screaming in my soul.

As the foot increased its pressure, perhaps for the final time, all indecision cast aside, I wrenched my head to the right, sucked in one desperate tiny breath, and forced from my constricted throat one hoarse word: "Lestat!" all the while desperately pointing to myself with my right hand and first finger.

It was the last gesture of which I was capable. I was suffocating, and the darkness came rolling over me. Indeed it was bringing a total strangling nausea with it, and just at the moment when I ceased to care in the most lovely light-headed fashion, the pressure ceased, and I found myself rolling over and rising up on my hands, one frantic cough tearing loose from me after another.

"For the love of God," I cried, spitting the words in between my hoarse painful choking breaths, "I'm Lestat. I'm Lestat in this body! Couldn't you have given me a chance to speak? Do you kill any hapless mortal who blunders into your little house? What of the ancient laws of hospitality, you bloody fool! Why the hell don't you put iron bars on your doors!" I struggled to my knees, and suddenly the nausea won out. I vomited a filthy stream of spoiled food into the dirt and the dust, and then shrank back from it, chilled and miserable, staring up at him.

"You killed the dog, didn't you? You monster!" I flung myself forward on Mojo's inert body. But he wasn't dead, merely unconscious, and at once, I felt the slow pumping of his heart. "Oh, thank God, if you'd done that, I would never, never, never have forgiven you."

A faint moan came from Mojo, and then his left paw moved, and then slowly his right. I laid my hand between his ears. Yes, he was coming back. He was unhurt. But oh, what a wretched experience this had been! Here of all places to come to the very brink of mortal death! Enraged again, I glared up at Louis.

How still he was as he stood there, how quietly astonished. The pounding of the rain, the dark lively sounds of the winter night—all seemed to evaporate suddenly as I looked at him. Never had I seen him with mortal eyes. Never had I beheld this wan, phantom beauty. How could mortals believe this was a human when their eyes passed over him? Ah, the hands—like those of plaster saints come to life in shadowy grottoes. And how utterly devoid of feeling the face, the eyes not windows of the soul at all, but fine jewel-like snares of illumination.

"Louis," I said. "The worst has happened. The very worst. The Body Thief made the switch. But he's stolen my body and has no intention of giving it back to me."

Nothing palpable quickened in him as I spoke. Indeed so lifeless and menacing did he seem, that I suddenly broke into a stream of French, pouring forth every image and detail which I could recall in the hopes of wringing recognition from him. I spoke of our last conversation in this very house, and the brief meeting at the foyer of the Cathedral. I recalled his warning to me that I must not speak to the

Body Thief. And I confessed that I had found the man's offer impossible to resist, and had gone north to meet with him, and to accept his proposal.

Still, nothing of vitality sparked the merciless face, and suddenly, I fell silent. Mojo was trying to stand, occasional little moans coming from him, and slowly I wrapped my right arm around his neck, and leaned against him, struggling to catch my breath, and telling him in a soothing voice that everything was fine now, we were saved. No more harm would come to him.

Louis shifted his gaze slowly to the animal, then back to me. Then gradually, the set of his mouth softened ever so slightly. And then he reached for my hand, and pulled me up—quite without my cooperation or consent—to a standing position.

"It really is you," he said in a deep, raw whisper.

"You're damned right it's me. And you nearly killed me, you realize that! How many times will you try that little trick before all the clocks of the earth tick to the finish? I need your help, damn you! And, *once again*, you try to kill me! Now, will you please close whatever shutters still hang on these damned windows, and make a fire of some sort in that miserable little hearth!"

I flopped down again in my red velvet chair, still laboring for breath, and a strange lapping sound suddenly distracted me. I looked up. Louis had not moved. Indeed he was staring at me, as if I were a monster. But Mojo was patiently and steadily devouring all of the vomit I had spilt upon the floor.

I gave a little delighted laugh, which threatened to become a fit of perfect hysteria.

"Please, Louis, the fire. Make the fire," I said. "I'm freezing in this mortal body! Move!"

"Good God," he whispered. "What have you done now!"

EIGHTEEN

IT WAS two by the watch on my wrist. The rain had slackened beyond the broken shutters which covered both doors and windows, and I sat huddled in the red velvet chair, enjoying the little blaze from the brick fireplace, yet badly chilled again, and suffering the same old racking cough. But the moment was at hand, surely, when such a thing would no longer be of concern.

I had poured out the whole tale.

In a frenzy of mortal candor, I had described each and every dreadful and bewildering experience, from my conversations with Raglan James to the very last sad farewell to Gretchen. I had told even of my dreams, of Claudia and me in the long-ago little hospital, of our conversation in the fantasy parlour of the eighteenth-century hotel suite, and of the sad terrible loneliness I'd felt in loving Gretchen, for I knew that she believed at heart that I was mad, and only for that reason had she loved me. She had seen me as some sort of beatific idiot, and no more.

It was finished and done. I had no idea where to find the Body Thief. But I must find him. And this search could only begin when I was once again a vampire, when this tall powerful body was pumped with preternatural blood.

Weak as I would be with only the power Louis could give me, I would nevertheless be some twenty times stronger than I was now, and capable perhaps of summoning help from the others, for who knew what manner of fledgling I would become. Once the body was transformed, surely I'd have some telepathic voice. I could beg Marius for his help; or call out to Armand, or even Gabrielle—as yes, my beloved Gabrielle—for she would no longer be my fledgling, and she could hear me, which in the ordinary scheme of things—if such a word can be used—she could not.

He sat at his desk, as he had the entire time, oblivious to the draughts, of course, and the rain splattering on the slats of the shutters, and listening without a word as I'd spoken, watching with a pained and amazed expression as I'd climbed to my feet and paced in my excitement, as I had rambled on and on.

"Judge me not for my stupidity," I implored him. I told him again of my ordeal in the Gobi, of my strange conversations with David, and David's vision in the Paris café. "I was in a state of desperation when I did this. You know why I did it. I don't have to tell you. But now, it must be undone."

I was now coughing almost continuously, and blowing my nose frantically with those miserable little paper handkerchiefs.

"You cannot imagine how absolutely revolting it is to be in this body," I said. "Now, please, do it quickly, do it with your greatest skill. It's been a hundred years since you did it last. Thank God for that. The power is not dissipated. I'm ready now. There need be no preparations. When I regain my form, I'll fling him into this one and burn him to a cinder."

He made no reply.

I stood up, pacing again, this time to keep warm and because a terrible apprehension was taking hold of me. After all, I was about to die, was I not, and be born again, as it had happened over two hundred years ago. Ah, but there would be no pain. No, no pain . . . only those awful discomforts which were nothing compared to the chest pain I felt now, or the chill knotted in my fingers, or in my feet.

"Louis, for the love of God, be quick," I said. I stopped and looked at him. "What is it? What's the matter with you."

In a very low and uncertain voice he answered:

"I cannot do this."

"What!"

I stared at him, trying to fathom what he meant, what possible doubt he could have, what possible difficulty we must now dispose of. And I realized what a dreadful change had come over his narrow face—that all its smoothness had been lost, and that indeed it was a perfect mask of sorrow. Once again, I realized that I was seeing him as human beings saw him. A faint red shimmer veiled his green eyes. Indeed, his entire form, so seemingly solid and powerful, was trembling.

"I cannot do it, Lestat," he said again, and all his soul seemed to come out in the words. "I can't help you!"

"What in the name of God are you saying to me!" I demanded. "I made you. You exist tonight because of me! You love me, you spoke those very words to me. Of course you will help me."

I rushed towards him, slamming my hands down on the desk and looking into his face.

"Louis, answer me! What do you mean, you can't do it!"

"Oh, I don't blame you for what you've done. I don't. But can't you see what's happened? Lestat, you have done it. You have been reborn a mortal man."

"Louis, this is no time to sentimentalize the transformation. Don't throw my own words back at me! I was wrong."

"No. You weren't wrong."

"What are you trying to tell me! Louis, we are wasting time. I have to go after that monster! He has my body."

"Lestat, the others will deal with him. Perhaps they already have."

"Already have! What do you mean, already have!"

"Don't you think they know what's happened?" He was deeply distressed but also angry. How the human lines of expression appeared and disappeared in his supple flesh as he spoke. "How could such a thing have taken place without their knowing?" he said, as if he were pleading with me to understand. "You spoke of this Raglan James as a sorcerer. But no sorcerer can veil himself entirely from creatures as powerful as Maharet or her sister, as powerful as Khayman and Marius, or even Armand. And what a clumsy sorcerer—to murder your mortal agent in such a bloody and cruel way." He shook his head, his hands suddenly pressed to his lips. "Lestat, they know! They must know. And it could well be that your body has already been destroyed."

"They wouldn't do that."

"Why wouldn't they? You surrendered an engine of destruction to this demon—"

"But he didn't know how to use it! It was only for thirty-six hours of mortal time! Louis, whatever the case, you must give me the blood. Lecture me afterwards. Work the Dark Trick and I'll find the answers to all these questions. We're wasting precious minutes, hours."

"No, Lestat. We are not. That's my entire point! The question of this Body Thief and the body he stole from you isn't what must concern us here. It's what's happening to you—your soul—in this body now."

"All right. Have it your way. Now make this body a vampire now."

"I can't. Or more truly, I will not."

I rushed at him. I couldn't prevent myself. And in an instant I had both hands on the lapels of his miserable dusty black coat. I pulled at the cloth, ready to tear him up and out of the chair, but he remained absolutely unmovable, looking at me quietly, his face still stricken and sad. In impotent fury, I let go of him, and stood there, trying to still the confusion in my heart.

"You can't mean what you're saying!" I pleaded, slamming my fists again on the desk in front of him. "How can you deny me this?"

"Will you let me be one who loves you now?" he asked, his voice once again infused with emotion, his face still deeply and tragically sad.

"I wouldn't do it no matter how great your misery, no matter how strongly you pleaded, no matter what awful litany of events you set down before me. I wouldn't do it because I will not make another one of us for any reason under God. But you have brought me no great misery! You are not beset by any awful litany of disasters!" He shook his head, overcome as if he couldn't continue, and then: "You have triumphed in this as only you could."

"No, no, you're not understanding . . ."

"Oh, yes, I am. Do I need to push you in front of a mirror?" He rose slowly from behind the desk and faced me eye-to-eye. "Must I sit you down and make you examine the lessons of the tale I've heard from your own lips? Lestat, you have fulfilled our dream! Don't you see it. You have done it. You have been reborn a mortal man. A strong and beautiful mortal man!"

"No," I said. I backed away from him, shaking my head, my hands up to implore him. "You're mad. You don't know what you're saying. I loathe this body! I loathe being human. Louis, if you have an ounce of compassion in you throw aside these delusions and listen to my words!"

"I've heard you. I've heard it all. Why can't you hear it? Lestat, you've won. You're free from the nightmare. You're alive again."

"I'm miserable!" I cried at him. "Miserable! Dear God, what must I do to convince you?"

"There is nothing. It is I who must convince you. What have you lived in this body? Three? Four days? You speak of discomforts as if they were deathly afflictions; you talk of physical limits as if they were malicious and punitive restraints.

"And yet through all your endless complaining, you yourself have told me that I must refuse you! You yourself have implored me to turn you away! Lestat, why did you tell me the story of David Talbot and his obsessions with God and the Devil? Why tell me all the things that the nun Gretchen said to you? Why describe the little hospital you saw in your fever dream? Oh, I know it wasn't Claudia who came to you. I don't say God put this woman Gretchen in your path. But you love this woman. By your own admission, you love her. She's waiting for you to return. She can be your guide through the pains and annoyances of this mortal life—"

"No, Louis, you've misunderstood everything. I don't want her to guide me. I don't want this mortal life!"

"Lestat, can't you see the chance you've been given? Can't you see the path laid out for you and the light ahead?"

"I'm going to go mad if you don't stop saying these things . . ."

"Lestat, what can any of us do to redeem ourselves? And who has been more obsessed with this very question than you?"

"No, no!" I threw my arms up and crossed them, back and forth, repeatedly, as if trying to head off this dump truck of mad philosophy which was driving right down upon me. "No! I tell you, this is false. This is the worst of all lies."

He turned away from me, and again I rushed at him, unable to stop myself, and would have grabbed him by the shoulders and shaken him, but with a gesture too quick for my eye, he hurled me backwards against the chair.

Stunned, one ankle painfully twisted, I fell down on the cushions, and then made my right hand into a fist and drove it into the palm of my left. "Oh, no, not sermons, not now." I was almost weeping. "Not platitudes and pious recommendations."

"Go back to her," he said.

"You're mad!"

"Imagine it," he went on, as if I hadn't spoken, his back turned to me, his eyes fixed perhaps on the distant window, his voice almost inaudible, his dark form outlined against the running silver of the rain. "All the years of inhuman craving, of sinister and remorseless feeding. And you are reborn. And there—in that little jungle hospital you could conceivably save a human life for every one you've ever taken. Oh, what guardian angels look over you. Why are they so merciful? And you come to me and you beg me to bring you back into this horror, yet with every word you affirm the splendour of all you've suffered and seen."

"I bare my soul to you and you use it against me!"

"Oh, I do not, Lestat. I seek to make you look into it. You are begging me to drive you back to Gretchen. Am I perhaps the only guardian angel? Am I the only one who can confirm this fate?"

"You miserable bastard son of a bitch! If you don't give me the blood . . ."

He turned around, his face like that of ghost, eyes wide and hideously unnatural in their beauty. "I will not do it. Not now, not tomorrow, not ever. Go back to her, Lestat. Live this mortal life."

"How dare you make this choice for me!" I was on my feet again, and finished with whining and begging.

"Don't come at me again," he said patiently. "If you do, I shall hurt you. And that I don't wish to do."

"Ah, you've killed me! That's what you've done. You think I believe all your lies! You've condemned me to this rotting, stinking, aching body, that's what you've done! You think I don't know the depth of hatred in you, the true face of retribution when I see it! For the love of God, speak the truth."

"It isn't the truth. I love you. But you are blind with impatience now, and overwrought with simple aches and pains. It is you who will never forgive me if I rob you of this destiny. Only it will take time for you to see the true meaning of what I've done."

"No, no, please." I came towards him, only this time not in anger. I approached slowly, until I could lay my hands on his shoulders and smell the faint fragrance of dust and the grave that clung to his clothes. Lord God, what was our skin that it drew the light to itself so exquisitely? And our eyes. Ah, to look into his eyes.

"Louis," I said. "I want you to take me. Please, do as I ask you. Leave the interpretations of all my tales to me. Take me, Louis, look at me." I snatched up his cold, lifeless hand and laid it on my face. "Feel the blood in me, feel the heat. You want me, Louis, you know you do. You want me, you want me in your power the way I had you in my power so long, long ago. I'll be your fledgling, your child, Louis. Please, do this. Don't make me beg you on my knees."

I could sense the change in him, the sudden predatory glaze that covered his eyes. But what was stronger than his thirst? His will.

"No, Lestat," he whispered. "I can't do it. Even if I'm wrong and you are right, and all your metaphors are meaningless, I can't do it."

I took him in my arms, oh, so cold, so unyielding, this monster which I had made out of human flesh. I pressed my lips against his cheek, shuddering as I did so, my fingers sliding around his neck.

He didn't move away from me. He couldn't bring himself to do it. I felt the slow silent heave of his chest against mine.

"Do it to me, please, beautiful one," I whispered in his ear. "Take this heat into your veins, and give me back all the power that I once gave to you." I pressed my lips to his cold, colorless mouth. "Give me the future, Louis. Give me eternity. Take me off this cross."

In the corner of my eye, I saw his hand rise. Then I felt the satin fingers against my cheek. I felt him stroke my neck. "I can't do it, Lestat."

"You can, you know you can," I whispered, kissing his ear as I spoke to him, choking back the tears, my left arm slipping around his waist. "Oh, don't leave me in this misery, don't do it."

"Don't beg me anymore," he said sorrowfully. "It's useless. I'm going now. You won't see me again."

"Louis!" I held fast to him. "You can't refuse me."

"Ah, but I can and I have."

I could feel him stiffening, trying to withdraw without bruising me. I held him ever more tightly, refusing to back away.

"You won't find me again here. But you know where to find her. She's waiting for you. Don't you see your own victory? Mortal again, and so very, very young. Mortal again, and so very, very beautiful. Mortal again, with all your knowledge and with the same indomitable will."

Firmly and easily he removed my arms and pushed me back, closing his hands over mine as he held me away from him.

"Good-bye, Lestat," he said. "Perhaps the others will come to you. In time, when they feel you've paid enough."

I gave one last cry, trying to free my hands, trying to fix upon him, for I knew full well what he meant to do.

In a dark flash of movement, he was gone, and I was lying on the floor.

The candle had fallen over on the desk and had gone out. Only the light of the dying fire filled the little room. And the shutters of the door stood open, and the rain was falling, thin and quiet, yet steady. And I knew I was completely alone.

I had fallen to one side, my hands out before me to break the fall. And as I rose now, I cried out to him, praying that somehow he could hear me, no matter how far away he'd gone.

"Louis, help me. I don't want to be alive. I don't want to be mortal! Louis, don't leave me here! I can't bear it! I don't want it! I don't want to save my soul!"

How long I repeated these themes I don't know. Finally, I was too exhausted to continue; and the sounds of this mortal voice and all its desperation were hurtful to my own ears.

I sat on the floor, one leg crooked beneath me, my elbow resting on my knee, my fingers in my hair. Mojo had come forward, fearfully, and lay now beside me, and I leaned down and pressed my forehead into his fur.

The little fire was almost gone out. The rain hissed and sighed and redoubled its strength, but falling straight from the heavens without a breath of hateful wind.

Finally I looked up at this dark, dismal little place, at its jumble of books and old statues, at the dust and filth everywhere, and at the glowing embers heaped in the little hearth. How weary I was; how seared from my own anger; how close to despair.

Had I ever in all my misery been this completely without hope?

My eyes moved sluggishly to the doorway, and to the steady downpour, and the menacing darkness which lay beyond. Yes, go out in it, you and Mojo, who will of course love it as he loved the snow. You have to go out in it. You have to get out of this absmyal little house, and find some comfortable shelter where you can rest.

My rooftop apartment, surely there was some way I could break into it. Surely . . . some way. And then the sun was coming in a few hours, wasn't it? Ah, this my lovely city, beneath the warm light of the sun.

For God's sake, don't start weeping again. You need to rest and to think.

But first, before you go, why don't you burn down his house! Let the big Victorian alone. He doesn't love it. But burn his little shack!

I could feel myself breaking into an irresistible and malicious smile, even as the tears still hovered in my eyes.

Yes, burn it down! He deserves it. And of course he's taken his writings with him, yes, indeed he has, but all his books will go up in smoke! And that's exactly what he deserves.

At once I gathered up the paintings—a gorgeous Monet, a couple of small Picassos, and a ruby-red egg tempera panel of the medieval period, all deteriorating badly, of course—and I rushed out and into the old empty Victorian mansion, and stashed these in a darkened corner which seemed both safe and dry.

Then I went back into the little house, snatched up his candle, and thrust it into the remains of the fire. At once the soft ashes exploded with tiny orange sparks; and the sparks fastened themselves upon the wick.

"Oh, you deserve this, you treacherous ungrateful bastard!" I seethed as I put the flame to the books piled against the wall, carefully ruffling their pages to get them going. And then to an old coat thrown over a wooden chair, which went up like straw, and then to the red velvet cushions of the chair that had been mine. Ah, yes, burn it, all of it.

I kicked a pile of moldering magazines beneath his desk and ignited them. I touched the flame to one book after another, and tossed these like flaming coals into all parts of the little house.

Mojo edged away from these little bonfires, and finally went out into the rain, where he stood at a distance, gazing at me through the open door.

Ah, but things were moving too slowly. And Louis has a drawer full of candles; how could I have forgotten them—curse this mortal brain!—and now I drew them out, some twenty of them, and started setting the wax to burning fiercely, never mind the wick, and flinging them into the red velvet chair to make a great heat. I hurled them at the heaps of debris that remained, and I flung burning books at the wet shutters, and ignited the old fragments of curtain which here and there hung forgotten and neglected from old rods. I kicked out holes in the rotted plaster and threw the burning candles in upon the old lathing, and then I leant down and set afire the worn threadbare rugs, wrinkling them to let the air move underneath.

Within minutes the place was full of raging blazes, but the red chair and the desk were the greatest of all. I ran out into the rain, and I saw the fire flickering through the dark broken slats.

A damp ugly smoke rose as the fire licked at the wet shutters, as it curled up and out of the windows into the wet mass of the Queen's Wreath! Oh, cursed rain! But then as the blaze of the desk and chair grew ever brighter, the entire little building exploded with orange flames! Shutters were blown into the darkness; a great hole burst in the roof.

"Yes, yes, burn!" I shouted, the rain pelting my face, my eyelids. I was practically jumping up and down with joy. Mojo backed towards the darkened mansion, lowering his head. "Burn, burn," I declared. "Louis, I wish I could burn you! I'd do it! Oh, if only I knew where you lie by day!"

But even in my glee I realized I was weeping. I was wiping at my mouth with the back of my hand, and crying. "How could you leave me like this! How could you do it! I curse you." And dissolving into tears, I went down on my knees again against the rainy earth.

I sank back on my heels, hands folded in front of me, beaten and miserable and staring at the great fire. Lights were snapping on in distant houses. I could hear the thin scream of a siren coming. I knew I should go.

Yet still I knelt there, and I felt almost stuporous when Mojo suddenly roused me with one of his deep, most menacing growls. I realized he had come to stand beside me, and was pressing his wet fur to my very face, and that he was peering off towards the burning house.

I moved to catch hold of his collar and was about to retreat when I made out the source of his alarm. It was no helpful mortal. But rather an unearthly and dim white figure standing still as an apparition near the burning building, luridly illuminated by the blaze.

Even with these weak mortal eyes, I saw it was Marius! And I saw the expression of wrath stamped on his face. Never have I seen such a perfect reflection of fury, and there was not the slightest doubt that it was what he meant for me to see.

My lips parted but my voice had died in my throat. All I could do was stretch out my arms to him, to send from my heart a silent plea for mercy and for help.

Again the dog gave his fierce warning and seemed about to spring.

And as I watched helplessly, and trembling uncontrollably, the figure turned its back slowly, and giving me one last angry, disdainful look, disappeared.

It was then that I sprang to life, crying his name. "Marius!" I rose to my feet, calling louder and louder. "Marius, don't leave me here. Help me!" I reached up into the skies. "Marius," I roared.

But it was useless and I knew it.

The rain soaked through my coat. It soaked into my shoes. My hair was slick and wet with it, and it didn't matter now whether or not I'd been crying, because the rain had washed away the tears.

"You think I'm defeated," I whispered. What need was there to shout for him? "You think you've passed your judgment, and that's the end of it. Oh, you think it is as simple as that. Well you are wrong.

I shall never have vengeance for this moment. But you will see me again. You will see me again."

I bowed my head.

The night was full of mortal voices, the sounds of running feet. A great noisy engine had come to a halt on the distant corner. I had to force these miserable mortal limbs to move.

I motioned for Mojo to follow, and off we crept past the ruins of the little house, still burning merrily, and over a low garden wall and through an overgrown alley and away.

ONLY later did I think how close we had probably come to capture— the mortal arsonist and his menacing dog.

But how could such a thing matter? Louis had cast me out, and so had Marius—Marius, who might find my preternatural body before I did, and destroy it on the spot. Marius, who might already have destroyed it so that I was left forever within this mortal frame.

Oh, if ever I'd known such misery in my mortal youth, I didn't remember it. And if I had, it would have been little consolation to me now. As for my fear, it was unspeakable! Reason couldn't compass it. Round and round I went with my hopes and feeble plans.

"I have to find the Body Thief, I have to find him and you must give me time, Marius, if you will not help me, you must grant me that much."

Over and over I said it like the Hail Mary of a rosary as I trudged on through the bitter rain.

Once or twice I even shouted my prayers in the darkness, standing beneath a high dripping oak tree, and trying to see the approaching light coming down through the wet sky.

Who in all the world would help me?

David was my only hope, though what he could do to help me, I couldn't even imagine. David! And what if he, too, turned his back on me?

NINETEEN

I WAS sitting in the Café du Monde as the sun came up, thinking, how shall I get into my rooftop rooms? This little problem was preventing me from losing my mind. Was that the key to mortal survival? Hmmm. How to breach my luxurious little apartment? I myself had fitted the entry to the roof garden with an impassable iron gate. I myself secured the doors of the penthouse itself with numerous and complex locks. Indeed, the windows were barred against intruding mortals, though how they could have possibly reached the windows, I never truly considered before.

Ah, well, I shall have to get through the gate. I shall work some verbal magic on the other tenants of the building—all tenants of the blond Frenchman Lestat de Lioncourt, who treats them very well, I might add. I shall convince them I am a French cousin of the landlord, sent to take care of the penthouse in his absence, and that I must be allowed in at all costs. Never mind that I must use a crowbar! Or an ax! Or a buzz saw. Only a technicality, as they say in this age. I must get in.

And then what will I do? Pick up a kitchen knife—for the place has such things, though God knows I never had need of a kitchen—and slit my mortal throat?

No. Call David. There is no one else in this world to whom you can turn, and oh, think of the dreadful things David is going to say!

When I ceased to think of all this, I fell immediately into the crushing despair.

They had cast me out. Marius. Louis. In my worst folly, they had refused me help. Oh, I had mocked Marius, true. I had refused his wisdom, his company, his rules.

Oh, yes, I had asked for it, as mortals so often declare. And I had done this despicable thing of letting loose the Body Thief with my powers. True. Guilty again of spectacular blunders and experiments. But had I ever dreamed of what it would truly mean to be stripped utterly of my powers and on the outside looking in? The others knew; they must know. And they had let Marius come to render the judgment, to let me know that for what I had done, I was cast out!

But Louis, my beautiful Louis, how *could* he have spurned me! I would have defied heaven to help Louis! I had so counted upon Louis, I had so counted upon waking this night with the old blood running powerful and true in my veins.

Oh, Lord God—I was no longer one of them. I was not anything but this mortal man, sitting here in the smothering warmth of the café, drinking this coffee—ah, yes, nice-tasting coffee, of course—and munching on the sugar doughnuts with no hope of ever regaining his glorious place in the dark Elohim.

Ah, how I hated them. How I wished to harm them! But who was to blame for all this? Lestat—now six feet two inches tall, with brown eyes and rather dark skin and a nice mop of wavy brown hair; Lestat, with muscular arms and strong legs, and another severe mortal chill sickening and weakening him; Lestat, with his faithful dog, Mojo— Lestat pondering how in the world he would catch the demon who had run off, not with his soul as so often happens, but with his body, a body which might have already been—don't think of it—destroyed!

Reason told me it was a little too early to plot anything. Besides, I have never had a deep interest in revenge. Revenge is the concern of those who are at some point or other beaten. I am not beaten, I told myself. No, not beaten. And victory is far more interesting to contemplate than revenge.

Ah, best to think of little things, things which can be changed. David had to listen to me. He had at least to give me his advice! But what else could he give? How could two mortal men go after that despicable creature. Ahhh . . .

And Mojo was hungry. He was looking up at me with his large clever brown eyes. How people in the café stared at him; what a wide berth they gave him, this ominous furry creature with his dark muzzle, tender pink-lined ears, and enormous paws. Really ought to feed Mojo. After all, the old cliché was true. This great hunk of dog flesh was my only friend!

Did Satan have a dog when they hurled him down into hell? Well, the dog would probably have gone with him, that much I knew.

"How do I do it, Mojo?" I asked. "How does a mere mortal catch the Vampire Lestat? Or have the old ones burnt my beautiful body to ashes? Was that the meaning of Marius's visit, to let me know it was done? Oooooh, God. What does the witch say in that ghastly film? How could you do this to my beautiful wickedness. Aaah, I have a fever again, Mojo. Things are going to take care of themselves. I'M GOING TO DIE!"

But Lord in heaven, behold the sun crashing down silently on the dirty pavements, look at my shabby and charming New Orleans waking to the beauteous Caribbean light.

"Let's go, Mojo. Time to break and enter. And then we can be warm and we can rest."

Stopping by the restaurant opposite the old French Market, I bought a mess of bones and meat for him. Surely it would do. Indeed, the kindly little waitress filled a sack with scraps from last night's garbage, with the lusty little affirmation that the dog was going to like that a lot! What about me? Didn't I want some breakfast? Wasn't I hungry on a beautiful winter morning like this?

"Later, darling." I placed a large bill in her hand. I was still rich, that was one consolation. Or at least I thought I was. I wouldn't know for certain until I reached my computer, and tracked the activities of the loathsome swindler for myself.

Mojo consumed his meal in the gutter without a single solitary complaint. That's a dog for you. Why wasn't I born a dog?

Now, where the hell was my penthouse apartment! I had to stop and to think, and then to wander two blocks out of my way, and back again before I found it, getting colder by the minute, though the sky was blue and the sun very bright now, for I almost never entered the building from the street.

Getting into the building was very easy. Indeed the door on Dumaine Street was very simple to force and then slam shut. Ah, but that gate, that will be the worst part, I thought, as I dragged my heavy legs up the stairs, one flight after another, Mojo waiting kindly at the landings for me to catch up.

At last I saw the bars of the gate, and the lovely sunlight streaming into the stairwell from the roof garden, and the flutter of the large green elephant ears, which were only a little bruised at the edges from the cold.

But this lock, how would I ever break this lock? I was in the process of estimating what tools I would need—how about a small bomb?—when I realized that I was looking at the door to my apartment some fifty feet away, and that it was not closed.

"Ah, God, the wretch has been here!" I whispered. "Damn him, Mojo, he's sacked my lair."

Of course that might be construed as a hopeful sign. The wretch still lived; the others hadn't done away with him. And I could still catch him! But how. I kicked the gate, sending a riot of pain through my foot and leg.

Then I grabbed hold of it and rattled it mercilessly but it was as secure in its old iron hinges as I had designed it to be! A weak revenant such as Louis couldn't have broken it, let alone a mortal man. Undoubtedly the fiend had never even touched it but made his entry as I did, out of the skies.

All right, stop this. Obtain some tools and do it quickly, and discover the extent of the damage which the fiend has done.

I turned to go, but just as I did so, Mojo stood at attention and gave his warning growl. Someone was moving inside the apartment. I saw a bit of shadow dance on the foyer wall.

Not the Body Thief, that was impossible, thank God. But who?

In an instant the question was answered. David appeared! My beautiful David, dressed in a dark tweed suit and overcoat and peering at me with his characteristic expression of curiosity and alertness over the length of the garden path. I don't think I have ever been so glad to see another mortal being in all my long accursed life.

I called his name at once. And then in French declared that it was I, Lestat. Please open the gate.

He did not immediately respond. Indeed, never had he seemed so dignified, self-possessed and so truly the elegant British gentleman as he stood there, staring at me, his narrow heavily lined face registering nothing but mute shock. He stared at the dog. Then he stared at me again. And then once more at the dog.

"David, it's Lestat, I swear to you!" I cried in English. "This is the body of the mechanic! Remember the photograph! James did it, David. I'm trapped in this body. What can I tell you to make you believe me? David, let me in."

He remained motionless. Then all of a sudden, he came forward with swift determined steps, his face quite unreadable as he stopped before the gate.

I was near to fainting with happiness. I clung to the bars still, with both hands as if I were in prison, and then I realized I was staring directly into his eyes—that for the first time we were the same height.

"David, you don't know how glad I am to see you," I said, lapsing into French again. "How did you ever get in? David, it's Lestat. It's me. Surely you believe me. You recognize my voice. David, God and the Devil in the Paris café! Who else knows but me!"

But it was not my voice to which he responded; he was staring into my eyes, and listening as if to distant sounds. Then quite suddenly his entire manner was altered and I saw the clear signs of recognition in his face.

"Oh, thank heaven," he said with a small, very polite British sigh.

He reached into his pocket for a small case, quickly removing from it a thin piece of metal which he inserted into the lock. I knew enough of the world to realize this was a burglar's tool of some sort. He swung the gate back for me, and then opened his arms.

Our embrace was long and warm and silent, and I fought furiously not to give way to tears. Only very seldom in all this time had I ever actually touched this being. And the moment was charged with an emotion which caught me somewhat off guard. The drowsy warmth of my embraces with Gretchen came back to me. I felt safe. And just for an instant, perhaps, I did not feel so utterly alone.

But there was no time now to enjoy this solace.

Reluctantly, I drew back, and thought again how splendid David looked. Indeed, so impressive was he to me that I could almost believe I was as young as the body I now inhabited. I needed him so.

All the little flaws of age which I naturally saw in him through my vampire eyes were invisible. The deep lines of his face seemed but part of his great expressive personality, along with the quiet light in his eyes. He looked entirely vigorous as he stood there in his very proper attire, the little gold watch chain glittering on his tweed waistcoat—so very solid and resourceful and grave.

"You know what the bastard's done," I said. "He's tricked me and abandoned me. And the others have also abandoned me. Louis, Marius. They've turned their backs on me. I'm marooned in this body, my friend. Come, I have to see if the monster has robbed my rooms."

I hurried towards the apartment door, scarce hearing the few words he uttered, to the effect that he thought the place was quite undisturbed.

He was right. The fiend had not rifled the apartment! Everything was exactly as I'd left it, down to my old velvet coat hanging on the open closet door. There was the yellow pad on which I'd made notes before my departure. And the computer. Ah, I had to go into the computer immediately and discover the extent of his thievery. And my

Paris agent, the poor man might still be in danger. I must contact him at once.

But I was distracted by the light pouring through the glass walls, the soft warm splendour of the sun spilling down upon the dark couches and chairs, and on the lush Persian carpet with its pale medallion and wreaths of roses, and even upon the few large modern paintings—furious abstracts all—which I had long ago chosen for these walls. I felt myself shudder at the sight of it, marveling again that electric illumination could never produce this particular sense of well-being which filled me now.

I also noted that there was a blazing fire going in the large white-tiled fireplace—David's doing, no doubt—and the smell of coffee coming from the nearby kitchen, a room I had scarce entered in the years I had inhabited this place.

At once David stammered an apology. He hadn't even checked into his hotel, so anxious was he to find me. He'd come here direct from the airport, and only gone out for a few little provisions so that he might spend a comfortable night keeping watch that I might come or think to call.

"Wonderful, very glad that you did," I said, a little amused by his British politeness. I was so glad to see him, and here he was apologizing for making himself at home.

I tore off the wet overcoat and sat down at the computer.

"This will take only a moment," I said, keying in the various commands, "and then I'll tell you about everything. But what made you come? Did you suspect what happened!"

"Of course I did," he said. "Don't you know of the vampire murder in New York? Only a monster could have wrecked those offices. Lestat, why didn't you call me? Why didn't you ask my help?"

"One moment," I said. Already the little letters and figures were coming up on the screen. My accounts were in order. Had the fiend been into this system, I would have seen preprogrammed signals of invasion throughout. Of course there was no way to know for certain that he hadn't attacked my accounts in European banks until I went into their files. And damn, I couldn't remember the code words, and in fact, I was having a difficult time managing the simplest commands.

"He was right," I muttered. "He warned me my thinking processes wouldn't be the same." I switched from the finances program into Wordstar, my means of writing, and immediately typed out a communication to my Paris agent, sending it through the phone modem, asking him for an immediate status report, and reminding him to take the utmost personal care as to his own safety. Over and out.

I sat back, heaving a deep breath, which immediately brought on a little fit of coughing, and realized that David was staring at me as if the sight were too shocking for him to absorb. Indeed, it was almost comical the way he was looking at me. Then again, he looked at Mojo, who was inspecting the place silently and a little sluggishly, eyes turning to me over and over for some command.

I snapped my fingers for Mojo to come to me and gave him a deep strong hug. David watched all this as if it were the weirdest thing in the world.

"Good Lord, you are really in that body," he whispered. "Not just hovering inside, but anchored into the cells."

"You're telling me," I said disgustedly. "It's dreadful, the whole mess. And the others won't help, David. I'm cast out." I gritted my teeth in rage. "Cast out!" I went into a seething growl which inadvertently excited Mojo so that he at once licked my face.

"Of course I deserve it," I said, stroking Mojo. "That's the simplest thing about dealing with me, apparently. I always deserve the worst! The worst disloyalty, the worst betrayal, the worst abandonment! Lestat the scoundrel. Well, they have left this scoundrel entirely on his own."

"I've been frantic to reach you," he said, his voice at once controlled and subdued. "Your agent in Paris swore he couldn't help me. I was going to try that address in Georgetown." He pointed to the yellow pad on the table. "Thank God you're here."

"David, my worst fear is that the others have destroyed James and my body with him. This may be the only body I now possess."

"No, I don't think so," he said with convincing equanimity. "Your little body borrower has left quite a trail. But come, get out of these wet clothes. You're catching cold."

"What do you mean, trail?"

"You know we keep track of such crimes. Now, please, the clothes."

"More crimes after New York?" I asked excitedly. I let him coax me towards the fireplace, immediately glad of the warmth. I pulled off the damp sweater and shirt. Of course there was nothing to fit me in my various closets. And I realized I had forgotten my valise somewhere on Louis's property last night. "New York was Wednesday night, was it not?"

"My clothes will fit you," David said, immediately snatching the thought from my mind. He headed for a mammoth leather suitcase in the corner.

"What's happened? What makes you think it's James?"

"Has to be," he answered, popping open the suitcase and removing several folded garments, and then a tweed suit very like his own, still on its hanger, which he laid over the nearest chair. "Here, change into these. You're going to catch your death."

"Oh, David," I said, continuing to undress. "I've almost caught my death repeatedly. In fact, I've spent my whole brief mortal life nearly dying. The care of this body is a revolting nuisance; how do living people endure this endless cycle of eating, pissing, sniveling, defecating, and then eating again! When you mix in fever, headache, attacks of coughing, and a runny nose, it becomes a penitential sentence. And prophylactics, good Lord. Removing the ugly little things is worse than having to put them on! Whatever made me think I wanted to do this! The other crimes—when did they take place! When is more important than where."

He had fallen into staring at me again, too purely shocked to answer. Mojo was giving him the eye now, sizing him up more or less, and offering a friendly lick of his pink tongue to David's hand. David petted him lovingly, but continued to stare blankly at me.

"David," I said, as I took off the wet socks. "Speak to me. The other crimes! You said that James had left a trail."

"It's so wildly uncanny," he said in a stunned voice. "I have a dozen pictures of this face. But to see you inside it. Oh, I simply couldn't imagine it. Not at all."

"When did this fiend strike last?"

"Ah . . . The last report was from the Dominican Republic. That was, let me see, two nights ago."

"Dominican Republic! Why in the world would he go there?"

"Exactly what I would like to know. Before that he struck near Bal Harbour in Florida. Both times it was a high-rise condominium, and entry was the same as in New York—through the glass wall. Furniture smashed to pieces at all three crime scenes; wall safes ripped from their moorings; bonds, gold, jewelry taken. One man dead in New York, a bloodless corpse, of course. Two women left drained in

Florida, and a family killed in Santo Domingo, with only the father drained in classic vampire style."

"He can't control his strength. He's blundering about like a robot!"

"Exactly what I thought. It was the combination of destructiveness and sheer force which first alerted me. The creature's unbelievably inept! And the whole operation is so stupid. But what I can't figure is why he's chosen these locations for his various thefts." Suddenly he broke off and turned away, almost shyly.

I realized I had stripped off all the garments and was standing there naked, and this had produced in him a strange reticence, and a near blush to his face.

"Here, dry socks," he said. "Don't you know better than to go about in soaking wet garments?" He tossed the socks to me without looking up.

"I don't know much of anything," I said. "That's what I've discovered. I see what you mean about the locations. Why in the world would he journey to the Caribbean when he might steal to his heart's content in the suburbs of Boston or New York?"

"Yes. Unless the cold is giving him considerable discomfort, but does that make sense?"

"No. He doesn't feel it that keenly. It's just not the same."

It felt good to pull on the dry shirt and pants. And these garments did fit, though they were loose in a rather old-fashioned way—not the slim tailored clothes more popular with the young. The shirt was heavy broadcloth, and the tweed pants were pleated, but the waistcoat felt snug and warm.

"Here, I can't tie this tie with mortal fingers," I declared. "But why am I dressing up like this, David? Don't you ever go around in anything casual, as the expression goes? Good Lord, we look like we're going to a funeral. Why must I wear this noose around my neck?"

"Because you'll look foolish in a tweed suit without it," he answered in a slightly distracted voice. "Here, let me help you." Once again, he had that shy look about him as he drew close to me. I realized that he was powerfully drawn to this body. In the old one, I had amazed him; but this body truly ignited his passion. And as I studied him closely, as I felt the busy work of his fingers on the knot of the tie—that keen little pressure—I realized that I was powerfully attracted to him.

I thought of all the times I'd wanted to take him, enfold him in my arms, and sink my teeth slowly and tenderly into his neck, and drink his blood. Ah, now I might have him in a sense without having him—in the mere human tangling with his limbs, in whatever combination of intimate gestures and delectable little embraces he might like. And I might like.

The idea paralyzed me. It sent a soft chill over the surface of my human skin. I felt *connected* to him, connected as I had been to the sad unfortunate young woman whom I'd raped, to the wandering tourists of the snow-covered capital city, my brothers and sisters—connected as I had been to my beloved Gretchen.

Indeed so strong was this awareness—of being human and being with a human—that I feared it suddenly in all its beauty. And I saw that the fear was part of the beauty.

Ah, yes, I was mortal now as he was. I flexed my fingers, and slowly straightened my back, letting the chill become a deep erotic sensation.

He broke away from me abruptly, alarmed and vaguely determined, picked up the jacket from the chair, and helped me to put it on.

"You have to tell me all that's happened to you," he said. "And within an hour or so we may have news from London, that is, if the bastard has struck again."

I reached out and clamped my weak, mortal hand on his shoulder, drew him to me, and kissed him softly on the side of his face. Once again, he backed away.

"Stop all this nonsense," he said, as if reproving a child. "I want to know everything. Now, have you had breakfast? You need a handkerchief. Here."

"How will we get this news from London?"

"Fax from the Motherhouse to the hotel. Now come, let's have something to eat together. We have a day of work ahead to figure this all out."

"If he isn't already dead," I said with a sigh. "Two nights ago in Santo Domingo." I was again filled with a crushing and black despair. The delicious and frustrating erotic impulse was threatened.

David removed a long wool scarf from the suitcase. He placed this around my neck.

"Can't you call London again now by phone?" I asked.

"It's a bit early, but I'll give it a try."

He found the phone beside the couch, and was in fast conversation with someone across the sea for about five minutes. No news yet.

Police in New York, Florida, and Santo Domingo were not in communication with each other, apparently, as no connections regarding these crimes had yet been made.

At last he hung up. "They'll fax information to the hotel as soon as they receive it. Let's go there, shall we? I myself am famished. I've been here all night long, waiting. Oh, and that dog. What will you do with that splendid dog?"

"He's had breakfast. He'll be happy in the roof garden. You're very anxious to be out of these rooms, aren't you? Why don't we simply get into bed together? I don't understand."

"You're serious?"

I shrugged. "Of course." Serious! I was beginning to be obsessed with this simple little possibility. Making love before anything else happened. Seemed like a perfectly marvelous idea!

Again, he fell to staring at me in maddening trancelike silence.

"You do realize," he said, "that this is an absolutely magnificent body, don't you? I mean, you aren't insensible to the fact that you've been deposited in a . . . a most impressive piece of young male flesh."

"I looked it over well before the switch, remember? Why is it you don't want to . . ."

"You've been with a woman, haven't you?"

"I wish you wouldn't read my mind. It's rude. Besides, what does that matter to you?"

"A woman you loved."

"I have always loved both men and women."

"That's a slightly different use of the word 'love.' Listen, we simply can't do it now. So behave yourself. I must hear everything about this creature James. It's going to take us time to make a plan."

"A plan. You really think we can stop him?"

"Of course I do!" He beckoned for me to come.

"But how?" I asked. We were going out the door.

"We must look at the creature's behavior. We must assess his weaknesses and his strengths. And remember there are two of us against him. And we have a powerful advantage."

"But what advantage?"

"Lestat, clear your mortal brain of all these rampant erotic images and come. I can't think on an empty stomach, and obviously you're not thinking straight at all."

Mojo came padding to the gate to follow us, but I told him to stay.

I kissed him tenderly on the side of his long black nose, and he lay down on the wet concrete, and merely peered at me in solemn disappointed fashion as we went down the stairs.

IT WAS only a matter of several blocks to the hotel, and the walk beneath the blue sky was not intolerable, even with the biting wind. I was too cold, however, to begin my story, and also the sight of the sunlighted city kept tearing me out of my thoughts.

Once again, I was impressed with the carefree attitudes of the people who roamed by day. All the world seemed blessed in this light, regardless of the temperature. And a sadness was growing in me as I beheld it, because I really didn't want to remain in this sunlighted world no matter how beautiful it was.

No, give me back my preternatural vision, I thought. Give me back the dark beauty of the world by night. Give me back my unnatural strength and endurance, and I shall cheerfully sacrifice this spectacle forever. The Vampire Lestat—*c'est moi.*

Stopping at the hotel desk, David left word that we would be in the coffee shop, and any fax material which came in must be brought to us at once.

Then we settled at a quiet white-draped table in the corner of the vast old-fashioned room with its fancy plaster ceiling and white silk draperies, and commenced to devour an enormous New Orleans breakfast of eggs, biscuits, fried meats, gravy, and thick buttery grits.

I had to confess that the food situation had improved with the journey south. Also I was better at eating now, and wasn't choking so much, or scraping my tongue on my own teeth. The thick syrupy coffee of my home city was past perfection. And the dessert of broiled bananas and sugar was enough to bring any sensible human being to his knees.

But in spite of these tantalizing delights, and my desperate hope that we would soon have a report from London, my main concern was that of pouring out for David the entire woeful tale. Again, and again, he pushed for details, and interrupted me with questions, so it became in fact a far more thorough account than I had ever given Louis, and one that wrung from me considerably more pain.

It was agony to relive my naive conversation with James in the town house, to confess that I had not cared sufficiently to be suspicious of him, that I'd been too satisfied that a mere mortal could never trick me.

And then came the shameful rape, the poignant account of my time with Gretchen, the awful nightmares of Claudia, and the parting from Gretchen to come home to Louis, who misunderstood all that I laid before him, and insisted upon his own interpretation of my words as he refused to give me what I sought.

No small part of the pain was that my anger had left me, and I felt only the old crushing grief. I saw Louis again in my mind's eye, and he was not my tender, embraceable lover any longer, so much as an unfeeling angel who had barred me from the Dark Court.

"I understand why he refused," I said dully, barely able to speak about it. "Perhaps I should have known. And very truly, I can't believe he will hold out against me forever. He's simply carried away with this sublime idea of his that I ought to go save my soul. It's what he would do, you see. And yet, in a way, he himself would never do it. And he's never understood me. Never. That's why he described me so vividly yet poorly in his book over and over again. If I am trapped in this body, if it becomes quite plain to him that I don't intend to go off into the jungles of French Guiana with Gretchen, I think he will give in to me eventually. Even though I did burn his house. It might take years, of course! Years in this miserable—"

"You're getting furious again," said David. "Calm down. And what in the world do you mean—you burnt his house."

"I was angry!" I said in a tense whisper. "My God. Angry. That isn't even the word."

I thought I had been too unhappy to be angry. I realized this wasn't so. But I was too unhappy to carry the point further. I took another bracing swallow of the thick black coffee and as best I could, I went on to describe how I had seen Marius by the light of the burning shack. Marius had wanted for me to see him. Marius had rendered a judgment, and I did not know truly what that judgment was.

Now the cold despair did come over me, obliterating the anger quite completely, and I stared listlessly at the plate before me, at the half-empty restaurant with its shining silver and napkins folded at so many empty places like little hats. I looked beyond to the muted lights of the lobby, with that awful gloom closing upon everything, and then I looked at David, who for all his character, his sympathy, and his charm was not the marvelous being he would have been to me with my vampire eyes, but only another mortal, frail and living on the edge of death as I did.

I felt dull and miserable. I could say no more.

"Listen to me," said David. "I don't believe that your Marius has destroyed this creature. He would not have revealed himself to you if he'd done such a thing. I can't imagine the thoughts or feelings of such a being. I can't even imagine yours, and I know you as I know my dearest and oldest friends. But I don't believe he would do it. He came to display his anger, to refuse assistance, and that was his judgment, yes. But I wager he's giving you time to recover your body. And you must remember: however you perceived his expression, you saw it through a human being's eyes."

"I've considered this," I said listlessly. "To tell the truth, what else can I do but believe that my body is still there to be reclaimed?" I shrugged. "I don't know how to give up."

He smiled at me, a lovely deep warm smile.

"You've had a splendid adventure," he said. "Now before we plot to catch this glorified purse snatcher, allow me to ask you a question. And don't lose your temper, please. I can see that you don't know your own strength in this body any more than you did in the other."

"Strength? What strength! This is a weak, flopping, sloshy, repulsive collection of nerves and ganglia. Don't even mention the word 'strength.' "

"Nonsense. You're a big strapping healthy young male of some one hundred and ninety pounds, without an ounce of spare fat on you! You have fifty years of mortal life ahead of you. For the love of heaven, realize what advantages you possess."

"All right. All right. It's jolly. So happy to be alive!" I whispered, because if I hadn't whispered, I would have howled. "And I could be smashed by a truck outside in the street at half past noon today! Good God, David, don't you think I despise myself that I cannot endure these simple trials? I hate it. I hate being this weak and cowardly creature!"

I sat back in the chair, eyes roving the ceiling, trying not to cough or sneeze or weep or make a fist out of my right hand which I might drive through the tabletop or perhaps the nearby wall. "I loathe cowardice!" I whispered.

"I know," he said kindly. He studied me for a few quiet moments, and then blotted his lips with his napkin, and reached for his coffee. Then he spoke again. "Assuming that James is still running about in your old body, you are absolutely certain that you want to make the switch back into it—that you *do* want to be Lestat in his old body again."

I laughed sadly to myself. "How can I make that any plainer?" I asked wearily. "*How* in the hell *can* I make the switch again! That is the question upon which my sanity depends."

"Well, first we must locate James. We shall devote our entire energy to finding him. We shall not give up until we are convinced that there is no James to be found."

"Again, you're making it sound so simple! How can such a thing be done?"

"Shhh, you're attracting needless attention," he said with quiet authority. "Drink the orange juice. You need it. I'll order some more."

"I don't need the orange juice and I don't need any more nursing," I said. "Are you seriously suggesting that we have a chance of catching this fiend?"

"Lestat, as I told you before—think on the most obvious and unchangeable limitation of your former state. A vampire cannot move about in the day. A vampire is almost entirely helpless in the day. Granted, there is a reflex to reach out for and harm anyone disturbing his rest. But otherwise, he is helpless. And for some eight to twelve hours he must remain in one place. That gives us the traditional advantage, especially since we know so much about the being in question. And all we require is an opportunity to confront the creature, and confuse him sufficiently for the switch to be made."

"We can force it?"

"Yes, I know that we can. He can be knocked loose from that body long enough for you to get in."

"David, I must tell you something. In this body I have no psychic power at all. I didn't have any when I was a mortal boy. I don't think I can . . . rise out of this body. I tried once in Georgetown. I couldn't budge from the flesh."

"Anyone can do this little trick, Lestat; you were merely afraid.

And some of what you learned in the vampiric body, you now carry with you. Obviously the preternatural cells gave you an advantage, but the mind itself does not forget. Obviously James took his mental powers from body to body. You must have taken some part of your knowledge with you as well."

"Well, I was frightened. I've been afraid to try since—afraid I'd get out and then couldn't get back in."

"I'll teach you how to rise out of the body. I'll teach you how to make a concerted assault upon James. And remember, there are two of us, Lestat. You and I together will make the assault. And I do have considerable psychic power, to use the simplest descriptive words for it. There are many things which I can do."

"David, I shall be your slave for eternity in exchange for this. Anything you wish I will get for you. I shall go to the ends of the earth for you. If only this can be done."

He hesitated as if he wanted to make some small jesting comment, but then thought the better of it. And went right on.

"We will begin with our lessons as soon as we can. But the more I consider it, I think it's best I jolt him out of the body. I can do it before he even realizes that you are there. Yes, that must be our game plan. He won't suspect me when he sees me. I can veil my thoughts from him easily enough. And that's another thing you must learn, to veil your thoughts."

"But what if he recognizes you. David, he knows who you are. He remembers you. He spoke of you. What's to stop him from burning you alive the minute he sees you?"

"The place where the meeting occurs. He won't risk a little conflagration too near his person. And we shall be sure to ensnare him where he would not dare to show his powers at all. We may have to lure him into position. This requires thinking. And until we know how to find him, well, that part can wait."

"We approach him in a crowd."

"Or very near to sunrise, when he cannot risk a fire near his lair."

"Exactly."

"Now, let's try to make a fair assessment of his powers from the information we have in hand."

He paused as the waiter swooped down upon the table with one of those beautiful heavy silver-plated coffeepots which hotels of quality always possess. They have a patina like no other silver, and always several tiny little dents. I watched the black brew coming out of the little spout.

Indeed, I realized I was watching quite a few little things as we sat there, anxious and miserable though I was. Merely being with David gave me hope.

David took a hasty sip of the fresh cup as the waiter went away, and then reached into the pocket of his coat. He placed in my hand a little bundle of thin sheets of paper. "These are newspaper stories of the murders. Read them carefully. Tell me anything that comes to your mind."

The first story, "Vampire Murder in Midtown," enraged me beyond words. I noted the wanton destruction which David had described. Had to be clumsiness, to smash the furniture so stupidly. And the theft—how silly in the extreme. As for my poor agent, his neck had been broken as he'd been drained of his blood. More clumsiness.

"It's a wonder he can use the power of flight at all," I said angrily. "Yet here, he went through the wall on the thirtieth floor."

"That doesn't mean he can use the power over really great distances," David replied.

"But how then did he get from New York to Bal Harbour in one night, and more significantly, why? If he is using commercial aircraft, why go to Bal Harbour instead of Boston? Or Los Angeles, or Paris, for heaven's sakes. Think of the high stakes for him were he to rob a great museum, an immense bank? Santo Domingo I don't understand. Even if he has mastered the power of flight, it can't be easy for him. So why on earth would he go there? Is he merely trying to scatter the kills so that no one will put together all the cases?"

"No," said David. "If he really wanted secrecy, he wouldn't operate in this spectacular style. He's blundering. He's behaving as if he's intoxicated!"

"Yes. And it does feel that way in the beginning, truly it does. You're overcome by the effect of your heightened senses."

"Is it possible that he is traveling through the air and merely striking wherever the winds carry him?" David asked. "That there is no pattern at all?"

I was considering the question as I read the other reports slowly, frustrated that I could not scan them as I would have done with my vampire eyes. Yes, more clumsiness, more stupidity. Human bodies crushed by "a heavy instrument," which was of course simply his fist.

"He likes to break glass, doesn't he?" I said. "He likes to surprise his victims. He must enjoy their fear. He leaves no witnesses. He steals everything of obvious value. And none of it is very valuable at all. How I hate him. And yet . . . I have done things as terrible myself."

I remembered the villain's conversations with me. How I had failed to see through his gentlemanly manner! But David's early descriptions of him, of his stupidity, and his self-destructiveness, also came back. And his clumsiness, how could I ever forget that?

"No," I said, finally. "I don't believe he can cover these distances. You have no idea how terrifying this power of flight can be. It's twenty times more terrifying than out-of-body travel. All of us loathe it. Even the roar of the wind induces a helplessness, a dangerous abandon, so to speak."

I paused. We know this flight in our dreams, perhaps because we knew it in some celestial realm beyond this earth before we were ever born. But we can't conceive of it as earthly creatures, and only I could know how it had damaged and torn my heart and soul.

"Go on, Lestat. I'm listening. I understand."

I gave a little sigh. "I learnt this power only because I was in the grip of one who was fearless," I said, "for whom it was nothing. There are those of us who never use this power. No. I can't believe he's mastered it. He's traveling by some other means and then taking to the air only when the prey is near at hand."

"Yes, that would seem to square with the evidence, if only we knew—"

He was suddenly distracted. An elderly hotel clerk had just appeared in the distant doorway. He came towards us with maddening slowness, a genial kindly man with a large envelope in his hand.

At once David brought a bill out of his pocket, and held it in readiness.

"Fax, sir, just in."

"Ah, thank you so much."

He tore open the envelope.

"Ah, here we are. News wire via Miami. A hilltop villa on the island of Curaçao. Probable time early yesterday evening, not discovered till four a.m. Five persons found dead."

"Curaçao! Where the hell is that?"

"This is even more baffling. Curaçao is a Dutch island—very far south in the Caribbean. Now, that really makes no sense at all."

We scanned the story together. Once again robbery was apparently the motive. The thief had come crashing through a skylight, and had demolished the contents of two rooms. The entire family had been killed. Indeed, the sheer viciousness of the crime had left the island in the grip of terror. There had been two bloodless corpses, one that of a small child.

"Surely the devil isn't simply moving south!"

"Even in the Caribbean there are far more interesting places," said David. "Why, he's overlooked the entire coast of Central America. Come, I want to get a map. Let's have a look at this pattern flat out. I spied a little travel agent in the lobby. He's bound to have some maps for us. We'll take everything back to your rooms."

The agent was most obliging, an elderly bald-headed fellow with a soft cultured voice, who groped about in the clutter of his desk for several maps. Curaçao? Yes, he had a brochure or two on the place. Not a very interesting island, as the Caribbean islands go.

"Why do people go there?" I asked.

"Well, in the main they don't," he confessed, rubbing the top of his bald head. "Except for the cruise ships, of course. They've been stopping there again these last few years. Yes, here." He placed a little folder in my hand for a small ship called the *Crown of the Seas*, very pretty in the picture, which meandered all through the islands, its final stop Curaçao before it started home.

"Cruise ships!" I whispered, staring at the picture. My eyes moved to the giant posters of ships which lined the office walls. "Why, he had pictures of ships all over his house in Georgetown," I said. "David, that's it. He's on some sort of ship! Don't you remember what you told me. His father worked for some shipping company. He himself said something about wanting to sail to America aboard a great ship."

"My God," David said. "You may be right. New York, Bal Harbour . . ." He looked at the agent. "Do cruise ships stop at Bal Harbour?"

"Port Everglades," said the agent. "Right near it. But not very many start from New York."

"What about Santo Domingo?" I asked. "Do they stop there?"

"Yes, that's a regular port all right. They all vary their itineraries. What sort of ship do you have in mind?"

Quickly David jotted down the various points and the nights

upon which the attacks had happened, without an explanation, of course.

But then he looked crestfallen.

"No," he said, "I can see it's impossible, myself. What cruise ship could possibly make the journey from Florida all the way to Curaçao in three nights?"

"Well, there is one," said the agent, "and as a matter of fact, she sailed from New York this last Wednesday night. It's the flagship of the Cunard Line, the *Queen Elizabeth 2.*"

"That's it," I said. "The *Queen Elizabeth 2*. David, it was the very ship he mentioned to me. You said his father—"

"But I thought the *QE2* makes the transatlantic crossing," said David.

"Not in winter," said the agent, agreeably. "She's in the Caribbean until March. And she's probably the fastest ship sailing any sea anywhere. She can do twenty-eight knots. But here, we can check the itinerary right now."

He went into another seemingly hopeless search through the papers on his desk, and at last produced a large handsomely printed brochure, opening it and flattening it with his right hand.

"Yes, left New York Wednesday. She docked at Port Everglades Friday morning, sailed before midnight, then on to Curaçao, where she arrived yesterday morning at five a.m. But she didn't stop in the Dominican Republic, I'm afraid, can't help you there."

"Never mind that, she passed it!" David said. "She passed the Dominican Republic the very next night! Look at the map. That's it, of course. Oh, the little fool. He all but told you himself, Lestat, with all his mad obsessive chatter! He's on board the *QE2,* the ship which mattered so much to his father, the ship upon which the old man spent his life."

We thanked the agent profusely for the maps and brochures, then headed for the taxis out front.

"Oh, it's so bloody typical of him!" David said as the car carried us towards my apartment. "Everything is symbolic with this madman. And he himself was fired from the *QE2* amid scandal and disgrace. I told you this, remember? Oh, you were so right. It's all a matter of obsession, and the little demon gave you the clue himself."

"Yes. Oh, definitely yes. And the Talamasca wouldn't send him to America on the *Queen Elizabeth 2*. He never forgave you for that."

"I hate him," David whispered, with a heat that amazed me even given the circumstances in which we were involved.

"But it isn't really so foolish, David," I said. "It's devilishly clever, don't you see? Yes, he tipped his hand to me in Georgetown, chattering away about it, and we can lay that down to his self-destructiveness, but I don't think he expected me to figure it out. And frankly, if you hadn't laid out the news stories for me of the other murders, maybe I never would have thought of it on my own."

"Possibly. I think he wants to be caught."

"No, David. He's hiding. From you, from me, and from the others. Oh, he's very smart. Here we have this beastly sorcerer, capable of cloaking himself entirely, and where does he conceal himself—amid a whole teeming little world of mortals in the womb of a fast-moving ship. Look at this itinerary! Why, every night she's sailing. Only by day does she remain in port."

"Have it your way," said David, "but I prefer to think of him as an idiot! And we're going to catch him! Now you told me you gave him a passport, did you not?"

"Clarence Oddbody was the name. But surely he didn't use it."

"We'll soon find out. My suspicion is that he boarded in New York in the usual way. It would have been crucial to him to be received with all due pomp and consideration—to book the finest suite and go parading up to the top deck, with stewards bowing to him. Those suites on the Signal Deck are enormous. No problem whatsoever for him to have a large trunk for his daylight hiding place. No cabin steward would trouble such a thing."

We had come around again to my building. He pulled out some bills to pay the driver, and up the stairs we went.

As soon as we reached the apartment, we sat down with the printed itinerary and the news stories and worked out a schedule of how the killings had been done.

It was plain the beast had struck my agent in New York only hours before the ship sailed. He'd had plenty of time to board before eleven p.m. The murder near Bal Harbour had been committed only hours before the ship docked. Obviously he covered a small distance by the power of flight, returning to his cabin or other hiding place before the sun rose.

For the Santo Domingo murder, he had left the ship for perhaps an hour, and then caught up with her on her journey south. Again, these distances were nothing. He did not even need preternatural sight to spot the giant *Queen Elizabeth 2* steaming across the open sea. The murders on Curaçao had taken place only a little while after the ship sailed. He'd probably caught up with the ship within less than an hour, laden with his loot.

The ship was now on her way north again. She had docked at La Guaira, on the coast of Venezuela, only two hours ago. If he struck tonight in Caracas or its environs, we knew we had him for certain. But we had no intention of waiting for further proof.

"All right, let's think this out," I said. "Dare we board this vessel ourselves?"

"Of course, we must."

"Then we should have fake passports for this. We may leave behind a great deal of confusion. David Talbot mustn't be implicated. And I can't use the passport he gave me. Why, I don't know where that passport is. Perhaps still in the town house in Georgetown. God knows why he used his own name on it, probably to get me in trouble first time I went through customs."

"Absolutely right. I can take care of the documents before we leave New Orleans. Now, we can't get to Caracas before the ship leaves at five o'clock. No. We'll have to board her in Grenada tomorrow. We'll have until five p.m. Very likely there are cabins available. There are always last-minute cancellations, sometimes even deaths. In fact, on a ship as expensive as the *QE2* there are always deaths. Undoubtedly James knows this. He can feed anytime he wishes if he takes the proper care."

"But why? Why deaths on the *QE2*?"

"Elderly passengers," David said. "It's a fact of cruise life. The *QE2* has a large hospital for emergencies. This is a floating world, a ship of this size. But no matter. Our investigators will clarify everything. I'll get them on it at once. We can easily make Grenada from New Orleans, and we have time to prepare for what we must do.

"Now, Lestat, let's consider this in detail. Suppose we confront this fiend right before sunup. And suppose we send him right straight back into this mortal body, and cannot control him after that. We need a hiding place for you . . . a third cabin, booked under a name which is in no way connected with either one of us."

"Yes, something deep in the center of the ship, on one of the lower decks. Not the very lowest. That would be too obvious. Something in the middle, I should think."

"But how fast can you travel? Can you make it within seconds to a lower deck?"

"Without question. Don't even worry about such a thing. An inside cabin, that's important, and one large enough to include a trunk. Well, the trunk isn't really essential, not if I've fitted a lock to the door beforehand, but the trunk would be a fine idea."

"Ah, I see it. I see it all. I see now what we must do. You rest, drink your coffee, take a shower, do whatever you wish. I'm going in the next room and make the calls I must make. This is Talamasca, and you must leave me alone."

"You're not serious," I said. "I want to hear what you're—"

"You'll do as I say. Oh, and find someone to care for that beautiful canine. We can't take him with us! That's patently absurd. And a dog of such character mustn't be neglected."

Off he hurried, closing me out of the bedroom, so that he might make all these exciting little calls alone.

"And just when I was beginning to enjoy this," I said.

I sped off to find Mojo, who was sleeping in the cold wet roof garden as if it were the most normal thing in the world. I took him down with me to the old woman on the first floor. Of all my tenants she was the most agreeable, and could certainly use a couple of hundred dollars for boarding a gentle dog.

At the mere suggestion, she was beside herself with joy. Mojo could use the courtyard behind the building, and she needed the money and the company, and wasn't I a nice young man? Just as nice as my cousin, Monsieur de Lioncourt, who was like a guardian angel to her, never bothering to cash the checks she gave him for her rent.

I WENT back up to the apartment, and discovered that David was still at work, and refusing to let me listen. I was told to make coffee, which of course I didn't know how to make. I drank the old coffee and called Paris.

My agent answered the phone. He was just in the process of sending me the status report I'd requested. All was going well. There had been no further assaults from the mysterious thief. Indeed the last had occurred on Friday evening. Perhaps the fellow had given up. An enormous sum of money was waiting for me now at my New Orleans bank.

I repeated all my cautions to the man, and told him that I would call soon again.

Friday evening. That meant James had tried his last assault before the *Queen Elizabeth 2* left the States. He had no means while at sea to consider his computer thievery. And surely he had no intention of hurting my Paris agent. That is, if James was still content with his little vacation on the *Queen Elizabeth 2*. There was nothing to stop him from jumping ship whenever he pleased.

I went into the computer again and tried to access the accounts of Lestan Gregor, the alias who had wired the twenty million to the Georgetown bank. Just as I suspected. Lestan Gregor still existed but he was virtually penniless. Bank balance zero. The twenty million wired to Georgetown for the use of Raglan James had indeed reverted back to Mr. Gregor at Friday noon, and then been immediately withdrawn from his account. The transaction assuring this withdrawal had been set up the preceding night. By one p.m. on Friday, the money was gone on some untraceable path. The whole story was there, embedded in various numerical codes and general bank gibberish, which any fool could see.

And surely there was a fool staring at this computer screen right now.

The little beast had warned me that he could steal through computers. No doubt he'd wheedled information from the people at the Georgetown bank, or raped their unsuspecting minds with his telepathy, to gain the codes and numbers he required.

Whatever the case he had a fortune at his disposal which had once been my fortune. I hated him all the more. I hated him for killing my man in New York. I hated him for smashing all the furniture when he did it, and for stealing everything else in the office. I hated him for his pettiness and his intellect, his crudeness and his nerve.

I sat drinking the old coffee, and thinking about what lay ahead.

Of course I understood what James had done, stupid though it seemed. From the very first I'd known that his stealing had to do with some profound hunger in his soul. And this *Queen Elizabeth 2* had been the world of his father, the world from which he, caught in an act of thievery, had been *cast out*.

Oh, yes, cast out, the way the others had cast me out. And how eager he must have been to return to it with his new power and his new wealth. He'd probably planned it down to the very hour, as soon as we'd agreed upon a date for the switch. No doubt if I had put him off, he would have picked up the ship at some later harbour. As it was, he was able to begin his journey only a short distance from George-town, and strike my mortal agent before the ship sailed.

Ah, the way he'd sat in that grimly lighted little Georgetown kitchen, staring again and again at his watch. I mean, this watch.

At last David emerged from the bedroom, notebook in hand. Everything had been arranged.

"There is no Clarence Oddbody on the *Queen Elizabeth 2*, but a mysterious young Englishman named Jason Hamilton booked the lavish Queen Victoria Suite only two days before the ship sailed from New York. For the moment we must assume that this is our man. We'll have more information about him before we reach Grenada. Our investigators are already at work.

"We ourselves are booked out of Grenada in two penthouse suites on the same deck as our mysterious friend. We must board anytime tomorrow before the ship sails at five p.m.

"The first of our connecting flights leaves New Orleans in three hours. We will need at least one of those hours to obtain a pair of false passports from a gentleman who's been highly recommended for this sort of transaction and is in fact waiting for us now. I have the address here."

"Excellent. I've plenty of cash on hand."

"Very good. Now, one of our investigators will meet us in Gre-nada. He's a very cunning individual and I've worked with him for years. He's already booked the third cabin—inside, deck five. And he will manage to smuggle a couple of small but sophisticated firearms into that cabin, as well as the trunk we will need later on."

"Those weapons will mean nothing to a man walking around in my old body. But of course afterwards . . ."

"Precisely," said David. "After the switch, I will need a gun to protect myself against this handsome young body here." He gestured to me. "Now, to continue. My investigator will slip off the ship after he has officially boarded, leaving the cabin and the guns to us. We ourselves will go through the regular boarding process with our new identification. Oh, and I've selected our names already. Afraid I had to do it. I do hope you don't mind. You're an American named Sheridan Blackwood. And I'm a retired English surgeon named Alexander Stoker. It's always best to pose as a doctor on these little missions. You'll see what I mean."

"I'm thankful you didn't pick H. P. Lovecraft," I said with an exaggerated sigh of relief. "Do we have to leave now?"

"Yes, we do. I've already called the taxi. We must get some tropical clothing before we go, or we'll look perfectly ridiculous. There isn't a moment to lose. Now, if you will use those strong young arms of yours to help me with this suitcase, I shall be forever obliged."

"I'm disappointed."

"In what?" He stopped, stared at me, and then almost blushed as he had earlier that day. "Lestat, there is no time for that sort of thing."

"David, assuming we succeed, it may be our last chance."

"All right," he said, "there is plenty of time to discuss it at the beachside hotel in Grenada tonight. Depending of course on how quick you are with your lessons in astral projection. Now, do please show some youthful vim and vigor of a constructive sort, and help me with this suitcase. I'm a man of seventy-four."

"Splendid. But I want to know something before we go."

"What?"

"Why are you helping me?"

"Oh, for the love of heaven, you know why."

"No, I don't."

He stared at me soberly for a long moment, then said, "I care for you! I don't care what body you're in. It's true. But to be perfectly honest, this ghastly Body Thief, as you call him, frightens me. Yes, frightens me to the marrow of my bones.

"He's a fool, and he always brings about his own ruin, that's true. But this time I think you're right. He's not at all eager to be apprehended, if in fact he ever was. He's planning on a long run of success, and he may tire of the *QE2* very soon. That's why we must act. Now pick up this suitcase. I nearly killed myself hauling it up those stairs."

I obeyed.

But I was softened and saddened by his words of feeling, and plunged into a series of fragmentary images of all the little things we might have done in the large soft bed in the other room.

And what if the Body Thief had jumped ship already? Or been destroyed this very morning—after Marius had looked upon me with such disdain?

"Then we'll go on to Rio," said David, leading the way to the gate. "We'll be in time for the carnival. Nice vacation for us both."

"I'll die if I have to live that long!" I said, taking the lead down the stairs. "Trouble with you is you've gotten used to being human because you've done it for so damned long."

"I was used to it by the time I was two years old," he said dryly.

"I don't believe you. I've watched two-year-old humans with interest for centuries. They're miserable. They rush about, fall down, and scream almost constantly. They hate being human! They know already that it's some sort of dirty trick."

He laughed to himself but didn't answer me. He wouldn't look at me either.

The cab was already waiting for us when we reached the front door.

TWENTY

THE plane ride would have been another absolute nightmare, had I not been so tired that I slept. A full twenty-four hours had passed since my last dreamy rest in Gretchen's arms, and indeed I fell so deep into sleep now that when David roused me for the change of planes in Puerto Rico, I scarce knew where we were or what we were doing, and for an odd moment, it felt entirely normal to be lugging about this huge heavy body in a state of confusion and thoughtless obedience to David's commands.

We did not go outside the terminal for this transfer of planes. And when at last we did land in the small airport in Grenada, I was surprised by the close and delicious Caribbean warmth and the brilliant twilight sky.

All the world seemed changed by the soft balmy embracing breezes which greeted us. I was glad we had raided the Canal Street shop in New Orleans, for the heavy tweed clothes felt all wrong. As the cab bounced along the narrow uneven road, carrying us to our beachfront hotel, I was transfixed by the lush forest around us, the big red hibiscus blooming beyond little fences, the graceful coconut palms bending over the tiny tumbledown hillside houses, and eager to see, not with this dim frustrating mortal night vision, but in the magical light of the morning sun.

There had been something absolutely penitential about my undergoing the transformation in the mean cold of Georgetown, no doubt of it at all. Yet when I thought of it—that lovely white snow, and the warmth of Gretchen's little house, I couldn't truly complain. It was only that this Caribbean island seemed the true world, the world for real living; and I marveled, as I always did when in these islands, that they could be so beautiful, so warm, and so very poor.

Here one saw the poverty everywhere—the haphazard wooden houses on stilts, the pedestrians on the borders of the road, the old rusted automobiles, and the total absence of any evidence of affluence, making of course for a quaintness in the eye of the outsider, but something of a hard existence perhaps for the natives, who had never gathered together enough dollars to leave this place, even perhaps for a single day.

The evening sky was a deep shining blue, as it is often in this part of the world, as incandescent as it can be over Miami, and the soft white clouds made the same clean and dramatic panorama on the far edge of the gleaming sea. Entrancing, and this is but one tiny part of the great Caribbean. Why do I ever wander in other climes at all?

The hotel was in fact a dusty neglected little guesthouse of white stucco under a myriad complex of rusted tin roofs. It was known only to a few Britishers, and very quiet, with a rambling wing of rather old-fashioned rooms looking out over the sands of Grand Anse Beach. With profuse apologies for the broken air-conditioning machines, and the crowded quarters—we must share a room with twin beds, I almost burst into laughter, as David looked to heaven as if to say silently that his persecution would never end!—the proprietor demonstrated that the creaky overhead fan created quite a breeze. Old white louvered shutters covered the windows. The furniture was made of white wicker, and the floor was old tile.

It seemed very charming to me, but mostly on account of the sweet warmth of the air around me, and the bit of jungle creeping down around the structure, with its inevitable snaggle of banana leaf and Queen's Wreath vine. Ah, that vine. A nice rule of thumb might be: Don't ever live in a part of the world which will not support that vine.

At once we set about to changing clothes. I stripped off the tweeds, and put on the thin cotton pants and shirt I'd bought in New Orleans before we left, along with a pair of white tennis shoes, and deciding against an all-out physical assault upon David, who was changing with his back turned to me, I went out under the graceful arching coconut palms, and made my way down onto the sand.

The night was as tranquil and gentle as any night I've ever known. All my love of the Caribbean came back to me—along with painful and blessed memories. But I longed to see this night with my old eyes. I longed to see past the thickening darkness, and the shadows that shrouded the embracing hills. I longed to turn on my preternatural hearing and catch the soft songs of the jungles, to wander with vampiric speed up the mountains of the interior to find the secret little valleys and waterfalls as only the Vampire Lestat could have done.

I felt a terrible, terrible sadness for all my discoveries. And perhaps it hit me in its fullness for the first time—that all of my dreams of mortal life had been a lie. It wasn't that life wasn't magical; it wasn't that creation was not a miracle; it wasn't that the world was not fundamentally good. It was that I had taken my dark power so for granted that I did not realize the vantage point it had given me. I had failed to assess my gifts. And I wanted them back.

Yes, I had failed, hadn't I? Mortal life should have been enough!

I looked up at the heartless little stars, such mean guardians, and I prayed to the dark gods who don't exist to understand.

I thought of Gretchen. Had she already reached her rain forests, and all the sick ones waiting for the consolations of her touch? I wished I knew where she was.

Perhaps she was already at work in a jungle dispensary, with gleaming vials of medicine, or trekking to nearby villages, with miracles in a pack on her back. I thought of her quiet happiness when she'd described the mission. The warmth of those embraces came back to me, the drowsy sweetness of it, and the comfort of that small room. I saw the snow falling once more beyond the windows. I saw her large hazel eyes fixed on me, and heard the slow rhythm of her speech.

Then again I saw the deep blue evening sky above me; I felt the breeze that was moving over me as smoothly as if it were water; and I thought of David, David who was here with me now.

I was weeping when David touched my arm.

For a moment, I couldn't make out the features of his face. The beach was dark, and the sound of the surf so enormous that nothing in me seemed to function as it ought to do. Then I realized that of course it was David standing there looking at me, David in a crisp white cotton shirt and wash pants and sandals, managing somehow to look elegant even in this attire—David asking me gently to please come back to the room.

"Jake's here," he said, "our man from Mexico City. I think you should come inside."

The ceiling fan was going noisily and cool air moved through the shutters as we came into the shabby little room. A faint clacking noise came from the coconut palms, a sound I rather liked, rising and falling with the breeze.

Jake was seated on one of the narrow saggy little beds—a tall lanky individual in khaki shorts and a white polo shirt, puffing on an odoriferous little brown cigar. All of his skin was darkly tanned, and he had a shapeless thatch of graying blond hair. His posture was one of complete relaxation, but beneath this facade, he was entirely alert and suspicious, his mouth a perfectly straight line.

We shook hands as he disguised only a little the fact that he was looking me up and down. Quick, secretive eyes, not unlike David's eyes, though smaller. God only knows what he saw.

"Well, the guns won't be any problem," he said with an obvious Australian accent. "There are no metal detectors at ports such as this. I'll board at approximately ten a.m., plant your trunk and your guns for you in your cabin on Five Deck, then meet you in the Café Centaur in St. George's. I do hope you know what you're doing, David, bringing firearms aboard the *Queen Elizabeth 2.*"

"Of course I know what I'm doing," said David very politely, with a tiny playful smile. "Now, what do you have for us on our man?"

"Ah, yes. Jason Hamilton. Six feet tall, dark tan, longish blond hair, piercing blue eyes. Mysterious fellow. Very British, very polite. Rumors as to his true identity abound. He's an enormous tipper, and a day sleeper, and apparently doesn't bother to leave the ship when she's in port. Indeed he gives over small packages to be mailed to his cabin steward every morning, quite early, before he disappears for the day. Haven't been able to discover the post box but that's a matter of time. He has yet to appear in the Queens Grill for a single meal. It's rumored he's seriously ill. But with what, no one knows. He's the picture of health, which only adds to the mystery. Everyone says so. A powerfully built and graceful fellow with a dazzling wardrobe, it seems. He gambles heavily at the roulette wheel, and dances for hours with the ladies. Seems in fact to like the very old ones. He'd arouse suspicion on that account alone if he weren't so bloody rich himself. Spends a lot of time simply roaming the ship."

"Excellent. This is just what I wanted to know," said David. "You have our tickets."

The man gestured to a black leather folder on the wicker dressing table. David checked the contents, then gave him an approving nod.

"Deaths on the *QE2* so far?"

"Ah, now that's an interesting point. They have had six since they left New York, which is a little more than usual. All very elderly women, and all apparent heart failure. This is the sort of thing you want to know?"

"Certainly is," said David.

The "little drink," I thought.

"Now you ought to have a look at these firearms," said Jake, "and know how to use them." He reached for a worn little duffel bag on the floor, just the sort of beat-up sack of canvas in which one would hide expensive weapons, I presumed. Out came the expensive weapons—one a large Smith & Wesson revolver. The other a small black automatic no bigger than the palm of my hand.

"Yes, I'm quite familiar with this," David said, taking the big silver gun and making to aim it at the floor. "No problem." He pulled out the clip, then slipped it back in. "Pray I don't have to use it, however. It will make a hell of a noise."

He then gave it to me.

"Lestat, get the feel of it," he said. "Of course there's no time to practice. I asked for a hair trigger."

"And that you have," said Jake, looking at me coldly. "So please watch out."

"Barbarous little thing," I said. It was very heavy. A nugget of destructiveness. I spun the cylinder. Six bullets. It had a curious smell.

"Both the guns are thirty-eights," said the man, with a slight note of disdain. "Those are man-stoppers." He showed me a small cardboard box. "You'll have plenty of ammunition available to you for whatever it is that you are going to do on this boat."

"Don't worry, Jake," said David firmly. "Things will probably go without a hitch. And I thank you for your usual efficiency. Now, go have a pleasant evening on the island. And I shall see you at the Centaur Café before noon."

The fellow gave me a deep suspicious look, then nodded, gathered up the guns and the little box of bullets, put them back in his canvas bag, and offered his hand again to me and then to David, and out he went.

I waited until the door had closed.

"I think he dislikes me," I said. "Blames me for involving you in some sort of sordid crime."

David gave a short little laugh. "I've been in far more compromising situations than this one," he said. "And if I worried about what our investigators thought of us, I would have retired a long time ago. What do we know now from this information?"

"Well, he's feeding on the old women. Probably stealing from them also. And he's mailing home what he steals in packages too small to arouse suspicion. What he does with the larger loot we'll never know. Probably throws it into the ocean. I suspect there's more than one post box number. But that's no concern of ours."

"Correct. Now lock the door. It's time for a little concentrated witchcraft. We'll have a nice supper later on. I have to teach you to veil your thoughts. Jake could read you too easily. And so can I. The Body Thief will pick up your presence when he's still two hundred miles out to sea."

"Well, I did it through an act of will when I was Lestat," I said. "I haven't the faintest idea how to do it now."

"Same way. We're going to practice. Until I can't read a single image or random word from you. Then we'll get to the out-of-body travel." He looked at his watch, which reminded me of James suddenly, in that little kitchen. "Slip that bolt. I don't want any maid blundering in here later on."

I obeyed. Then I sat on the bed opposite David, who had assumed a very relaxed yet commanding attitude, rolling up the stiff starched cuffs of his shirt, which revealed the dark fleece of his arms. There was also quite a bit of dark hair on his chest, bubbling up through the open collar of the shirt. Only a little gray mixed in with it, like the gray that sparkled here and there in his heavy shaven beard. I found it quite impossible to believe he was a man of seventy-four.

"Ah, I caught that," he said with a little lift of the eyebrows. "I catch entirely too much. Now. Listen to what I say. You must fix it in your mind that your thoughts remain within you, that you are not attempting to communicate with other beings—not through facial expression or body language of any sort; that indeed you are impenetrable. Make an image of your sealed mind if you must. Ah, that's good. You've gone blank behind your handsome young face. Even your eyes have changed ever so slightly. Perfect. Now I'm going to try to read you. Keep it up."

By the end of forty-five minutes, I had learned the trick fairly painlessly, but I could pick up nothing of David's thoughts even when he tried his hardest to project them to me. In this body, I simply did not have the psychic ability which he possessed. But the veiling we had achieved, and this was a crucial step. We would continue to work on all this throughout the night.

"We're ready to begin on the out-of-body travel," he said.

"This is going to be hell," I said. "I don't think I can get out of this body. As you can see, I just don't have your gifts."

"Nonsense," he said. He loosened his posture slightly, crossing his ankles and sliding down a bit in the chair. But somehow, no matter what he did, he never lost the attitude of the teacher, the authority, the priest. It was implicit in his small, direct gestures and above all in his voice.

"Lie down on that bed, and close your eyes. And listen to every word I say."

I did as I was told. And immediately felt a little sleepy. His voice became even more directive in its softness, rather like that of a hypnotist, bidding me to relax completely, and to visualize a spiritual double of this form.

"Must I visualize myself with this body?"

"No. Doesn't matter. What matters is that you—your mind, your soul, your sense of self—are linked to the form you envision. Now picture it as congruent with your body, and then imagine that you want to lift it up and out of the body—that *you* want to go up!"

For some thirty minutes David continued this unhurried instruction, reiterating in his own fashion the lessons which priests had taught to their initiates for thousands of years. I knew the old formula. But I also knew complete mortal vulnerability, and a crushing sense of my limitations, and a stiffening and debilitating fear.

We had been at it perhaps forty-five minutes when I finally sank into the requisite and lovely vibratory state on the very cusp of sleep. My body seemed in fact to have become this delicious vibratory feeling, and nothing more! And just when I realized this, and might have remarked upon it, I suddenly felt myself break loose and begin to rise.

I opened my eyes; or at least I thought I did. I saw I was floating directly above my body; in fact, I couldn't even see the real flesh-and-blood body at all. "Go up!" I said. And instantly I traveled to the ceiling with the exquisite lightness and speed of a helium balloon! It was nothing to turn completely over and look straight down into the room.

Why, I had passed through the blades of the ceiling fan! Indeed, it was in the very middle of my body, though I could feel nothing. And down there, under me, was the sleeping mortal form I had inhabited so miserably all of these strange days. Its eyes were closed, and so was its mouth.

I saw David sitting in his wicker chair, right ankle on his left knee, hands relaxed on his thighs, as he looked at the sleeping man. Did he know I had succeeded? I couldn't hear a word he was speaking. Indeed, I seemed to be in a totally different sphere from these two solid figures, though I felt utterly complete and entire and real myself.

Oh, how lovely this was! This was so near to my freedom as a vampire that I almost began to weep again. I felt so sorry for the two solid and lonely beings down there. I wanted to pass up through the ceiling and into the night.

Slowly I went up, and then out over the roof of the hotel, until I was hovering above the white sand.

But this was enough, wasn't it? Fear gripped me, the fear I'd known when I did this little trick before. What in the name of God was keeping me alive in this state! I needed my body! At once I plummeted, blindly, back into the flesh. I woke up, tingling all over, and staring at David as he sat staring back at me.

"I did it," I said. I was shocked to feel these tubes of skin and bone enclosing me again, and to see my fingers moving when I told them to do it, to feel my toes come alive in my shoes. Lord God, what an experience! And so many, many mortals had sought to describe it. And so many more, in their ignorance, did not believe that such a thing could be.

"Remember to veil your thoughts," David said suddenly. "No matter how exhilarated you become. Lock your mind up tight!"

"Yes, sir."

"Now let's do it all again."

By midnight—some two hours later—I had learned to rise at will. Indeed, it was becoming addictive—the feeling of lightness, the great swooshing ascent! The lovely ease of passing through walls and ceiling; and then the sudden and shocking return. There was a deep throbbing pleasure to it, pure and shining, like an eroticism of the mind.

"Why can't a man die in this fashion, David? I mean why can't one simply rise into the heavens and leave the earth?"

"Did you see an open doorway, Lestat?" he asked.

"No," I said sadly. "I saw this world. It was so clear, so beautiful. But it was this world."

"Come now, you must learn to make the assault."

"But I thought you would do it, David. You'd jolt him and knock him out of his body and . . ."

"Yes, and suppose he spots me before I can do it, and makes me into a nice little torch. What then? No, you must learn the trick as well."

This was far more difficult. Indeed it required the very opposite of the passivity and relaxation which we had employed and developed before. I had now to focus all my energy upon David with the avowed purpose of knocking him out of his body—a phenomenon which I could not hope to see in any real sense—and then go into his body myself. The concentration demanded of me was excruciating. The timing was critical. And the repeated efforts produced an intense and exhausting nervousness rather like that of a right-handed person trying to write perfectly with the left hand.

I was near to tears of rage and frustration more than once. But David was absolutely adamant that we must continue and that this could be done. No, a stiff drink of Scotch wouldn't help. No, we couldn't eat until later. No, we couldn't break for a walk on the beach or a late swim.

The first time I succeeded, I was absolutely aghast. I went speeding towards David, and felt the impact in the same purely mental fashion in which I felt the freedom of the flight. Then I was inside David, and for one split second saw myself—slack-jawed and staring dully—through the dim lenses of David's eyes.

Then I felt a dark shuddering disorientation, and an invisible blow as if someone had placed a huge hand on my chest. I realized that he had returned and pushed me out. I was hovering in the air, and then back in my own sweat-drenched body, laughing near hysterically from mad excitement and sheer fatigue.

"That's all we need," he said. "Now I know we can pull this off. Come, once again! We're going to do it twenty times if we have to, until we know that we can achieve it without fail."

On the fifth successful assault, I remained in his body for a full thirty seconds, absolutely mesmerized by the different feelings attendant to it—the lighter limbs, the poorer vision, and the peculiar sound of my voice coming out of his throat. I looked down and saw his hands—thin, corded with blood vessels, and touched on the backs of the fingers with dark hair—and they were my hands! How hard it was to control them. Why, one of them had a pronounced tremour which I had never noticed before.

Then came the jolt again, and I was flying upwards, and then the plummet, back into the twenty-six-year-old body once more.

We must have done it twelve times before the slave driver of a Candomble priest said it was time for him to really fight my assault.

"Now, you must come at me with much greater determination. Your goal is to claim the body! And you expect a fight."

For an hour we battled. Finally, when I was able to jolt him out and keep him out for the space of ten seconds, he declared that this would be enough.

"He told you the truth about your cells. They will know you. They will receive you and strive to keep you. Any adult human knows how to use his own body much better than the intruder. And of course you know how to use those preternatural gifts in ways of which he can't possibly even dream. I think we can do it. In fact, I'm certain now that we can."

"But tell me something," I said. "Before we stop, don't you want to jolt me out of this body and go into it? I mean, just to see what it's like?"

"No," he said quietly. "I don't."

"But aren't you curious?" I asked him. "Don't you want to know . . ."

I could see that I was taxing his patience.

"Look, the real truth is, we don't have time for that experience. And maybe I don't want to know. I can remember my youth well enough. Too well, in fact. We aren't playing little games here. You can make the assault now. That's what counts." He looked at his watch. "It's almost three. We'll have some supper and then we'll sleep. We've a full day ahead, exploring the ship and confirming our plans. We must be rested and in full control of our faculties. Come, let's see what we can rustle up in the way of food or drink."

We went outside and along the walk until we reached the little kitchen—a funny, damp, and somewhat cluttered room. The kindly proprietor had left two plates for us in the rusted, groaning refrigerator, along with a bottle of white wine. We sat down at the table and commenced to devour every morsel of rice, yams, and spiced meat, not caring at all that it was very cold.

"Can you read my thoughts?" I asked, after I'd consumed two glasses of wine.

"Nothing, you've got the trick."

"So how do I do it in my sleep? The *Queen Elizabeth 2* can't be more than a hundred miles out now. She's to dock in two hours."

"Same way you do it when you're awake. You shut down. You close up. Because, you see, no one is ever completely asleep. Not even those in a coma are completely asleep. Will is always operative. And will is what this is about."

I looked at him as we sat there. He was obviously tired, but he did not look haggard or in any way debilitated. His thick dark hair obviously added to the impression of vigor; and his large dark eyes had the same fierce light in them which they always had.

I finished quickly, shoved the dishes into the sink, and went out on the beach without bothering to say what I meant to do. I knew he would say we had to rest now, and I didn't want to be deprived of this last night as a human being under the stars.

Going down to the lip of the water, I peeled off the cotton clothes, and went into the waves. They were cool but inviting, and then I stretched out my arms and began to swim. It was not easy, of course. But it wasn't hard either, once I resigned myself to the fact that humans did it this way—stroke by stroke against the force of the water, and letting the water buoy the cumbersome body, which it was entirely willing to do.

I swam out quite far, and then rolled over on my back and looked at the sky. It was still full of fleecy white clouds. A moment of peace came over me, in spite of the chill on my exposed skin, and the dimness all around me, and the strange feeling of vulnerability I experienced as I floated on this dark treacherous sea. When I thought of being back in my old body, I could only be happy, and once again, I knew that in my human adventure, I had failed.

I had not been the hero of my own dreams. I had found human life too hard.

Finally I swam back into the shallows and then walked up onto the beach. I picked up my clothes, shook off the sand, slung them over my shoulder, and walked back to the little room.

Only one lamp burned on the dressing table. David was sitting on his bed, closest to the door, and dressed only in a long white pajama shirt and smoking one of those little cigars. I liked the scent of it, dark and sweet.

He looked his usual dignified self, arms folded, eyes full of normal curiosity as he watched me take a towel from the bath and dry off my hair and my skin.

"Just called London," he said.

"What's the news?" I wiped my face with the towel, then slung it over the back of the chair. The air felt so good on my naked skin, now that it was dry.

"Robbery in the hills above Caracas. Very similar to the crimes in Curaçao. A large villa full of artifacts, jewels, paintings. Much was smashed; only small portables were stolen; three people dead. We should thank the gods for the poverty of the human imagination—for the sheer meanness of this man's ambitions—and that our opportunity to stop him has come so soon. In time, he would have wakened to his monstrous potential. As it is, he is our predictable fool."

"Does any being use what he possesses?" I asked. "Perhaps a few brave geniuses know their true limits. What do the rest of us do but complain?"

"I don't know," he said, a sad little smile passing over his face. He shook his head and looked away. "Some night, when this is all over, tell me again how it was for you. How you could be in that beautiful young body and hate this world so much."

"I'll tell you, but you'll never understand. You're on the wrong side of the dark glass. Only the dead know how terrible it is to be alive."

I pulled a loose cotton T-shirt out of my little suitcase, but I didn't put it on. I sat down on the bed beside him. And then I bent down and kissed his face again gently, as I had in New Orleans, liking the feel of his roughly shaven beard, just as I liked that sort of thing when I was really Lestat and I would soon have that strong masculine blood inside.

I moved closer to him, when suddenly he grasped my hand, and I felt him gently push me away.

"Why, David?" I asked him.

He didn't answer. He lifted his right hand and brushed my hair back out of my eyes.

"I don't know," he whispered. "I can't. I simply can't."

He got up gracefully, and went outside into the night.

I was too furious with pure stymied passion to do anything for a moment. Then I followed him out. He had gone down on the sand a ways and he stood there alone, as I had done before.

I came up behind him.

"Tell me, please, why not?"

"I don't know," he said again. "I only know I can't. I want to. Believe me, I do. But I can't. My past is . . . so close to me." He let out a long sigh, and for a while was silent again. Then he went on. "My memories of those days are so clear. It's as if I'm in India again, or Rio. Ah, yes, Rio. It's as if I am that young man again."

I knew I was to blame for this. I knew it, and that it was useless to say apologetic words. I also sensed something else. I was an evil being, and even when I was in this body, David could sense that evil. He could sense the powerful vampiric greed. It was an old evil, brooding and terrible. Gretchen hadn't sensed it. I had deceived her with this warm and smiling body. But when David looked at me, he saw that blond blue-eyed demon whom he knew very well.

I said nothing. I merely looked out over the sea. Give me back my body. Let me be that devil, I thought. Take me away from this paltry brand of desire and this weakness. Take me back into the dark heavens where I belong. And it seemed suddenly that my loneliness and my misery were as terrible as they had ever been before this experiment, before this little sojourn into more vulnerable flesh. Yes, let me be outside it again, please. Let me be a watcher. How could I have been such a fool?

I heard David say something to me, but I didn't really catch the words. I looked up slowly, pulling myself out of my thoughts, and I saw that he had turned to face me, and I realized that his hand was resting gently on my neck. I wanted to say something angry—Take your hand away, don't torment me—but I didn't speak.

"No, you're not evil, that's not it," he whispered. "It's me, don't you understand. It's my fear! You don't know what this adventure has meant to me! To be here again in this part of the great world—and with you! I *love* you. I love you desperately and insanely, I love the soul inside you, and don't you see, it's not evil. It's not greedy. But it's immense. It overpowers even this youthful body because it is your soul, fierce and indomitable and outside time—the soul of the true Lestat. I can't give in to it. I can't . . . do it. I'll lose myself forever if I do it, as surely as if . . . as if . . ."

He broke off, too shaken obviously to go on. I'd hated the pain in his voice, the faint tremour undermining its deep firmness. How could I ever forgive myself? I stood still, staring past him into the darkness. The lovely pounding of the surf and the faint clacking of the coconut palms were the only sounds. How vast were the heavens; how lovely and deep and calm these hours just before dawn.

I saw Gretchen's face. I heard her voice.

There was a moment this morning when I thought I could throw up everything—just to be with you . . . I could feel it sweeping me away, the way the music once did. And if you were to say "Come with me," even now, I might go . . . The meaning of chastity is not to fall in love . . . I could fall in love with you. I know I could.

And then beyond this burning image, faint yet undeniable, I saw the face of Louis, and I heard words spoken in his voice that I wanted to forget.

Where was David? Let me wake from these memories. I don't want them. I looked up and I saw him again, and in him the old familiar dignity, the restraint, the imperturbable strength. But I saw the pain too.

"Forgive me," he whispered. His voice was still unsteady, as he struggled to preserve the beautiful and elegant facade. "You drank from the fountain of youth when you drank the blood of Magnus. Really you did. You'll never know what it means to be the old man that I am now. God help me, I loathe the word, but it's true. I'm old."

"I understand," I said. "Don't worry." I leant forward and kissed him again. "I'll leave you alone. Come on, we should sleep. I promise. I'll leave you alone."

TWENTY-ONE

GOOD Lord, look at it, David." I had just stepped out of the taxi onto the crowded quai. The great blue and white *Queen Elizabeth 2* was far too big to come into the little harbour. She rested at anchor a mile or two out—I could not gauge—so monstrously large that she seemed the ship out of a nightmare, frozen upon the motionless bay. Only her row upon row of myriad tiny windows prevented her from seeming the ship of a giant.

The quaint little island with its green hills and curved shore reached out towards her, as if trying to shrink her and draw her nearer, all in vain.

I felt a spasm of excitement as I looked at her. I had never been aboard a modern vessel. This part was going to be fun.

A small wooden launch, bearing her name in bold painted letters, and obviously laden with but one load of her many passengers, made its way to the concrete dock as we watched.

"There's Jake in the prow of the launch," said David. "Come on, let's go into the café."

We walked slowly under the hot sun, comfortable in our short-sleeve shirts and dungarees—a couple of tourists—past the dark-skinned vendors with their seashells for sale, and rag dolls, and tiny steel drums, and other souvenirs. How pretty the island appeared. Its forested hills were dotted with tiny dwellings, and the more solid buildings of the town of St. George's were massed together on the steep cliff to the far left beyond the turn of the quai. The whole prospect had almost an Italian hue to it, what with so many dark and stained reddish walls and the rusted roofs of corrugated tin which in the burning sun looked deceptively like roofs of baked tile. It seemed a lovely place to go exploring—at some other time.

The dark café was cool inside with only a few brightly painted tables and straight-back chairs. David ordered bottles of cold beer, and within minutes Jake came sauntering in—wearing the very same khaki shorts and white polo shirt—and carefully chose a chair from which he might watch the open door. The world out there seemed made of glittering water. The beer tasted malty and rather good.

"Well, the deed is done," Jake said in a low voice, his face rather rigid and abstracted as though he were not with us at all, but deep in thought. He took a gulp from the brown beer bottle, and then slipped a couple of keys across the table to David. "She's carrying over one thousand passengers. Nobody will notice that Mr. Eric Sampson doesn't reboard. The cabin's tiny, inside as you requested, right off the corridor, midship, Five Deck, as you know."

"Excellent. And you obtained two sets of keys. Very good."

"The trunk's open, with half the contents scattered on the bed. Your guns are inside the two books inside the trunk. Hollowed them out myself. The locks are there. You ought to be able to fit the big one to the door easily enough but I don't know if the staff will care much for it when they see it. Again, I wish you the best of luck. Oh, and you heard the news about the robbery this morning on the hill? Seems we have a vampire in Grenada. Maybe you should plan to stay here, David. Sounds like just your sort of thing."

"This morning?"

"Three o'clock. Right up there on the cliff. Big house of a rich Austrian woman. Everyone murdered. Quite a mess. The whole island's talking about it. Well, I'm off."

It was only after Jake had left us that David spoke again.

"This is bad, Lestat. We were standing out on the beach at three this morning. If he sensed even a glimmer of our presence, he may not be on the ship. Or he may be ready for us when the sun sets."

"He was far too busy this morning, David. Besides, if he'd sensed our presence, he would have made a bonfire of our little room. Unless he doesn't know how to do it, but that we simply cannot know. Let's board the bloody ship now. I'm tired of waiting. Look, it's starting to rain."

We gathered up our luggage, including the monstrous leather suitcase David had brought from New Orleans, and hurried to the launch. A crowd of frail elderly mortals seemed to appear from everywhere—out of taxis and nearby sheds and little shops—now that the rain was really coming down, and it took us some minutes to get inside the unsteady little wooden boat, and take a seat on the wet plastic bench.

As soon as she turned her prow towards the *Queen Elizabeth 2*, I felt a giddy excitement—fun to be riding this warm sea in such a small craft. I loved the movement as we gained speed.

David was quite tense. He opened his passport, read the information for the twenty-seventh time, and then put it away. We had gone over our identities this morning after breakfast, but hoped that we would never need to use the various details.

For what it was worth, Dr. Stoker was retired and on vacation in the Caribbean but very concerned about his dear friend Jason Hamilton, who was traveling in the Queen Victoria Suite. He was eager to see Mr. Hamilton, and so he would tell the cabin stewards of the Signal Deck, though cautioning them not to let Mr. Hamilton know of this concern.

I was merely a friend he'd met at the guesthouse the night before, and with whom he'd struck up an acquaintance on account of our sailing together on the *Queen Elizabeth 2*. There was to be no other connection between us, for James would be in this body once the switch was done, and David might have to vilify him in some fashion if he could not be controlled.

There was more to it, in the event we were questioned about any sort of row that might occur. But in general, we did not think our plan could possibly lead to such a thing.

Finally the launch reached the ship, docking at a broad opening in the very middle of the immense blue hull. How utterly preposterously enormous the vessel appeared from this angle! She really did take my breath away.

I scarce noticed as we gave over our tickets to the waiting crew members. Luggage would be handled for us. We received some vague directions as to how we were to reach the Signal Deck, and then we were wandering down an endless corridor with a very low ceiling and door after door on either side of us. Within minutes, we realized we were quite lost.

On we walked until suddenly we reached a great open place with a sunken floor and, of all things, a white grand piano, poised on its three legs as if ready for a concert, and this within the windowless womb of this ship!

"It's the Midships Lobby," said David, pointing to a great colored diagram of the vessel in a frame upon the wall. "I know where we are now. Follow me."

"How absurd all this is," I said, staring at the brightly colored carpet, and the chrome and plastic everywhere I looked. "How utterly synthetic and hideous."

"Shhh, the British are very proud of this ship, you're going to offend someone. They can't use wood anymore—it has to do with fire regulations." He stopped at an elevator and pushed the button. "This will take us up to the Boat Deck. Didn't the man say we must find the Queens Grill Lounge there?"

"I have no idea," I said. I was like a zombie wandering into the elevator. "This is unimaginable!"

"Lestat, there have been giant liners like this one since the turn of the century. You've been living in the past."

The Boat Deck revealed an entire series of wonders. The ship housed a great theatre, and also an entire mezzanine of tiny elegant shops. Below the mezzanine was a dance floor, with a small bandstand, and a sprawling lounge area of small cocktail tables and squat comfortable leather chairs. The shops were shut up since the vessel was in port, but it was quite easy to see their various contents through the airy grilles which closed them off. Expensive clothing, fine jewelry, china, black dinner jackets and boiled shirts, sundries, and random gifts were all on display in the shallow little bays.

There were passengers wandering everywhere—mostly quite old men and women dressed in scant beach clothing, many of whom were gathered in the quiet daylighted lounge below.

"Come on, the rooms," said David, pulling me along.

It seems the penthouse suites, to which we were headed, were somewhat cut off from the great body of the ship. We had to slip into the Queens Grill Lounge, a long narrow pleasantly appointed bar reserved entirely for the top-deck passengers, and then find a more or less secret elevator to take us to these rooms. This bar had very large windows, revealing the marvelous blue water and the clear sky above.

This was all the province of first class on the transatlantic crossing. But here in the Caribbean it lacked this designation, though the lounge and restaurant locked out the rest of the little floating world.

At last we emerged on the very top deck of the ship, and into a corridor more fancily decorated than those below. There was an art deco feel to its plastic lamps, and the handsome trim on the doors. There was also a more generous and cheerful illumination. A friendly cabin steward—a gentleman of about sixty—emerged from a small curtained galley and directed us to our suites near the far end of the hall.

"The Queen Victoria Suite, where is it?" asked David.

The steward answered at once in a very similar British accent, that indeed, the Victoria Suite was only two cabins away. He pointed to the very door.

I felt the hair rise on my neck as I looked at it. I knew, absolutely knew, that the fiend was inside. Why would he bother with a more difficult hiding place? No one had to tell me. We would find a large trunk sitting near the wall in that suite. I was vaguely conscious of David using all his poise and charm upon the steward, explaining that he was a physician and how he meant to have a look at his dear friend Jason Hamilton as soon as he could. But he didn't want to alarm Mr. Hamilton.

Of course not, said the cheerful steward, who volunteered that Mr. Hamilton slept throughout the day. Indeed, he was asleep in there now. Behold the "Do Not Disturb" sign hanging on the doorknob. But come, didn't we want to settle into our rooms? Here was our luggage coming right along.

Our cabins surprised me. I saw both as the doors were opened, and before I retired into my own.

Once again, I spied only synthetic materials, looking very plastic and lacking altogether the warmth of wood. But the rooms were quite large, and obviously luxurious, and opened to each other with a connecting door to make one grand suite. This door was now closed.

Each room was furnished identically except for small differences of color, and rather like streamlined hotel rooms, with low king-sized beds, draped in soft pastel bedspreads, and narrow dressing tables built into the mirrored walls. There was the de rigueur giant television set, and the cleverly concealed refrigerator, and even a small sitting area with pale tastefully shaped little couch, coffee table, and upholstered chair.

The real surprise, however, was the verandas. A great glass wall with sliding doors opened upon these small private porches, which were wide enough to contain a table and chairs of their own. What a luxury it was to walk outside, and stand at the railing and look out upon the lovely island and its sparkling bay. And of course this meant the Queen Victoria Suite would have a veranda, through which the morning sun would very brightly shine!

I had to laugh to myself remembering our old vessels of the nineteenth century, with their tiny portholes. And though I much disliked the pale, spiritless colors of the decor, and the total absence of any vintage surface materials, I was beginning to understand why James had remained fascinated with this very special little realm.

Meantime I could plainly hear David talking away to the cabin steward, their lilting British accents seeming to sharpen in response to one another, their speech becoming so rapid that I couldn't entirely follow what was being said.

Seems it all had to do with poor ailing Mr. Hamilton, and that Dr. Stoker was eager to slip in and have a look at him as he slept but the steward was terribly afraid to allow such a thing. In fact, Dr. Stoker wanted to obtain and keep a spare key to the suite, so that he might keep a very close watch on his patient just in case . . .

Only gradually, as I unpacked my suitcase, did I realize that this little conversation with all its lyrical politeness was moving towards the question of a bribe. Finally David said in the most courteous and considerate fashion that he understood the man's discomfort, and look, he wanted the good fellow to have a supper at his expense first time he went into port. And if things did go wrong and Mr. Hamilton was upset, well, David would take the entire blame. He'd say he'd taken the key from the galley. The steward wouldn't be implicated at all.

It seemed the battle was won. Indeed, David seemed to be using his near-hynotic power of persuasion. Yet there followed some polite and very convincing nonsense about how sick Mr. Hamilton was, on how Dr. Stoker had been sent by the family to look after him, and how important it was for him to have a look at the man's skin. Ah, yes, the skin. Undoubtedly the steward inferred a life-threatening ailment. And finally, he confessed that all the other stewards were at lunch, he was alone on the Signal Deck just now, and yes, he'd turn his back, if Dr. Stoker was absolutely sure . . .

"My dear man, I take responsibility for everything. Now, here, you must take this for all the trouble I've caused you. Have supper in some nice . . . No, no, now don't protest. Now leave things to me."

Within seconds the narrow bright corridor was deserted. With a tiny triumphant smile David beckoned for me to come out and join him. He held up the key to the Queen Victoria Suite. We crossed the passage and he fitted it into the lock.

The suite was immense, and split between two levels separated by four or perhaps five carpeted steps. The bed rested upon the lower level, and was quite mussed, with pillows plumped up beneath the covers to make it appear that indeed someone was there fast asleep with a hood of covers carelessly drawn over his head.

The upper level contained the sitting area and the doors to the veranda, over which the thick draperies had been pulled, admitting almost no visible light. We slipped into the suite, snapped on the overhead lamp, and closed the door.

The pillows piled on the bed made an excellent ruse for anyone peeking in from the hallway, but on closer inspection did not appear to be a contrivance at all. Merely a messy bed.

So where was the devil? Where was the trunk?

"Ah, there," I whispered. "On the far side of the bed." I had mistaken it for some sort of table, as it was almost entirely draped with a decorative cloth. Now I could see that it was a large black metal locker, trimmed in brass, and very shiny, and easily big enough to accommodate a man with his knees crooked and lying upon his side. The thick drapery of decorative fabric was no doubt held in place upon the lid with a bit of glue. In the old century, I had often used this trick myself.

Everything else was quite immaculate, though the closets veritably bulged with fine clothes. A quick search of the dresser drawers revealed no documents of importance. Obviously he carried what few papers he required on his person, and his person was concealed inside that trunk. There were no jewels or gold hidden in this room as far as we could determine. But we found the stack of prestamped mailing envelopes which the fiend was using to get rid of the stolen treasures, and these were quite thick and large.

"Five post boxes," I said, as I went through them. David noted all the numbers in his small leatherbound book, then slipped it back in his pocket and looked at the trunk.

I warned him in a whisper to be careful. The fiend can sense danger even in his sleep. Don't think of touching the lock.

David nodded. He knelt down silently beside the trunk and gently laid his ear against the lid, and then he drew back rather fast and stared at it with a fierce and excited expression on his face.

"He's in there all right," he said, eyes still fixed on the trunk.

"What did you hear?"

"His heartbeat. Go listen for yourself if you wish. It's your heart."

"I want to see him," I said. "Stand over there, out of the way."

"I don't think you should do this."

"Ah, but I want to. Besides, I must assess that lock just in case." I approached the trunk and realized as soon as I saw it closely that the lock had not even been turned. He either could not do it telepathically or had never bothered. Standing well to one side, I reached down with my right hand and jerked at the brass edge of the lid. Then I threw it back against the wall.

It struck the paneling with a dull sound, remaining open, and I realized that I was looking at a mass of soft black fabric, folded loosely and completely hiding the contents below. Nothing stirred beneath this fabric.

No powerful white hand suddenly reached for my throat!

Standing as far back as I could, I reached out and snatched up the cloth and drew it back in a great black flash of silk. My mortal heart was pounding miserably, and I almost lost my balance as I put several feet of space between myself and the trunk. But the body which lay there, quite visibly, with its knees drawn up just as I'd imagined, and its arms folded around its knees, did not move.

Indeed, the sunburnt face was as still as that of a mannequin, with its eyes closed and its familiar profile burning against the funereal padding of white silk beneath it. My profile. My eyes. My body dressed in formal evening black—a vampire's black, if you will—with stiff white shirtfront and shining black tie at the neck. My hair, loose and full and golden in the dim light.

My body!

And I, standing there in a trembling mortal frame, with this bolt of loose black silk hanging like a matador's cape from my trembling hand.

"Hurry!" David whispered.

Even as the syllables left his lips, I saw the crooked arm inside the trunk begin to move. The elbow tightened. The hand was sliding loose from its grip on the bent knee. At once I hurled the fabric back over the body, seeing it slip into the same shapeless covering it had been before. And with a quick swipe of my left fingers, I threw the lid up away from the wall so that it fell shut with a dull sound.

Thank God the fancy outer cloth did not catch in it, but tumbled down into place, covering the unsnapped lock. I moved backwards away from the locker, almost sick with fear and amazement, and felt the reassuring pressure of David's hand on my arm.

Together we stood there silent for a long moment until we were
certain that the preternatural body was at rest again.

Finally, I had collected myself sufficiently to take one more quiet
look about. I was still trembling, but powerfully excited by the tasks
that lay ahead.

Even with their thick layer of synthetic materials, these quarters
were sumptuous by any standards. They represented the sort of luxury
and privilege which very few mortals can ever attain. How he must
have reveled in it. Ah, and to look at all those fine evening clothes.
Black velvet dinner jackets as well as the more familiar style, and even
an opera cape, he had indulged himself in that as well. There were
shiny shoes galore on the floor of the closet, and a great wealth of
expensive liquor exposed upon the bar.

Did he lure the women here for cocktails as he took his little
drink?

I looked at the large stretch of glass wall, quite visible on account
of the seam of light at the top and bottom edges of the draperies. Only
now did I realize that this room was facing the southeast.

David squeezed my arm. Wasn't it safe now to go?

We left the Signal Deck immediately without encountering the
steward again. David had the key in his inside pocket.

Down we went now to Five Deck, which was the very last deck
of cabins, though not of the ship itself, and we found the little inside
stateroom of Mr. Eric Sampson, who did not exist, and where another
trunk was waiting to be occupied by that body upstairs when it once
again belonged to me.

Nice small, windowless chamber. Of course it had the regular
lock, but what of the others, which Jake had brought aboard at our
request?

They were entirely too cumbersome for our purposes. But I saw
that the door could be made quite impassable if I pushed the trunk
against it. That would keep out any troublesome steward, or James if
he managed to be prowling about after the switch. He could not
possibly move the door back. Indeed, if I wedged the trunk between
the door and the end of the bunk, no one could move it. Excellent. So
that part of the plan was complete.

Now to plot a route from the Queen Victoria Suite to this deck.
As diagrams of the ship were hung in every small lobby and foyer, this
was not difficult at all.

I quickly realized that Stairway A was the best interior route. Indeed it was perhaps the only stairway which went directly from the deck below ours all the way to Five Deck without a break. As soon as we reached the foot of this stairway, I knew that it would be nothing for me to drop from the very top of it, down through the well of turning railings to this very spot. Now, I must climb it to the Sports Deck, and see how to reach it from our deck above.

"Ah, you can do that, my dear young fellow," said David. "I'm taking the elevator up those eight flights."

By the time we met again in the quiet sunlight of the Queens Grill Lounge, I had plotted every step. We ordered a couple of gin and tonics—a drink that I found fairly tolerable—and went over the entire scheme in final detail.

We'd wait the night in hiding until James decided to retire for the approaching day. If he came early, we would wait until the crucial moment before we moved in upon him, throwing back the lid of his trunk.

David would have the Smith & Wesson leveled upon him as we both attempted to jolt his spirit out of the body, at which point I would rush in. Timing was crucial. He would be feeling the danger of the sunlight, and knowing that he could not possibly remain in the vampiric body; but he must not have sufficient opportunity to harm either of us.

If the first assault failed, and an argument did ensue, we would make plain to him the vulnerability of his position. If he tried to destroy either of us, our inevitable shouts or screams would bring help at once. And any dead body would be left lying in James's stateroom. Where at the eleventh hour was James to go himself? It was very doubtful he knew how long he could remain conscious as the sun was rising. Indeed, I was sure he had never pushed it to the limit, as I had done many a time.

Surely given his confusion, a second assault upon him would be successful. And then as David held the large revolver on the mortal body of James, I would dart with preternatural swiftness down the corridor of the Signal Deck, down the interior stairway to the deck below, then run the length of it, passing out of the narrow corridor and into a wider one behind the Queens Grill Restaurant, where I would find the top of Stairway A, and then drop eight floors to Five Deck, rush down the corridor, and enter the small inside cabin and bolt the door. The trunk would then be shoved between bed and door, and I would climb inside it, bringing down the lid.

Even if I encountered a horde of sluggish mortals in my path it would take me no more than a few seconds, and almost all of that time I should be safe within the interior of the ship, insulated from the sun's light.

James—back in this mortal body and no doubt furious—would have no clue as to where I'd gone. Even if he overpowered David, he could not conceivably locate my cabin without an exhaustive search which would be quite beyond his ability to undertake. And David would be rousing security against him, accusing him of all sorts of sordid crimes.

Of course David had no intention of being overpowered. He would keep the powerful Smith & Wesson trained on James until the ship docked in Barbados, at which time he would escort the man to the gangway and invite him to go ashore. David would then take up his watch to see that James did not return. At sunset I would rise from the trunk and meet David, and we would enjoy the night's voyage to the next port.

David sat back in the pale green armchair, drinking the remainder of his gin and tonic, and obviously pondering the plan.

"You realize of course that I cannot execute the little devil," he said. "Gun or no gun."

"Well, you can't do it on board, that's for certain," I said. "The shot would be heard."

"And what if he realizes it? What if he goes for the weapon?"

"Then he finds himself in the same predicament. Surely he's smart enough to know that."

"I'll shoot him if I have to. That's the thought he can read from me with all his psychic skill. I will do it if I have to. Then I'll make the appropriate accusations. He was trying to rob your cabin. I was waiting for you when he came in."

"Look, suppose we make this switch soon enough before sunrise for me to hurl him over the side."

"No good. There are officers and passengers everywhere. He's sure to be seen by someone and it will be 'Man overboard' and mayhem all around."

"Of course I could crush his skull."

"Then I would have to conceal the body. No, let's hope the little monster realizes his good luck and cheerfully goes ashore. I don't want to have to . . . I don't like the thought of . . ."

"I know, I know, but you could simply shove him into that trunk. Nobody would find him."

"Lestat, I don't want to frighten you, but there are excellent reasons why we mustn't try to kill him! He told you those reasons himself. Don't you recall? Threaten that body and he'll rise out of it and make another assault. In fact, we'd be giving him no choice. And we'd be prolonging the psychic battle at the worst possible moment. It isn't inconceivable that he could follow you on your path to Five Deck, and try to get in again. Of course he'd be foolish to do it with no hiding place. But suppose he does have an alternative hiding place. Think on that."

"You're probably right on that."

"And we don't know the extent of his psychic power," he said. "And we must remember that this is his specialty—switching and possession! No. Don't try to drown him or crush him. Let him climb back into that mortal body. I'll keep the gun on him until you've had time to vanish from the scene altogether, and he and I shall have a round of conversation about what lies ahead."

"I see your point."

"Then if I do have to shoot him, very well. I'll do it. I'll put him into the trunk, and hope the sound of the shot goes unnoticed. Who knows? It might."

"God, I'm leaving you with this monster, you realize it? David, why don't we move on him as soon as the sun sets."

"No. Absolutely not. That means an all-out psychic battle! And he can hold the body sufficiently to take flight and simply leave us on board this ship, which will be at sea for the entire night. Lestat, I've thought all this through. Every part of the plan is crucial. We want him at his weakest, just before dawn, with the ship about to dock so that once he is in his mortal body, he can cheerfully and gratefully disembark. Now, you must trust that I'll handle this fellow. You don't know how much I despise him! If you did, perhaps you wouldn't worry at all."

"Be assured I shall kill him when I find him."

"All the more reason for him to willingly go ashore. He'll want a head start, and I shall advise him to be quick."

"The Big-Game Hunt. I shall love it. I'll find him—even if he hides in another body. What a lovely game it will be."

David fell quiet for a moment.

"Lestat, there is one other possibility, of course . . ."

"What? I don't understand you."

He looked away as if he were trying to choose just the right words. Then he looked directly at me. "We could destroy that thing, you know."

"David, are you mad to even . . . ?"

"Lestat, the two of us could do it. There are ways. Before sunset, we could destroy that thing, and you would be . . ."

"Say no more!" I was angry. But when I saw the sadness in his face, the concern, the obvious moral confusion, I sighed and sat back and took a softer tone. "David," I said, "I'm the Vampire Lestat. That's my body. We're going to get it back for me."

For a moment he didn't respond, and then he nodded rather emphatically and said in a half whisper, "Yes. Correct."

A pause fell between us, during which time I began to go over each and every step of the plan.

When I looked at him again, he seemed similarly thoughtful, in fact rather deeply engaged.

"You know I think it will go smoothly," he said. "Especially when I remember your descriptions of him in that body. Awkward, uncomfortable. And of course we must remember what sort of human he is—his true age, his old modus operandi, so to speak. Hmmm. He isn't going to get that gun away from me. Yes, I think it's all going to work as planned."

"So do I," I said.

"And all things considered," he added, "well, it's the only chance we've got!"

TWENTY-TWO

FOR the next two hours we went exploring the ship. It was imperative that we be able to hide in it during the nighttime hours when James might be roaming the various decks. For this, we had to know it, and I must confess that my curiosity about the vessel was extreme.

We wandered out of the quiet and narrow Queens Grill Lounge, and back into the main body of the vessel, past many cabin doors before we reached the circular mezzanine with its village of fancy shops. Then down a large circular stairway we went and across a vast polished dance floor through the main lounge, and off to other darkened bars and lounges, each with its own great spread of dizzying carpet and throbbing electronic music, and then past an indoor pool around which hundreds lunched at large circular tables, and then outside to yet another pool in the open, where countless passengers sunned themselves in beach chairs, snoozing or reading their folded papers or little paperback books.

Eventually we came upon a small library, full of quiet patrons, and a darkened casino, not to be opened until the ship had left the port. Here stood banks of somber darkened slot machines, and tables for blackjack and roulette.

At one point, we peeked into the darkened theatre, and found it to be enormous, though only some four or five people were watching the film upon a giant screen.

Then there was another lounge, and yet another, some with windows, and some utterly dark, and a fine fancy restaurant for passengers of middle rank, reached by a winding stairs. Yet a third—also quite handsome—served the patrons of the very lowest decks. Down we went, past my secret cabin hiding place. And there we discovered not one but two health spas, with their machines for building muscles and rooms for cleansing the pores of the skin with jets of steam.

Somewhere we stumbled upon the small hospital, with nurses in white uniforms, and tiny brightly lighted rooms; at another juncture a large windowless chamber full of computers at which several persons were working quietly away. There was a beauty salon for women, and a similar grooming establishment for men. We came upon a travel desk at one time, and at another what seemed a sort of bank.

And always we were walking in narrow corridors to which we could not quite see the end. The dull beige walls and ceilings were forever close around us. One hideous color of carpet gave way to another. Indeed, sometimes the garish modern patterns met with such violence at various doorways that I all but laughed out loud. I lost count of the many stairways with their shallow padded steps. I could not distinguish one bank of elevators from another. Everywhere I looked there were numbered cabin doors. The framed pictures were bland and indistinguishable one from another. I had again and again to seek the diagrams to determine where exactly I had been and might be going now, or how to escape some circular path in which I found myself wandering for the fourth or fifth time.

David thought it powerfully amusing, especially since we encountered other passengers who were lost at almost every turn. At least six different times, we helped these very old individuals find their way to a certain place. And then became lost ourselves again.

Finally, by some miracle, we found our way back through the narrow Queens Grill Lounge and up to the secret Signal Deck and to our cabins. It was only an hour before sunset, and the giant engines were already roaring.

As soon as I had on my clothes for the evening—a white turtleneck and light seersucker suit—I headed out on the veranda to see the smoke pouring from the great chimney above. The entire ship had begun to vibrate with the power of the engines. And the soft Caribbean light was waning over the distant hills.

A fierce churning apprehension gripped me. It was as if my entrails had been caught by the vibration of the engine. But it had nothing to do with such things. I was merely thinking that I should never see this brilliant natural light again. I should see the light of only moments from now—twilight—but never this splash of the dying sun on the tessellated water, never this gleam of gold in distant windows, or the blue sky shining so clear in its last hour, above the rolling clouds.

I wanted to cling to the moment, to savor every soft and subtle change. Then again, I did not. Centuries ago, there had been no farewell to the daylight hours. As the sun set on that last fateful day, I had not even dreamed that I would never see it until this time. Never even dreamed!

Surely I should stand here, feeling the last of its sweet warmth, enjoying these precious moments of wholesome light.

But I really didn't want to. I really didn't care. I had seen it at moments far more precious and wondrous. It was over, wasn't it? I would soon be the Vampire Lestat again.

I passed slowly back through the stateroom. I looked at myself in the large mirror. Oh, this would be the longest night of my existence, I thought—longer even than that awful night of cold and sickness in Georgetown. And what if we fail!

David was waiting for me in the corridor, looking his very proper self in white linen. We must get away from here, he said, before the sun went down below the waves. I wasn't so anxious. I didn't think that slovenly idiot creature would hop right from the trunk into the burning twilight as I so loved to do. On the contrary, he would probably lie there fearfully in the dark for some time before he emerged.

Then what would he do? Open the draperies to his veranda and leave the ship by that means to rob some doomed family on the distant shore? Ah, but he had struck Grenada. Maybe he meant to rest.

We couldn't know.

We slipped off down to the Queens Grill Lounge again and then out onto the windy deck. Many passengers had come outside to see the ship leave port. The crew was making ready. Thick gray smoke poured from the chimney into the waning light of the sky.

I leant my arms against the rail and looked out towards the distant curve of land. The infinitely changing waves caught and held the light with a thousand different shades and degrees of opacity. But how much more varied and translucent it would appear to my eyes when tomorrow night came! Yet as I looked at it, I lost all thought of the future. I lost myself in the sheer majesty of the sea, and the firey pink light now suffusing and changing the azure of the endless sky.

All around me, mortals seemed subdued. There was little talk. People were gathered up on the windy prow to pay homage to this moment. The breeze here was silken and fragrant. The dark orange sun, visible as a peeping eye on the horizon, suddenly sank beyond sight. A glorious explosion of yellow light caught the underside of the great stacks of blowing clouds. A rosy light moved up and up into the limitless and shining heavens, and through this glorious mist of color came the first twinkling glimmer of the stars.

The water darkened; the waves struck the hull below with greater violence. I realized the big ship was moving. And suddenly a deep violent throbbing whistle broke from her, a cry striking both fear and excitement in my bones. So slow and steady was her movement that I had to keep my eyes on the far shore to gauge it. We were turning to the west and into the dying light.

I saw that David's eyes were glazed over. With his right hand, he gripped the railing. He looked at the horizon, at the rising clouds and the deep pink sky beyond.

I wanted to say something to him—something fine and important, and indicative of the deep love I felt. My heart seemed to be breaking with it suddenly, and I turned slowly to him, and laid my left hand upon his right, which held the rail.

"I know," he whispered. "Believe me, I know. But you must be clever now. Keep it locked inside."

Ah, yes, bring down the veil. Be one among the countless hundreds, shut off and silent and alone. Be alone. And this my last day as a mortal man, had come to a close.

Once again the great throbbing whistle sounded.

The ship had almost completed her about-face. She was moving towards open sea. The sky was now darkening swiftly and it was time for us to retreat to the lower decks, and find some corner of a noisy lounge where we would not be observed.

I took one last look at the sky, realizing that all the light had now fled, utterly and completely, and my heart grew cold. A dark chill passed over me. But I couldn't regret the loss of the light. I couldn't. All I wanted with my whole monstrous soul was to have my vampire powers once more. Yet the earth itself seemed to demand something finer—that I weep for what was forsworn.

I couldn't do it. I felt sadness, and the crushing failure of my human venture weighed upon me in the silence as I stood there motionless, feeling the warm tender breeze.

I felt David's hand, tugging gently at my arm.

"Yes, let's go on in," I said, and I turned my back on the soft Caribbean sky. Night had already fallen. And my thoughts were with James and James alone.

Oh, how I wished I could glimpse the fool when he rose from his silken hiding place. But it was far too risky. There was no vantage point from which we could watch in safety. Our only move was to conceal ourselves now.

The ship itself changed with the fall of darkness.

The small glittering shops of the mezzanine were doing a busy and noisy trade as we passed them. Men and women clad in shiny fabrics for evening were already taking their places in the Theatre Lounge below.

The slot machines had come alive with flashing lights in the casino; there was a crowd around the roulette table. And the elderly couples were dancing to the soft slow music of a band in the vast shadowy Queens Room.

Once we had found a likely little corner in the dark Club Lido, and ordered a pair of drinks to keep us company, David commanded me to stay there as he ventured up to the Signal Deck alone.

"Why? What do you mean, stay here?" I was instantly furious.

"He'll know you the minute he sees you," he said dismissively, as if he were talking to a child. He fitted a pair of dark glasses over his face. "He's not likely to notice me at all."

"All right, boss," I said disgustedly. I was outraged to have to wait here in silence while he went adventuring about!

I slumped back in the chair, drank another deep cold antiseptic swallow of my gin and tonic, and strained to see through the annoying darkness as several young couples moved out over the flashing lights of the electrically illuminated dance floor. The music was intolerably loud. But the subtle vibratory movement of the giant ship was delicious. She was already tearing along. Indeed, when I looked to the far left out of this little pit of contrived shadows, and through one of the many vast glass windows, I could see the cloud-filled sky, still luminous with the light of early evening, simply flying by.

A mighty ship, I thought. I must give her that. For all her flashy little lights and ugly carpet, her oppressively low ceilings and endlessly boring public rooms, she is a mighty ship indeed.

I was reflecting upon it, trying not to go mad with impatience, and attempting in fact to see it from the point of view of James, when I was distracted by the distant appearance, in the far corridor, of a magnificently handsome blond-haired young man. He was dressed all in evening clothes, except for an incongruous pair of violet-tinted glasses, and I was drinking up his appearance in characteristic fashion when I suddenly realized with stultifying horror that I was gazing at myself!

It was James in his black dinner jacket and boiled shirt, scanning the place from behind those fashionable lenses, and making his way slowly to this lounge.

The tightening in my chest was unbearable. Every muscle of my frame began to spasm in my anxiety. Very slowly I lifted my hand to support my forehead and bowed my head just a little, looking again to the left.

But how could he not see me with those sharp preternatural eyes! This darkness was nothing to him. Why, surely he could pick up the scent of fear that emanated from me as the sweat poured down beneath my shirt.

But the fiend did not see me. Indeed, he had settled at the bar with his back to me, and turned his head to the right. I could make out only the line of his cheek and his jaw. And as he fell into a state of obvious relaxation, I realized that he was posing as he sat there, his left elbow leaning on the polished wood, his right knee crooked ever so slightly, his heel hooked into the brass rail of the stool upon which he sat.

He moved his head gently with the rhythm of the slow, woozy music. And a lovely pride emanated from him, a sublime contentment in what and where he was.

Slowly I took a deep breath. Far across the spacious room, and well beyond him, I saw the unmistakable figure of David stop for an instant in the open door. Then the figure moved on. Thank God, he had seen the monster, who must have looked to all the world as completely normal now—except for his excessive and flashy beauty— as he did to me.

When the fear crested in me again, I deliberately imagined a job I did not have, in a town where I had never lived. I thought of a fiancée named Barbara, most beautiful and maddening, and an argument be- tween us which of course had never taken place. I cluttered my mind with such images, and thought of a million other random things— tropical fish I should like to have in a little tank someday, and whether or not I should go to the Theatre Lounge and see the show.

The creature took no notice of me. Indeed, I soon realized he was taking no notice of anyone. There was something almost poignant in the way he sat there, face slightly uplifted, apparently enjoying this dark and fairly ordinary and certainly ugly little place.

He loves it here, I thought. These public rooms with their plastic and tinsel represent some pinnacle of elegance, and he is silently thrilled merely to be here. He does not even need to be noticed. He takes no notice of anyone who might notice. He is a little world unto himself as this ship is such a world, speeding along so very fast through the warm seas.

Even in my fear, I found it heartbreaking suddenly and tragic. And I wondered had I not seemed the very same tiresome failure to others when I was in that shape? Had I not seemed just as sad?

Trembling violently, I picked up the glass and downed the drink as if it were medicine, receding behind those contrived images again, cloaking my fear with them, and even humming a little with the music, watching almost absently the play of the soft-colored lights on that lovely head of golden hair.

Suddenly he slipped off the stool and, turning to the left, walked very slowly through the dark bar, and past me without seeing me, and into the brighter lights around the enclosed pool. His chin was lifted; his steps so slow and careful as to seem painful, his head turning from right to left as he surveyed the space through which he passed. Then with the same careful manner, indeed a manner more indicative of weakness than strength, he pushed open the glass door to the outer deck and slipped into the night.

I had to follow him! I shouldn't and I knew it, but I was on my feet before I could stop myself, my head thick with the same cloud of false identity as I moved after him, and then stopped inside the door. I could see him very far away at the very end of the deck itself, arms leaning on the railing, wind blowing hard through his loose hair. He was looking heavenward as he stood there, and once again he seemed lost in pride and in contentment, loving the wind and the darkness, perhaps, and swaying just a little, as blind musicians sway when they play their music, as if he relished every ticking second in that body, simply swimming in pure happiness as he stood on that spot.

The heartbreaking sense of recognition passed over me again. Did I seem the same wasteful fool to those who had known me and condemned me? Oh, pitiful, pitiful creature to have spent his preternatural life in this of all places, so painfully artificial, with its old and sad passengers, in unremarkable chambers of tawdry finery, insulated from the great universe of true splendours that lay beyond.

Only after a great while did he bow his head just a little, and run the fingers of his right hand slowly down his jacket lapel. A cat licking its own fur had never looked more relaxed or self-indulgent. How lovingly he stroked this bit of unimportant cloth! It was more eloquent of the whole tragedy than any other single thing he had done.

Then, rolling his head to one side and then the other, and seeing only a couple of passengers to his far right, who were facing an entirely different direction, he suddenly rose off the boards and immediately disappeared!

Of course, no such thing had really happened. He had merely taken to the air. And I was left shuddering inside the glass door, the sweat breaking out all over my face and back as I looked at the empty place beyond, and felt David's quick whisper in my ear.

"Come, old chap, let's go on to the Queens Grill and have our supper."

I turned and saw the forced expression on his face. Of course James was still within range to hear both of us! To hear anything out of the ordinary without so much as a deliberate scan.

"Yes, the Queens Grill," I said, trying not to consciously think of Jake's words of last night that the fellow had yet to appear for a meal in that room. "I'm not really hungry, but it's awfully tiresome, isn't it, hanging around here?"

David, too, was trembling. But he was powerfully excited, as well.

"Oh, I must tell you," he said, carrying on the same false manner, as we walked back through the lounge and towards the nearby stairway. "They're all in black tie up there, but they have to serve us, as we've just come aboard."

"I don't care if they're all naked. It's going to be a hell of a night."

The famous first-class dining room was a bit more subdued and civilized than other rooms through which we'd passed. All done in white upholstery and black lacquer, it was quite pleasant with its generous blaze of warm light. The decor had a hard brittle quality to it, but then so did everything aboard the vessel; it wasn't at all ugly, however, and the carefully prepared food was quite good.

When some twenty-five minutes had passed since the dark bird had flown, I ventured several quick remarks. "He can't use a tenth of his strength! He's terrified of it."

"Yes, I agree with you. So frightened is he that he actually moves as if he were drunk."

"Ah, that's it, you have it. And he wasn't twenty feet away from me, David. And he had absolutely no sense that I was there."

"I know, Lestat, believe me, I know. My God, there's so much I haven't taught you. I stood there watching you, terrified he'd try some telekinetic mischief, and I hadn't given you the slightest instruction on how to fend him off."

"David, if he really uses his power, nothing can fend him off. But you see, he can't use it. And if he had taken a stab, I'd draw on instinct, because that's all you've been teaching me to do."

"Yes, that's true. It's all a matter of the same tricks which you knew and understood in the other form. I had the feeling last night that you achieved the surest victories when you forgot you were mortal and lapsed into behaving as if you were your old self."

"Perhaps so," I said. "I honestly don't know. Oh, just the sight of him in my body!"

"Shhh, eat your last meal, and keep your voice down."

"My last meal." I gave a little chuckle. "I'll make a meal of him when I finally catch him." Then I stopped, realizing with distaste that I was speaking of my own flesh. I looked down at the long dark-skinned hand which was holding the silver knife. Did I feel any affection for this body? No. I wanted my own body, and I could not bear the thought that we had some eight hours to wait before it would again be mine.

WE DIDN'T see him again until well past one o'clock.

I knew enough to avoid the little Club Lido, as it was the best place for dancing, which he liked to do, and it was also comfortably dark. Instead I hung about in the larger lounge areas, dark glasses securely in place, and hair plastered back with a thick dollop of grease which a confused young steward had obligingly given me upon request. I didn't mind looking so dreadful. I felt more anonymous and safe.

When we spotted him he was again in one of the outer corridors, moving this time into the casino. It was David who went after him to watch and principally because he couldn't resist.

I wanted to remind him that we didn't have to follow the monster. All we had to do was move upon the Queen Victoria Suite at the appropriate time. The ship's little newspaper, which had already been issued for the following morning, gave the exact time of sunrise as 6:21 a.m. I laughed when I saw it, but then I couldn't tell such a thing so easily now, could I? Well, by 6:21 a.m. I would be myself again.

At last David returned to his chair beside me and picked up the newspaper he'd been doggedly reading by the small table light.

"He's at the roulette wheel and he's winning. The little beast is using his telekinetic power to win! How stupid he is."

"Yes, you keep saying that," I said. "Shall we talk now about our favorite films? Haven't seen anything with Rutger Hauer lately. I miss that chap."

David gave a little laugh. "Yes, I'm rather fond of that Dutch actor myself."

We were still talking quietly at twenty-five minutes past three when we happened to see the handsome Mr. Jason Hamilton pass by again. So slow, so dreamy, so doomed. When David moved to follow, I laid my hand on his.

"No need, old boy. Just three more hours. Tell me the plot of that old film, *Body and Soul,* you remember it, the one about the boxer, and isn't there a line in it about the tyger from Blake?"

AT TEN past six, the milky light was already filling the sky. This was exactly the moment when I usually sought my resting place, and I couldn't imagine that he had not already sought his. We should find him in his shiny black trunk.

We had not seen him since a little past four o'clock when he'd been dancing in his slow drunken fashion on the little floor of the deserted Club Lido with a smallish gray-haired woman in a lovely soft red gown. We'd stood some distance away, outside the bar, our backs to the wall, listening to the brisk flow of his oh, so proper British voice. Then we had both fled.

Now the moment was at hand. No more running from him. The long night was coming to its close. It occurred to me several times that I might perish within the next few minutes, but never in my life had such a thought stopped me from doing anything. If I thought of David being hurt, I would entirely lose my nerve.

David had never been more determined. He had only just taken the big silver gun from the cabin on Five Deck, and was carrying it in the pocket of his coat. We had left the trunk open there in readiness for me; and the door wore its little "Do Not Disturb" sign to keep the stewards out. We had also determined that I could not carry the black gun with me, for after the switch the weapon would then be in the hands of James. The little cabin was left unlocked. Indeed the keys were inside it, for I could not risk carrying these either. If some helpful steward did lock the door, I should have to move the lock with my mind, which would not be difficult for the old Lestat at all.

What I did carry on my person now was the bogus Sheridan Blackwood passport in my coat pocket along with enough money for the fool to get out of Barbados and to whatever part of the world he wished to flee. The ship was already making its way into the harbour of Barbados. God willing, it would not take her too long to dock.

As we'd hoped, the broad brightly lighted passage of the Signal Deck was deserted. I suspected that the steward was behind the galley curtains, catching a little sleep.

Quietly we proceeded to the door of the Queen Victoria Suite, and David slipped the key in the lock. Immediately we were inside. The trunk lay open and empty. The lamps were burning. The fiend had not yet come.

Without a word, I turned off these lights one by one and went to the veranda doors and drew back the drapes. The sky was still the shining blue of night but growing paler by the second. A gentle and pretty illumination filled the room. It would burn his eyes when he saw it. It would bring an immediate flush of pain to his exposed skin.

No doubt he was on his way here now, he had to be, unless he did have another hiding place of which we didn't know.

I went back to the door, and stood to the left of it. He would not see me when he entered, for the door itself would cover me from view when he pushed it back.

David had moved up the steps, to the raised sitting room, and was turned with his back to the glass wall, and facing the cabin door, the big gun held firmly in both hands.

Suddenly, I heard the rapid steps drawing nearer and nearer. I didn't dare signal to David, but I could see that he, too, heard the approach. The creature was almost running. His daring surprised me. Then David lifted the gun and aimed it, as the key ground in the lock.

The door swung back against me and then slammed as James all but staggered into the room. His arm was up to shade his eyes from the light coming through the glass wall, and he uttered a half-strangled curse, clearly damning the stewards for not having closed the draperies as they'd been told to do.

In the usual awkward fashion, he turned towards the steps, and then came to a halt. He saw David above, holding the gun on him, and then David cried out:

"Now!"

With my whole being, I made the assault upon him, the invisible part of me flying up and out of my mortal body and hurtling towards my old form with incalculable force. Instantly, I was thrown backwards! I went down into my mortal body again with such speed that the body itself was slammed in defeat against the wall.

"Again!" David shouted, but once more I was repelled with dizzying rapidity, struggling to regain control of my heavy mortal limbs and scramble to my feet.

I saw my old vampire face looming over me, blue eyes reddened and squinting as the light grew ever more bright throughout the room. Ah, I knew the pain he suffered! I knew the confusion. The sun was searing that tender skin, which had never completely healed from the Gobi! His limbs were probably already growing weak with the inevitable numbness of the coming day.

"All right, James, the game's over," David said in obvious fury. "Use your clever little brain!"

The creature turned as if jerked to attention by David's voice, and then shrank back against the night table, crumpling the heavy plastic material with a loud ugly noise, his arm thrown up again to shield his eyes. In panic, he saw the destruction he'd wrought, and then tried to look again at David, who stood with his back to the coming sun.

"Now what do you mean to do?" demanded David. "Where can you go? Where can you hide? Harm us and the cabin will be searched as soon as the bodies are discovered. It's over, my friend. Give it up now."

A deep growl came from James. He ducked his head as if he were a blind bull about to charge. I felt absolutely desperate as I saw his hands curl into fists.

"Give it up, James," David shouted.

And as a volley of oaths came from the being, I made for him once more, panic driving me as surely as courage and plain mortal will. The first hot ray of the sun cut across the water! Dear God, it was now or never and I couldn't fail. I couldn't. I collided with him full force, feeling a paralytic electric shock as I passed through him and then I could see nothing and I was being sucked as if by a giant vacuum down and down into the darkness, crying, "Yes, into him, into me! Into my body, yes!" Then I was staring directly into a blaze of golden light.

The pain in my eyes was unbearable. It was the heat of the Gobi. It was the great and final illumination of hell. But I'd done it! I was inside my own body! And that blaze was the sun rising, and it was scalding my lovely priceless preternatural face and my hands.

"David, we've won!" I shouted, and the words leapt out at freakish volume. I sprang up from the floor where I'd fallen, possessed once more of all my delicious and glorious quickness and strength. In a blind rush, I made for the door, catching one flickering glimpse of my old mortal body struggling on hands and knees towards the steps.

The room veritably exploded with heat and light as I gained the passage. I could not remain there one second longer, even though I heard the powerful gun go off with a deafening crack.

"God help you, David," I whispered. I was instantly at the foot of the first flight of steps. No sunlight penetrated this inside passage, thank heaven, but my strong familiar limbs were already growing weak. By the time the second shot was fired, I'd vaulted the railing of Stairway A, and plunged all the way down to Five Deck, where I hit the carpet at a run.

I heard yet another shot before I reached the little cabin. But it was oh, so faint. The dark sunburnt hand which snatched open the door was almost incapable of turning the knob. I was struggling against a creeping cold again as surely as if I were wandering in the Georgetown snows. But the door was jerked open, I fell on my knees inside the little room. Even if I collapsed I was safe from the light.

With one last thrust of sheer will, I slammed the door, and shoved the open trunk into place and toppled into it. Then it was all I could do to reach up for the lid. I could feel nothing any longer as I heard it fall into place. I was lying there motionless, a ragged sigh escaping my lips.

"God help you, David," I whispered. Why had he fired? Why? And why so many shots from that great powerful gun? How could the world have not heard that big noisy gun!

But no power on earth could enable me to help him now. My eyes were closing. And then I was floating in the deep velvet darkness I had not known since that fateful meeting in Georgetown. It was over, it was finished. I was the Vampire Lestat again, and nothing else mattered. Nothing.

I think my lips formed the word "David" one more time as if it were a prayer.

TWENTY-THREE

A S SOON as I awoke, I sensed that David and James were not
on the ship.

I'm not certain how I knew. But I did.

After straightening my clothes somewhat and indulging myself in
a few moments of giddy happiness as I looked in the mirror, and flexed
my marvelous fingers and toes, I went out to make certain that the two
men were not on board. James I did not hope to find. But David. What
had happened to David after firing that gun?

Surely three bullets would have killed James! And of course all
this had happened in *my* cabin—indeed I found *my* passport with the
name of Jason Hamilton securely in my pocket—and so I proceeded
to the Signal Deck with the greatest of care.

The cabin stewards were rushing to and fro, delivering evening
cocktails, and straightening the rooms of those who had already ventured out for the night. I used my utmost skill to move swiftly along
the passage and into the Queen Victoria Suite without being seen.

The suite had obviously been put in order. The black lacquered
locker which James had used as his coffin was closed, with the cloth
smoothed over the lid. The battered and broken bedside table had been
cleared away, leaving a scar upon the wall.

There was no blood on the carpet. Indeed, there was no evidence
of any kind that the horrific struggle had taken place. And I could see
through the glass windows to the veranda that we were moving out
of Barbados harbour under a glorious and shining veil of twilight,
towards the open sea.

I stepped outside on the veranda for a moment, just to look up into
the limitless night and feel the joy of my old true vampiric vision once
again. On the distant glittering shores I saw a million tiny details which
no mortal could ever see. I was so thrilled to feel the old physical
lightness, the sense of dexterity and grace, that I wanted to start
dancing. Indeed, it would be lovely to do a little tap dance up one side
the ship and down the other, snapping my fingers and singing songs
all the while.

But there was no time for all this. I had to find out what had happened to David at once.

Opening the door to the passage, I quickly and silently worked the lock on David's cabin across the way. Then in a little spurt of preternatural speed I entered it, unseen by those moving down the hall.

Everything was gone. Indeed, the cabin had been sanitized for a new passenger. Obviously David had been forced to leave the ship. He might now be in Barbados! And if he was, I could find him quickly enough.

But what about the other cabin—the one that had belonged to my mortal self? I opened the connecting door without touching it, and I found that this cabin had also been emptied and cleaned.

How to proceed. I didn't want to remain on this ship any longer than I had to, for certainly I would be the center of attention as soon as I was discovered. The debacle had taken place in my suite.

I heard the easily identifiable tread of the steward who had been of such service to us earlier, and I opened the door just as he meant to pass by. When he saw me he was powerfully confused and excited. I beckoned for him to come inside.

"Oh, sir, they are looking for you! They thought you'd left the ship in Barbados! I must contact security at once."

"Ah, but tell me what happened," I said, peering directly into his eyes, and beyond his words. I could see the charm working on him as he softened and fell into a complete state of trust.

There had been a dreadful incident in my cabin at sunrise. An elderly British gentleman—who had earlier claimed to be my physician, by the way—had fired several shots at a young assailant who—he claimed—had tried to murder him, but none of these shots had struck the mark. Indeed, no one had ever been able to locate the young assailant. On the basis of the elderly gentleman's description, it was determined that the young man had occupied this very cabin in which we were now standing, and that he had boarded the ship under an assumed name.

Indeed so had the elderly British gentleman. In fact, the confusion of names was no small part of the entire affair. The steward really didn't know all that had taken place, except that the elderly British gentleman had been held in custody until he was finally escorted ashore.

The steward was puzzled. "I think they were rather relieved to have him off the ship. But we must call the security officer, sir. They are very concerned about your welfare. It's a wonder they didn't stop you when you came aboard again in Barbados. They've been searching for you all day."

I wasn't at all sure that I wanted to endure any close scrutiny on the part of the security officers, but the matter was quickly decided for me when two men in white uniforms appeared before the door of the Queen Victoria Suite.

I thanked the steward and approached these two gentlemen, inviting them into the suite, and moving deeply into the shadows as was my custom during such encounters, and begging them to forgive me for not turning on the lights. Indeed, the light coming through the veranda doors was quite enough, I explained, considering the poor condition of my skin.

Both these men were deeply troubled and suspicious, and once again I did my best to work the persuasive charm on them as I spoke.

"What has happened to Dr. Alexander Stoker?" I asked. "He is my personal physician, and I'm deeply concerned."

The younger of the two men, a very red-faced man with an Irish accent, clearly did not believe what I was saying to him, and he could sense that something was very wrong with my manner and my speech. My only hope was to sink this individual into confusion so that he remained quiet.

But the other, the tall and educated Englishman, was much easier to spellbind, and he began to pour out the whole tale without guile.

Seems Dr. Stoker was not really Dr. Stoker, but a man from England named David Talbot, though why he had used the assumed name, he refused to say.

"You know, this Mr. Talbot had a gun on board this vessel, sir!" said the tall officer, while the other continued to stare at me in deep inarticulate distrust. "Of course this organization in London, this Talamasca, or whatever it is, was most apologetic, and eager to make things right. It was settled with the captain finally, and some persons at the home offices of Cunard. No charges were brought against Mr. Talbot when Mr. Talbot agreed to pack his belongings and allow himself to be escorted ashore and to a plane leaving immediately for the United States."

"To where in the United States?"

"Miami, sir. In fact, I saw him to the flight myself. He insisted upon giving me a message for you, sir, that you should meet him in Miami, at your convenience. At the Park Central Hotel? He gave me this message any number of times."

"I see," I answered. "And the man who attacked him? The man at whom he fired the gun?"

"We haven't found any such person, sir, though undoubtedly this man was seen on this ship earlier by any number of persons, and in the company of Mr. Talbot, it seems! As a matter of fact, that is the young gentleman's cabin over there, and I believe you were in it, talking to the steward, when we arrived?"

"The whole thing is most puzzling," I said in my most intimate and confiding manner. "You think this brown-haired young man is no longer on the ship?"

"We're fairly certain of it, sir, though of course it's quite impossible to engage in an all-out search of a vessel such as this. The young man's belongings were still in the cabin when we opened it. We did have to open it, of course, what with Mr. Talbot insisting he'd been assaulted by the young man, and that the young man was also traveling under an assumed name! We have his luggage in safekeeping, of course. Sir, if you would come with me to the captain's office, I think perhaps you could shed some light upon—"

I quickly averred that I knew nothing about all this, really. I hadn't been in the cabin at the time. Indeed, I'd gone ashore yesterday in Grenada without ever knowing that either man was boarding the vessel. And I had disembarked this morning in Barbados for a day of sightseeing without ever knowing this shooting incident had taken place.

But all this calm clever chatter on my part was a cover for the persuasion I continued to use on both of them—that they must leave me now, so that I might change clothes and have some rest.

When I shut the door on them, I knew they were on their way to the captain's quarters, and that I had only minutes before they returned. It didn't really matter. David was safe; he'd left the ship and gone on to Miami, where I was to meet him. That was all I wanted to know. Thank God he'd gotten an immediate flight out of Barbados. For God only knew where James might be at this time.

As for Mr. Jason Hamilton, whose passport I was carrying in my pocket, he still had a closet full of clothes in this suite and I intended to avail myself of some of them at once. I stripped off the rumpled dinner jacket, and other nighttime finery—vampire drag, par excellence!—and found a cotton shirt, decent linen jacket, and pants. Of course everything was exquisitely tailored for this body. Even the canvas shoes were a comfortable fit.

I took along the passport with me, and a sizable sum of American dollars which I had found in the old clothes.

Then I went back out on the veranda and stood still in the sweet caressing breeze, eyes moving dreamily over the deeply blue and luminous sea.

The *Queen Elizabeth 2* was now thundering along at her famed twenty-eight knots, the bright translucent waves crashing into her mighty bow. The island of Barbados had completely disappeared from view. I looked up at the great black smokestack, which seemed in its immensity to be the very chimney of hell. It was a splendid sight to see the thick gray smoke gushing from it, and then arching back and down to the very water in the continuous blast of the wind.

I looked again at the distant horizon. All the world was filled with fine and beauteous azure light. Beyond a thin haze which mortals could not have detected I saw the tiny twinkling constellations, and the somber shining planets drifting ever so slowly by. I stretched my limbs, loving the feel of them, and the sweet ripples of sensation which moved down my shoulders and back. I shook myself all over, loving the feel of my hair on the back of my neck, and then I rested my arms upon the rail.

"I'll catch up with you, James," I whispered. "You can be certain of it. But I have other things I must do now. For the moment plot your little schemes in vain."

Then I went upwards slowly—indeed as slowly as I could manage it—until I was very high over the vessel, and I gazed down at her, admiring her many decks stacked one atop the other, and trimmed in so many tiny yellow lights. How festive she looked, and how removed from all care. Bravely she advanced through the rolling sea, mute and powerful and carrying her whole little realm with her of dancing and dining and chattering beings, of busy security officers and rushing stewards, of hundreds upon hundreds of happy creatures who knew not at all that we had ever been there to trouble them with our little drama, or that we were gone as swiftly as we had come, leaving only the smallest bit of confusion in our wake. Peace to the happy *Queen*

Elizabeth 2, I thought, and then again, I knew why the Body Thief had loved her, and hidden himself within her, sad and tawdry though she was.

After all, what is our entire world to the stars above? What do they think of our tiny planet, I wondered, full of mad juxtaposition, happenstance, and endless struggle, and the deep crazed civilizations sprawled upon the face of it, and held together not by will or faith or communal ambition but by some dreamy capacity of the world's millions to be oblivious to life's tragedies and again and again sink into happiness, just as the passengers of that little ship sank into it—as if happiness were as natural to all beings as hunger or sleepiness or love of warmth and fear of the cold.

I rose higher and higher until I could no longer see the ship at all. Clouds raced across the face of the world below me. And above, the stars burned through in all their cold majesty, and for once I didn't hate them; no, I couldn't hate them; I could hate nothing; I was too full of joy and dark bitter triumph. I was Lestat, drifting between hell and heaven, and content to be so—*perhaps for the first time.*

TWENTY-FOUR

THE rain forest of South America—great deep tangle of woods and jungle that covers miles upon miles of the continent, blanketing mountain slopes and crowding into deep valleys, and breaking only for broad glittering rivers and shimmering lakes— soft and verdant and lush and seemingly harmless when seen through the drifting clouds from high above.

The darkness is impenetrable when one stands upon the soft, moist ground. The trees are so high there is no heaven above them. Indeed, creation is nothing but struggle and menace amid these deep moist shadows. It is the final triumph of the Savage Garden, and not all the scientists of civilization will ever classify every species of painted butterfly or speckled cat or flesh-eating fish or giant coiling snake, which thrives in this place.

Birds with feathers the color of the summer sky or the burning sun streak through the wet branches. Monkeys scream as they reach out with their tiny clever little hands for vines as thick as hemp rope. Sleek and sinister mammals of a thousand shapes and sizes crawl in remorseless search of one another over monstrous roots and half-buried tubers, under giant rustling leaves and up the twisted trunks of saplings dying in the fetid darkness, even as they suck their last nourishment from the reeking soil.

Mindless and endlessly vigorous is the cycle of hunger and satiation, of violent and painful death. Reptiles with eyes as hard and shining as opals feast eternally upon the writhing universe of stiff and crackling insects as they have since the days when no warm-blooded creature ever walked the earth. And the insects—winged, fanged, pumped with deadly venom, and dazzling in their hideousness and ghastly beauty, and beyond all cunning—ultimately feast upon all.

There is no mercy in this forest. No mercy, no justice, no worshipful appreciation of its beauty, no soft cry of joy at the beauty of the falling rain. Even the sagacious little monkey is a moral idiot at heart.

That is—there was no such thing until the coming of man.

How many thousands of years ago that was, no one can tell you for certain. The jungle devours its bones. It quietly swallows up sacred manuscripts as it gnaws on the more stubborn stones of the temple. Textiles, woven baskets, painted pots, and even ornaments of hammered gold ultimately dissolve on its tongue.

But the small-bodied, dark-skinned peoples have been there for many centuries, that is beyond question, forming their friable little villages of palm-frond huts and smoky cooking fires, and hunting the abundant and lethal game with their crude spears and their deadly poison-tipped darts. In some places they make their orderly little farms as they have always done, to grow thick yams, or lush green avocados, red peppers, and corn. Lots of sweet, tender yellow corn. Little hens peck at the dust outside the small carefully constructed houses. Fat, glossy pigs snuffle and snuggle in their pens.

Are these humans the best thing in this Savage Garden, warring as they have done so long upon one another? Or are they simply an undifferentiated part of it, no more complex ultimately than the crawling centipede or the slinky satin-skinned jaguar or the silent big-eyed frog so very toxic that one touch of his spotted back brings certain death?

What have the many towers of great Caracas to do with this endless sprawling world that comes so close to it. Wence came this metropolis of South America, with its smog-filled skies and its vast teeming hillside slums? Beauty is beauty where you find it. At night, even these *ranchitos* as they call them—the thousands upon thousands of shacks that cover the steep slopes on either side of the roaring freeways—are beautiful, for though they have no water, and no sewerage, and they are crowded beyond all modern questions of health or comfort, they are nevertheless strung with bright, shining electric lights.

Sometimes it seems that light can transform anything! That it is an undeniable and irreducible metaphor for grace. But do the people of the *ranchitos* know this? Is it for beauty that they do it? Or do they merely want a comfortable illumination in their little shacks?

It doesn't matter.

We can't stop ourselves from making beauty. We can't stop the world.

Look down upon the river that flows past the small outpost of St. Laurent, a ribbon of light glimpsed here and there for an instant from the treetops as it makes its way deeper and deeper into the forest, coming at last upon the little Mission of St. Margaret Mary—a gathering of dwellings in a clearing around which the jungle patiently waits. Isn't it beautiful, this little cluster of tin-roofed buildings, with their whitewashed walls and crude crosses, with their small lighted windows, and the sound of a single radio playing a thin song of Indian lyrics and merrily beating drums?

How pretty the deep porches of the little bungalows, with their scattering of painted wooden swings and benches and chairs. The screens over the windows give the rooms a soft drowsy prettiness, for they make a tiny tight grid of fine lines over the many colors and shapes and thereby somehow sharpen them and render them more visible and vibrant, and make them look more deliberate—like the interiors in an Edward Hopper painting, or in a child's bright picture book.

Of course there is a way to stop the rampant spread of beauty. It has to do with regimentation, conformity, assembly-line aesthetics, and the triumph of the functional over the haphazard.

But you won't find much of that here!

This is Gretchen's destiny, from which all the subtleties of the modern world have been eliminated—a laboratory for a single repetitive moral experiment—Doing Good.

The night sings its song of chaos and hunger and destruction in vain around this little encampment. What matters here is the care of a finite number of humans who have come for vaccination, surgery, antibiotics. As Gretchen herself has said—to think about the larger picture is a lie.

For hours, I wandered in a great circle through the dense jungle, carefree and strong as I moved through impassable foliage, as I climbed over the high fantastical roots of the rain trees, as I stood still here and there to listen to the deep tangled chorus of the savage night. So tender the wet waxen flowers growing in the higher more verdant branches, slumbering in the promise of the morning light.

Once again, I was beyond all fear at the wet, crumbling ugliness of process. The stench of decay in the pocket of swamp. The slithering things couldn't harm me and therefore they did not disgust me. Oh, let the anaconda come for me, I would love to feel that tight, swiftly moving embrace. How I savored the deep, shrill cry of the birds, meant surely to strike terror in a simpler heart. Too bad the little hairy-armed monkeys slept now in the darkest hours, for I should have loved to catch them long enough to bestow kisses upon their frowning foreheads or their lipless chattering mouths.

And those poor mortals, slumbering within the many small houses of the clearing, near to their neatly tilled fields, and to the school, and the hospital, and the chapel, seemed a divine miracle of creation in every tiny common detail.

Hmmm. I missed Mojo. Why was he not here, prowling this jungle with me? I had to train him to become the vampire's dog. Indeed, I had visions of him guarding my coffin during the daylight hours—an Egyptian-style sentinel, commanded to tear the throat out of any mortal intruder who ever found his way down the sanctuary stairs.

But I would see him soon enough. The whole world waited beyond these jungles. When I closed my eyes and made of my body a subtle receiver, I could hear over the miles the dense noisy traffic of Caracas, I could hear the sharp accents of her amplified voices, I could hear the thick pounding music of those dark air-conditioned dens where I draw the killers to me, like the moths to the bright candle, so that I might feed.

Here peace reigned as the hours ticked away in the soft purring tropic silence. A shimmer of rain fell from the low and cloudy sky, tamping down the dust of the clearing, speckling the clean-swept steps of the schoolhouse, tapping ever so lightly upon the corrugated tin roofs.

Lights winked off in the small dormitories, and in the outlying houses. Only a dull red illumination flickered deep inside the darkened chapel, with its low tower and big shiny silent bell. Small yellow bulbs in their rounded metal shades shone upon the clean paths and white-washed walls.

Lights went dim in the first of the little hospital buildings, where Gretchen worked alone.

Now and then I saw her profile against the window screens. I caught a glimpse of her just inside the doorway, seated at a desk long enough to scratch some notes on paper, her head bent, her hair gathered at the nape of her neck.

Finally I moved silently towards the doorway, and slipped into the small, cluttered office, with its one glaring lamp, and to the door of the ward itself.

Children's hospital! They were all small beds. Crude, simple, in two rows. Was I seeing things in this deep semidarkness? Or were the beds made of crude wood, lashed at the joints, and hung with netting? And on the small colorless table, was that not a stub of candle on a small plate?

I felt dizzy suddenly; the great clarity of vision left me. *Not this hospital!* I blinked, trying to tear loose the timeless elements from those that made sense. Plastic sacks of intravenous food glistening on their chrome racks at bedside, weightless nylon tubing shining as it descended to the tiny needles stuck in thin fragile little arms!

This wasn't New Orleans. This wasn't that little hospital! Yet look at the walls! Are they not stone? I wiped the thin sheen of blood sweat from my forehead, staring at the stain on the handkerchief. Was that not a blond-haired child lying in that distant little bed? Again, the dizziness swept over me. I thought I heard a dim, high-pitched laughter, full of gaiety and easy mockery. But that was a bird surely in the great outer darkness. There was no old female nurse in homespun skirts to her ankles, and kerchief about her shoulders. She'd been gone for centuries, along with that little building.

But the child was moaning; the light gleamed on her small rounded head. I saw her chubby hand against the blanket. Again, I tried to clear my vision. A deep shadow fell over the floor beside me. Yes, look, the apnea alarm with its tiny glowing digits, and the glass-doored cabinets of medicines! Not that hospital, but this hospital.

So you've come for me, Father? You said you would do it again.

"No, I won't hurt her! I don't want to hurt her." Was I whispering aloud?

Far, far down at the end of the narrow room, she sat on the small chair, her little feet kicking back and forth, her hair in fancy curls against her puff sleeves.

Oh, you've come for her. You know you have!

"Shhh, you'll wake the children! Go away. You're not there!"

Everyone knew you would be victorious. They knew you'd beat the Body Thief. And here you are . . . come for her.

"No, not to hurt her. But to lay the decision in her hands."

"Monsieur? May I help you?"

I looked up at the old man standing in front of me, the doctor, with the stained whiskers and the tiny spectacles. No, not this doctor! Where had he come from? I stared at the name tag. This is French Guiana. That's why he's speaking French. And there is no child at the end of the ward, sitting in any chair.

"To see Gretchen," I whispered. "Sister Marguerite." I had thought she was in this building, that I'd glimpsed her through the windows. I knew she was here.

Dull noises at the far end of the ward. He can't hear them but I can hear them. She's coming. I caught her scent suddenly, mingled with the scent of the children, of the old man.

But even with these eyes, I couldn't see in the intolerable gloom. Where was the light in this place coming from? She had just extinguished the tiny electric lamp at the far door, and she came now down the length of the ward past bed after bed, her steps quick though dogged, her head bowed. The doctor made a little weary gesture, and shuffled past me.

Don't stare at the stained whiskers; don't stare at the spectacles, or the rounded hump of his bent back. Why, you saw the plastic name tag on his pocket. He is no ghost!

The screen door thumped softly behind him, as he shambled away.

In the thin darkness, she stood. How beautiful her wavy hair, pulled back from her smooth forehead and her large steady eyes. She saw my shoes before she saw me. Sudden awareness of the stranger, the pale soundless figure—not so much as a breath comes from me—in the absolute stillness of the night, where he does not belong.

The doctor had vanished. It seemed the shadows had swallowed him, but surely he was out there somewhere in the dark.

I stood against the light from the office. Her scent was overpowering me—blood and the clean perfume of a living being. God, to see her with this vision—to see the glistening beauty of her cheeks. But I was blocking the light, wasn't I, for the door was very small. Could she see the features of my face clearly enough? Could she see the eerie unnatural color of my eyes?

"Who are you?" It was a low, wary whisper. She stood far away from me, stranded in the aisle, looking up at me from beneath her dark knitted brows.

"Gretchen," I answered. "It's Lestat. I've come as I promised I would come."

Nothing stirred in the long narrow ward. The beds appeared frozen behind their veils of netting. Yet the light moved in the sparkling sacks of fluid, like so many silvery little lamps glimmering in the dull close dark. I could hear the faint, steady respiration of the small sleeping bodies. And a dull rhythmic sound like a child playfully thumping the leg of chair over and over with the back of her tiny heel.

Slowly, Gretchen raised her right hand and laid her fingers instinctively and protectively against her chest, at the base of her throat. Her pulse quickened. I saw her fingers close as if over a locket, and then I saw the light glinting on the thin little thread of gold chain.

"What is that around your neck?"

"Who are you?" she asked again, her whisper scraping bottom, her lips trembling as she spoke. The dim light from the office behind me caught in her eyes. She stared at my face, my hands.

"It's me, Gretchen. I won't hurt you. It's the farthest thing from my mind to hurt you. I've come because I promised I would come."

"I . . . I don't believe you." She backed away on the wooden floor, her rubber heels making the softest sound.

"Gretchen, don't be frightened of me. I wanted you to know that what I told you was true." I spoke so softly. Could she hear me?

I could see her struggling to clear her vision as only seconds ago I had struggled to clear my own. Her heart beat fiercely inside her, breasts moving beautifully beneath the stiff white cotton, the rich blood rising suddenly in her face.

"I'm here, Gretchen. I've come to thank you. Here, let me give you this for your mission."

Stupidly, I reached into my pockets; I withdrew the lucre of the Body Thief in thick handfuls and held it out, my fingers trembling as her fingers trembled, the money looking soiled and foolish, like so much rubbish.

"Take it, Gretchen. Here. It will help the children." I turned and saw the candle again—that same candle! Why the candle? I laid the money down beside it, hearing the boards creak under my weight as I stepped to the little table.

As I turned to look back at her, she came towards me, fearfully, eyes wide.

"Who are you?" she whispered for the third time. How large her eyes, how dark the pupils, as they danced over me, like fingers drawn to something that would burn them. "I'm asking you again to tell me the truth!"

"Lestat, whom you nursed in your own house, Gretchen. Gretchen, I've recovered my true form. I came because I promised you I would come."

I could scarcely bear it, my old anger kindling as the fear intensified in her, as her shoulders stiffened and her arms came tightly together, and the hand clenching the chain at her neck began to shake.

"I don't believe you," she said, in the same strangled whisper, her entire body recoiling though she did not even take a step.

"No, Gretchen. Don't look at me in fear or as if you despise me. What have I done to you that you should look at me that way? You know my voice. You know what you did for me. I came to thank you—"

"*Liar!*"

"No, that's not true. I came because . . . because I wanted to see you again."

Lord God, was I weeping? Were my emotions now as volatile as my power? And she would see the blood in streaks on my face and it would scare her even more. I could not bear the look in her eyes.

I turned, and stared at the little candle. I struck the wick with my invisible will and saw the flame leap up, a tiny yellow tongue. *Mon Dieu, that same play of shadow on the wall.* She gasped as she stared at it and back at me, as the illumination spread around us and she saw for the first time very clearly and unmistakably the eyes that were fixed upon her, the hair that framed the face which looked at her, the gleaming fingernails of my hands, the white teeth just visible perhaps behind my parted lips.

"Gretchen, don't be afraid of me. In the name of truth, look at me. You made me promise I would come. Gretchen, I didn't lie to you. You saved me. I am here, and there is no God, Gretchen, you told me so. From anyone else it wouldn't have mattered, but you said it yourself."

Her hands went to her lips as she drew back, the little chain falling loose so that I saw the gold cross in the candle's light. Oh, thank God, a cross not a locket! She stepped back again. She could not stop the impulsive motion.

Her words came in a low faltering whisper:

"Get away from me, unclean spirit! Get out of this house of God!"

"I won't hurt you!"

"Get away from these little ones!"

"Gretchen. I won't hurt the children."

"In the name of God, get away from me . . . go." Her right hand groped again for the cross and she held it towards me, her face flushed and her lips wet and loose and trembling in her hysteria, her eyes devoid of reason as she spoke again. I saw it was a crucifix with the tiny twisted body of the dead Christ.

"Go out of this house. God himself protects it. He protects the children. Go."

"In the name of truth, Gretchen," I answered, my voice as low as hers, and as full of feeling. "I lay with you! I am here."

"Liar," she hissed. "Liar!" Her body was shaking so violently, it seemed she would lose her balance and fall.

"No, it's the truth. If nothing else is true, it's true. Gretchen, I won't hurt the children. I won't hurt you."

In another instant, surely, she would lose her reason altogether, helpless screams would break from her, and the whole night would hear her, and every poor soul of the compound would come outdoors to heed her, to take up perhaps the very same cry.

But she remained there, shaking all over, and only dry sobs came suddenly from her open mouth.

"Gretchen, I'll go now, I'll leave you if that's what you really want. But I kept my promise to you! Is there nothing more I can do?"

A little cry came from one of the beds behind her, and then a moan from another, and she turned her head frantically this way and that.

Then she bolted towards me, and past me through the small office, papers flying off the desk as she brushed past it, the screen door banging behind her as she ran out into the night.

I heard her distant sobbing as, in a daze, I turned around.

I saw the rain falling in a thin soundless mist. I saw her far across the clearing already and racing towards the chapel doors.

I told you you would hurt her.

I turned back and looked down the shadowy length of the ward.

"You're not there. I'm done with you!" I whispered.

The light of the candle showed her clearly now even though she remained at the far end of the room. She was swinging her white-stockinged leg still, heel of her black slipper striking the leg of the chair.

"Go away," I said as gently as I could. "It's over."

The tears *were* running down my face, blood tears. Had Gretchen seen them?

"Go away," I said again. "It's finished and I'm going too."

It seemed she smiled, but she did not smile. Her face became the picture of all innocence, the face of the dream locket. And in the stillness, as I stood transfixed, looking at her, the entire image remained but ceased altogether to move. Then it dissolved.

I saw only an empty chair.

Slowly I turned back to the door. I wiped at my tears again, hating them, and put the handkerchief away.

Flies buzzed against the screen of the door. How clear the rain was, pelting the earth now. There came that soft swelling sound as the rain came down harder, as if the sky had slowly opened its mouth and sighed. Something forgotten. What was it? The candle, ah, blow out the candle, lest a fire start and hurt these tender little ones!

And look at the far end—the little blond child in the oxygen tent, the sheet of crinkled plastic flashing as if made up of bits and pieces of light. How could you have been so foolish as to make a flame in this room?

I put out the light with a pinch of my fingers. I emptied all my pockets. I laid down all the soiled and curling bills, hundreds upon hundreds of dollars, and the few coins I found as well.

And then I went out, and I walked slowly past the chapel with its open doors. Through the gentle downpour, I heard her praying, her low rapid whispers, and then through the open entrance, I saw her kneeling before the altar, the reddened fire of a candle flickering beyond her, as she held her arms outstretched in the form of a cross.

I wanted to go. It seemed in the depths of my bruised soul I wanted nothing more. But something again held me. I had smelled the sharp unmistakable scent of fresh blood.

It came from the chapel, and it was not the blood pumping within her, it was blood that was flowing free from a new wound.

I drew closer, careful not to make the slightest noise, until I stood in the chapel door. The smell grew stronger. And then I saw the blood dripping from her outstretched hands. I saw it on the floor, flowing in rivulets from her feet.

"Deliver me from Evil, O Lord, take me to you, Sacred Heart of Jesus, gather me into your arms . . ."

She did not see or hear me as I drew closer. A soft glow suffused her face, made of the light of the flickering candle, and of the radiance from inside her, the great consuming rapture which held her now, and removed her from all around her, including the dark figure at her side.

I looked at the altar. I saw the giant crucifix high above it, and below, the tiny gleaming tabernacle, and the burning candle deep in its red glass which meant the Blessed Sacrament was there. A gust of breeze moved through the open chapel doors. It caught the bell above and a faint tinny peal broke from it, barely audible above the sound of the breeze itself.

I looked down at her again, at her upturned face with its blind eyes at half mast, and her mouth so slack though the words still came from it.

"Christ, my beloved Christ, gather me into your arms."

And through the haze of my tears, I watched the red blood welling and flowing red and thick and copious from her open palms.

There were hushed voices in the compound. Doors opened and closed. I heard the sound of people running on the packed earth. When I turned I saw that dark shapes had gathered at the entrance—a cluster of anxious female figures. I heard a whispered word in French which meant "stranger." And then the muffled cry:

"Devil!"

Down the aisle I went, right towards them, forcing them perhaps to scatter, though I never touched them or looked at them, and hurried past them and out into the rain.

Then I turned and looked back. I saw her kneeling still, as they gathered around her, and I heard their soft reverent cries of "Miracle!" and "Stigmata!" They were making the Sign of the Cross and dropping to their knees around her, as the prayers continued to fall in that dull trancelike voice from her lips.

"And the Word was with God, and the Word was God, and the Word was made flesh."

"Good-bye, Gretchen," I whispered.

And then I was gone, free and alone, into the warm embrace of savage night.

TWENTY-FIVE

I SHOULD have gone on to Miami that night. I knew that David might need me. And of course I had no idea where James might be.

But I had no heart for it—I was far too badly shaken—and I found myself before morning quite far east of the little country of French Guiana, yet still in the hungry sprawling jungles, and thirsting, but with no hope of satisfaction on that account.

About an hour before dawn I came upon an ancient temple—a great rectangle of pitted stone—so overgrown with vines, and other rankled foliage that it was perhaps altogether invisible even to mortals who might pass a few feet away. But as there was no road or even a footpath through this part of the jungle, I sensed that no one had passed here in centuries. It was my secret, this place.

Except for the monkeys, that is, who had waked with the coming light. A veritable tribe of them had laid siege to the crude building, whooping and screeching and swarming all over the long flat roof, and the sloping sides. In a dull listless fashion I watched them, even smiling, as they went about their antics. Indeed, the whole jungle had gone into a rebirth. The chorus of the birds was much louder than it had been in the hours of total darkness, and as the sky paled, I saw myriad shades of green all around me. And with a shock I realized I wasn't going to see the sun.

My stupidity on this count surprised me somewhat. But what creatures of habit we are. Ah, but wasn't this early light enough? It was pure joy to be in my old body . . .

. . . unless I remembered the look of pure revulsion on Gretchen's face.

A thick mist rose from the floor of the jungle, catching this precious illumination and diffusing it even to the tiniest nooks and crannies beneath shuddering flowers and leaves.

My sadness deepened as I looked around me; or more truly I felt raw and as if I'd been skinned alive. "Sadness" is too mild and sweet a word. I thought again and again of Gretchen, but only in wordless images. And when I thought of Claudia I felt a numbness, a silent obdurate remembrance of the words I'd spoken to her in my fever dreams.

Like a nightmare the old doctor with the stained whiskers. The doll-child in the chair. No, not there. Not there. Not there.

And what did it matter if they had been? It didn't matter at all.

Beneath these deep enervating emotions, I was not unhappy; and to be aware of this, to know it truly, was perhaps a wondrous thing. Ah, yes, just my old self again.

Had to tell David all about this jungle! David must go to Rio before he returned to England. I would go with him, perhaps.

Perhaps.

I found two doors in the temple. The first was blocked with heavy irregular stones. But the other lay open, for the stones had long ago fallen away into a shapeless heap. Climbing over them, I made my way down a deep staircase, and then through several passages, until I came upon chambers to which no light penetrated at all. It was in one of these, very cool and utterly removed from the noises of the jungle, that I lay down to sleep.

Tiny slithering things dwelt there. As I laid my face against the damp cool floor, I felt these little creatures moving around the tips of my fingers. I heard their rustling. And then the heavy silken weight of a snake moved across my ankle. All this made me smile.

How my old mortal body would have cringed and shaken. But then my mortal eyes could have never seen into this deep place.

I began to tremble suddenly, to cry again softly, thinking of Gretchen. I knew there would never again be a dream of Claudia.

"What did you want of me?" I whispered. "Did you really think I could save my soul?" I saw her as I had in my delirium, in that old New Orleans hospital when I'd taken her by the shoulders. Or had we been in the old hotel? "I told you I would do it again. I told you."

Something had been saved at that moment. The dark damnation of Lestat had been saved, and was now forever intact.

"Good-bye, darlings," I whispered again.

And then I slept.

TWENTY-SIX

MIAMI—ah, my beautiful southern metropolis, lying under the polished sky of the Caribbean, no matter what say the various maps! The air seemed sweeter even than in the islands—sweeping gently over the inevitable crowds of Ocean Drive.

Hurrying through the fancy art deco lobby of the Park Central, and to the rooms I kept there, I stripped off my jungle-worn clothes, and went into my own closets for a white turtleneck shirt, belted khaki jacket and pants, and a pair of smooth brown leather boots. It felt good to be free of clothing purchased by the Body Thief, well fitted or not.

Then I immediately rang the desk and discovered that David Talbot had been in the hotel since yesterday and was now waiting for me on the porch of Bailey's Restaurant down the street.

I had no spirit for crowded public places. I'd persuade him to come back to my rooms. Surely he was still exhausted from the whole ordeal. The table and chairs here before the front windows would be a much better place for us to talk, as we were surely meant to do.

Out I went and up the busy sidewalk north until I saw Bailey's with the inevitable sign in fancy neon script above its handsome white awnings, and all its little tables draped in pink linen and set with candles, already busy with the first wave of the evening crowd. There was the familiar figure of David in the farthest corner of the porch, very proper in the suit of white linen he'd worn on the ship. He was watching for my approach with the usual quick and curious expression on his face.

In spite of my relief, I deliberately took him by surprise, slipping into the chair opposite so quickly that he gave a little start.

"Ah, you devil," he whispered. I saw a little stiffening about his mouth for a minute as though he were really annoyed, but then he smiled. "Thank God you're all right."

"You really think that's appropriate?" I asked.

When the handsome young waiter appeared I told him I wanted a glass of wine, just so that he would not continue to ask me about such things as the time passed. David had already been served some loathsome-colored exotic drink.

"What in the hell actually happened?" I asked, leaning in a little closer over the table to shut out some of the general noise.

"Well, it was mayhem," he said. "He tried to attack me, and I had no choice but to use the gun. He got away, over the veranda, as a matter of fact, because I couldn't hold the bloody gun steady. It was simply too big for these old hands." He gave a sigh. He seemed tired, frayed at the edges. "After that, it was really a matter of calling the Motherhouse, and having them bail me out. Calls back and forth to Cunard in Liverpool." He made a dismissive gesture. "I was on a plane for Miami at noon. Of course I didn't want to leave you unattended aboard the vessel, but there really was no choice."

"I was never in the slightest danger," I said. "I feared for you. I told you not to fear for me."

"Well, that's what I thought would be the case. I sent them after James, of course, hoping to drive him from the ship. It became plain they could not even consider undertaking a cabin-by-cabin search of the vessel. So I thought you'd be left alone. I'm almost certain James disembarked right after the melee. Otherwise they would have apprehended him. I gave them a full description of course."

He stopped, took a gingerly little sip of his fancy drink, and then laid it down.

"You don't really like that, do you? Where's your disgusting Scotch?"

"The drink of the islands," he said. "No, I don't like it, but it doesn't matter. How did it go with you?"

I didn't answer. I was of course seeing him with my old vision, and his skin was more translucent, and all the little infirmities of his body were plain. Yet he possessed the aura of the marvelous as do all mortals to a vampire's eyes.

He seemed weary, racked with nervous tension. Indeed, his eyes were red around the edges, and again I saw that stiffness about his mouth. I also noted a sagging to his shoulders. Had this awful ordeal aged him further? I couldn't bear to see this in him. But his face was full of concern now as he looked at me.

"Something bad has happened with you," he said, softening even more and reaching across the table and laying his fingers on my hand. How warm they felt. "I can see this in your eyes."

"I don't want to talk here," I said. "Come up to my rooms at the hotel."

"No, let's stay here," he said very gently. "I feel anxious after all that's happened. It was quite an ordeal, really, for a man my age. I'm exhausted. I hoped you would come last night."

"I'm sorry I didn't. I should have. I knew this was a terrible trial for you, even though you enjoyed it so much when it was going on."

"You thought so?" He gave a slow sad smile. "I need another drink. What did you say? Scotch?"

"What did *I* say? I thought that was your favorite drink."

"Now and then," he said. He gestured to the waiter. "Sometimes it's a bit too serious." He asked for a single malt if they had it. They didn't. Chivas Regal would be fine. "Thank you for indulging me. I like it here. I like the quiet commotion. I like the open air."

Even his voice sounded tired; it lacked some bright spark. This was hardly the time to suggest a trip to Rio de Janeiro, obviously. And it was all my fault.

"Anything you wish," I said.

"Now, tell me what happened," he said, solicitously. "I can see it's weighing on your soul."

And then I realized how much I wanted to tell him about Gretchen, that indeed, this is why I'd rushed here as much as any concern I felt for him. I was ashamed, and yet I couldn't prevent myself from telling him. I turned towards the beach, my elbow on the table, and my eyes sort of misted so that the colors of the evening world became muted and more luminescent than before. I told him that I'd gone to Gretchen because I'd promised to do it, though deep within myself, I was hoping and praying to take her into my world with me. And then I explained about the hospital, the pure strangeness of it—the similarity of the doctor to the one of centuries ago, and the little ward itself, and that mad, crazy notion that Claudia was there.

"It was baffling," I whispered. "I never dreamed that Gretchen would turn me away. You know what I thought? It sounds so foolish now. I thought she would find me irresistible! I thought it couldn't possibly be any other way. I thought when she looked into my eyes—my eyes now, not those mortal eyes!—she'd see the true soul which she'd loved! I never imagined that there would be revulsion, or that it could be so total—both moral and physical—and that in the very moment of understanding what we are, she would recoil completely and turn away. I can't understand how I could have been foolish, how I persist in my illusions! Is it vanity? Or am I simply mad? You've never found me repellent, have you, David? Or am I deluded on that score as well?"

"You are beautiful," he whispered, the words softened with feeling. "But you are unnatural, and that is what this woman saw." How deeply distressed he seemed. He had never sounded more solicitous in all his patient talks with me. Indeed, he looked as if he felt the pain I felt—acutely and totally. "She was no fit companion for you, don't you see?" he said kindly.

"Yes, I see. I see." I rested my forehead against my hand. I wished we were in the quiet of my rooms, but I didn't push the matter. He was being my friend again, as no other being on earth had ever been, really, and I would do as he wished. "You know you are the only one," I said suddenly, my own voice sounding ragged and tired. "The only one who will let me be my defeated self without turning away."

"How so?"

"Oh. All the others must damn me for my temper, my impetuosity, my will! They enjoy it. But when I show the weakness in myself, they shut me out." I thought then of Louis's rejection, and that I would very soon see him again, and an evil satisfaction filled me. Ah, he would be so very surprised. Then a little fear came over me. How would I forgive him? How would I keep my precious temper from exploding like a great wanton flame?

"We would make our heroes shallow," he answered, the words very slow and almost sad. "We would make them brittle. It is they who must remind us of the true meaning of strength."

"Is that it?" I asked. I turned, and folded my arms on the table, facing him, staring at the finely turned glass of pale yellow wine. "Am I truly strong?"

"Oh, yes, strength you've always had. And that's why they envy you and despise you and become so cross with you. But I needn't tell you these things. Forget about the woman. It would have been wrong, so very wrong."

"And what about you, David? It wouldn't be wrong with you." I looked up, and to my surprise, I saw his eyes were moist now, and truly reddened, and again came that stiffening of his mouth. "What is it, David?" I asked.

"No, it wouldn't be wrong," he said. "I do not think now that it would be wrong at all."

"You're saying . . . ?"

"Bring me into it, Lestat," he whispered, and then he pulled back, the proper English gentleman, shocked and disapproving of his own emotions, and he looked out over the milling crowd and towards the distant sea.

"You mean this, David? You're certain?" In truth I didn't want to ask. I didn't want to speak another word. And yet why? Why had he come to this decision? What had I done to him with this mad escapade? I wouldn't be the Vampire Lestat now if it weren't for him. But what a price he must have paid.

I thought of him on the beach in Grenada, and how he had refused the simple act of making love. He was in pain now as he had been then. And it seemed no mystery at all suddenly that he had come to this. I had brought him to it with our little adventure together to defeat the Body Thief.

"Come," I said to him. "It *is* time to go now, away from all this and to where we can be alone." I was trembling. How many times had I dreamed of this moment.

And yet it had come so quickly, and there were so many questions I should ask.

A sudden terrible shyness fell over me. I couldn't look at him. I thought of the intimacy we would soon experience, and I couldn't meet his gaze. My God, I was acting the way he had in New Orleans when I'd been in that strapping mortal body and pelting him with my rampant desire.

My heart was hammering with expectation. David, David in my

arms. The blood of David passing into me. And mine into David, and then we would stand on the edge of the sea together as dark immortal brothers. I could scarce speak or even think.

I got up without looking at him, and I walked across the porch and down the steps. I knew he was following me. I was like Orpheus. One backward glance and he'd be torn away from me. Perhaps the glaring lights of a passing car would flash on my hair and eyes in such a way that he would suddenly be paralyzed with fear.

I led the way back down the pavement, past the sluggish parade of mortals in their beach finery, past the little sidewalk tables of the cafés. I went directly into the Park Central and through the lobby again with all its sparkling high-toned glamour and up the stairs to my rooms.

I heard him close the door behind me.

I stood at the windows, looking out again at that shining evening sky. My heart, be quiet! Do not hurry it. It is too important that each step be made with care.

Look at the clouds scudding so quickly away from paradise. Stars mere specks of glitter struggling in the pale flood of evening light.

There were things I must tell him, things I must explain. He would be the same for all time as he was at this moment; was there any small physical thing he wished to change? Shave the beard closer; trim the hair.

"None of that matters," he said, in that soft cultured English voice. "What's wrong?" So kind, as if I were the one who needed reassurance. "Isn't it what you wanted?"

"Oh, yes, truly yes. But you have to be sure you want it," I said, and only now I turned around.

He stood there in the shadows, so composed in his trim white linen suit, pale silk tie properly knotted at the neck. The light from the street shone brightly on his eyes, and flashed for one instant on the tiny gold stud in the tie.

"I can't explain it," I whispered. "It's happened so quickly, so suddenly, when I was sure it wouldn't. I'm afraid for you. Afraid you're making a terrible mistake."

"I want it," he said, but how strained his voice was, how dark, how without that bright lyric note. "I want it more than you can know. Do it now, please. Don't prolong my agony. Come to me. What can I do to invite you? To assure you? Oh, I've had longer than you know to brood on this decision. Remember how long I've known your secrets, all of you."

How strange his face looked, how hard his eyes, and how stiff and bitter his mouth.

"David, something is wrong," I said. "I know it is. Listen to me. We must talk it out together. It is the most crucial conversation perhaps that we will ever have. What's happened to make you want it? What was it? Our time on the island together? Spell it out for me. I must understand."

"You waste time, Lestat."

"Oh, but for this, one must take time, David, it's the very last time that time really matters."

I drew closer to him, deliberately letting his scent fill my nostrils, deliberately letting the scent of his blood come to me, and awaken the desire in me which cared little who he was or what I was—the sharp hunger for him that wanted only his death. The thirst twisted and snapped inside me like a great whip.

He stepped backwards. I saw fear in his eyes.

"No, don't be frightened. You think I would hurt you? How could I have beaten that stupid little Body Thief if it hadn't been for you?"

His face stiffened all over, eyes becoming smaller, his mouth stretching in what seemed a grimace. Why, how dreadful and unlike himself he looked. What in God's name was going on in his mind? Everything was wrong about this moment, this decision! There was no joy, no intimacy. It was wrong.

"Open to me!" I whispered.

He shook his head, eyes flashing as they narrowed again. "Won't it happen when the blood flows?" Brittle, his voice!

"Give me an image, Lestat, to hold in mind. An image to hold against fear."

I was confused. I wasn't sure I knew what he meant.

"Shall I think of you and how beautiful you are," he said tenderly, "and that we shall be together, companions always? Will that bring me through?"

"Think of India," I whispered. "Think of the mangrove forest, and when you were most happy . . ."

I wanted to say more, I wanted to say, no, not that, but I didn't know why! And the hunger surged in me, and the burning loneliness mingled with it, and once again I saw Gretchen, saw the pure horror in her face. I moved closer to him. David, David at last . . . *Do it!* and be done with talking, what do the images matter, do it! What's wrong with you that you fear to do it?

And this time I caught him firmly in my embrace.

There came his fear again, a spasm, but he did not truly struggle against me, and I savored it for one moment, this lush physical intimacy, the tall regal body in my arms. I let my lips move over his dark gray hair, breathing in the familiar fragrance, I let my fingers cradle his head. And then my teeth broke through the surface of the skin before I meant to do it and the hot salted blood flowed over my tongue and filled my mouth.

David, David at last.

In a torrent the images came—the great forests of India, and the great gray elephants thundering past, knees lifted awkwardly, giant heads wagging, tiny ears flapping like loose leaves. Sunlight striking the forest. *Where is the tiger? Oh, dear God, Lestat, you are the tiger! You've done it to him! That's why you didn't want him to think of this!* And in a flash I saw him staring at me in the sunlit glade, David of years ago in splendid youth, smiling, and suddenly, for a split second, superimposed upon the image, or springing from within it like an unfolding flower, there appeared another figure, another man. It was a thin, emaciated creature with white hair, and cunning eyes. And I knew, before it vanished once more into the faltering and lifeless image of David, that it had been James!

This man in my arms was James!

I hurled him backwards, hand up to wipe the spilling blood from my lips.

"James!" I roared.

He fell against the side of the bed, eyes dazed, blood trickling onto his collar, one hand flung out against me. "Now don't be hasty!" he cried in that old familiar cadence of his own, chest heaving, sweat gleaming on his face.

"Damn you into hell," I roared again, staring at those frenzied glittering eyes in David's face.

I lunged at him, hearing a sudden spurt from him of desperate crazed laughter, and more slurred and hurried words.

"You fool! It's Talbot's body! You don't want to hurt Talbot's—"

But it was too late. I tried to stop myself but my hand had closed around his throat, and I'd already flung the body at the wall!

In horror, I saw him slam into the plaster. I saw the blood splatter from the back of his head, and I heard the ugly crunch of the broken wall behind him, and when I reached out to catch him, he fell directly into my arms. In a wide bovine stare he looked at me, his mouth working desperately to make the words come out.

"Look what you've done, you fool, you idiot. Look what . . . look what . . ."

"Stay in that body, you little monster!" I said between my clenched teeth. "Keep it alive!"

He was gasping. A thin tiny stream of blood poured out of his nose and down into his mouth. His eyes rolled. I held him up, but his feet were dangling as if he were paralyzed. "You . . . you fool . . . call Mother, call her . . . Mother, Mother, Raglan needs you . . . Don't call Sarah. Don't tell Sarah. Call Mother—" And then, he lost consciousness, head flopping forward as I held him and then laid him down on the bed.

I was frantic. What was I to do! Could I heal his wounds with my blood! No, the wound was inside, in his head, in his brain! Ah, God! The brain. David's brain!

I grabbed up the telephone, stammered the number of the room and that there was an emergency. A man was badly hurt. A man had fallen. A man had had a stroke! They must get an ambulance for this man at once.

Then I put down the phone and went back to him. David's face and body lying helplessly there! His eyelids were fluttering, and his left hand opened, and then closed, and opened again. "Mother," he whispered. "Get Mother. Tell her Raglan needs her . . . Mother."

"She's coming," I said, "you must wait for her!" Gently, I turned his head to the side. But in truth what did it matter? Let him fly up and out of it if he could! This body wasn't going to recover! This body could be no fit host to David ever again!

And where the hell was David!

Blood was spreading all over the coverlet of the bed. I bit into my wrist. I let the drops fall on the puncture wounds in the neck. Maybe a few drops on the lips would help somehow. But what could I do about the brain! Oh, God, how could I have done it . . .

"Foolish," he whispered, "so foolish. Mother!"

The left hand began to flop from side to side on the bed. Then I saw that his entire left arm was jerking, and indeed, the left side of his mouth was pulling to the side over and over again in the same repetitive pattern, as his eyes stared upwards and pupils ceased to move. The blood continued to flow from the nose and down into the mouth and over the white teeth.

"Oh, David, I didn't mean to do it," I whispered. "Oh, Lord God, he's going to die!"

I think he said the word "Mother" once more.

But I could hear the sirens now, screaming towards Ocean Drive. Someone was pounding on the door. I slipped to the side as it was flung open, and I darted from the room, unseen. Other mortals were rushing up the stairway. They saw no more than a quick shadow as I passed. I stopped once in the lobby, and in a daze I watched the clerks scurrying about. The awful scream of the siren grew louder. I turned and all but stumbled out the doors and down into the street.

"Oh, Lord God, David, what have I done?"

A car horn startled me, then another blast jogged me loose from my stupor. I was standing in the very middle of the traffic. I backed away, and up onto the sand.

Suddenly a large stubby white ambulance came rattling to a halt directly before the hotel. One hulking young man jumped from the front seat and rushed into the lobby, while the other went to throw open the rear doors. Someone was shouting inside the building. I saw a figure at the window of my room above.

I backed further away, my legs trembling as if I were mortal, my hands clutching stupidly at my head as I peered at the horrid little scene through the dim sunglasses, watching the inevitable crowd gather as people stopped in their meandering, as they rose from the tables of the nearby restaurants and approached the hotel doors.

Now it was quite impossible to see anything in normal fashion, but the scene materialized before me as I snatched the images from mortal minds—the heavy gurney being carried through the lobby, with David's helpless body strapped to it, the attendants forcing people to the side.

The doors of the ambulance were slammed shut. Again the siren began its frightful peal, and off the vehicle sped, carrying David's body inside it to God only knows where!

I had to do something! But what could I do? Get into that hospital; work the change upon the body! What else can save it? And then you have James inside it? Where is David? Dear God, help me. But why should you?

At last I sprang into action. I hurried up the street, sprinting easily past the mortals who could scarcely see me, and found a glass-walled phone booth and slipped into it and slammed the door.

"I have to reach London," I told the operator, spilling out the information: the Talamasca, collect. Why was it taking so long! I pounded upon the glass with my right fist in my impatience, the receiver pressed to my ear. At last one of those kindly patient Talamasca voices accepted the call.

"Listen to me," I said, blurting out my name in full as I began. "This isn't going to make sense to you, but it's dreadfully important. The body of David Talbot has just been rushed to a hospital in the city of Miami. I don't even know which hospital! But the body is badly wounded. The body may die. But you must understand. David is not inside this body. Are you listening? David is someplace . . ."

I stopped.

A dark shape had appeared in front of me on the other side of the glass. And as my eyes fell on it, fully prepared to dismiss it—for what did I care if some mortal man were pressing me to hurry?—I realized it was my old mortal body standing there, my tall young brown-haired mortal body, in which I had lived long enough to know every small particular, every weakness and strength. I was staring into the very face I had seen in the mirror only two days ago! Only it was now two inches taller than I. I was looking up into those familiar brown eyes.

The body wore the same seersucker suit with which I had last clothed it. Indeed, there was the same white turtleneck shirt that I had pulled over its head. And one of those familiar hands was lifted now in a calm gesture, calm as the expression on the face, giving me the unmistakable command to hang up the phone.

I put the receiver back into its hook.

In a quiet fluid movement, the body came around to the front of the booth and opened the door. The right hand closed on my arm, drawing me out with my full cooperation onto the sidewalk and into the gentle wind.

"David," I said. "Do you know what I've done?"

"I think so," he said with a little lift to the eyebrows, the familiar

English voice issuing confidently from the young mouth. "I saw the ambulance at the hotel."

"David, it was a mistake, a horrible, horrible mistake!"

"Come on, let's get away from here," he said. And this *was* the voice I remembered, truly comforting and commanding and soft.

"But, David, you don't understand, your body . . ."

"Come, you can tell me all about it," he said.

"It's dying, David."

"Well, there isn't much we can do about it, then, is there?"

And to my utter amazement, he put his arm around me, and leant forward in his characteristic authoritative manner, and pressed me to come along with him, down the pavement to the corner, where he put up his hand to signal a cab.

"I don't know which hospital," I confessed. I was still shaking violently all over. I couldn't control the tremours in my hands. And the sight of him looking down at me so serenely was shocking me beyond endurance, especially when the old familiar voice came again from the taut, tanned face.

"We're not going to the hospital," he said, as if deliberately trying to calm a hysterical child. He gestured to the taxi. "Please get in."

Sliding onto the leather seat beside me, he gave the driver the address of Grand Bay Hotel in Coconut Grove.

TWENTY-SEVEN

I WAS still in a pure mortal state of shock as we entered the large marble-tiled lobby. In a haze, I saw the sumptuous furnishings, the immense vases of flowers, and the smartly dressed tourists drifting past. Patiently, the tall brown-haired man who had been my former self guided me to the elevator, and we went up in swooshing silence to a high floor.

I was unable to tear my eyes off him, yet my heart was throbbing from what had only just taken place. I could still taste the blood of the wounded body in my mouth!

The suite we entered now was spacious and full of muted colors, and open to the night through a great wall of floor-length windows which looked out upon the many lighted towers along the shores of dark serene Biscayne Bay.

"You do understand what I've been trying to tell you," I said, glad to be alone with him at last, and staring at him as he settled opposite me at the small round wooden table. "I hurt him, David, I hurt him in a rage. I . . . I flung him at the wall."

"You and your dreadful temper, Lestat," he said, but again it was the voice one uses to calm an overwrought child.

A great warm smile fired the beautifully molded face with its clear graceful bones, and broad serene mouth—David's unmistakable smile.

I couldn't respond. Slowly, I lowered my eyes from the radiant face to the powerful straight shoulders settling against the back of the chair, and the entire relaxed form.

"He led me to believe he was you!" I said, trying to focus again. "He pretended to be you. Oh, God, I poured out all my woe to him, David. He sat there listening to me, suckering me on. And then he asked for the Dark Gift. He told me he'd changed his mind. He lured me up to the rooms to give it to him, David! It was ghastly. It was everything I had wanted, and yet I knew something wasn't right! Something about him was so sinister. Oh, and there were clues, and I didn't see them! What a fool I was."

"Body and soul," said the smooth-skinned, poised young man opposite. He removed the seersucker jacket, tossing it on the nearby chair, and sat back again, folding his arms across his chest. The fabric of the turtleneck shirt showed his muscles to great advantage, and the clean white cotton made his skin seem all the more richly colored, almost a dark golden brown.

"Yes, I know," he said, the lovely British voice flowing naturally. "It's quite shocking. I had the very same experience, only a few days ago in New Orleans, when the only friend I have in the world appeared before me in this body! I sympathize completely. And I do understand—you needn't ask me again—that my old body is probably dying. It's just I don't know what either of us can do."

"Well, we can't go near it, that's certain! If you were to come within a few feet of it, James might sense your presence and focus sufficiently to get out."

"You think James is still in the body?" he asked, the eyebrows lifting again, precisely as David always lifted them when he spoke, the head tipping forward ever so slightly, and the mouth on the edge of a smile.

David in that face! The timbre of the voice was almost exactly the same.

"Ah . . . what . . . oh, yes, James. Yes, James is in the body! David, it was a blow to the head! You remember our discussion. If I was to kill him, it ought to be a swift blow to the head. He was stammering something about his mother. He wanted her. He kept saying to tell her that Raglan needed her. He was in that body when I left the room."

"I see. This means the brain is functioning but the brain is severely impaired."

"Exactly! Don't you see? He thought he would stop me from hurting him because it was your body. He had taken refuge in your body! Oh, he figured wrong! Wrong! And to try to lure me into the Dark Trick! What vanity! He should have known better. He should have confessed his little scheme the moment he saw me. Damn him. David, if I haven't killed your body, I've wounded it beyond repair."

He had drifted into his thoughts precisely the way he always did in the midst of conversation, the eyes soft and wide and looking off into the distance through the floor-length windows, and over the dark bay.

"I must go to the hospital, mustn't I?" he whispered.

"For God's sakes, no. Do you want to be plunged into that body as it dies! You can't be serious."

He climbed to his feet with an easy grace, and moved to the windows. He stood there staring out into the night, and I saw the characteristic posture in him, I saw the unmistakable expression of David in troubled reflection in the new face.

What absolute magic it was to see this being with all his poise and wisdom shining from within this young form. To see the soft intelligence behind the clear young eyes as he looked down at me again.

"My death's waiting for me, isn't it?" he whispered.

"Let it wait. It was an accident, David. It's not an inevitable death. Of course there is one alternative. We both know what it is."

"What?" he asked.

"We go there together. We get into the room somehow by bewitching a few medical persons of various rank. You push him out of the body, and you go into it, and then I give you the blood. I bring you to me. There is no conceivable injury that the full infusion of blood won't heal."

"No, my friend. You should know better by now than to suggest it. That I cannot do."

"I knew you'd say it," I said. "Then don't go near the hospital. Don't do anything to rouse him from his stupor!"

And then we both fell silent, looking at one another. The alarm was fast draining out of me. I was no longer trembling. And I realized quite suddenly that he had never been alarmed.

He wasn't alarmed now. He did not even look sad. He was looking at me, as if asking me silently to understand. Or perhaps he wasn't thinking of me at all.

Seventy-four years old he was! And he had gone out of a body full of predictable aches and pains and dulling vision and into this hardy and beautiful form.

Why, I could have no idea at all of what he was really feeling! I'd swapped a god's body for those limbs! He had swapped the body of an aged being, with death ever present at his shoulder, a man for whom youth was a collection of painful and tormenting memories, a man so shaken by those memories that his peace of mind was fast crumbling away entirely, threatening to leave him bitter and discouraged in the few years he had left.

Now he had been given back his youth! He might live another whole lifetime! And it was a body that he himself had found enticing, beautiful, even magnificent—a body for which he himself had felt carnal desire.

And here I'd been crying anxiously about the aged body, battered and losing its life drop by drop, in a hospital bed.

"Yes," he said, "I'd say that is the situation, exactly. And yet I know that I should go to that body! I know that it is the proper home of this soul. I know that every moment I wait, I risk the unimaginable—that it will expire, and I will have to remain in this body. Yet I brought you here. And here is exactly where I intend to remain."

I shuddered all over, staring at him, blinking as if to wake myself from a dream, and then shuddering again. Finally I laughed, a crazed ironic laugh. And then I said:

"Sit down, pour yourself some of your bloody miserable Scotch and tell me how this came about."

He wasn't ready to laugh. He appeared mystified, or merely in a great state of passivity, peering at me and at the problem and at the whole world from within that marvelous frame.

He stood a moment longer at the windows, eyes moving over the distant high-rises, so very white and clean looking with their hundreds of little balconies, and then at the water stretching on to the bright sky.

Then he went to the small bar in the corner, without the slightest awkwardness, and picked up the bottle of Scotch, along with a glass, and brought these back to the table. He poured himself a good thick swallow of the stinking stuff, and drank half of it, making that lovely little grimace with his tight new facial skin, exactly the way he had with the older, softer face, and then he flashed his irresistible eyes on me again.

"Well, he was taking refuge," he said. "It was exactly what you said. I should have known he would do it! But damn, it never occurred to me. We had our hands full, so to speak, dealing with the switch. And God knows, I never thought he'd try to seduce you into the Dark Trick. What made him think he could fool you when the blood started to flow?"

I made a little desperate gesture.

"Tell me what happened," I said. "He knocked you out of your body!"

"Completely. And for a moment I couldn't imagine what had happened! You can't conceive of his power! Of course he was desperate, as were we all! Of course I tried to reclaim myself at once, but he repelled me and then he started firing that gun at you!"

"At me? He couldn't have hurt me with it, David!"

"But I didn't know that for certain, Lestat. Suppose one of those bullets had struck you in the eye! I didn't know but that he might shock your body with one good shot and somehow manage to get back into it himself! And I can't claim to be an experienced spirit traveler. Certainly not on a level with him. I was in a state of plain fear. Then you were gone, and I still couldn't recapture my own body, and he turned that gun on the other, lying on the floor.

"I didn't even know if I could take possession of it. I've never done this. I wouldn't even attempt it when you invited me to do so. Possession of another body. It's as morally loathsome to me as deliberately taking human life. But he was about to blow the head off that body—that is, if he could get proper control of the gun. And where was I? And what was to happen to me? That body was my only chance of reentrance into the physical world.

"I went into it exactly the way I'd instructed you to enter your own. And I had it up and on its feet instantly, knocking him backwards, and almost dislodging the gun from his hand. By that time the passage outside was full of panic-stricken passengers and stewards! He fired another bullet as I fled over the veranda and dropped down to the lower deck.

"I don't think I realized what had happened until I hit those boards. The fall would have broken my ankle in my old body! Probably even my leg. I was prepared for that inevitable splitting pain, and suddenly I realized I wasn't hurt at all, that I'd climbed to my feet almost effortlessly, and I ran down the length of the deck and into the door to the Queens Grill Lounge.

"And of course that was the very wrong way to go. The security officers were on their way through that room to the Signal Deck stairs. I had no doubt they would apprehend him. They had to. And he'd been so awkward with that gun, Lestat. It was the way you described him before. He really doesn't know how to move in these bodies he steals. He remains too much himself!"

He stopped, took another drink of the Scotch, and then filled the glass again. I was mesmerized watching him, and listening to him—to the authoritative voice and manner combined with the glistening and innocent face. Indeed, late adolescence had only just completed itself in this young male form, though I hadn't thought about it before. It was in every sense only just finished, like a coin with the first clear impression stamped upon it and not a single tiny scratch of true wear.

"You don't get as drunk in this body, do you?" I asked.

"No," he said. "I don't. Nothing is the same, actually. Nothing. But let me go on. I didn't mean to leave you on the ship. I was frantic for your safety. But I had to."

"I told you not to worry on my account," I said. "Oh, Lord God, those are almost the same words I used to him . . . when I thought he was you. But go on. What happened then?"

"Well, I stepped back out into the hallway behind the Queens Grill Lounge, where I could still see inside through the little glass window in the door. I figured they had to bring him down that way. I didn't know of any other way. And I had to know if he had been caught. Understand, I'd made no decision as to what to do. Within seconds, a whole contingent of officers appeared, with me—David Talbot—in the very midst of them, and they ushered him—the old

me—hastily and grimly through the Queens Grill itself and towards
the front of the ship. And oh, to see him struggling to preserve his
dignity, talking at them rapidly and almost cheerfully, as if he were a
gentleman of great wealth and influence, caught up in some sordid
annoying little affair."

"I can imagine it."

"But what is his game, I thought. I didn't realize of course that
he was thinking of the future, how to take refuge from you. All I could
think was, What is he up to now? Then it occurred to me that he
would send them to search for me. He'd blame me for the entire
incident, of course.

"At once, I checked my pockets. I had the passport of Sheridan
Blackwood, the money you'd left to help him get clear of the boat, and
the key to your old cabin upstairs. I was trying to think what I should
do. If I went to that cabin they would come to look for me. He didn't
know the name on the passport. But the cabin stewards would put it
all together, of course.

"I was still utterly confused when I heard his name coming over
the loudspeakers. A quiet voice was asking for Mr. Raglan James to
report to any available officer of the ship at once. So he had implicated
me, believing me to have that passport which he gave to you. And it
would only be a matter of time before the name Sheridan Blackwood
was connected to it. He was probably giving them a physical description of me now.

"I didn't dare go down to Five Deck to try to see if you'd made
your hiding place safely. I might be leading them there if I tried. There
was only one thing I could do, as I saw it, and that was to hide
somewhere until I knew that he was off the ship.

"It seemed entirely logical to me that he'd be taken into custody
in Barbados on account of the firearm. And then he probably didn't
know what name was on his passport, and they would have a look at
it before he could pull it out.

"I went down to the Lido Deck, where the great majority of the
passengers were having breakfast, got myself a cup of coffee, and crept
into a corner, but within minutes I knew this wasn't going to work.
Two officers appeared and were obviously looking for someone. I
barely escaped notice. I started talking to two kindly women next to
me, and more or less slipped into their little group.

"Within seconds after these officers moved on, but another announcement came over the public address system. This time they had the name right. Would Mr. Sheridan Blackwood report to any officer of the ship at once? And another dreadful possibility occurred to me! I was in the body of this London mechanic who'd murdered his entire family and escaped from a madhouse. The fingerprints of this body were probably on file. James wasn't past making that known to the authorities. And here we were docking now in British Barbados! Not even the Talamasca could get this body out of custody if I were taken. Much as I feared to leave you, I had to try to get off the ship."

"You should have known I'd be all right. But why didn't they stop you at the gangway?"

"Ah, they almost did, but it was sheer confusion. Bridgetown harbour is quite large, and we were properly docked at the pier. No need for the little launch. And it had taken so long for the customs officials to clear the ship for disembarkation that there were hundreds waiting in the aisles of the lower deck to go ashore.

"The officers were checking boarding passes as best they could, but I managed again to slip in with a little group of English ladies, and I began talking quite loudly to them about the sights of Barbados and the lovely weather, and I managed to get through.

"I walked right down and onto the concrete wharf and towards the customs building. My next fear was that they would check my passport in that building before I'd be allowed through.

"And of course you have to remember, I'd been in this body for less than an hour! Every step felt completely strange to me. Over and over I looked down and saw these hands, and there came the shock— Who am I? I would look into people's faces, as if peering out of two holes in a blank wall. I couldn't imagine what they saw!"

"I know, believe me."

"Oh, but the strength, Lestat. That you cannot know. It was as if I'd drunk some overwhelming stimulant which had saturated every fiber! And these young eyes, ah, how far and how clearly they can see."

I nodded.

"Well, to be perfectly frank," he said, "I was scarcely reasoning at all. The customs building was very crowded. There were several cruise ships in port, as a matter of fact. The *Wind Song* was there, and so was the *Rotterdam*. And I think the *Royal Viking Sun* was also tied up, just across from the *Queen Elizabeth 2*. Whatever, the place was swarming with tourists, and I soon realized that passports were being checked only for those returning to their ships.

"I went into one of the little shops—you know the sort, full of horrible merchandise—and I bought a big pair of mirrored sunglasses, the kind you used to wear when your skin was so pale, and a hideous shirt with a parrot on it.

"Then taking off my jacket and turtleneck, I put on that horrible shirt, and the glasses, and I took up a station from which I could see the length of the wharf through the open doors. I didn't know what else to do. I was terrified that they would start searching the cabins! What would they do when they couldn't open that little door on Five Deck, or if they did find your body in that trunk? Then on the other hand, how could they make such a search? And what would prompt them to do it? They had the man with the gun."

He paused again to take another swallow of the Scotch. He looked truly innocent in his distress as he described all this, innocent in the way he never could have looked in the older flesh.

"I was mad, absolutely mad. I tried to use my old telepathic powers, and it took me some time to discover them, and the body was more involved with it than I would have thought."

"No surprise to me," I said.

"And then all I could pick up were various thoughts and pictures from passengers nearest me. It was no good at all. But fortunately my agony came abruptly to an end.

"They brought James ashore. He had the same enormous contingent of officers with him. They must have thought him the most dangerous criminal in the Western world. And he had my luggage with him. And again he was the very image of British propriety and dignity, chatting away with a gay smile, even though the officers were obviously deeply suspicious and profoundly uncomfortable as they ushered him to the customs people and laid his passport in their hands.

"I realized that he was being forced to permanently leave the ship. They even searched his luggage before the party was allowed to go through.

"All this time I was cleaving to the wall of the building, a young bum, if you will, with my jacket and shirt over my arm, staring at my old dignified self through those awful glasses. What is his game, I thought. Why does he want that body! As I told you, it simply never occurred to me what a clever move it had been.

"I followed the little troop outside, where a police car was waiting, into which they put his luggage as he stood rattling on and shaking hands now with those officers who were to stay behind.

"I drew near enough to hear his profuse thanks and apologies, the dreadful euphemisms and meaningless language, and his enthusiastic statements as to how much he'd enjoyed his brief voyage. How he seemed to enjoy this masquerade."

"Yes," I said dismally. "That's our man."

"Then the strangest of all moments occurred. He stopped all this chatter as they held the door of the car open for him, and turned around. He looked directly at me, as if he'd known I was there all along. Only he disguised this gesture quite cleverly, letting his eyes drift over the crowds coming and going through the enormous entrances, and then he looked at me again, very quickly, and he smiled.

"Only when the car drove off did I realize what had occurred. He had willingly driven away in my old body, leaving me with this twenty-six-year-old hunk of flesh."

He lifted the glass again, took a sip, and stared at me.

"Maybe the switch at such a moment would have been absolutely impossible. I really don't know. But the fact was, he wanted that body. And I was left standing there, outside the customs building, and I was . . . a young man again!"

He stared fixedly at the glass, obviously not seeing it at all, and then again his eyes looked into mine.

"It was *Faust*, Lestat. I'd bought youth. But the strange part was . . . I hadn't sold my soul!"

I waited as he sat there in confounded silence, and shook his head a little, and seemed on the verge of beginning again. Finally he spoke:

"Can you forgive me for leaving then? There was no way I could return to the ship. And of course James was on his way to jail, or so I believed."

"Of course I forgive you. David, we knew this might happen. We expected you might be taken into custody just as he was! It's absolutely unimportant. What *did* you do? Where did you go?"

"I went into Bridgetown. It wasn't even really a decision. A young very personable black cabdriver came up to me, thinking I was a cruise passenger, which of course I was. He offered me a tour of the city at a good price. He'd lived for years in England. Had a nice voice. I don't even think I answered him. I simply nodded and climbed into the back seat of the little car. For hours he drove me around the island. He must have thought me a very strange individual, indeed.

"I remember we drove through the most beautiful sugarcane fields. He said the little road had been built for the horse and carriage. And I thought that these fields probably looked the way they did two hundred years ago. Lestat could tell me. Lestat would know. And then I'd look down at my hands again. I'd move my foot, or tense my arms, or any small gesture; and I'd feel the sheer health and vigor of this body! And I'd fall back into a state of wonder, utterly oblivious to the poor man's voice or the sights we passed.

"Finally we came to a botanical garden. The gentlemanly black driver parked the little car and invited me to go in. What did it matter to me? I bought the admission with some of the money you'd so kindly left in your pockets for the Body Thief, and then I wandered into the garden and soon found myself in one of the most beautiful places I had ever seen in all the world.

"Lestat, all this was like a potent dream!

"I must take you to this place, you must see it—you who love the islands so very much. In fact, all I could think of . . . was you!

"And I must explain something to you. Never in all this time since you first came to me, never once have I ever looked into your eyes or heard your voice, or even thought of you, without feeling pain. It's the pain connected to mortality, to realizing one's age and one's limits, and what one will never have again. Do you see my meaning?"

"Yes. And as you walked around the botanical garden, you thought of me. And you didn't feel the pain."

"Yes," he whispered. "I didn't feel the pain."

I waited. He sat in quiet, drinking the Scotch again in a deep greedy gulp, and then he pushed the glass away. The tall muscular body was completely controlled by his elegance of spirit, moving with his polished gestures, and once again there came the measured, even tones of his voice.

"We must go there," he said. "We must stand on that hill over the sea. You remember the sound of the coconut palms in Grenada, that clicking sound as they moved in the wind? You've never heard such music as you will hear in that garden in Barbados, and oh, those flowers, those mad savage flowers. It's your Savage Garden, and yet so tame and soft and safe! I saw the giant traveler's palm with its branches seemingly braided as they came out of the stalk! And the lobster claw, a monstrous and waxen thing; and the ginger lilies, oh, you must see them. Even in the light of the moon it must all be beautiful, beautiful to your eyes.

"I think I would have stayed there forever. It was a busload of tourists which shook me out of my dreams. And do you know, they were from our ship? They were the folks from the *QE2.* " He gave a bright laugh and the face became too exquisite to describe. The whole powerful body shook with soft laughter. "Oh, I got out of there then very fast indeed.

"I went back out, found my driver, and then let him take me down to the west coast of the island, past the fancy hotels. Lots of British people there on vacation. Luxury, solitude—golf courses. And then I saw this one particular place—a resort right on the water that was everything I dream of when I want to get away from London and jet across the world to some warm and lovely spot.

"I told him to take me up the drive so that I might have a look. It was a rambling place of pink stucco, with a charming dining room under a bungalow roof and open all along the white beach. I thought things over as I roamed about, or rather I tried to, and I decided I would stay for the time being in this hotel.

"I paid off the driver, and checked into a fine little beachfront room. They took me through the gardens to reach it, and then admitted me to a small building, and I found myself inside with the doors open to a small covered porch from which a little path went right down to the sand. Nothing between me and the blue Caribbean but the coconut palms and a few great hibiscus shrubs, covered with unearthly red blooms.

"Lestat, I began to wonder if I'd died and all this wasn't the mirage before the curtain drops at last!"

I nodded in understanding.

"I sank down on the bed, and you know what happened? I went to sleep. I lay there in this body and I went to sleep."

"It's no wonder," I said, with a little smile.

"Well, it's a wonder to me. It really is. But how you would love that little room! It was like a silent shell turned to the trade winds. When I woke in the middle of the afternoon the water was the very first thing I saw.

"Then came the shock of realizing I was still in this body! I realized I'd feared all along that James would find me and push me out of it, and that I'd end up roaming around, invisible and unable to find a physical home. I was sure something like that would happen. It even occurred to me that I would simply become unanchored on my own.

"But there I was, and it was past three o'clock by this ugly watch of yours. I called London at once. Of course they had believed James was David Talbot when he'd called earlier, and only by listening patiently did I piece together what had happened—that our lawyers had gone at once to Cunard headquarters and straightened out everything for him, and that he was indeed on the way to the United States. Indeed, the Motherhouse thought I was calling from the Park Central Hotel in Miami Beach, to say that I had arrived safely and received their wire of emergency funds."

"We should have known he would think of that."

"Oh, yes, and such a sum! And they'd sent it right on, because David Talbot is still Superior General. Well, I listened to all this, patiently, as I said, then asked to speak to my trusted assistant, and told him more or less what was actually going on. I was being impersonated by a man who looked exactly like me and could imitate my voice with great skill. Raglan James was the very monster, but if and when he called again they were not to let on that they were wise to him, but rather pretend to do whatever he asked.

"I don't suppose there is another organization in the entire world where such a story, coming even from the Superior General, would be accepted as fact. Indeed, I had to do some heavy convincing myself. But really it was a lot simpler than one would suppose. There were so many little things known only to me and my assistant. Identification was no real problem. And then of course I didn't tell him that I was firmly ensconced in the body of a twenty-six-year-old man.

"I did tell him I needed to obtain a new passport immediately. I had no intention of trying to leave Barbados with the name Sheridan Blackwood stamped on my picture. My assistant was instructed to call good old Jake in Mexico City, who would of course supply me with the name of a person in Bridgetown who could do the necessary work that very afternoon. And then I needed some money myself.

"I was about to ring off when my assistant told me the impostor had left a message for Lestat de Lioncourt—that he was to meet him at the Park Central in Miami as soon as possible. The impostor had said that Lestat de Lioncourt would surely call for this message. That it must be given to him without fail."

He broke off again, and this time with a sigh.

"I know I should have gone on to Miami. I should have warned you that the Body Thief was there. But something occurred in me when I received this information. I knew that I could reach the Park Central Hotel, and confront the Body Thief, probably before you could, if I were to move on it right away."

"And you didn't want to do it."

"No. I didn't."

"David, it's all entirely understandable."

"Is it?" He looked at me.

"You're asking a little devil like me?"

He gave a wan smile. And then shook his head again, before going on:

"I spent the night on Barbados, and half of this day. The passport was ready well in time yesterday for the last flight to Miami. But I didn't go. I stayed in that beautiful seaside hotel. I dined there, and I wandered in the little city of Bridgetown. I didn't leave until noon today."

"I told you, I understand."

"Do you? What if the fiend had assaulted you again?"

"Impossible! We both know that. If he could have done it successfully with force, he would have done it the first time around. Stop tormenting yourself, David. I didn't come last night myself, though I thought you might need me. I was with Gretchen." I made a little sad shrug. "Stop worrying about what does not matter. You know what matters. It's what's happening to your old body right now. It hasn't penetrated to you, my friend. I've dealt a death blow to that body! No, I can see that you haven't grasped it. You think you have, but you're still in a daze."

These words must have struck him hard.

It broke my heart to see the pain in his eyes, to see them clouded, and see the sharp lines of distress in this new and unmarred skin. But once again, the mix of a vintage soul and a youthful form was so wondrous and beguiling that I could only stare at him, thinking vaguely of the way he had stared at me in New Orleans and how impatient with it I had become.

"I have to go there, Lestat. To that hospital. I have to see what's taken place."

"I'll go. You can come with me. But I alone will go into the hospital room itself. Now where is the phone? I must call the Park Central and find out where they took Mr. Talbot! And again, they're probably looking for me. The incident happened in my room. Perhaps I should simply call the hospital."

"No!" He reached out and touched my hand. "Don't. We should go there. We should . . . see . . . for ourselves. I should see for myself. I have . . . I have a feeling of foreboding."

"So do I," I said. But it was more than foreboding. After all, I had seen that old man with the iron-gray hair passing into silent convulsions on the bloodstained bed.

TWENTY-EIGHT

IT WAS a vast general hospital to which all emergency cases were taken, and even at this late hour of the night, the ambulances were busy at its entrances, and white-jacketed doctors were hard at work as they received the victims of traffic violence, sudden heart attack, the bloody knife or the common gun.

But David Talbot had been taken quite far away from the glaring lights and the relentless noise, to the silent precincts on a higher floor known simply as Intensive Care.

"You wait here," I said to David firmly, directing him into a sterile little parlour with dismal modern furnishings and a scattering of tattered magazines. "Don't move from this place."

The broad corridor was absolutely silent. I walked towards the doors at the far end.

It was only a moment later that I returned. David sat staring into space, long legs crossed before him, arms folded once more across his chest.

As if waking from a dream, he finally looked up.

I began to tremble again all over, almost uncontrollably, and the serene quiet of his face only worsened my dread and the awful agonizing remorse.

"David Talbot's dead," I whispered, struggling to made the words plain. "He died half an hour ago."

He registered no visible response whatever. It was as if I hadn't spoken at all. And all I could think was, I made this decision for you! I did it. I brought the Body Thief into your world, though you warned me against it. And it was I who struck down that other body! And God knows what you will feel when you realize what's happened. You don't really know.

Slowly he climbed to his feet.

"Oh, but I do know," he said in a small and reasonable voice. He came towards me and placed his hands on my shoulders, his entire demeanor so much that of his old self that it was as if I were looking at two beings who had been fused into one. "It's *Faust*, my beloved friend," he said. "And you weren't Mephistopheles. You were only Lestat, striking out in anger. And now it's done!"

He took a slow step backwards, and stared off in that dazed fashion again, his face at once losing its marks of distress. He was immersed in his thoughts, isolated, and cut off from me, as I stood there trembling, trying to regain control, trying to believe it was what he wanted.

And then again, I saw it from his perspective. How could he not want it? And I knew something else as well.

I'd lost him forever. He would never, never consent to come with me now. Any remnant of a chance had been blown completely away by this miracle. How could that not be so? I felt it penetrate, deeply and silently. I thought of Gretchen again, and the expression on her face. And for one flashing moment I was in the room again with the false David, and he was looking at me with those dark beautiful eyes and saying that he wanted the Dark Gift.

A shimmer of pain passed through me, and then it grew brighter and stronger, as if my body were suffering a ghastly and all-consuming inner fire.

I said nothing. I stared at the ugly fluorescent lights embedded in the tiled ceiling; I stared at the meaningless furniture, with its stains and its torn threads; at a soiled magazine with a grinning child on its cover. I stared at him. Slowly the pain died away into a dull ache. I waited. I could not have spoken a word for any reason, not just then.

After a long time of musing in silence, he appeared to wake from a spell. The quiet feline grace of his movements bewitched me again as it had all along. He said in a murmur that he must see the body. Surely that could be done.

I nodded.

Then he reached into his pocket and drew out a little British passport—the fake he'd obtained on Barbados, no doubt—and he looked at it as if he were trying to fathom a small but very important mystery. Then he held it out to me, though why, I couldn't imagine. I saw the handsome young face with all its quiet attributes of knowledge; why must I see the picture? But I looked at it, as he obviously wanted me to do, and I saw there—beneath the new face—the old name.

David Talbot.

He had used his own name on the false document, as if . . .

"Yes," he said, "as if I knew I would never, never be the old David Talbot again."

THE deceased Mr. Talbot had not yet been taken to the morgue, for a dear friend was on his way from New Orleans—a man named Aaron Lightner, coming by chartered plane, who should arrive very soon.

The body lay in a small immaculate room. An old man with full dark gray hair, still, as if sleeping, with his large head on a plain pillow, and his arms at his sides. Already the cheeks were a little sunken, elongating the face, and the nose in the yellow light of the lamp appeared slightly sharper than it really was, and hard as if made not of cartilage but of bone.

They had removed the linen suit from the body, washed it and groomed it and clothed it in a simple cotton gown. The covers were laid over it, the hem of pale blue sheet covering the edge of the white blanket and perfectly smooth across the chest. The eyelids were molded too closely over the eyes, as if the skin were already flattening and even melting. To a vampire's keen senses, it already gave off the fragrance of death.

But this David would not know, nor catch that scent.

He stood at the bedside looking down at the body, at his own still face with the skin faintly yellow, and the crust of beard looking somehow soiled and unkempt. With an uncertain hand he touched his own gray hair, letting his fingers linger on the curling strands just before the right ear. Then he drew back and stood collected, merely looking, as though he were at a funeral and paying his respects.

"It's dead," he murmured. "Really and truly dead." He gave a deep sigh and his eyes moved over the ceiling and the walls of the little chamber, over the window with its drawn blinds and then over the dull linoleum tile of the floor. "I sense no life in it or near it," he said, with the same subdued voice.

"No. There's nothing," I answered. "The process of decay has already begun."

"I thought he'd be here!" he whispered. "Like a bit of smoke in this room. I thought surely I'd feel him near me, struggling to get back in."

"Perhaps he is here," I said. "And he cannot do it. How ghastly even for him."

"No," he said. "There's no one here." Then he stared at his old body as if he could not tear his eyes away.

Minutes ticked by. I watched the subtle tension in his face, the fine plastic skin infused with the expression of emotion, and then smoothing itself again. Was he resigned now? He was as closed to me as he had ever been, and seemed even more deeply lost in this new body, even though his soul shone through with such fine light.

Again, he sighed, and drew back, and we walked together out of the room.

We stood in the dull beige corridor together, beneath the grim and yellowish fluorescent lights. Beyond the glass window, with its thin dark screen, Miami flickered and blazed; a dull roar came from the nearby freeway, its cascade of burning headlamps sliding perilously close before the road swerved and rose again on its long thin concrete legs and shot away.

"You realize you've lost Talbot Manor," I said. "It belonged to that man there."

"Yes, I've thought of that," he answered listlessly. "I'm the sort of Englishman who would. And to think it goes to such a dreary little cousin, who will only want to put it on the market at once."

"I shall buy it back for you."

"The order may do it. They are in my will for most of the estate."

"Don't be so sure. Even the Talamasca might not be ready for this! And besides, humans can be perfect beasts when it comes to money. Call my agent in Paris. I'll instruct him to give you absolutely anything that you wish. I'll see to it your fortune is restored to you, to the very last pound, and most definitely the house. You can have anything that is mine to give."

He looked faintly surprised. And then deeply moved.

I couldn't help but wonder, Had *I* had ever seemed so completely at ease in this tall limber body? Surely my movements had been more impulsive and even a little violent. Indeed, the strength had wrung from me a certain carelessness. He seemed on the other hand to have assimilated a knowledge of every sinew and bone.

I saw him in my mind's eye, old David, striding through the narrow cobblestone streets of Amsterdam, sidestepping the whizzing bicycles. He'd had the same poise even then.

"Lestat, you are not responsible for me now," he said. "You didn't cause this to happen."

How miserable I was suddenly. But there were words, weren't there, which had to be said.

"David," I began, trying not to show the soreness. "I couldn't have beaten him if it hadn't been for you. I told you in New Orleans I would be your slave for eternity if only you helped me to get my body away from him. And that you did." My voice was quavering. I hated it. But why not say it all now? Why prolong the pain? "Of course I know I've lost you forever, David. I know you'll never take the Dark Gift from me now."

"But why say you've lost me, Lestat?" he said in a low fervent voice. "Why must I die to love you?" He pressed his lips together, trying to suppress his sudden surge of feeling. "Why that price, especially now when I am alive as never before? Lord God, surely you grasp the magnitude of what's taken place! I've been reborn."

He placed his hand on my shoulder, fingers trying to close on the hard alien body which barely felt his touch, or rather felt it in such a wholly different way that he would never know. "I love you, my friend," he said in the same ardent whisper. "Please, don't leave me now. All this has brought us so close."

"No, David. It has not. In these last few days, we were close because we were both mortal men. We saw the same sun and the same twilight, we felt the same pull of the earth beneath our feet. We drank together and broke bread together. We might have made love together, if you had only allowed such a thing. But that's all changed. You have your youth, yes, and all the dizzying wonder that accompanies the miracle. But I still see death when I look at you, David. I see one who walks in the sun with death right at his shoulder. I know now I cannot be your companion, and you cannot be mine. It simply costs me too much pain."

He bowed his head, silently and valiantly struggling to maintain an inner control. "Don't leave me yet," he whispered. "Who else in all the world can understand?"

I wanted suddenly to plead with him. *Think, David, immortality in this beautiful young form.* I wanted to tell him of all the places we might go, immortals together, and the wonders we might see. I wanted to describe to him that dark temple I'd discovered in the very depths of the rain forest, and tell him of what it had been like to roam the jungle, fearless, and with a vision that could penetrate the darkest corners . . . Oh, all this threatened to break loose from me in a rush of words, and I made no effort to veil my thoughts or my feelings. Oh, yes, you are young again, and now you can be young for all time. It is the finest vehicle for your travel into darkness that anyone could have fashioned; it is as if the dark spirits had done all this to prepare you! Wisdom and beauty are both yours. Our gods have worked the charm. Come, come with me now.

But I didn't speak. I didn't plead. As I stood silent in the corridor, I let myself breathe the blood scent rising from him, the scent that rises from all mortals, and which is different with each in its own way. How it tormented me to mark this new vitality, this sharper heat, and the sounder, slower heartbeat which I could hear as if the body itself were speaking to me in a manner in which it could not speak to him.

In that café in New Orleans, I had caught the same sharp scent of life from this physical being, but it had *not* been the same. No, not at all the same.

It was a simple thing to shut this off. I did it. I shrank back into the brittle lonely quiet of an ordinary man. I avoided his eyes. I didn't want to hear any more apologetic and imperfect words.

"I'll see you soon," I said. "I know you will need me. You'll need your only witness when the horror and mystery of all this is too much. I'll come. But give me time. And remember. Call my man in Paris. Don't rely upon the Talamasca. Surely you don't mean to give them this life too?"

As I turned to go, I heard the distant muffled sound of the elevator doors. His friend had come—a smallish white-haired man, dressed as David had so often dressed, in a proper old-fashioned suit, complete with vest. How concerned he looked as he came towards us with quick sprightly steps, and then I saw his eyes close on me, and he slowed his pace.

I hurried away, ignoring the annoying realization that the man knew me, knew what I was and who I was. So much the better, I thought, for he will surely believe David when David begins his strange tale.

The night was waiting for me as always. And my thirst could wait no longer. I stood for a moment, head thrown back, eyes closed, and mouth open, feeling the thirst, and wanting to roar like a hungry beast. Yes, blood again when there is nothing else. When the world seems in all its beauty to be empty and heartless and I myself am utterly lost. Give me my old friend, death, and the blood that rushes with it. The Vampire Lestat is here, and he thirsts, and tonight of all nights, he will not be denied.

But I knew as I sought the dingy back streets, in search of the cruel victims I so loved, that I had lost my beautiful southern city of Miami. At least for a little while.

I kept seeing again in my mind's eye that smart little room in the Park Central, with its windows open to the sea, and the false David telling me he wanted the Dark Gift from me! And Gretchen. Would I ever think of those moments that I didn't remember Gretchen, and pouring out my story of Gretchen to the man I believed to be David before we climbed those steps to that chamber, as my heart had knocked inside me, and I had thought: At last! At last!

Bitter, and angry, and empty, I never wanted to see the pretty hotels of South Beach again.

I I

ONCE
OUT OF NATURE

The Dolls

by W. B. Yeats

A doll in the doll-maker's house
Looks at the cradle and bawls:
"That is an insult to us."
But the oldest of all the dolls,
Who had seen, being kept for show,
Generations of his sort,
Out-screams the whole shelf: "Although
There's not a man can report
Evil of this place,
The man and the woman bring
Hither, to our disgrace,
A noisy and filthy thing."
Hearing him groan and stretch
The doll-maker's wife is aware
Her husband has heard the wretch,
And crouched by the arm of his chair,
She murmurs into his ear,
Head upon shoulder leant:
"My dear, my dear, O dear,
It was an accident."

TWENTY-NINE

IT WAS two nights later that I returned to New Orleans. I'd been wandering in the Florida Keys, and through quaint little southern cities, and walking for hours on southern beaches, even wriggling my naked toes in the white sand.

At last I was back, and the cold weather had been blown away by the inevitable winds. The air was almost balmy again—my New Orleans—and the sky was high and bright above the racing clouds.

I went immediately to my dear old lady tenant, and called to Mojo, who was in the back courtyard sleeping, for he found the little apartment too warm. He gave no growl when I stepped into the courtyard. But it was the sound of my voice which triggered recognition. As soon as I said his name he was mine again.

At once he came to me, leaping up to throw his soft heavy paws on my shoulders and lick my face again with his great ham-pink tongue. I nuzzled him and kissed him and buried my face in his sweet shining gray fur. I saw him again as I had that first night in Georgetown—his fierce stamina and his great gentleness.

Had ever a beast looked so frightening yet been so full of calm, sweet affection? It seemed a wondrous combination. I knelt down on the old flags, wrestling with him, rolling him over on his back, and burying my head in the big collar of fur on his chest. He gave forth all those little growls and squeaks and high-pitched sounds that dogs give when they love you. And how I loved him in return.

As for my tenant, the dear old woman, who watched all this from the kitchen doorway, she was in tears to have him gone. At once we struck a bargain. She would be his keeper, and I should come for him through the garden gate whenever I wished. How perfectly divine, for surely it was not fair to him to expect him to sleep in a crypt with me, and I had no need of such a guardian, did I, no matter how graceful the image now and then seemed.

I kissed the old woman tenderly and quickly, lest she sense she was in close proximity to a demon, and then away I went with Mojo, walking the narrow pretty streets of the French Quarter and laughing to myself at how mortals stared at Mojo, and gave him a wide berth and seemed indeed to be terrified of him, when guess who was the one to fear?

My next stop was the building on Rue Royale where Claudia and Louis and I had spent those splendid, luminous fifty years of earthly existence together in the early half of the old century—a place partially in ruins, as I have described.

A young man had been told to meet me on the premises, a clever individual with a great reputation for turning dismal houses into palatial mansions, and I led him now up the stairs and into the decayed flat.

"I want it all as it was over a hundred years ago," I said to him. "But mind you, nothing American, nothing English. Nothing Victorian. It must be entirely French." Then I led him on a merry march through room after room, as he scribbled hastily in his little book, scarce able to see in the darkness, while I told him what wallpaper I should want here, and which shade of enamel on this door, and what sort of bergère he might round up for this corner, and what manner of Indian or Persian carpet he must acquire for this or that floor.

How keen my memory was.

Again and again, I cautioned him to write down every word I spoke. "You must find a Greek vase, no, a reproduction will not do, and it must be this high and have upon it dancing figures." Ah, wasn't it the ode by Keats which had inspired that long-ago purchase? Where had the urn gone? "And that fireplace, that is not the original mantel. You must find one of white marble, with scrollwork like so, and arched over the grate. Oh, and these fireplaces, they must be repaired. They must be able to burn coal.

"I will live here again as soon as you are finished," I said to him. "So you must hurry. And, another caution. Anything you find in these premises—hidden in the old plaster—you must give to me."

What a pleasure it was to stand beneath these high ceilings, and what a joy it would be to see them when the soft crumbling moldings were once more restored. How free and quiet I felt. The past was here, but it wasn't here. No whispering ghosts anymore, if there had ever been.

Slowly I described the chandeliers I wanted; when the proper labels eluded me, I drew pictures in words for him of what had once been there. I would have oil lamps here and there, also, though of course there must be limitless electricity, and we would conceal the various television screens in handsome cabinets, not to mar the effect. And there, a cabinet for my videotapes and laser disks, and again, we should find something suitable—a painted Oriental press would do the trick. Hide the telephones.

"And a facsimile machine! I must have one of those little marvels! Find someplace to conceal it as well. Why, you can use that room as an office, only make it gracious and beautiful. Nothing must be visible which is not made of polished brass, fine wool, or lustrous wood, or silk or cotton lace. I want a mural in that bedroom. Here, I shall show you. But look, see the wallpaper? That's the very mural. Bring in a photographer and record every inch and then begin your restoration. Work diligently but very fast."

Finally we were finished with the dark damp interior. It was time to discuss the courtyard in the back with its broken fountain, and how the old kitchen must be restored. I would have bougainvillea and the Queen's Wreath, how I love the Queen's Wreath, and the giant hibiscus, yes, I had just seen this lovely flower in the Caribbean, and the moonflower, of course. Banana trees, give me those as well. Ah, the old walls are tumbling. Patch them. Shore them up. And on the back porch above, I want ferns, all manner of delicate ferns. The weather's warming again, isn't it? They will do well.

Now, upstairs, once more, through the long brown hollow of the house and to the front porch.

I broke open the French doors and went out on the rotted boards. The fine old iron railings were not so badly rusted. The roof would have to be remade of course. But I would soon be sitting out here as I did now and then in the old days, watching the passersby on the other side of the street.

Of course the faithful and zealous readers of my books would spot me here now and then. The readers of Louis's memoir, come to find the flat where we had lived, would surely recognize the house.

No matter. They believed in it, but that's different from believing it. And what was another young blond-faced man, smiling at them from a high balcony, his arms resting on the rail? I should never feed upon those tender, innocent ones—even when they bare their throats at me and say, "Lestat, right here!" (This has happened, reader, in Jackson Square, and more than once.)

"You must hurry," I told the young man, who was still scribbling, and taking measurements, and murmuring about colors and fabrics to himself, and now and then discovering Mojo beside him, or in front of him, or underfoot, and giving a start. "I want it finished before summer." He was in quite a dither when I dismissed him. I remained behind in the old building with Mojo, alone.

The attic. In the olden times, I'd never gone there. But there was an old staircase hidden off the rear porch, just beyond the back parlour, the very room where Claudia had once sliced through my thin fledgling white skin with her great flashing knife. I went there now and climbed up into the low rooms beneath the sloping roof. Ah, it was high enough for a man of six feet to walk here, and the dormer windows on the very front let in the light from the street.

I should make my lair here, I thought, in a hard plain sarcophagus with a lid no mortal could hope to move. Easy enough to build a small chamber beneath the gable, fitted with thick bronze doors which I should design myself. And when I rise, I shall go down into the house and find it as it was in those wondrous decades, save I shall have everywhere about me the technological marvels I require. The past will not be recovered. The past will be perfectly eclipsed.

"Won't it, Claudia?" I whispered, standing in the back parlour. Nothing answered me. No sounds of a harpsichord or the canary singing in its cage. But I should have songbirds again, yes, many of them, and the house would be full of the rich rampaging music of Haydn or Mozart.

Oh, my darling, wish you were here!

And my dark soul is happy again, because it does not know how to be anything else for very long, and because the pain is a deep dark sea in which I would drown if I did not sail my little craft steadily over the surface, steadily towards a sun which will never rise.

It was past midnight now; the little city was humming softly around me, with a chorus of mingled voices, and the soft clickety-clack of a distant train, with the low throb of a whistle on the river, and the rumble of traffic on the Rue Esplanade.

I went into the old parlour, and stared at the pale luminous patches of light falling through the panes of the doors. I lay down on the bare wood, and Mojo came to lie down beside me, and there we slept.

I dreamed no dreams of her. So why was I weeping softly when it came time finally to seek the safety of my crypt? And where was my Louis, my treacherous and stubborn Louis? Pain. Ah, and it would get worse, wouldn't it, when I saw him soon enough?

With a start, I realized that Mojo was lapping the blood tears from my cheeks. "No. That you must never do!" I said, closing my hand over his mouth. "Never, never that blood. That evil blood." I was badly shaken. And he was at once obedient, backing off just a little from me in his unhurried and dignified way.

How perfectly demonic his eyes seemed as he gazed at me. What a deception! I kissed him again, on the tenderest part of his long, furry face, just beneath his eyes.

I thought again of Louis, and the pain hit me as if I'd been dealt a hard blow by one of the ancients, right in the chest.

Indeed, my emotions were so bitter, and so beyond my control, that I felt frightened and for a moment thought of nothing and felt nothing but this pain.

In my mind's eye, I saw all the others. I brought up their faces as if I were the Witch of Endor standing over the cauldron invoking the images of the dead.

Maharet and Mekare, the red-haired twins, I beheld together—the oldest of us, who might not have even known of my dilemma, so remote were they in their great age and wisdom, and so deeply wrapped in their own inevitable and timeless concerns; Eric and Mael and Khayman I pictured, who held scant interest for me even if they had knowingly refused to come to my aid. They had never been my companions. What did I care for them? Then I saw Gabrielle, my beloved mother, who surely could not have known of my terrible jeopardy, who was no doubt wandering some distant continent, a ragged goddess, communing only with the inanimate, as she had always done. I did not know if she fed any longer on humans; some dim memory came to me of her describing the embrace of some dark woodland beast. Was she mad, my mother, wherever she had gone? I did not think so. That she existed still, I was certain. That I could never find her, I had no doubt.

It was Pandora I pictured next. Pandora, the lover of Marius, might have perished long ago. Made by Marius in Roman times, she had been on the verge of despair when last I saw her. Years ago, she had wandered away, without warning, from our last true coven on the Night Island—one of the first to depart.

As for Santino, the Italian, I knew almost nothing of him. I had expected nothing. He was young. Perhaps my cries had never reached him. And why should he listen if they had?

Then I envisioned Armand. My old enemy and friend Armand. My old adversary and companion Armand. Armand, the angelic child who had created the Night Island, our last home.

Where was Armand? Had Armand deliberately left me to my own devices? And why not?

Let me turn now to Marius, the great ancient master who had made Armand in love and tenderness so many centuries ago; Marius, for whom I'd searched so many decades; Marius, the true child of two millennia, who had led me down into the depths of our meaningless history, and bid me worship at the shrine of Those Who Must Be Kept.

Those Who Must Be Kept. Dead and gone as was Claudia. For kings and queens among us can perish as surely as tender childlike fledglings.

Yet I go on. I am here. I am strong.

And Marius, like Louis, had known of my suffering! He'd known and he'd refused to help.

The rage in me grew stronger, ever more dangerous. Was Louis somewhere near in these very streets? I clenched my fists, struggling against this rage, struggling against its helpless and inevitable expression.

Marius, you turned your back on me. That came as no surprise, really. You were always the teacher, the parent, the high priest. I don't despise you for it. But Louis! My Louis, I could never deny you anything, and you turned me away!

I knew I could not remain here. I did not trust myself to lay eyes on him. Not yet.

An hour before dawn, I took Mojo back to his little garden, kissed him good-bye, and then I walked fast to the outskirts of the old city, and through the Faubourg Marigny, and finally into the swamplands, and then I raised my arms towards the stars, swimming so brilliant beyond the clouds, and I went up, and up, and up until I was lost in the song of the wind and tumbling on the thinnest currents, and the joy I felt in my gifts filled my entire soul.

THIRTY

I T MUST have been a full week that I traveled the world. First I'd gone to snowy Georgetown and found that frail, pathetic young woman whom my mortal self had so unforgivably raped. Like an exotic bird, she looked to me now, struggling to see me well in the smelly dark of the quaint little mortal restaurant, not wanting to admit that this encounter with "my French friend" had ever happened, and then stunned as I placed an antique rosary made of emeralds and diamonds in her hand. "Sell it, if you like, chérie," I said. "He wanted you to have it for whatever purpose you wish. But tell me one thing. Did you conceive a child?"

She shook her head and whispered the word "no." I wanted to kiss her, she was beautiful again to me. But I dared not risk it. It wasn't only that I would have frightened her, it was that the desire to kill her was almost overpowering. Some fierce purely male instinct in me wanted to claim her now simply because I had claimed her in another way before.

I was gone from the New World within hours, and night after night, I wandered, hunting in the seething slums of Asia—in Bangkok and Hong Kong and Singapore—and then in the dreary and frozen city of Moscow, and in the charming old cities of Vienna and Prague. I went to Paris for a short time. I did not go to London. I pushed my speed to the limits; I rose and plunged in the darkness, sometimes alighting in towns of which I did not know the name. I fed ceaselessly among the desperate and the vicious and, now and then, the lost and the mad and the purely innocent who fell under my gaze.

I tried not to kill. I tried not to. Except when the subject was damn near irresistible, an evildoer of the first rank. And then the death was slow and savage, and I was just as hungry when it was over, and off to find another before the sun rose.

I had never been so at ease with my powers. I had never risen so high into the clouds, nor traveled so fast.

I walked for hours among mortals in the narrow old streets of Heidelberg, and of Lisbon, and of Madrid. I passed through Athens and Cairo and Marrakesh. I walked on the shores of the Persian Gulf and the Mediterranean and the Adriatic Sea.

What was I doing? What was I thinking? That the old cliché was true—*the world was mine.*

And everywhere I went I let my presence be known. I let my thoughts emanate from me as if they were notes played on a lyre.

The Vampire Lestat is here. The Vampire Lestat is passing. Best give way.

I didn't want to see the others. I didn't really look for them, or open my mind or my ears to them. I had nothing to say to them. I only wanted them to know that I had been there.

I did pick up the sound of nameless ones in various places, vaga-bonds unknown to us, random creatures of the night who had escaped the late massacre of our kind. Sometimes it was a mere mental glimpse of a powerful being who, at once, veiled his mind. Other times it was the clear sound of a monster plodding through eternity without guile or history or purpose. Maybe such things will always be there!

I had eternity now to meet such creatures, if ever the urge came over me. The only name on my lips was Louis.

Louis.

I could not for a moment forget Louis. It was as if someone else were chanting his name in my ear. What would I do if ever again I laid eyes on him? How could I curb my temper? Would I even try?

At last I was tired. My clothes were rags. I could stay away no longer. I wanted to be home.

THIRTY-ONE

I WAS sitting in the darkened cathedral. Hours ago it had been locked, and I had entered surreptitiously through one of the front doors, quieting the protective alarms. And left it open for him.

Five nights had passed since my return. Work was progressing wonderfully well on the flat in the Rue Royale, and of course he had not failed to notice it. I'd seen him standing under the porch opposite, staring up at the windows, and I'd appeared on the balcony above for only an instant—not even enough for a mortal eye to see.

I'd been playing cat and mouse with him since.

Tonight, I'd let him see me near the old French Market. And what a start it gave him, to actually lay eyes upon me, and to see Mojo with me, to realize as I gave him a little wink that it was truly Lestat whom he saw.

What had he thought in that first instant? That it was Raglan James in my body come to destroy him? That James was making a home for himself in the Rue Royale? No, he'd known it was Lestat all along.

Then I had walked slowly towards the church, Mojo coming along smartly at my side. Mojo, who kept me anchored to the good earth.

I wanted him to follow me. But I wouldn't so much as turn my head to see whether or not he was coming.

It was warm this night, and it had rained earlier enough to darken the rich, rose-colored walls of the old French Quarter buildings, to deepen the brown of the bricks, and to leave the flags and the cobblestones with a fine and lovely sheen. A perfect night for walking in New Orleans. Wet and fragrant, the flowers blooming over the garden walls.

But to meet with him again, I needed the quiet and silence of the darkened church.

My hands were shaking a little, as they had been off and on since I had come back into my old form. There was no physical cause for it, only my anger coming and going, and long spells of contentment, and then a terrifying emptiness which would open around me, and then the happiness coming again, quite complete, yet fragile, as though it were but a thin fine veneer. Was it fair to say I didn't know the full state of my soul? I thought of the unbridled rage with which I'd smashed the head of David Talbot's body, and I shuddered. Was I still afraid?

Hmmm. Look at these dark sunburnt fingers with their gleaming nails. I felt the tremour as I pressed the tips of my right fingers to my lips.

I sat in the dark pew, several rows back from the railing before the altar, looking at the dark statues, and the paintings, and all the gilded ornament of this cold and empty place.

It was past midnight. The noise from the Rue Bourbon was as loud as ever. So much simmering mortal flesh there. I'd fed earlier. I would feed again.

But the sounds of the night were soothing. Throughout the narrow streets of the Quarter, in her small apartments, and atmospheric little taverns, in her fancy cocktail lounges, and in her restaurants, happy mortals laughed and talked, and kissed and embraced.

I slumped back comfortably in the pew, and stretched out my arms on the back of it as if it were a park bench. Mojo had already gone to sleep in the aisle near me, long nose resting on his paws.

Would that I were you, my friend. Looking like the very devil, and full of big lumbering goodness. Ah, yes, goodness. It was goodness that I felt when I locked my arms around him, and buried my face in his fur.

But now *he* had come into the church.

I sensed his presence though I could pick up no glimmer of thought or feeling from him, or even hear his step. I had not heard the outer door open or close. Somehow I knew he was there. Then I saw the shadow moving in the corner of my left eye. He came into the pew and sat beside me, a little distance away.

We sat there in silence for many long moments, and then he spoke.

"You burnt my little house, didn't you?" he asked in a small, vibrant voice.

"Can you blame me?" I asked with a smile, eyes still on the altar. "Besides, I was a human when I did that. It was human weakness. Want to come and live with me?"

"This means you've forgiven me?"

"No, it means I'm playing with you. I may even destroy you for what you did to me. I haven't made up my mind. Aren't you afraid?"

"No. If you meant to do away with me, it would already be done."

"Don't be so certain. I'm not myself, and yet I am, and then I am not again."

Long silence, with only the sounds of Mojo breathing hoarsely and deeply in his sleep.

"I'm glad to see you," he said. "I knew you would win. But I didn't know how."

I didn't answer. But I was suddenly boiling inside. Why were both my virtues and my faults used against me?

But what was the use of it—to make accusations, to grab him and shake him and demand answers from him? Maybe it was better not to know.

"Tell me what happened," he said.

"I will not," I replied. "Why in the world do you want to know?"

Our hushed voices echoed softly in the nave of the church. The wavering light of the candles played upon the gilt on the tops of the columns, on the faces of the distant statues. Oh, I liked it here in this silence and coolness. And in my heart of hearts I had to admit I was so very glad that he had come. Sometimes hate and love serve exactly the same purpose.

I turned and looked at him. He was facing me, one knee drawn up on the pew and his arm resting on the back of it. He was pale as always, an artful glimmer in the dark.

"You were right about the whole experiment," I said. At least my voice was steady, I thought.

"How so?" No meanness in his tone, no challenge, only the subtle desire to know. And what a comfort it was—the sight of his face, and the faint dusty scent of his worn garments, and the breath of fresh rain still clinging to his dark hair.

"What you told me, my dear old friend and lover," I said. "That I didn't really want to be human. That it was a dream, and a dream built upon falsehood and fatuous illusion and pride."

"I can't claim that I understood it," he said. "I don't understand it now."

"Oh, yes, you did. You understand very well. You always have. Maybe you lived long enough; maybe you have always been the stronger one. But you knew. I didn't want the weakness; I didn't want the limitations; I didn't want the revolting needs and the endless vulnerability; I didn't want the drenching sweat or the searing cold. I didn't want the blinding darkness, or the noises that walled up my hearing, or the quick, frantic culmination of erotic passion; I didn't want the trivia; I didn't want the ugliness. I didn't want the isolation; I didn't want the constant fatigue."

"You explained this to me before. There must have been something . . . however small . . . that was good!"

"What do you think?"

"The light of the sun."

"Precisely. The light of the sun on snow; the light of the sun on water; the light of the sun . . . on one's hands and one's face, and opening up all the secret folds of the entire world as if it were a flower, as if we were all part of one great sighing organism. The light of the sun . . . on snow."

I stopped. I really didn't want to tell him. I felt I had betrayed myself.

"There were other things," I said. "Oh, there were many things. Only a fool would not have seen them. Some night, perhaps, when we're warm and comfortable together again as if this never happened, I'll tell you."

"But they were not enough."

"Not for me. Not now."

Silence.

"Maybe that was the best part," I said, "the discovery. And that I no longer entertain a deception. That I know now I truly love being the little devil that I am."

I turned and gave him my prettiest, most malignant smile.

He was far too wise to fall for it. He gave a long near-silent sigh, his lids lowered for a moment, and then he looked at me again.

"Only you could have gone there," he said. "And come back."

I wanted to say this wasn't true. But who else would have been fool enough to trust the Body Thief? Who else would have plunged into the venture with such sheer recklessness? And as I thought this over, I realized what ought to have been plain to me already. That I'd known the risk I was taking. I'd seen it as the price. The fiend told me he was a liar; he told me he was a cheat. But I had done it because there was simply no other way.

Of course this wasn't really what Louis meant by his words; but in a way it was. It was the deeper truth.

"Have you suffered in my absence?" I asked, looking back at the altar.

Very soberly he answered, "It was pure hell."

I didn't reply.

"Each risk you take hurts me," he said. "But that is my concern and my fault."

"Why do you love me?" I asked.

"You know, you've always known. I wish I could be you. I wish I could know the joy you know all the time."

"And the pain, you want that as well?"

"Your pain?" He smiled. "Certainly. I'll take your brand of pain anytime, as they say."

"You smug, cynical lying bastard," I whispered, the anger cresting in me suddenly, the blood even rushing into my face. "I needed you and you turned me away! Out in the mortal night you locked me. You refused me. You turned your back!"

The heat in my voice startled him. It startled me. But it was there and I couldn't deny it, and once again my hands were trembling, these hands that had leapt out and away from me at the false David, even when all the other lethal power in me was kept in check.

He didn't utter a word. His face registered those small changes which shock produces—the slight quiver of an eyelid, the mouth lengthening and then softening, a subtle clabbering look, vanishing as quickly as it appeared. He held my accusing glance all through it, and then slowly looked away.

"It was David Talbot, your mortal friend, who helped you, wasn't it?" he asked.

I nodded.

But at the mere mention of the name, it was as if all my nerves had been touched by the tip of a heated bit of wire. There was enough suffering here as it was. I couldn't speak anymore of David. I wouldn't speak of Gretchen. And I suddenly realized that what I wanted to do most in the world was to turn to him and put my arms around him and weep on his shoulder as I'd never done.

How shameful. How predictable! How insipid. And how sweet. I didn't do it.

We sat there in silence. The soft cacophony of the city rose and fell beyond the stained-glass windows, which caught the faint glow from the street lamps outside. The rain had come again, the gentle warm rain of New Orleans, in which one can walk so easily as if it were nothing but the gentlest mist.

"I want you to forgive me," he said. "I want you to understand that it wasn't cowardice; it wasn't weakness. What I said to you at the time was the truth. I couldn't do it. I can't bring someone into this! Not even if that someone is a mortal man with you inside him. I simply could not."

"I know all that," I said.

I tried to leave it there. But I couldn't. My temper wouldn't cool, my wondrous temper, the temper which had caused me to smash David Talbot's head into a plaster wall.

He spoke again. "I deserve whatever you have to say."

"Ah, more than that!" I said. "But this is what I want to know." I turned and faced him, speaking through my clenched teeth. "Would you have refused me forever? If they'd destroyed my body, the others—Marius, whoever knew of it—if I'd been trapped in that mortal form, if I'd come to you over and over and over again, begging you and pleading with you, would you have shut me out forever! Would you have held fast?"

"I don't know."

"Don't answer so quickly. Look for the truth inside yourself. You do know. Use your filthy imagination. You do know. Would you have turned me away?"

"I don't know the answer!"

"I despise you!" I said in a bitter, harsh whisper. "I ought to destroy you—finish what I started when I made you. Turn you into ashes and sift them through my hands. You know that I could do it! Like that! Like the snap of mortal fingers, I could do it. Burn you as I burnt your little house. And nothing could save you, nothing at all."

I glared at him, at the sharp graceful angles of his imperturbable face, faintly phosphorescent against the deeper shadows of the church. How beautiful the shape of his wide-set eyes, with their fine rich black lashes. How perfect the tender indentation of his upper lip.

The anger was acid inside me, destroying the very veins through which it flowed, and burning away the preternatural blood.

Yet I couldn't hurt him. I couldn't even conceive of carrying out such awful, cowardly threats. I could never have brought harm to Claudia. Ah, to make something out of nothing, yes. To throw up the pieces to see how they will fall, yes. But vengeance. Ah, arid awful distasteful vengeance. What is it to me?

"Think on it," he whispered. "Could you make another, after all that's passed?" Gently he pushed it further. "Could you work the Dark Trick again? Ah—*you* take *your* time before answering. Look deep inside you for the truth as you just told me to do. And when you know it, you needn't tell it to me."

Then he leant forward, closing the distance between us, and pressed his smooth silken lips against the side of my face. I meant to pull away, but he used all his strength to hold me still, and I allowed it, this cold, passionless kiss, and he was the one who finally drew back like a collection of shadows collapsing into one another, with only his hand still on my shoulder, as I sat with my eyes on the altar still.

Finally I rose slowly, stepping past him, and motioned for Mojo to wake and come.

I moved down the length of the nave to the front doors of the church. I found that shadowy nook where the vigil candles burn beneath the statue of the Virgin, an alcove full of wavering and pretty light.

The scent and sound of the rain forest came back to me, the great enclosing darkness of those powerful trees. And then the vision of the little whitewashed chapel in the clearing with its doors thrown open, and the eerie muted sound of the bell in the vagrant breeze. And the scent of blood coming from the wounds in Gretchen's hands.

I lifted the long wick that lay there for the lighting of candles, and I dipped it into an old flame, and made a new one burst into being, hot and yellow and finally steady, giving off the sharp perfume of burnt wax.

I was about to say the words "For Gretchen," when I realized that it was not for her at all that I had lighted the candle. I looked up at the face of the Virgin. I saw the crucifix above Gretchen's altar. Again, I felt the peace of the rain forest around me, and I saw that little ward with those small beds. For Claudia, my precious beautiful Claudia? No, not for her either, much as I loved her . . .

I knew the candle was for me.

It was for the brown-haired man who had loved Gretchen in Georgetown. It was for the sad lost blue-eyed demon I had been before I became that man. It was for the mortal boy of centuries ago who went off to Paris with his mother's jewels in his pocket, and only the clothes on his back. It was for the wicked impulsive creature who had held the dying Claudia in his arms.

It was for all those beings, and for the devil who stood here now, because he loved candles, and he loved the making of light from light. Because there was no God in whom he believed, and no saints, and no Queen of Heaven.

Because he had kept his bitter temper and he had not destroyed his friend.

Because he was alone, no matter how near to him that friend. And because happiness had returned to him, as if it were an affliction he'd never fully conquer, the impish smile already spreading on his lips, the thirst leaping inside him, and the desire in him rising just to step outside again and wander in the slick and shining city streets.

Yes. For the Vampire Lestat, that little candle, that miraculous tiny candle, increasing by that small amount all the light in the universe! And burning in an empty church the night long among those other little flames. It would be burning on the morrow when the faithful came; when the sun shone through these doors.

Keep your vigil, little candle, in darkness and in sunshine.

Yes, for me.

THIRTY-TWO

DID you think the story was finished? That the fourth installment of the Vampire Chronicles had come to a close?

Well, the book should be ended. It really should have ended when I lit that small candle, but it didn't. I realized that the following night when I first opened my eyes.

Pray continue to Chapter Thirty-three to discover what happened next. Or you can quit now, if you like. You may come to wish that you had.

THIRTY-THREE

BARBADOS.

He was still there when I caught up with him. In a hotel by the sea.

Weeks had passed, though why I let so much time go by, I don't know. Kindness was no part of it, nor cowardice either. Nevertheless I had waited. I had watched the splendid little flat in the Rue Royale being restored, step by step, until there were at least some exquisitely furnished rooms in which I could spend my time, thinking about all that had happened, and which might yet take place. Louis had returned to take up residence with me, and was busy searching for a desk very like the one which had once stood in the parlour over a hundred years before.

David had left many messages with my man in Paris. He would be leaving soon for the carnival in Rio. He missed me. He wished I would come join him there.

All had gone well with the settlement of his estate. He was David Talbot, a young cousin of the older man who had died in Miami, and the new owner of the ancestral home. The Talamasca had accomplished these things for him, restoring to him the fortune he had left to them, and settling upon him a generous pension. He was no longer their Superior General, though he maintained his quarters in the Motherhouse. He would be forever under their wing.

He had a small gift for me, if I wanted it. It was the locket with the miniature of Claudia. He'd found it. Exquisite portrait; fine gold chain. He had it with him, and would send it to me if I liked. Or would I not come to see him, and accept it from his hands myself?

Barbados. He had felt compelled to return to the scene of the crime, so to speak. The weather was beautiful. He was reading *Faust* again, he wrote to me. He had so many questions he wanted to ask me. When would I come?

He had *not* seen God or the Devil again, though he had, before leaving Europe, spent a long time in various Paris cafés. He wasn't going to spend this lifetime searching for God or the Devil either. "Only you can know the man I am now," he wrote. "I miss you, I want to talk to you. Can you not remember that I helped you, and forgive me everything else?"

It was that seaside resort he'd described to me, of handsome pink stucco buildings, and great sprawling bungalow roofs, and soft fragrant gardens, and endless vistas of the clean sand and the sparkling translucent sea.

I didn't go there until I'd been in the gardens up the mountain, and had stood on those very cliffs he had visited, looking out over the forested mountains, and listening to the wind in the branches of the noisy clacking coconut palms.

Had he told me about the mountains? That you could look immediately down into the deep soft valleys and that the neighboring slopes seemed so close you thought you could touch them, though they were far, far away?

I don't think so, but he had described well the flowers—the shrimp plant with its tiny blossoms, and the orchid tree and the ginger lilies, yes, those fierce red lilies with their delicate shivering petals, and the ferns nestled in the deep glades, and the waxen bird-of-paradise and the tall stiff pussy willows, and the tiny yellow-throated blossoms of the trumpet vine.

We should walk there together, he had said.

Well, that we would do. Soft the crunch of the gravel. And oh, never had the high swaying coconut palms looked so beautiful as on these bluffs.

I waited until it was past midnight before I made my descent upon the sprawling seaside hotel. The courtyard was as he had said, full of pink azaleas and large waxen elephant ears and dark glossy shrubs.

I passed through the empty darkened dining room and its long open porches and went down on the beach. I went far out in the shallows, so that I might look back from a distance upon the bungalow rooms with their roofed verandas. I found him at once.

The doors to the little patio were completely pulled back, and the yellow light spilled out on the small paved enclosure with its painted table and chairs. Inside, as if on a lighted stage, he sat at a small desk, facing the night and the water, typing away on a small portable computer, the tight small clicking of the keys carrying in the silence, even over the whisper of the lazy softly foaming surf.

He was naked except for a pair of white beach shorts. His skin was very darkly golden as though he spent his days sleeping in the sun. Streaks of yellow shone in his dark brown hair. There was a glow to his naked shoulders and smooth, hairless chest. Very firm muscles at his waist. A slight golden sheen came from the down on his thighs and legs and the very scant bits of hair on the backs of his hands.

I hadn't even noticed that hair when I was alive. Or maybe I hadn't liked it. Didn't really know. I liked it now well enough. And that he seemed a little more slender than I had been in that frame. Yes, all the bones of the body were more visible, conforming I suppose to some modern style of health which says we must be fashionably underfed. It suited him; it suited the body; I suppose it suited them both.

The room was very neat behind him and rustic in the style of the islands with its beamed ceiling and rose-tiled floor. The bed was covered in a gay pastel fabric printed with a jagged geometric Indian design. The armoire and chests were white and decorated with brightly painted flowers. The many simple lamps gave off a generous light.

I had to smile though that he sat amid all this luxury, typing away—David the scholar, dark eyes dancing with the ideas inside his head.

Drawing nearer, I noted that he was very clean-shaven. His nails had been trimmed and buffed, perhaps by a manicurist. His hair was still the same full wavy mop I'd worn so carelessly when I'd been in this body, but it, too, had been trimmed and had an altogether more pleasing shape. There lay his copy of Goethe's *Faust* beside him, open, a pen lying across it, and many of the pages folded, or marked with small silver paper clips.

I was still taking my time with this inspection—noting the bottle of Scotch beside him, and the thick-bottomed crystal glass, and the pack of small thin cigars—when he looked up and saw me there.

I stood on the sand, well outside the little porch with its low cement railing, but quite visible in the light.

"Lestat," he whispered. His face brightened beautifully. He rose at once and came towards me with the familiar graceful stride. "Thank God you've come."

"You think so?" I said. I thought of that moment in New Orleans when I'd watched the Body Thief scurrying out of the Café du Monde and thought that body could move like a panther with someone else inside.

He wanted to take me in his arms, but when I stiffened and moved just a little away, he stood still, and folded his arms across his chest—a gesture that seemed to belong entirely to this body, as I couldn't remember ever seeing him do it before we'd met in Miami. These arms were heavier than his old arms. The chest was broader too.

How naked it looked. How darkly pink the nipples. How fierce and clear his eyes.

"I've missed you," he said.

"Really? Surely you haven't been living as a recluse here?"

"No, I've seen too much of others, I think. Too many little supper parties in Bridgetown. And my friend Aaron has come and gone several times. Other members have been here." He paused. "I can't bear to be around them, Lestat. I can't bear to be at Talbot Manor among the servants, pretending to be a cousin of my old self. There's something really appalling about what's happened. Sometimes I can't bear to look in the mirror. But I don't want to talk about that side of it."

"Why not?"

"This is a temporary period, one of adjustment. These shocks will eventually pass. I have so much to do. Oh, I'm so glad you've come. I had a feeling you would. I almost left for Rio this morning, but I had the distinct feeling I'd see you tonight."

"Is that so."

"What's the matter? Why the dark face? Why are you angry?"

"I don't know. I don't really require a reason to be angry these days. And I ought to be happy. I will be soon. Always happens, and after all—it's an important night."

He stared at me, trying to figure what I meant by these words, or more properly what was the right thing for him to reply.

"Come inside," he said finally.

"Why not sit here on the porch in the shadows? I like the breeze."

"Certainly, as you say."

He went into the little room to take up the bottle of Scotch, pour himself a drink, and then he joined me at the wooden table. I had just seated myself in one of the chairs and was looking directly out over the sea.

"So what *have* you been doing?" I asked.

"Ah, where do I begin?" he asked. "I've been writing about it continuously—trying to describe all the little sensations, the new discoveries."

"Is there any doubt that you're securely anchored in the body?"

"None." He took a deep drink of his Scotch. "And there seems to be no deterioration of any kind. You know, I feared that. I feared it even when you were in this body, but I didn't want to say it. We had enough to worry about, didn't we?" He turned and looked at me, and quite suddenly he smiled. In a low stunned voice he said, "You're looking at a man you know from the inside out."

"No, not really," I said. "Tell me, how do you deal with the perception of strangers . . . those who don't guess. Do women invite you into their bedrooms? What about young men?"

He looked out to the sea, and there was a little bitterness in his face suddenly. "You know the answer. I can't make a vocation of those encounters. They mean nothing to me. I don't say I haven't enjoyed a few safaris into the bedroom. I have more important things to do, Lestat, far more important things to do.

"There are places I want to go—lands and cities I always dreamt

I would visit. Rio is only the beginning. There are mysteries I must solve; things I must find out."

"Yes, I can imagine."

"You said something very important to me when we were together last. You said, surely you won't give the Talamasca this life too. Well, I won't give it to them. What's paramount in my mind is that I must not waste it. That I must do something of absolute importance with it. Of course the direction won't come to me all at once. There has to be a period of traveling, of learning, of evaluation, before I make a decision as to direction. And as I engage in my studies, I write. I write everything down. Sometimes the record itself seems the goal."

"I know."

"There are many things I want to ask you. I've been plagued with questions."

"Why? What sort of questions?"

"About what you experienced those few days, and whether you have the slightest regret that we ended the venture so soon."

"What venture? You mean my life as a mortal man?"

"Yes."

"No regret."

He started to speak again, and then broke off. Then again he spoke. "What did you take back with you?" he asked in a low fervent voice.

I turned and looked at him again. Yes, the face was definitely more angular. Was it personality which had sharpened it and given it more definition. Perfect, I thought.

"I'm sorry, David, my mind wandered. Ask me this question again."

"What did you take back with you?" he said, with his old familiar patience. "What lesson?"

"I don't know that it was a lesson," I said. "And it may take time for me to understand whatever I learnt."

"Yes, I see, of course."

"I can tell you that I'm aware of a new lust for adventure, for wandering, the very things you describe. I want to go back to the rain forests. I saw them so briefly when I went to visit Gretchen. There was a temple there. I want to see it again."

"You never told me what happened."

"Ah, yes, I told you but you were Raglan at the time. The Body Thief witnessed that little confession. Why on earth would he want to steal such a thing? But I'm drifting off the point. There are so many places that I, too, want to go."

"Yes."

"It's a lust again for time and for the future, for the mysteries of the natural world. For being the watcher that I became that long-ago night in Paris, when I was forced into it. I lost my illusions. I lost my favorite lies. You might say I revisited that moment and was reborn to darkness of my own free will. And such a will!"

"Ah, yes, I understand."

"Do you? That's good if you do."

"Why do you speak that way?" He lowered his voice and spoke slowly. "Do you need my understanding as much as I need yours?"

"You've never understood me," I said. "Oh, it's not an accusation. You live with illusions about me, which make it possible for you to visit with me, to speak with me, even to shelter me and help me. You couldn't do that if you really knew what I was. I tried to tell you. When I spoke of my dreams . . ."

"You're wrong. That's your vanity talking," he said. "You love to imagine you're worse than you are. What dreams? I don't remember your ever speaking to me of dreams."

I smiled. "You don't? Think back, David. My dream of the tiger. I was afraid for you. And now the menace of the dream will be fulfilled."

"What do you mean?"

"I'm going to do it to you, David. I'm going to bring you to me."

"What?" His voice dropped to a whisper. "What are you saying to me?" He leant forward, trying to see clearly the expression on my face. But the light was behind us, and his mortal vision wasn't sharp enough for that.

"I just told you. I'm going to do it to you, David."

"Why, why are you saying this?"

"Because it's true," I said. I stood up and pushed the chair aside with my leg.

He stared up at me. Only now did his body register the danger. I saw the fine muscles of his arms tense. His eyes were fixed on mine.

"Why are you saying this? You couldn't do this to me," he said.

"Of course I could. And I shall. Now. All along I've told you I was evil. I've told you I'm the very devil. The devil in your *Faust,* the devil of your visions, the tiger in my dream!"

"No, that's not true." He climbed to his feet, knocking the chair over behind him, and almost losing his balance. He stepped back into the room. "You're not the devil, and you know that you're not. Don't do this to me! I forbid it!" He clenched his teeth on the last words. "You are in your own heart as human as I am. And you will not do it."

"The hell I won't," I said. I laughed. I couldn't help it suddenly. "David the Superior General," I said. "David the Candomble priest."

He backed across the tiled floor, the light fully illuminating his face, and the tense powerful muscles of his arms.

"Want to fight me? It's useless. There's no force on earth that can stop me from doing this."

"I'll die first," he said, in a low strangled voice. His face was darkening, flushed with blood. Ah, David's blood.

"I won't let you die. Why don't you call on your old Brazilian spirits? You don't remember how to do it, do you? Your heart's not in it. Well, it wouldn't do you the slightest good if you did."

"You can't do this," he said. He was struggling for calm. "You can't repay me in this fashion."

"Oh, but this is how the devil repays his helpers!"

"Lestat, I helped you against Raglan! I helped you recover this body, and what was your pledge to me of loyalty! What were your words?"

"I lied to you, David. I lie to myself and to others. That's what my little excursion in the flesh taught me. I lie. You surprise me, David. You're angry, so very angry, but you're not afraid. You're like me, David—you and Claudia—the only ones who really have my strength."

"Claudia," he said, with a little nod. "Ah, yes, Claudia. I have something for you, my dear friend." He moved away, deliberately turning his back on me, letting me see the fearlessness of this gesture, and he went slowly, refusing to hurry, to the chest beside the bed. When he turned around again he had a small locket in his hands. "From the Motherhouse. The locket you described to me."

"Oh, yes, the locket. Give it to me."

Only now did I see how his hands shook as he struggled with the little oval gold case. And the fingers, he did not know them so very well, did he? At last he had it opened and he thrust it at me, and I looked down at the painted miniature—her face, her eyes, her golden curls. A child staring back at me out of the mask of innocence. Or was this a mask?

And slowly, out of the vast dim vortex of memory, came the moment when I had first laid eyes upon that trinket and upon its golden chain . . . when in the dark muddy street, I had happened upon the plague-ridden hovel where her mother lay dead, and the mortal child herself had become food for the vampire, a tiny white body shivering helplessly in Louis's arms.

How I'd laughed at him, how I'd pointed my finger, and then snatched up from the stinking bed the body of the dead woman—Claudia's mother—and danced with it round and round the room. And there gleaming on her throat had been the golden chain and the locket, for not even the boldest thief would have entered that hovel to steal the bauble from the very maw of the plague.

With my left hand I'd caught it, just as I let the poor body drop. The clasp had broken, and I'd swung the chain over my head as if waving a little trophy of the moment and then dropped it in my pocket as I stepped over the body of the dying Claudia and ran after Louis through the street.

It had been months after that I'd found it in that same pocket, and I'd held it to the light. The living child she'd been when that portrait was painted, but the Dark Blood had given her the very saccharine perfection of the artist. It was my Claudia, and in a trunk I'd left it, and how it came to be with the Talamasca, or anywhere, I did not know.

I held it in my hands. I looked up. It was as though I'd just been there, back in that ruined place, and now I was here, and staring at him. He'd been speaking to me but I hadn't heard him, and now his voice came clear:

"You would do it to me?" he demanded, the timbre betraying him now as his trembling hands betrayed him. "Look at her. You would do it to me?"

I looked at her tiny face, and back to him.

"Yes, David," I said. "I told her I would do it again. And I will do it to you."

I pitched the locket out of the room, over the porch, past the sand, and into the sea. The tiny chain was like a scratch of gold on the fabric of the sky for an instant then it disappeared as if into the luminous light.

He drew back with a speed that astonished me, cleaving to the wall.

"Don't do this, Lestat."

"Don't fight me, old friend. You waste your effort. You have a long night of discovery ahead."

"You won't do it!" he cried, voice so low it was a guttural roar. He lunged at me, as if he thought he could knock me off balance, and both his fists struck my chest, and I did not move. Back he fell, bruised from his efforts and staring at me with pure outrage in his watering eyes. Once again the blood had flooded into his cheeks, darkening his entire visage. And only now, as he saw for himself the sheer hopelessness of defense, did he try to flee.

I grabbed him by the neck before he reached the porch. I let my fingers massage the flesh as he struggled wildly, like an animal, to tear my grip away and pull himself loose. Slowly I lifted him, and cradling the back of his head effortlessly with my left hand, I drove my teeth through the fine, fragrant young skin of his neck, and caught the first bubbling jet of blood.

Ah, David, my beloved David. Never had I descended into a soul I knew so well. How thick and wondrous the images that enveloped me: the soft beautiful sunlight slicing through the mangrove forest, the crunch of the high grass on the veldt, the boom of the great gun, and the shiver of the earth beneath the elephant's pounding feet. It was all there: all the summer rains washing endlessly through the jungles, and the water swimming up the pilings and over the boards of the porch, and the sky flashing with lightning—and his heart pounding beneath it with rebellion, with recrimination, you betray me, you betray me, you take me against my will—and the deep rich salty heat of the blood itself.

I flung him backwards. That was enough for the first drink. I watched him struggle to his knees. What had he seen in those seconds? Did he know now how dark and willful was my soul?

"You love me?" I said. "I am your only friend in this world?"

I watched him crawl across the tiles. He grabbed for the footboard of the bed and raised himself, then fell back, dizzy, to the floor. Again, he struggled.

"Ah, let me help you!" I said. I spun him around and lifted him and sank my teeth in those very same tiny wounds.

"For love of God, stop, don't do it. Lestat, I'm begging you, don't do it."

Beg in vain, David. Oh, how scrumptious this young body, these hands shoving at me, even in the trance, what a will you have, my beautiful friend. And now we are in old Brazil, are we not, we are in the tiny room, and he is calling the names of the Candomble spirits, he is calling, and will the spirits come?

I let him go. Again he sank on his knees, then keeled over on his side, eyes staring forward. That's enough for the second assault.

There was a faint rattling sound in the room. A faint knocking.

"Oh, do we have company? We have little invisible friends? Yes, look, the mirror is wobbling. It's going to fall!" And then it hit the tiles and exploded like so many pieces of light coming loose from the frame.

He was trying to get up again.

"You know what they feel like, David? Can you hear me? They are like many silk banners unfurled around me. That weak."

I watched as he gained his knees again. Once more he was crawling across the floor. Suddenly he rose, pitching forward. He snatched up the book from beside the computer, and turning, hurled it at me. It fell at my feet. He was reeling. He could scarce keep standing, his eyes clouded.

And then he turned and almost fell forward into the little porch, stumbling over the rail and towards the beach.

I came behind him, following him as he staggered down the slope of white sand. The thirst rose, knowing only that the blood had come seconds before, and that it must have more. When he reached the water, he stood there, tottering, only an iron will keeping him from collapse.

I took him by the shoulder, tenderly, embracing him with my right arm.

"No, damn you, damn you into hell. No," he said. With all his waning strength he struck at me, shoving at my face with his doubled fist, tearing the flesh of the knuckles as it struck the unyielding skin.

I twisted him around, watching as he kicked at my legs, as he struck me again and again with those soft impotent hands; and again I nuzzled in against his neck, licking it, smelling it, and then sinking my teeth for the third time. Hmmm . . . this is ecstasy. Could that other body, worn with age, have ever yielded such a feast? I felt the heel of his hand against my face. Oh, so strong. So very strong. Yes, fight me, fight me as I fought Magnus. So sweet that you are fighting me. I love it. I do.

And what was it this time as I went into the swoon? The purest of prayers coming from him, not to gods we didn't believe in, not to a crucified Christ or an old Virgin Queen. But prayers to me. "Lestat, my friend. Don't take my life. Don't. Let me go."

Hmmm. I slipped my arm ever more tightly around his chest. Then drew back, licking at the wounds.

"You choose your friends badly, David," I whispered, licking the blood from my lips, and looking down into his face. He was almost dead. How beautiful these strong even white teeth of his, and the tender flesh of the lip. Only the whites showed beneath his eyelids. And how his heart fought—this young, flawless mortal heart. Heart that had sent the blood pumping through my brain. Heart that had skipped and stopped when I knew fear, when I saw the approach of death.

I laid my ear against his chest, listening. I heard the ambulance screaming through Georgetown. "Don't let me die."

I saw him in that dream hotel room of long ago with Louis and with Claudia. Are we all but random creatures in the devil's dreams?

The heart was slowing. The moment had almost come. One more little drink, my friend.

I lifted him and carried him up the beach and back into the room. I kissed the tiny wounds, licking at them and sucking them with my lips, and then letting my teeth go in again. A spasm passed through him, a little cry escaped his lips.

"I love you," he whispered.

"Yes, and I love you," I answered, words smothered against the flesh, as the blood spurted hot and irresistible once again.

The heartbeat came ever more slowly. He was tumbling through memories, back to the very cradle, beyond the sharp distinct syllables of language, and moaning to himself as if to the old melody of a song.

His warm heavy body was pressed against me, arms dangling, head held in my left fingers, eyes closed. The soft moaning died away, and the heart raced suddenly with tiny, muffled beats.

I bit into my tongue, until I couldn't stand the pain. Again and again I made the punctures with my own fang teeth, moving my tongue to the right and to the left, and then I locked my mouth to his, forcing his lips open, and let the blood flow onto his tongue.

It seemed that time stood still. There came that unmistakable taste of my own blood leaking into my own mouth, as it leaked into his. Then suddenly his teeth snapped closed on my tongue. They snapped down upon it menacingly and sharply, with all the mortal strength in his jaws, and scraped at the preternatural flesh, scraping the blood out of the gash I'd made, and biting so hard that it seemed they would sever the tongue itself if they could.

The violent spasm shot through him. His back arched against my arm. And when I drew back now, my mouth full of pain, my tongue hurting, he drew up, hungering, eyes still blind. I tore my wrist. Here it comes, my beloved. Here it comes, not in little droplets, but from the very river of my being. And this time when the mouth clamped down upon me, it was a pain that reached all the way down to the roots of my being, tangling my heart in its burning mesh.

For you, David. Drink deep. Be strong.

It could not kill me now, no matter how long it lasted. I knew it, and memories of those bygone times when I had done it in fear seemed clumsy and foolish, fading even as I recollected them, and leaving me here alone with him.

I knelt on the floor, holding him, letting the pain spread through every vein and every artery as I knew it must. And the heat and the pain grew so strong in me that I lay down slowly with him in my arms, my wrist sealed against his mouth, my hand still beneath his head. A dizziness came over me. The beating of my own heart grew perilously slow. On and on he pulled, and against the bright darkness of my closed eyes I saw the thousands upon thousands of tiny vessels emptied and contracted and sagging like the fine black filaments of a spider's wind-torn web.

We were in the hotel room again in old New Orleans, and Claudia sat quietly on the chair. Outside, the little city winked here and there with its dull lamps. How dark and heavy the sky overhead, with no hint of the great aurora of the cities to come.

"I told you I would do it again," I said to Claudia.

"Why do you bother to explain to me," she asked. "You know perfectly well that I never asked you any questions about it. I've been dead for years and years."

I opened my eyes.

I lay on the cold tiled floor of the room, and he was standing over me, looking down at me, and the electric light was shining on his face.

And now his eyes were brown no longer; they were filled with a soft dazzling golden light. An unnatural sheen had already invaded his sleek dark skin, paling it ever so slightly and rendering it more perfectly golden, and his hair had already taken on that evil, gorgeous luster, all the illumination gathered to him and reflected off him and playing around him as if it found him irresistible—this tall angelic man with the blank and dazed expression on his face.

He didn't speak. And I could not read his expression. Only I knew the wonders that he beheld. I knew when he looked around him—at the lamp, at the broken fragments of mirror, at the sky outside—what he saw.

Again he looked at me.

"You're hurt," he whispered.

I heard the blood in his voice!

"Are you? Are you hurt?"

"For the love of God," I answered in a raw, torn voice. "How can you care if I'm hurt?"

He shrank back away from me, eyes widening, as if with each passing second his vision expanded, and then he turned and it was as if he'd forgotten that I was there. He kept staring in the same enchanted fashion. And then, doubling over with pain, grimacing with it, he turned and made his way out over the little porch and to the sea.

I sat up. The entire room shimmered. I had given him every drop of blood that he could take. The thirst paralyzed me, and I could scarce remain steady. I wrapped my arm around my knee and tried to sit there without falling down again in sheer weakness on the floor.

I held my left hand up so that I might see it in the light. The little veins were raised on the back of it, yet they were smoothing out as I watched.

I could feel my heart pumping lustily. And keen and terrible though the thirst was, I knew that it could wait. I knew no more than a sick mortal as to why I was healing from what I had done. But some dark engine inside me was working busily and silently upon my restoration, as if this fine killing machine must be cured of all weakness so that it may hunt again.

When I finally climbed to my feet, I was myself. I had given him far more blood than ever I had given the others I'd made. It was finished. I'd done it right. He'd be so very strong! Lord God, he'd be stronger than the old ones.

But I had to find him. He was dying now. I had to help him, even if he tried to drive me away.

I found him waist deep in the water. He was shuddering, and in such pain that small gasps were coming from him, though he tried to keep quiet. He had the locket, and the gold chain was wrapped round his clenched hand.

I put my arm around him to steady him. I told him it would not last very long at all. And when it was gone, it would be gone forever. He nodded his head.

After a little while, I could feel his muscles loosening. I urged him to follow me into the shallow waves, where we could walk more easily, no matter what our strength, and together we walked down the beach.

"You're going to have to feed," I said. "Do you think you can do that alone?"

He shook his head no.

"All right, I'll take you and show you all you need to know. But first the waterfall up there. I can hear it. Can you hear it? You can wash yourself clean."

He nodded, and followed me, his head bowed, his arm still locked around his waist, his body now and then tensing with the last of the violent cramps which death always brings.

When we reached the waterfall, he stepped over the treacherous rocks easily and stripped away his shorts, and stood naked under the great rushing downpour, and let it pass over his face and all his body and his wide-open eyes. There was a moment when he shook himself all over, and spit out the water which had come accidentally into his mouth.

I watched, feeling stronger and stronger as the seconds passed. Then I leapt up, high above the waterfall, and landed upon the cliff. I could see him down there, a tiny figure, standing back, with the spray covering him, gazing up at me.

"Can you come to me?" I said softly.

He nodded. Excellent that he had heard it. He stood back and made a great leap, springing out of the water, and landing on the sloped face of the cliff only several yards below me, hands easily clutching the wet slippery rocks. Over these he climbed without once looking down until he stood at my side.

I was quite frankly astonished at his strength. But it was not merely his strength. It was his utter fearlessness. And he himself seemed to have forgotten about it entirely. He was merely looking off again, at the rolling clouds, and the soft shimmering sky. He was looking at the stars, and then inland at the jungle running down over the cliffs above.

"Can you feel the thirst?" I asked. He nodded, looking at me only in passing, and then looking out to the sea.

"All right, now we go back to your old rooms, and you dress properly to prowl the mortal world and we go into town."

"That far?" he asked. He pointed to the horizon. "There's a little boat out that way."

I scanned for it, and saw it through the eyes of a man on board. A cruel unsavory creature. It was a smuggling venture. And he was bitter that he'd been left by drunken cohorts to do it alone.

"All right," I said. "We'll go together."

"No," he said. "I think I should go . . . alone."

He turned without waiting for my answer, and quickly and gracefully descended to the beach. He moved out like a streak of light through the shallows and dove into the waves and began to swim with powerful swift strokes.

I walked down the edge of the cliff, found a small rugged path, and followed it listlessly until I reached the room. I stared at the wreckage—the broken mirror, the table overturned and the computer lying on its side, the book fallen on the floor. The chair lying on its back on the little porch.

I turned and went out.

I went back up to the gardens. The moon was risen very high, and I walked up the gravel path to the very edge of the highest point and stood there looking down on the thin ribbon of white beach and the soft soundless sea.

At last I sat down, against the trunk of a great dark tree with branches spreading over me in an airy canopy, and I rested my arm on my knee and my head on my arm.

An hour passed.

I heard him coming, walking up the gravel path fast and light, with a footfall no mortal ever made. When I looked up I saw he was bathed and dressed, and even his hair was combed, and the scent of the blood he'd drunk was lingering, perhaps coming from his lips. He was no weak and fleshly creature like Louis, oh, no, he was far stronger than that. And the process had not finished. The pains of his death had finished, but he was hardening even as I looked at him, and the soft golden gleam of his skin was enchanting to behold.

"Why did you do it?" he demanded. What a mask was this face. And then it flashed with anger as he spoke again. "Why did you do it?"

"I don't know."

"Oh, don't give me that. And don't give me those tears! Why did you do it!"

"I tell you the truth. I don't know. I could give you all the many reasons, but I don't know. I did it because I wanted to do it, because I wanted to. Because I wanted to see what would happen if I did it, I wanted to . . . and I couldn't not do it. I knew that when I went back to New Orleans. I . . . waited and I waited, but I couldn't not do it. And now it's done."

"You miserable, lying bastard. You did it from cruelty and meanness! You did it because your little experiment with the Body Thief went wrong! And out of it came this miracle to me, this youth, this rebirth, and it infuriated you that such a thing could happen, that I should profit when you had suffered so!"

"Maybe that's true!"

"It is true. Admit it. Admit the pettiness of it. Admit the meanness, that you couldn't bear to let me slip into the future with this body which you hadn't the courage to endure!"

"Perhaps so."

He drew in close and tried to drag me to my feet with a firm, insistent grip on my arm. Nothing happened, of course. He could not move me an inch.

"You're still not strong enough to play those games," I said. "If you don't stop, I'll hit you and knock you flat on your back. You won't like it. You're too dignified to like it. So leave off with the cheap mortal fisticuffs, please."

He turned his back on me, folding his arms, bowing his head. I could hear the small desperate noises that came from him, and I could almost feel the anguish. He walked away, and I buried my face again in my arm.

But then I heard him coming back.

"Why? I want something from you. I want an admission of some kind."

"No," I said.

He reached out and snatched at my hair, tangling his fingers in it, and jerking my head up as the pain shot over the surface of my scalp.

"You're really pushing it, David," I growled at him, pulling myself loose. "One more little trick like that and I'm going to drop you at the bottom of the cliff."

But when I saw his face, when I saw the suffering in him, I grew quiet.

He went down on his knees before me so that we were almost eye-to-eye.

"Why, Lestat?" he asked, and his voice was torn and sad, and it broke my heart.

Overcome with shame, overcome with misery, I pressed my closed eyes again on my right arm, and brought up my left to cover my head. And nothing, not all his pleas or curses or cries against me or his final quiet departure, could make me look up again.

WELL before morning I went to search for him. The little room was now straightened, and his suitcase lay on the bed. The computer had been folded up, and the copy of *Faust* lay upon its smooth plastic case.

But he was not there. I searched all about the hotel for him, but I couldn't find him. I searched the gardens, and then the woodlands in one direction and another, but with no luck.

At last I found a small cave high on the mountain, and dug down deep into it and slept.

What is the use of describing my misery? Of describing the dull dark pain I felt? What is the use of saying I knew the full measure of my injustice, my dishonor, and my cruelty? I knew the magnitude of what I'd done to him.

I knew myself and all my evil to the fullest and I expected nothing back from the world now except the very same evil in kind.

I woke as soon as the sun had gone into the sea. On a high bluff I watched the twilight and then went down into the streets of the town to hunt. It wasn't too long before the usual thief tried to lay hands on me and rob me, and I carried him with me into a little alleyway and there drained him slowly and very enjoyably, only steps from the tourists passing by. I concealed his body in the very depths of the alley and went on my way.

And what was my way?

I went back to the hotel. His possessions were still there but he was not. Once again, I searched, fighting an awful fear that he had already done away with himself, and then realizing that he was far too strong for that to be a simple thing. Even if he had lain out in the fury of the sun, which I strongly doubted, he could not have been wholly destroyed.

Yet I was plagued by every conceivable fear: Perhaps, he had been so burnt and crippled that he could not help himself. He had been discovered by mortals. Or perhaps the others had come, and stolen him completely away. Or he would reappear and curse me again. I feared that too.

Finally I made my way back down to Bridgetown, unable to leave the island until I knew what had become of him.

I was still there an hour before dawn.

And the next night I did not find him. Nor the night after that.

At last, bruised in mind and soul, and telling myself I deserved nothing but misery, I went home.

The warmth of spring had come to New Orleans, finally, and I found her swarming with the usual tourists beneath a clear and purple evening sky. I went first to my old house to take Mojo from the care of the old woman, who was not at all glad to give him up, save that he had obviously missed me very much.

Then he and I together proceeded to the Rue Royale.

I knew the flat wasn't empty even before I reached the top of the back stairs. I paused for a moment, looking down on the restored courtyard with its scrubbed flagstones and romantic little fountain, complete with cherubs and their great cornucopia-style shells pouring forth a splash of clean water into the basin below.

A bed of dark sweet flowers had been planted against the old brick wall, and a stand of bananas was already thriving in the corner, long graceful knifelike leaves nodding in the breeze.

This gladdened my vicious selfish little heart beyond words.

I went inside. The back parlour had finally been finished, and beautifully laid out with the fine antique chairs I'd selected for it, and the thick pale Persian carpet of faded red.

I looked up and down the length of the hallway, past the fresh wallpaper of gold and white stripes, and over the yards of dark carpet, and I saw Louis standing in the front parlour door.

"Don't ask me where I've been or what I've done," I said. I

walked towards him, brushed him aside, and went into the room. Ah, it surpassed all my expectations. There were a very replica of his old desk between the windows, and the camelback sofa of silver damask, and the oval table inlaid with mahogany. And the spinet against the far wall.

"I know where you've been," he said, "and I know what you've done."

"Oh? And what's to follow? Some stultifying and endless lecture? Tell me now. So I can go to sleep."

I turned around to face him, to see what effect this stiff rebuff had had, if any, and there stood David beside him, dressed very well in black fine-combed velvet, and with his arms folded across his chest, and leaning against the frame of the door.

They were both looking at me, with their pale, expressionless faces, David presenting the darker, taller figure, but how amazingly similar they appeared. It only penetrated to me slowly that Louis had dressed for this little occasion, and for once, in clothes which did not look as if they'd come from an attic trunk.

It was David who spoke first.

"The carnival starts tomorrow in Rio," he said, the voice even more seductive than it had ever been in mortal life. "I thought we might go."

I stared at him with obvious suspicion. It seemed a dark light infused his expression. There was a hard luster to his eyes. But the mouth was so gentle, without a hint of malevolence, or bitterness. No menace emanated from him at all.

Then Louis roused himself from his reverie and quietly moved away down the hall and into his old room. How I knew that old pattern of faintly creaking boards and steps!

I was powerfully confused, and a little breathless.

I sat down on the couch, and beckoned for Mojo to come, who seated himself right in front of me, leaning his heavy weight against my legs.

"You mean this?" I asked. "You want us to go there together?" I asked.

"Yes," he said. "And after that, the rain forests. What if we should go there? Deep into those forests." He unfolded his arms and, bowing his head, began to pace with long slow steps. "You said something to me, I don't remember when . . . Maybe it was an image I caught from you before it all happened, something about a temple which mortals didn't know of, lost in the depths of the jungle. Ah, think of how many such discoveries there must be."

Ah, how genuine the feeling, how resonant the voice.

"Why have you forgiven me?" I asked.

He stopped his pacing, and looked at me, and I was so distracted by the evidence of the blood in him, and how it had changed his skin and hair and eyes, that I couldn't think for a moment. I held up my hand, begging him not to speak. Why did I never get used to this magic? I dropped my hand, allowing him, nay, bidding him, to go on.

"You knew I would," he said, assuming his old measured and restrained tone. "You knew when you did it that I'd go on loving you. That I'd need you. That I would seek you out and cling to you of all the beings in this world."

"Oh, no. I swear I didn't," I whispered.

"I went off awhile to punish you. You're past all patience, really you are. You are the damnedest creature, as you've been called by wiser beings than I. But you knew I'd come back. You knew I'd be here."

"No, I never dreamt it."

"Don't start weeping again."

"I like to weep. I must. Why else would I do it so much?"

"Well, stop!"

"Oh, it's going to be fun, isn't it? You think you are the leader of this little coven, don't you, and you're going to start bossing me around."

"Come again?"

"You don't even look like the elder of the two of us anymore, and you never were the elder. You let my beautiful and irresistible visage deceive you in the simplest and most foolish way. I'm the leader. This is my house. I shall say if we go to Rio."

He began to laugh. Slowly at first, and then more deeply and freely. If there was menace in him it was only in the great flashing shifts of expression, the dark glint in his eyes. But I wasn't sure there was any menace at all.

"You are the leader?" he asked scornfully. The old authority.

"Yes, I am. So you ran off . . . you wanted to show me you could get along without me. You could hunt for yourself; you could find a hiding place by day. You didn't need me. But here you are!"

"Are you coming with us to Rio or not?"

"Coming with us! Did you say 'us'?"

"I did."

He walked over to the chair nearest the end of the couch and sat down. It penetrated to me that obviously he was already in full command of his new powers. And I, of course, couldn't gauge how strong he truly was merely by looking at him. The dark tone of his skin concealed too much. He crossed his legs and fell into an easy posture of relaxation, but with David's dignity intact.

Perhaps it was a matter of the way his back remained straight against the chair behind him, or the elegant way his hand rested on his ankle, and the other arm molded itself to the arm of the chair.

Only the thick wavy brown hair betrayed the dignity somewhat, tumbling down on his forehead so that finally he gave a little unconscious toss to his head.

But quite suddenly his composure melted; his face bore all the sudden lines of serious confusion, and then pure distress.

I couldn't stand it. But I forced myself to be silent.

"I tried to hate you," he confessed, the eyes widening even as the voice nearly died away. "I couldn't do it; it's as simple as that." And for one moment there was the menace, the great preternatural anger, glaring out of him, before the face became perfectly miserable and then merely sad.

"Why not?"

"Don't play with me."

"I've never played with you! I mean these things when I say them. How can you not hate me?"

"I'd be making the same mistake you made if I hated you," he said, eyebrows raised. "Don't you see what you've done? You've given me the gift, but you spared me the capitulation. You've brought me over with all your skill and all your strength, but you didn't require of me the moral defeat. You took the decision from me, and gave me what I could not help but want."

I was speechless. It was all true, but it was the damnedest lie I'd ever heard. "Then rape and murder are our paths to glory! I don't buy it. They are filthy. We are all damned and now you are too. And that's what I've done to you."

He bore that as if it were a series of soft slaps, merely flinching just a little and then fixing his eyes on me again.

"It took you two hundred years to learn that you wanted it," he said. "I knew the moment I woke out of the stupor and saw you lying there on the floor. You looked like an empty shell to me. I knew you'd gone too far with it. I was in terror for you. And I was seeing you with these new eyes."

"Yes."

"Do you know what went through my mind? I thought you'd found a way to die. You'd given me every drop of blood in you. And now you yourself were perishing before my very eyes. I knew I loved you. I knew I forgave you. And I knew with every breath I took and with every new color or shape I saw before me that I wanted what you'd given me—the new vision and life, which none of us can really describe! Oh, I couldn't admit it. I had to curse you, fight you for a little while. But that's all it was in the end—a little while."

"You're much smarter than I am," I said softly.

"Well, of course, what did you expect?"

I smiled. I settled back on the couch.

"Ah, this is the Dark Trick," I whispered. "How right they were, the old ones, to give it that name. I wonder if the trick's on me. For this is a vampire sitting here with me, a blood drinker of enormous power, my child, and what are old emotions to him now?"

I looked at him, and once more I felt the tears coming. They never let me down.

He was frowning, and his lips were slightly parted, and it seemed now I truly had dealt him a terrible blow. But he didn't speak to me. He seemed puzzled, and then he gave a little shake of his head as though he couldn't reply.

I realized that it wasn't vulnerability I saw in him now so much as compassion, and blatant concern for me.

He left the chair suddenly, dropping to his knees in front of me, and putting his hands on my shoulders, completely ignoring my faithful Mojo, who stared at him with indifferent eyes. Did he realize this was how I'd faced Claudia in my fever dream?

"You're the same," he said. He shook his head. "The very same."

"The same as what?"

"Oh, every time you ever came to me, you touched me; you wrung from me a deep protectiveness. You made me feel love. And it's the same now. Only you seem all the more lost and in need of me now. I'm to take you forward, I see it clearly. I'm your link with the future. It's through me that you'll see the years ahead."

"You're the same too. An absolute innocent. A bloody fool." I tried to brush his hand off my shoulder, but didn't succeed. "You're headed for great trouble. Just wait and see."

"Oh, how exciting. Now, come, we must go to Rio. We must not miss anything of the carnival. Though of course we can go again . . . and again . . . and again . . . But come."

I sat very still, looking at him for the longest time, until finally he became concerned again. His fingers were quite strong as they pressed my shoulders. Yes, I had done well with him in every step.

"What is it?" he asked timidly. "Are you grieving for me?"

"Perhaps, a little. As you've said, I'm not as clever as you are at knowing what I want. But I think I'm trying to fix this moment in my mind. I want to remember it always—I want to remember the way you are now, here with me . . . before things start to go wrong."

He stood up, pulling me suddenly to my feet, with scarcely any effort at all. There was a soft triumphant smile on his face as he noted my amazement.

"Oh, this is going to be really something, this little tussle," I said.

"Well, you can fight with me in Rio, while we are dancing in the streets."

He beckoned for me to follow him. I wasn't sure what we would do next or how we would make this journey, but I was wondrously excited, and I honestly didn't care about the small aspects of it at all.

Of course Louis would have to be persuaded to come, but we would gang up on him, and somehow lure him into it, no matter how reticent he was.

I was about to follow him out of the room, when something caught my eye. It was on Louis's old desk.

It was the locket of Claudia. The chain was coiled there, catching the light with its tiny gold links, and the oval case itself was open and propped against the inkwell, and the little face seemed to be peering directly at me.

I reached down and picked up the locket, and looked very closely at the little picture. And a sad realization came to me.

She was no longer the real memories. She had become those fever dreams. She was the image in the jungle hospital, a figure standing against the sun in Georgetown, a ghost rushing through the shadows of Notre Dame. In life she'd never been my conscience! Not Claudia, my merciless Claudia. What a dream! A pure dream.

A dark secret smile stole over my lips as I looked at her, bitter and on the edge, once more, of tears. For nothing had changed in the realization that I had given her the words of accusation. *The very same thing was true.* There had been the opportunity for salvation—and I had said no.

I wanted to say something to her as I held the locket; I wanted to say something to the being she had been, and to my own weakness, and to the greedy wicked being in me who had once again triumphed. For I had. I had won.

Yes, I wanted to say something so terribly much! And would that it were full of poetry, and deep meaning, and would ransom my greed and my evil, and my lusty little heart. For I was going to Rio, wasn't I, and with David, and with Louis, and a new era was beginning . . .

Yes, say something—for the love of heaven and the love of Claudia—to darken it and show it for what it is! Dear God, to lance it and show the horror at the core.

But I could not.

What more *is* there to say, really?

The tale is told.

Lestat de Lioncourt
New Orleans
1991

A NOTE ON THE TYPE

THIS BOOK was set in a digitized version of Janson. The hot-metal version of Janson was a recutting made direct from type cast from matrices long thought to have been made by the Dutchman Anton Janson, who was a practicing type founder in Leipzig during the years 1668 to 1687. However, it has been conclusively demonstrated that these types are actually the work of Nicholas Kis (1650–1702), a Hungarian, who most probably learned his trade from the master Dutch type founder Dirk Voskens. The type is an excellent example of the influential and sturdy Dutch types that prevailed in England up to the time William Caslon (1692–1766) developed his own incomparable designs from them.

Composed by ComCom, a division of
The Haddon Craftsmen,
Scranton, Pennsylvania
Printed and bound by Fairfield Graphics,
Fairfield, Pennsylvania
Designed by Virginia Tan